Hattie of Crawford Notch

A novel by Mary Anne Evans

ISBN: 979-8-9851642-2-0 (paperback)
ISBN: 979-8-9851642-3-7 (ebook)

Cover photo courtesy of Raymond Evans collection

Praise for Hattie of Crawford Notch

"Set in a remote corner of the White Mountains of New Hampshire with a framework of real-life events, this is a story of an amazing woman named Hattie Evans. Her story is one of enjoying many happy occasions, grieving the tragic loss of her husband, raising four children, and managing a section house on the tracks of the Maine Central Railroad. More importantly, though, this story is about a wife, widow, mother, and friend to many whose positive spirit and unselfish caring for those around her brings new meaning to the word 'remarkable.'"

- Phil Franklin
President, Bartlett Historical Society, Bartlett, NH

"This book brought my grandparents' lives to me, which allowed me to be there with my heart. I was actually able to grieve for my grandfather. I also felt the pain and joy of their lives by the tracks. Now as I visit the home site, or view the many family pictures, my emotions will be so much deeper and richer. I truly love this heartfelt, loving family story."

- Craig Robinson
Grandson of Hattie and Loring Evans

"I freely admit that I enjoy the ease and comfort of my life, with a connection to the world literally in the palm of my hand and the ability to get anything I need at the push of a virtual button. But the true story of Hattie Evans reminded me that I have lost much in the bargain: the joy of simple things, the dignity of hard labor in loving service to others, and the nobility of doing one's best in the day-to-day activities of life, even when it's hard. The author has a true gift for telling this story without romanticizing or pulling any punches, celebrating their victories and letting us feel their losses. I highly recommend it."

- Charles Smith
Dayton, OH

Other works
by Mary Anne Evans:

I LV ME: A Spiritual Journey of Healing

Embracing Our Final Days: A Journey of Care to the End
(co-authored with Rebecca McElfresh, Ph.D.
and Lucy Ellen Smith)

Are You Serious?

My Teen Teachers

Something of Value

Dedicated to my mother and father,
whose love of this story infected me.

"When life feels too big to handle, go outside.
Everything looks smaller when you're
standing under the sky."

-L.R. Knost

Overall Area Map

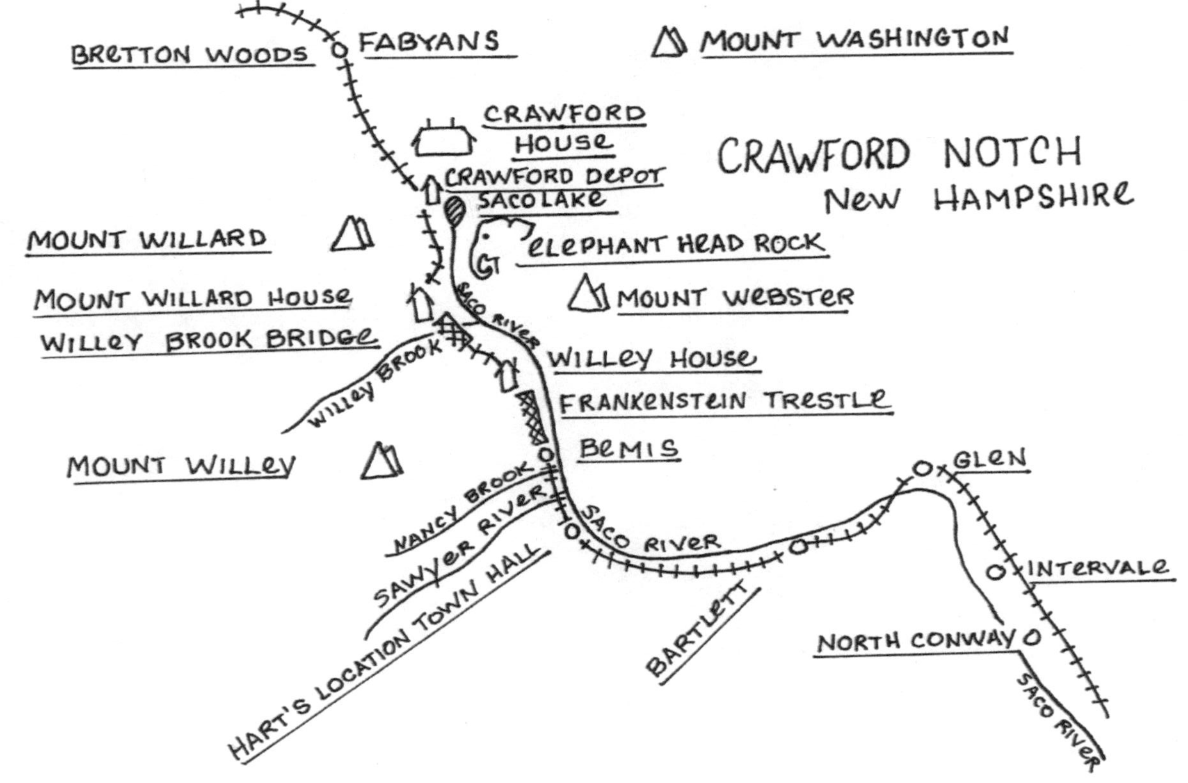

BRETTON WOODS
FABYANS
MOUNT WASHINGTON
CRAWFORD HOUSE
CRAWFORD DEPOT
SACO LAKE
CRAWFORD NOTCH
New Hampshire
MOUNT WILLARD
ELEPHANT HEAD ROCK
MOUNT WILLARD HOUSE
MOUNT WEBSTER
WILLEY BROOK BRIDGE
SACO RIVER
WILLEY BROOK
WILLEY HOUSE
FRANKENSTEIN TRESTLE
MOUNT WILLEY
BEMIS
GLEN
NANCY BROOK
SAWYER RIVER
SACO RIVER
HART'S LOCATION TOWN HALL
INTERVALE
BARTLETT
NORTH CONWAY
SACO RIVER
Detailed Map of Crawford Notch

Contents

One

~ Flood Week ~
Monday, October 31, 1927

Hattie had things on her mind besides her daily Monday routine as she dressed for the day ahead. First and foremost, she was looking forward to the weekend when all the children would be home again. They came home nearly every weekend, all of them, something for which she was always very grateful and tried very hard not to take for granted. She thought maybe she'd make some special food for their visit but wasn't sure yet what that might be. But behind those lovely thoughts lingered something she couldn't quite name.

Removing her nightcap and coaxing her long, still mostly brunette hair out of its nighttime twist, she thought about her richly blessed life. Her boys. Her girls. Her home in the Notch. She brushed her naturally wavy hair and then nimbly twisted it into its familiar position on her head as she'd done hundreds of times before. She wondered what tales the children would each tell when they came through the front door this weekend. Would Gordon say he still liked his new job? And had he looked into joining the Masons? *He does so love a cause.* Would Mildred find her classes thrilling? *Oh, how Mildred wants to be a teacher!* And what about the younger two still in high school? Was Raymond thinking ahead about what he wanted to do after graduating, as she'd prodded him to? *Likely not,* Hattie smiled to herself, pulling her dress on over her slip. *That boy prefers to live in the present. And there's nothing wrong with that.* And Enola. Sweet Enola. Hattie thought about the stray cat her youngest had befriended in Whitefield. *I know Enola wants to bring it home, but I think one cat and one dog is enough.*

Her thoughts brought warmth to her heart as she slid her stockinged feet into the shoes she had been fortunate enough to inherit from a bag of used clothing. She was told they were glacé kid shoes and she supposed she should keep them looking properly shiny, but she had acquired the pair of probably more than three-dollar shoes for free, so she gave herself permission to spend less time keeping their sheen and more time simply making sure they lasted as long as possible. The fact that they were stylish paled in comparison to their practicality. Finding shoes that could go the distance with her throughout a typical day was the goal and these had proven up to the task. Hattie turned and bent over her bed, pulling the sheets and spread up under her pillow. She made a mental note to retrieve a blanket from the old chest and air it out on the line as it would soon be time to pull it into service. She smoothed out the wrinkles and tucked the bedclothes neatly under the mattress. Finally, she folded her nightgown and cap and stowed them beneath her pillow.

As she turned again to reach for the lamp, her elbow bumped the framed picture she so loved. *Well, that was certainly clumsy of me.* It had only fallen on top of her brush and comb and not to the floor, thank goodness. She placed the lamp back down so she could set the picture to rights. As she fingered the dainty little pastel-colored shells around the frame's perimeter, Hattie's thoughts of the children shifted disturbingly close to the edge of an emotional place she preferred not to go. This mental ritual of keeping bleakness at bay was certainly not new. Hattie believed that to dwell on the past only hindered the present and she simply would not allow that. After tucking these forbidden thoughts safely back inside her deepest-most places within, strangely, she detected a twinge of fear she was not used to feeling and couldn't account for.

As if he knew how to quickly squelch her darker line of thought, Laddie came over to her, shaking the sleep from his thickening coat. He nudged her hand with his snout, making her smile again. "You're such a good boy, Laddie," Hattie crooned to this creature who was more family than dog, and her words set his tail in motion. "Let's just let you outside, hmm?" Laddie cocked his head, listening for understanding. "I've really no time to fritter away. There are things to be done." Sneakers stretched and meowed his own greeting and Hattie reached down to scratch him behind his ear. "Good morning to you, too, Sneakers." Then she put on her glasses, picked up the lamp, and followed the dog, who walked with a slow, steady gait, across the room toward the door. The sound of her shoes beat a rhythm that joined Laddie's nails click-clicking on the hardwood floor. Sneakers, as always, lived up to his name, the almost imperceptible sound of his footfalls giving him the edge over the long-tailed breakfast Hattie hoped he'd find. She opened the door to both animals and the pre-dawn darkness.

It was a new week. Hattie looked forward to seeing how the view out her kitchen window might have changed, as it would every single day if she were especially observant. Like an enormous window shade being slowly and meticulously pulled from the top of the mountains to the bottom, the once brilliant yellows, reds, and oranges of late September and mid-October gradually dulled, giving way to the evergreens and browns of winter. Now, at the end of October, the higher elevations were finished being showy. Their conifers provided a palette of various subtle shades of green while the deciduous trees stood stark naked, displaying their unique skeletons. The only remnants of the bright autumn colors were a stubborn dab here and there of rustic red, presented mostly by the oaks and sumacs, and bits of honey yellow, courtesy of the hickories and some of the birches laying low on the mountains' long skirts. The late autumn changes meant Hattie could pick out some familiar favorites growing near the house, like the old oak tree that stood in a permanent morning stretch.

No season here in the Notch was without its beauty. Each one was to be savored, not rushed. If she didn't adequately revel in autumn, she'd have no reserve for the harsh reality of winter, which would be upon them soon. Yet, after a significant snowstorm when the sky was blindingly blue and the sun birthed diamonds on top of the whipped layers of snow, there was an intensely quiet peace that filled Hattie's soul. Nature rested beneath its blanket and she, too, could rest from certain outdoor routines. Everything in its time, Hattie thought, watching Laddie sniff his way across the lawn. She closed the door to the chilly air. It was still too dark to tell if the weather would allow her to hang the clothes outside today. She turned and headed for the kitchen.

Donning her apron, Hattie checked the stove to see how the embers looked this morning. She shook down the ashes and added more coal. The copper boilers were nice and hot to start her laundry after breakfast. She pushed them to the back of the stove and checked her oats. They'd cooked nicely overnight and with a bit of stirring would be ready for the men who would be down soon. Their coffee would be ready as well. *Good old reliable stove,* Hattie thought with gratitude, not wishing for anything more modern. She retrieved the eggs she'd need from the pantry and began slicing bread.

Soon Laddie was making his presence known on the other side of the door. She never knew if the dog was reminding her to hoist the American flag—as if she could forget—or was simply prompting her to let him in. Perhaps both. She smiled and grabbed her well-worn sweater off the hook, then retrieved the flag from its drawer where it had been folded neatly yesterday to await another day's duty today. Opening the door, she and Laddie headed for the flagpole. Once the flag was hoisted, they both turned and went inside, Hattie to her breakfast-making and Laddie to a spot near the stove. As she made sandwiches for the men's dinner pails (ham today) and topped them off with nice big pieces of the apple pie she'd made Saturday, she hummed to herself, happy in her routine. There was always plenty to do each day, which might have been overwhelming to another woman, such as her beloved sister-in-law, Nell, whose love of life did not include a heavy load of housework. But Hattie managed well, keeping to a regular, predictable schedule. She found that by doing Monday's work Monday, there was time for the unexpected on Tuesday, should it present itself.

Before long she began to hear stirrings above her as the men readied themselves for their own workday. The trains heading east and west, looking more north and south in her particular section, waited for no man. The tracks had to be ready when those trains came through, and the next train of the day would be coming soon enough. Hattie was almost done making breakfast when she heard footfalls on the back stairs.

The first of the men entered the kitchen. "Good morning, John," Hattie greeted the section foreman with the familiarity of having known him nearly twenty-five years. She knew him well enough to count on him giving her whatever daily information she might need. "What do you think the weather will bring today?"

John knew that Hattie's question was primarily about whether she'd be able to hang her wash outside. He saw the sturdy, reliable woman before him and admired her fortitude. All the men respected Hattie as one of the crew. They relied on her to make their mountain home run smoothly so that they could do their own work. They knew they could count on her to keep clothes and bedding clean and the house organized, and Hattie made some of the best meals any of the train men in these parts could hope to enjoy. John may be foreman of Section 129, but Hattie was most definitely "foreman" of the house. They all worked well together and enjoyed one another's company, for the most part.

John always felt comfortable around Hattie and thought he knew her well, but sometimes he had to admit to himself that Hattie was a mystery, keeping her deepest thoughts and feelings to herself. When John saw Hattie this morning and heard her greeting, he felt somewhat embarrassed, even though he was still glad he had been honest with her last night. He hoped Hattie wouldn't sense anything amiss and kept his voice as even as he could. "I hear tell there may be rain coming, but perhaps not today. I imagine the wash will be fine outside."

Hattie smiled warmly, knowing John understood the intent of her question. Maybe he understood the words she'd needed to say to him last night as well, but when he ended his response abruptly this morning, continuing through the kitchen, Hattie wasn't sure. She watched the tall, thin man exit into the dining room. On another Monday he might have lingered to make small talk about her children's lives or comment on things they'd talked about previously. When he didn't, she knew that he was hiding at least some of his feelings and she honored that. John took a seat at the table as the other men, who had just arrived, did the same, greeting Hattie as they walked by. She returned their greeting in kind and served up their meal, the usual hearty breakfast they would need to begin their day. She ate her own breakfast in the kitchen, one bite at a time as she began cleaning up her pots and utensils.

When each man finished his breakfast, he left his dishes at the serving hatch—a show of respect for Hattie, more than a requirement she set—and, grabbing his dinner pail, wished Hattie a good day. They walked out through the back door, which also could have been called the side door. John, behind his men, made no further attempt to talk, but Hattie knew he'd have a lot on his mind, facing a new week. As foreman, John saw to the bigger picture of what needed to be done and when. He would assign his men their duties, knowing how each man worked. It was generally a good crew and for that he was grateful. He and his men were critical to the operation of the trains, both passenger and freight. The engineers needed to know the rails were clear. The crews, those on the tracks as well as those in the trains and at the station, knew each other well and counted on each man to do his job so that the whole operation worked like a well-oiled machine. In a sense, they were a family.

The section crew's days varied. Sometimes they would be close by and sometimes they would be working a mile from the house. Many days, Hattie didn't see them until supper. But her day would be full, too, and the time would go by quickly. With breakfast dishes to finish, a mound of laundry to clean, a shopping order to have ready, eggs to gather, and the supper meal to prepare, her time would be well spent. How often had she told the children, "Idle hands are the devil's playground"?

Hard work never hurt a soul, she thought, and began to hum once again as she busied herself. That evening, after the supper meal was finished and tomorrow's oats for breakfast and water for coffee sat on the back burners to warm throughout the night, Hattie banked the stove, then hung her apron back up on its hook. Laddie joined her in retrieving the flag from its pole, though he poked around near her flower garden first in case there might be a stray mouse or shrew that the cat hadn't found. Then the two of them went inside where she folded and put away the flag for use tomorrow. Only then did she retire to the front room with a cup of steeping tea, sitting down in her favorite chair with the sigh of a day gone well. Laddie also sighed, bent his legs, and curled up on the floor beside her. She scratched his now-graying muzzle, so much like her own hair beginning to gray with age. Hattie could hear the men upstairs walking around or moving a chair now and then. She assumed they were writing letters or reading or maybe playing cards. Whatever they were up to, it was soothing to hear them when the house was so devoid of her children's voices. She briefly wondered if John had talked to the others about his personal matters. Whether he did or not, she thought, was his prerogative.

Hattie caught Sneaker's eye. He needed no further persuasion to jump into her lap. She ran her chapped hands down the cat's dark-gray and white back, making his rump and tail rise. Studying her hands, she made a mental note to put some lanolin on them before bedtime. Sneakers purred his delight until Hattie stopped petting him and reached for the newspaper. Several of the men had looked at it already, she knew, but had left it neatly on the table by her chair. The weather forecast in the corner of the front page always won her attention first. Heaven only knew how each day's undertakings depended on the weather here in Crawford Notch, and there was only so much she could foresee on her own. Glancing at the paper now, she was compelled to acknowledge the twinge of fear she'd felt at the beginning of the day. Although there had been no rain, as John had predicted, and she'd been happy to hang the clothes outside in air she thought was a bit too sultry for this time of year, she fervently hoped there would be no more downpours. October had been unusually wet as it was.

Hattie, like everyone else living in this Notch, understood as much about the weather as Mother Nature would allow. No one could predict everything, but there were hints, along with a person's sixth sense, that accounted for a great deal of accuracy. The closeness or lightness of the air, patterns and colors of the clouds, and behaviors of the animals were often indicators of a change in weather. She turned the pages to find more detail and read about a late season tropical depression moving up the eastern coast. With a sudden chill, she realized the possible source of her anxiety. "Something just isn't right," Hattie muttered to the only pairs of ears nearby. If they had heard her or cared, they didn't show it. She decided to let go of her worried thoughts. If there was anything to them, she could always worry about them later.

Satisfied that she knew all she needed to know for the time being, Hattie folded up the paper she'd use for a number of other things, such as kindling or insulation from the cold, and picked up her knitting. A parade of thoughts marched through her mind as her needles clicked, everything from tomorrow's chores to giving more thought about what to make for the children's meals this weekend that they would especially love. Soon her eyes tired. Taking off her glasses and setting them down, she slowly rubbed her eyes, then rose to retire to her room, inviting Laddie and Sneakers to join her. She was too tired to return her teacup to the kitchen. *I'll get it first thing in the morning*, she thought, closing the bedroom door. She worked through her familiar nighttime routine, finally dressing in her nightgown and turning down the bed. Picking up her brush, she sat and took down her hair, brushing it thoroughly. Then she twisted it and put it underneath her nightcap. Her brush resumed its position on her bureau, and she slipped gratefully between the covers.

Before sleep overtook her, a thought from her day lingered. It concerned her that John had been so quiet around her after their supper. She wondered if her honesty had cost her a valued friendship. She sincerely hoped not. Then her thoughts drifted to something she'd not given in to all day long. "Good night, my dear Loring. Happy thirtieth anniversary. Where has all the time gone? And happy birthday. Fifty-four already. We're getting old, aren't we?" she whispered. "I'll be glad to see October leave us. Maybe November will bring drier weather." She turned down the lamp and, in the darkness, she knew it would not be long before five o'clock came again.

Two

~ 1897 ~
Musings in a Honeymoon Cabin

Hattie and Loring lay on their sides gazing into one another's eyes. The wool blankets were pulled up to keep them warm on this chilly last day of October. They hardly needed the covers, though, because the love they had for one another made them all but oblivious to the world around them. Still, it was cold enough that Loring knew he'd need to put more wood on the fire before it went out completely. It had been a wonderful day, the makings of a dream come true. For both of them.

"What's goin' on in that lovely head of yours, Mrs. Evans?" Loring asked his new wife tenderly, using her new name with profound joy. He could hardly believe his great fortune to have married this amazing and gorgeous woman. He watched the subtle movements of the smaller muscles in her cheeks and brow as she lay quiet and thoughtful, and he wondered what the small twitches meant.

"Oh, I was just thinking about the day. How beautiful it was. And our service. Didn't Nell sound lovely singing 'Oh Promise Me'? I'm glad she picked that song. And I'm glad we picked this date, even though at first I wasn't sure it was a good idea to pair it with your birthday. And a night in this cozy cabin? Well, I'm a lucky, lucky girl to be sure. Today couldn't have been more perfect, could it? Even the weather was perfect."

Loring murmured his agreement. "I'm not sure I even noticed the weather, to tell you the truth. You were the only beauty I was thinking about."

Hattie touched his face and played with his bushy mustache, "Honestly, Loring, you're making me blush."

"Good!" he teased. "Has anyone else ever told you how beautiful you are?"

"No, Loring. You're the first and I expect the only one from here on in." She was nothing if not realistic. "I love that you do, though." They kissed. Then Hattie pulled back slightly to say, "I love a lot of things about you, in fact."

"Oh? Like what?" Loring was lost in his own dreamy, all's-right-with-the-world place, just as Hattie was.

"Well, I love that you're a happy person."

"Why wouldn't I be?" he said playfully.

"No, I don't just mean tonight," she smirked, then became serious again. "You know how to enjoy life in a cheerful sort of way, as if all you can see is the best of things. I love life, too, don't get me wrong. But you are more…I don't know…more buoyant, I guess."

"I know you do," Loring said with conviction, fully aware that he wouldn't have chosen a woman who couldn't enjoy the very act of living right along with him. There was so much he wanted to experience with Hattie by his side.

"I'm more serious than you are, I think," Hattie continued her self-evaluation.

"I always was the class clown and that got me into trouble sometimes," Loring reminisced. With too much delight, Hattie thought.

"Really? How?" she said, intrigued.

Loring laughed and pretended that he wasn't going to divulge his secrets. This provoked Hattie into her own pretense of beating it out of him. Loring pulled her into him and hugged her all the more tightly, kissing her again. Hattie wiggled out of the embrace to look at him, eyebrows raised, imploring him to answer her question.

"Alright. With five of us boys and some of my cousins capering around one or the other of our parents' farms, we managed to pull a stunt or two. I guess that just naturally carried over into school. I didn't like farm chores or school well enough to be overly serious about either. It was more fun to make fun, like teasing the girls at school or even my sisters. I was most often the instigator," he said, rolling his eyes. "But I planned things out pretty well. If I could get others to do things we shouldn't be doing, I wasn't the one to get into trouble. Usually."

Hoping to let the subject go, Loring kissed Hattie a good long while. But Hattie wasn't ready to let her new husband off the hook quite yet. *He might never be so willing to talk about this again. Plus, I love hearing his accent. It's deeper Maine than mine,* she thought. "So, what exactly did you do in school that wasn't schoolwork?"

Loring gave her a look of resignation and said, "One time this boy who bragged about everything said his mother made him the best dinners. He opened his pail and showed us his sandwich, a hard-boiled egg, some vegetable or other, and a big piece of pie. I'd had about enough of him, I guess, and the next day I snatched an old egg ma was going to use for fertilizer and took it to school in my pail. When the bragger wasn't looking, I switched eggs on him. When we were all dismissed for dinner, I made sure to eat his hard-boiled egg first to get rid of the evidence. Then I just sat and watched him crack the rotten egg all over himself. It was awful funny, but I had to be careful not to be the one laughing the hardest."

"Loring! That's a terrible thing to do!" Hattie said, but her smile gave her away. She wasn't one to pull pranks, but there were times, she knew as well as anyone, when a good lesson went a long way. "Anything else you'd like to confess, Mr. Evans?"

"You mean besides getting everyone to switch seats when the teacher wasn't looking? That was especially fun when the teacher was new and trying to learn our names. Then there's the times growing up on the farm. Me and my brothers, especially Will and Charlie, were constantly picking on our sisters. I don't know why they didn't stop talkin' to us altogether. We'd get 'em to come in real close to the cow's bag when we were milking.

'Hey, Nell,' I'd say, 'look at this!' and she'd bend way down and then I'd squirt her in the face with warm, sticky milk. Oh, she'd get real angry and go stormin' off. Ma wouldn't do much about it, though. I think she just plain had too many other things to worry about. As long as we weren't bleeding to death, she'd shoo us back to work. Besides, Nell and Nora would get us back and even the score. Sometimes the girls would use only one sheet to make our beds up, you know, folding it in half and covering it with the blanket to make it look like two sheets. We'd crawl into bed real tired after working all day and hit the bottom of the sheet halfway down the bed. We'd either have to get out and fix it or, more often than not, we'd just lie on top of the whole mess and forget about it. I guess things evened out pretty good. I think, in the end, we all cared enough about each other not to let teasin' turn ugly. We were pretty protective of each other."

When Loring got going like this, talking about his growing up years—on the farm especially, with all those brothers and sisters—Hattie felt envious, even though she loved listening to him. She knew he was close to his family and that he loved being with them. Maybe that's why it seemed he was almost jolly at times. Things weren't like that for her. She couldn't say her childhood was bad, necessarily, but it wasn't fun like Loring's. Her parents and his had known each other, though their lives were very different. Where Loring lived on a farm, Hattie lived closer to town. Her father worked for the Portland and Ogdensburg Railroad when he married her mother. He was employed as part of the engine crew who lost their lives when an engine blew up one day. Hattie was only a year old. She'd lost her father so young she didn't remember him at all, but she'd heard the story. The father she had grown up with had married her mother more as a convenience than for true love. His first wife had died giving birth to a son, their only child. Since both her mother and stepfather had young children to raise, they figured they could do that better together than apart. Hattie might have been close to her stepbrother, but, for whatever reason, the chemistry between them wasn't there.

Hattie's mother, Abbie Smith, was a serious woman, at least as Hattie knew her. She seemed fearful, as though one tragedy begot another. What Hattie was too young to understand was that her mother had had difficulty coping with the loss of Hattie's father. Instead of developing an affectionate relationship with her daughter, Abbie remained aloof to protect her heart should she lose another person she loved. What Hattie did understand was that her mother needed to know where she was at all times. So she hardly dared stray, apart from the one thing her mother had insisted on (and Hattie was always very grateful for). She insisted that Hattie go to school. For Hattie, education was very important. She thrived on information and knowing the basics of reading, writing, and arithmetic.

Her more formal education stopped the year she turned twelve, when her mother died of a heart attack. With no mother or father to intervene, her stepfather insisted she work at home, keeping up with the housework and cooking. He also expected her to work for other people, to earn an income. He was not cruel, but practical and emotionally distant. Hattie suddenly felt like an island, alone in the middle of a vast ocean. She had no choice but to work as her stepfather had insisted. This was difficult for her at first. She missed learning new things at school and being with her friends all day. Worse still, she was unsure of herself and quite shy with adults she didn't know. It scared her to put herself out into the world, especially when she could no longer trust the world as she'd known it.

Her first job was cleaning house for an elderly couple in town. The only method for cleaning was the one her mother had taught her, and she hoped that was good enough. The elderly woman never complained, but Hattie would always wonder if that was because the woman's eyes and ears weren't working well. Nevertheless, the couple was sweet to her, and her stepfather seemed pleased with her earnings.

Her favorite job was being hired to work for a family of seven. The husband was a traveling merchant, and with five young children to see to, the wife needed an extra pair of hands. Hattie cleaned and cooked and was constantly on the go, either diapering or bathing the children or cleaning up little handprints all over the house. She helped with the piles of laundry each week, and when she'd been there a few years, she did all the laundry by herself. To Hattie, the saving grace about this job was the children with whom she enjoyed a mutually loving relationship. She especially loved the days she and the missus would take walks with the children. There seemed to be no end to the information this mother had about the flora and fauna of the area. In fact, the children's mother loved the outdoors and instilled in her children, as well as in Hattie, a deep appreciation for nature. While Hattie had had to cut her formal education short, she always knew she'd been given an education in life outside the classroom.

When Hattie was in her later teens, she began helping her young charges with their studies. Not only was she able to relearn much of her early educational work, but she found she truly loved teaching the children. Finally, when Hattie was almost twenty years old, she was relieved of her job, as by then the children were able to do the work she had been hired to do. Hattie could have been let go earlier, but the bond she'd made with the mother and children was so strong that no one wanted the arrangement to end. After leaving her work with the family, Hattie, still living at home, took a job at the Standish General Store in town. Until she married Loring.

"Loring," Hattie whispered, "I'm getting cold. Would you please put more wood on the fire, and then come right back?"

It didn't take him long to stoke the fire and return to their warm bed.

"Do you remember the night you asked to court me?" she asked, searching for his warm feet with her own cold ones. She loved those first days of courting, though there hadn't been so very many of them. Just a handful of sparse moments they stole to be alone, unchaperoned.

"Of course!" said Loring. "I was pretty nervous. It wasn't as easy to approach you as I would've thought, knowing you as I already did. I'd had a plan that night. I was going to go to the dance with Will and Charlie, then move around the dance hall until I found myself a pretty girl to dance with. And if I didn't find one, I'd just drink cider and enjoy the party." He was laughing at himself now. "I was going to be so smooth, so suave moving around that big room. I was going to sweep some gal right off her feet. But when I got to the hall and you were sitting outside on that bench, well, you completely took me by surprise. In fact, I darted into the shadows for a few moments to think, hoping you hadn't seen me."

"I hadn't. But why did you do that, and what did you need to think about?" Hattie asked, not realizing this fact but suddenly being very curious.

"Because until that moment, I hadn't thought of anything other than having a good time that night. Nothing specific. Nothing with a future. But when I saw you, I suddenly realized I wanted more. And I wanted it from you, which was odd because until then I'd only seen you as a girl, not a woman. But you were all grown up and looking awful fine," he said, twirling her hair around his fingers and looking lovingly and deeply into her eyes. "I remember wondering where those thoughts about you were coming from. It wasn't like I'd recently entertained them. And then it slowly dawned on me that I'd had passing daydreams about you years ago when we were still young. I guess all those passing thoughts bundled up together all at once when I saw you. I decided right then to ask you to dance. I didn't know what I'd do if you turned me down, though. I think that's what sent me into the shadows. Fear. I had to find my nerve." He paused a moment, then said, "Come to think of it, I don't think I've ever asked you why you weren't inside dancing."

Hattie said, "I'd had enough for one night and told my girlfriend I'd wait outside for her so we could go home together."

"Well, I'm glad you hadn't left already. But if you'd had enough dancing, why'd you go back inside?"

"I guess you weren't the only one wanting something more!" she answered cryptically, winking.

"Well," he said, "my jitters stuck around even after we went back in."

"Why's that?" Hattie probed further.

"Well, I didn't want that night to be the end of things. I suddenly wanted to court you, and I was afraid you'd never want to be with me again after that night."

"Why wouldn't I?" she asked again.

"I'm a rather rotund man, wouldn't you say?"

"What's that got to do with anything? I'd either like you or I wouldn't. You just looked like you enjoyed eating. A lot!" she said, poking his belly and grinning.

"So, what exactly did make you decide to go back into the dance with me?" Loring asked her.

"I must confess that I had liked you for some time. Even so, I was caught off guard when you asked to court me. I wasn't prepared to meet a man that night, I guess. Not one that I'd consider courting. And certainly not one that would find me attractive. I'm awfully glad you asked for more than just one dance!" Thinking further about Loring's nervousness that night, she asked, "Was there something else you were afraid of?"

"Ayuh, I guess there was," he admitted. "My biggest fear was that since your father died doing railroad work, you wouldn't want to court a railroad worker."

"Oh, yes, I remember now. It seems so long ago that we first talked about that."

"I just wouldn't have known how to react if you'd've told me you wanted nothing to do with a railroad man," he continued. "That's all I've ever done. Well, except for farming. But it's all I've ever really wanted to do and, as I said then, working on the rails is nothing like being in those engines. It's much safer."

"Do you know the first moment I knew I wanted you to propose to me?" Hattie was thoroughly enjoying this walk down memory lane.

"Am I supposed to pick from all the great romantic moments I never was quite able to make happen?" He quipped and chuckled.

"I never needed romance, Loring. I needed to know I was safe with you. It was when you took me to formally meet your family and introduce me as your girl that I knew I could trust you."

"Oh! That was a disaster as I recall."

"Well, in a way, I guess it was. At least from your perspective, I think," she admitted. "But when your brothers got to acting foolish and cavorting around, trying to win my favor, I got flustered. I felt embarrassed, too priggish and serious to be around your family. I didn't know what to say or what to do. I could tell your sisters felt bad for me, and I appreciated that, but it was you I needed to feel safe with. When you stopped your brothers' silliness and held me at your side, I felt safe. And I think I knew then that I always would if you were with me."

He ran his fingers through her long hair, barely capable of believing this woman had just married him. "And I can't even remember a time when you weren't the girl for me." He looked intensely into her sable-brown eyes, willing her to understand his sincerity. His natural jocularity sometimes covered his deeper, more tender feelings.

Hattie locked eyes with him in her own private ecstasy of understanding. "And then, on White's Bridge, with Mount Washington clearer than I can ever remember it being, you got down on one knee and asked me to be your wife. All I could think was finally, at long last. Yes, of course, *yes!*" He kissed her forehead. They were meant for one another.

It had been a long day of preparing for the wedding service and reception, then celebrating with his family and the friends they'd each invited, who had come to witness their marriage. Loring sensed that Hattie was almost asleep. He knew he wouldn't be awake long, either.

Barely speaking above a whisper, Hattie said, "And happy birthday, Loring."

He closed his eyes, and the last thing he remembered was holding Hattie close to him, feeling her heart beat, and listening to the fire crackle.

Three

~ 1898 ~
Attending to the Work of a Relationship

"How about," Loring said, first thing when he walked in their bedroom, "a hiking trip up near Mount Washington!" He lifted Hattie off her feet and swung her around in circles. If Loring hadn't been so excited, she might have told him she was getting dizzy.

"Wonderful!" she answered, meaning it. How she loved their hiking trips! "When?"

"How about the next good-weather Sunday?"

They'd been married six months, and everything had been all they had hoped. Loring had been working as the Maine Central Railroad foreman for Section 34 in Lewiston, Maine, for over a year. After they were married, Hattie had moved into the room he rented from Reverend Amos Boothby and his wife, Martha. *They look sweet together*, Hattie thought, *like matching salt and pepper shakers*. Both had graying hair and were considerably shorter than she was. The only obvious difference between them was that Amos was lean and Martha was pleasingly plump. Loring and Hattie shared the living space with the elderly couple, so it was only in their small bedroom that she and Loring were truly alone. But Hattie couldn't have been happier. She was Mrs. Loring Evans, and she loved the title.

The Reverend was retired, and the couple had no children. Renting the spare bedroom was a bit of extra income for them, although if they needed it badly, they never let on. Loring's rent included their room and meals, which meant that Hattie didn't have to work at all if she didn't want to. She was so used to being busy she wasn't sure what she'd do with so much free time on her hands, so she pitched in here and there, always making sure Martha didn't feel overstepped. But Martha always seemed to enjoy Hattie's company.

The older woman would sometimes play the pump organ that sat in their living room. She told Hattie that she had played it for many years in the church her husband served. When he retired, the church offered to give them the organ as a token of their thanks. Martha was thrilled to have this beautiful instrument in her own home. It may have been an older model, but it worked just fine under her deft fingers. At first, she had played it often, but when Martha learned that Hattie could play it, she told Hattie she'd welcome hearing someone else play for a change. Though that's what Martha said, Hattie wondered if Martha was becoming too winded to keep the organ pumped with air. In either case, Hattie was welcome to play the organ to her heart's content.

On many of Loring's days off, the couple went fishing, hiking, hunting, snowshoeing, or cross-country skiing. There was no end to the pleasure they had experiencing the world together. Neither had grown up attending church on a regular basis, but, in a profound way, the out-of-doors was church enough for them because nature is where they both saw and felt God's presence.

Loring had been pleasantly surprised to find that he'd met his match with almost everything the two of them did on Sundays. He'd been an outdoorsman for as long as he could remember. He would have expected as much from another man, but he was quite surprised to learn that Hattie was not only willing to be outdoors, but she also loved it as much as he did. She was a strong and able outdoorswoman, and he suspected that, besides simply loving the outdoors, she liked the challenge of any new outdoor adventure.

Some Sundays they would borrow the Reverend's horse and buggy and make a long day of it to go see Loring's family in Raymond. Hattie enjoyed being with Loring's family more and more each time they went, and his family soon became hers. At the Evans family farm, she could wander the acreage or play with the cats to her heart's content. She would help gather eggs, feed the animals, or muck out stalls, and she would even occasionally help with planting or harvesting. She truly loved being with animals and all sorts of nature. It was there that she found her peace.

Today they were celebrating May Day with Loring's family. Nell, the sister closest in age to Loring, was making her last May basket, this one to hang on her beau's door after dark. Hattie was helping her, though Nell didn't really need it. When they finished, Nell said, "May I ask you a rather personal question?" Nell suggested they sit on the settee while no one else was in the room.

Hattie was not particularly concerned about what Nell wanted to know. She and Nell had enjoyed one another's company from the first. Sometimes they cooked together, sometimes they took strolls around the property. Wherever they were, Hattie felt she'd found a sister and a friend in Nell, even though they were quite different in some ways.

"Well, I probably shouldn't pry, Hattie, but I wondered if you and Loring plan to have any children?" It had been several months since her brother's wedding and since Hattie and Loring were both in their mid-twenties, time was obviously marching on to start a family. At least Nell thought so, anyway.

Hattie took no offense and answered truthfully. "We both love children, but it just hasn't happened yet."

"Oh. Well," stammered Nell, trying to guide the conversation out of its sudden awkwardness, "I'm sure it will happen when it's meant to." Nell had asked in the hope of being the first to hear that she was going to have a new niece or nephew in the coming months. She hadn't expected Hattie's answer and quickly changed the subject. "So, do you two have any exciting plans this spring?"

"As a matter of fact, yes. Loring just asked me if I'd like to go hiking up near Mount Washington. I always loved looking at that mountain from White's Bridge when I lived in Standish, you know. I'd gaze at that mountain for as long as I could and imagine what it would be like to be way up there. From here, I've always thought that mountain has a mysterious look to it, being so far away and dreamlike. I can hardly imagine seeing it up close. I'm excited, of course, but I'm a little afraid that it will lose the mystique when we get up near it." Hattie paused a moment, lost in thought. "But, anyway, we plan to go sometime soon when the weather seems best."

"How wonderful! Loring really is such a good chap. He's a good brother, too," Nell said. Hattie thought about Loring's admission to teasing his sister when they were younger. It obviously hadn't damaged their relationship.

Later, on their way home, Hattie thought about Nell's question. She had had a similar one, but hers was directed to God. *Will we ever have children?* she wondered, sending the thought silently to God's ears. She, too, knew that time was not in their favor and would make matters worse before they'd get better. Loring hadn't talked about it after they'd broached the subject of having a family months ago and agreed to wanting several children.

Not having children wasn't Hattie's only concern, however. She was used to being busy, but renting a room from the Boothbys left her with little to do save for the bit of cooking and cleaning she did to help out. If she were more occupied, then perhaps she'd forget about having children and simply get on with the business of life.

"Loring?"

"Yes, dear one?" Loring said as he clucked to the horse to keep a steady pace.

"I'm thinking I need to get a job."

"A job? Why do you need one? I make enough money for both of us, don't I?" Loring said, with an edge to his voice. "And how long have you been thinking about this?"

"For a while now. It's not that I think you don't make enough money," she said, with matching edginess. "I feel the need because I'm used to being busy. I've been feeling so restless these days, but I'm just mentioning it now because Nell and I had a conversation today that got me thinking about it some more." She didn't mention Nell's inquiry about children. She didn't want to open that subject right now.

"Nell's a good woman and keeps a fine house, but she isn't exactly what I would call a busy bee. Why would a conversation with her make you think of getting a job?"

"Maybe just because she *isn't* a busy bee, as you say. I would have been busier today than she wanted to be. Our visit was all well and good and I enjoyed it, but I saw things at your parent's house that I would've liked to do to be helpful even while we talked. Since it isn't my house, I didn't say anything. Is it wrong to want to stay busy?"

"No," Loring answered, but said no more.

Hattie waited. Finally, she said, "So, you don't approve?"

Loring stayed quiet. Hattie also became quiet with growing anxiety. She'd never felt whatever this was coming from Loring. Normal silence was one thing, but this particular silence between them was so foreign and charged, it scared Hattie and she didn't know how to proceed. The last time she'd felt this kind of anxiety was around her stepfather when he was out of sorts. At such times, Hattie would simply busy herself with whatever she was doing or leave the house and take a walk, anything to remove the cloak of uneasiness she felt when she was near him. It wasn't that her stepfather was loud or physically abusive, thank goodness, but his terse responses created an emotional storm that always felt like his anger could escalate.

Along with her fear, she felt anger seeping in. *Why won't Loring answer me? What was so wrong about asking a question? He seemed threatened by it, but what on earth could be so threatening? Did he think I would accept no other answer than an affirmative one? Did he think I wouldn't discuss the subject logically? Did he think I couldn't be trusted to come to a fair resolution?* She folded her arms in tight to her body, as much to protect herself against the chill in the early spring air as to hold in her emotions. Her mood had changed, and she no longer wanted him to respond. She just wanted to get back to their room. She suddenly felt so tired and cold.

Finally, Loring said, "I'm not sure what I think right now."

Hattie didn't speak. They reached the Boothby's house in silence. Hattie retreated inside quickly, fervently hoping she wouldn't run into the Reverend or Martha. Loring took his time caring for the horse.

Hattie lay on their bed, working herself deeper and deeper into the story encircling her mind. As she angrily thought, for at least the third time, of Loring's unacceptable behavior, her eyes welled up. It dawned on her that their bed had never been a place of anything other than the words and actions of the love between them. She had felt only safety and the reality of their deep bond when she lay on their bed. Now the bed seemed tarnished by a much harsher reality. In fact, it had ceased to feel like their bed at all. Her disappointment and grief overflowed in tears that fell off her face and onto her pillow. She thought that in marrying Loring she would never again have to experience such a tension as she'd felt growing up.

Loring walked into the room. She hadn't even heard him. He took one look at Hattie's face, red, blotchy, and wet, and saw that her breathing was the ragged breath of weeping. His heart broke. He sat beside her and laid a hand on her shoulder. She turned her head to look up at him and saw the love in his eyes once again. The love that had drawn her to him from the beginning. She sat up and they embraced, wordlessly, while Hattie's sobs came naturally in Loring's arms.

"Hattie…" Loring tried to begin.

"No, Loring," Hattie said quietly, trying to force herself into a more normal rhythm of breath so that she could speak. "Let me explain something first. The issue of my working needs to wait until I clear the air about something else. I felt something this afternoon I hadn't considered even possible between us. When you didn't answer my question or want to discuss it, I felt alone all of a sudden, as if we were no longer the couple I thought we were. You know how I told you that I felt safe when you stood up for me around your family? That was one kind of safety that I felt for the first time. No one had ever stood up for me like that." His eyes drooped with failure, as though he'd irreparably broken something, so she quickly said, "And I still feel that. It was a kind of physical safety, I think. But I hadn't realized there is also an emotional safety. A kind when touch is not even necessary to feel the bond of compassion. When you weren't willing to discuss things with me, I felt like that bond had broken or evaporated, like it was gone, like I'd lost you. It made me angry at first to think our relationship was so easily vulnerable." Hattie paused, "No, that wasn't the primary anger. At first, I couldn't understand why you weren't the person I needed right then. The person you've always been, you know, right there for me. I guess I just trusted that you will always be someone I can talk to about anything."

"I'd like to be that person, Hattie," Loring said quietly. "I'm sorry I wasn't."

Without commenting, Hattie continued, "But then, after my anger cooled down, I realized that your distance scared me very, very much. I couldn't bear to lose you. Or to lose *us*. When I thought about it that way, I just started crying. Does that make any sense at all?"

"I know it makes sense to you. I've never felt exactly that, but I have felt the awful feeling of being without you. These past minutes, an hour, however long it was when we weren't talking, felt like an eternity. I felt so alone and that's not something I'd like to ever feel again. You know, it's funny. Until I met you, I'd always been alone and never gave it another thought. But without you, alone is…is…is really quite miserable."

They embraced, grateful to feel like-minded once more.

"Now, Hattie, let me explain something to *you*." She looked into his eyes which held a truth she knew she was about to hear. "The reason I didn't answer is because your question caught me off guard. I've never considered a working wife. My mother never worked. When I left home, I took a job so I could support a wife if I ever found a woman I wanted to marry. I just assumed I would work and my wife would tend to our home and babies. I have hoped to be able to buy a place of our own as soon as I could and that our room here would be temporary. It never occurred to me that we wouldn't have babies right away. I don't know," he paused, "I guess things haven't worked exactly as I'd thought. And as time goes by, I've just pushed that thought away. Your question felt like a stab in my already too big stomach," Hattie smiled with her husband, "as though I wasn't man enough to take care of you."

"Oh, Loring. I never, ever thought that."

"I'm glad," he said. "I think I can be man enough to let you work if that's what would make you happy. But if the Good Lord sees fit to give us children, I'd like to revisit this discussion, alright?"

"Yes, Loring, that's fine. So, you're really okay with me working, then?" she asked.

"I think that your wonderful meals make me fat!"

"It's not *my* hand that brings the fork to your mouth, Loring Staples Evans," she replied dryly, with a smirk. "But I don't understand how that answers my question."

"If you get a job, maybe the meals won't be so good," he answered, immediately realizing the statement's implication about Martha's cooking. Quickly he added, "Not that I think Martha would make something that *wasn't* good. What I mean is, you won't be able to make pie and, you know, other desserts that I love. Not that Martha's pies aren't..." Falling all over himself now, he said, "I'm getting nowhere fast, aren't I?"

By now, Hattie was laughing out loud at the mess he was making of his answer. Together, they decided that she would begin looking for a job after their planned hiking trip.

Four

~ 1898 ~
A Trip Through Crawford Notch

The very next Sunday looked promising for a hike in the White Mountains. A strong high-pressure system hung over the east coast, producing the bluest of New England skies. Early that day, Hattie and Loring boarded the Number 6 train out of Lewiston bound for Portland. It was Hattie's first time riding a train and she had mixed emotions. On one hand, she was thrilled to be going anywhere with Loring–another adventure with her beloved, especially sweet after their first real argument. On the other hand, she was somewhat anxious, still living some of her mother's fear of exploding engines. But she spoke about none of her fear to Loring, determined to enjoy her husband's excitement.

Loring had told her about his first railroad job in South Lunenburg, Vermont. He'd started there as a section man in 1891, maintaining that segment of Maine Central Railroad's Mountain Division tracks. One of the benefits of working for the railroad, besides being in the mountains, was that he, and now Hattie, as his wife, could ride the company's rails for free. By 1895, Loring was offered the foreman position of the Mount Willard section, but he hadn't felt ready to tackle what was known as the toughest section on the line. He did, however, take over as foreman of his Vermont section when it became available. He was not yet twenty-two years old and being the head of a crew was a lot of responsibility, but he liked working with people, and he was well liked in return.

In 1896, when he'd gone home for a visit, he went to a dance being held in Forest Hall in nearby North Gorham. Perhaps it was luck, perhaps fate, but Hattie had also gone to that dance. Because she agreed to let him court her, he decided to take a foreman position in a section closer to her. Section 34 in Lewiston, part of the Maine Central Portland Division, opened at the right time. Though by taking this section, he'd left the mountains behind.

Now it was 1898 and he and Hattie were on their way to the White Mountains of New Hampshire. The early morning air was chilly enough for the blanket she'd brought along to picnic on. As she wrapped her lap in it, she listened to the engine hissing and huffing in protest to having been asked to move, but slowly the train gained speed. They were aboard a mighty iron steed whose momentum seemed a miracle when Hattie considered the sheer size and weight of it. The rhythmic sounds of the wheels on the rails might have lulled her to sleep had she not been so excited.

As they traveled this first leg southwesterly toward Portland, Hattie snuggled close to Loring, with the food she'd packed sitting on the seat beside them. She entwined her arm in his. The conversation they had was theirs alone, or at least that's what it felt like to them. There may have been others in the car, but for them there was no one else. The engineer blew the whistle each time they approached a road crossing. What had always been a subdued, forlorn sound somewhere in the distance was now nearly ear-shattering. They had to cease talking when the whistle blew. The steam, which looked like a trailing gray cloud from miles away, was now spewing soot that rained down over them. They simply brushed it off, barely noticing it at all.

Though she had been to Portland, it was always a thrill to see the ocean, the mighty Atlantic that stretched three thousand miles to find significant land to the east. What an unfathomable distance! She couldn't imagine anyone ever being able to cross a body of water that large. When the train slowly pulled through the city and into Portland Union Station,

Loring said, "We get off here and switch to the 154 that will take us into New Hampshire." Hattie could hardly believe they were headed to the mountains she had always wished to see up close. And, just as importantly, they would be in the mountains Loring loved to talk about. She didn't yet know exactly where they would get off the train to begin their hike because Loring wanted to leave some of their day a mystery.

Their next train took them slowly back out of the city's neighborhoods before opening to the countryside. As Hattie dreamily watched a variety of wagons and horses, as well as walkers and bicyclists, she felt important somehow, though she didn't know why. There was just something about the grandeur of the train that she couldn't shake, no matter how much the memory of her mother's fears tried to rob her of her delight.

"And you should…" Loring started, turning toward her. "Hattie? Where on earth are you?"

"Oh, sorry. I was wondering where everyone out there is going on this fine day. And I was thinking that surely they aren't as fortunate as I am right now. What were you saying?"

"You should start recognizing where we…"

"Loring! There's White Rock Station! We must be close to Sebago Lake now!" Loring smiled, realizing she hadn't heard him at all. No matter. She was enjoying this even more than he had hoped she would. And he was enjoying her.

Before they reached the New Hampshire border, the spectacular view of the White Mountains captivated Hattie. Loring, hating to interrupt her reverie, said, "We'll be pulling into the North Conway Station soon and then head up into Crawford Notch. Along the way are some mighty fine hotels with coaches pulled by six or eight horses to take people from the station straight to the hotel. Pretty fancy. These hotels line the Saco River which is a beautiful sight in its own right. This is a popular area to visit, and you'll see why."

Indeed, once they'd pulled away from North Conway, the trees with newly greening leaves of spring, the rushing waters of the Saco in a hurry to get to the ocean, and the occasional wildlife she glimpsed in the distance were more than enough to thrill her. The hotels were lovely sights, to be sure. But her heart was coming alive in these mountains in a way it never had before. She shifted in her seat, first left, then right, trying to take in as much as she could.

When they stopped at Bartlett Station, Hattie remarked that the buildings in Bartlett looked new. Loring told her that a fire two years ago had taken most of the town, which had been rebuilt. She noticed the beautiful Bartlett train station as well and asked Loring if it, too, burned. "It did," he said, "and by the way, this station is very beautiful inside, too. Maybe another time we can get off here and go inside."

Then Hattie watched with fascination as a long freight train on one of the other tracks added another engine on back. "Why are they doing that, Loring?" she asked.

"Heavier trains need another engine to help push them up the mountain, or grade, as it's known. Once it gets to Crawford Station, the ground will level out again and the helper engine will probably come back here to Bartlett. This next section of track is the steepest grade in the country," Loring said with obvious pride, as though this set of tracks belonged to him.

"Getting this track laid into these mountains was quite an amazing feat. Many people said it couldn't be done. It wasn't built by the Maine Central Railroad, by the way. The Portland and Ogdensburg Railroad, the one your father worked for, built it just after the war. I think it's pretty amazing that they were able to lay these twenty miles of steep track in only two years. They had to cut a path into the sides of the next three mountains, Bemis, Willey, and Willard, for starters. And then there were two long bridges, or more specifically trestles, to build along the way."

"Why did they need this track to begin with if it was going to be so hard to do? I mean, couldn't they have gone an easier way?" Hattie asked, reasonably.

"Well, there already are tracks going an easier way. But the P&O president and his brother thought they could build a shortcut. Everyone thought they were crazy, that trains couldn't make the trip. But they tried anyway, and they succeeded. I can't imagine what would have happened if all that work had been for nothing. But when the first train made it up the mountain, the scoffers had nothing more to say about it! I sure wish I'd been old enough to watch that first train go up." Hattie watched Loring's face reflect his yearning. "But anyway, you'll be surprised how hard the engine has to work to pull us up this grade."

"Should I be afraid?" Hattie asked, imagining her back pinned to the seat in a near-vertical climb.

"No," Loring smiled, remembering how he had had to learn all this himself a few years ago. "You won't really feel the difference very much, but you'll hear the engine work harder. These engines have pulled trains up here hundreds of times. They make it just fine, even in the winter, believe it or not." Hattie relaxed into his confidence.

When they were off again, the path made by the tracks soon became quite narrow. Loring explained that they had entered the lower gateway of Crawford Notch. Hattie was spellbound. When she could see beyond the trees, the mountains were everywhere and she was *in* them. Loring pointed out that they were on Mount Willey and would soon be on Mount Willard. Opposite them was Mount Webster. By then she knew they had started to climb when she saw that the bottom of the valley had begun to drop away.

"I *can* hear the engine working harder!" Hattie said with childlike glee.

"Just wait. You should hear the engine work even harder the farther we go, and we'll slow down even more," Loring said.

Then she looked up and could see vast heights above them. "We have to climb up there?" she asked.

"No," he assured her, "but it should be getting steeper soon." And it did. There was no mistaking the work the engine was doing now.

Suddenly, Hattie's attention was not on the hard-working engine but on the terribly high bridge they were crossing. She couldn't even see the track bed out her window. One look below at the staggering depth was enough to send her stomach into somersaults. "We're crossing the Frankenstein Trestle," Loring explained.

Alarmed, Hattie's look told him what her next question was, so he said, "Nothing to do with the book. Look up." Hattie did and saw an enormous rock formation above them. "Some say those rocks look like a monster. But this bridge was actually named for the artist, Godfrey Frankenstein. He liked to paint around here years ago and was friends with the dentist, Doctor Bemis, who owned most of this Notch at one time. Both men died a few years ago, but it was Doctor Bemis who named the trestle after Mr. Frankenstein."

Hattie looked from the rocks high above to the deep chasm below and thought, *Such magnificence. Such power. It all looks indomitable. Man's ability to build a bridge across this expanse is impressive considering what Mother Nature gave them to work with.*

Before long they crossed yet another bridge, this time across Willey Brook that divided Mount Willey from the next mountain. On the other side of the bridge, when they began climbing Mount Willard, a single house came into view. "Loring! Who lives *there?* And *why?*" The house was sitting at the edge, the sheer drop-off on its backside, with the rest of the mountain not twenty feet from the front porch, towering above it. It was a grand-looking house, gray with dark green trim. And large, too, she noticed as they passed it slowly. A woman stood on the porch and waved as they went by. Hattie was on the wrong side of the train to wave back, but she was mesmerized by the fact that a real person lived in that house.

"This is the Mount Willard House, for Section 129, the one they offered me a few years ago. It's a tough section to be assigned to. Anyway, the Monahans live in the house with the section men who work here. Joe is the section foreman and that was Florence, his wife."

"My land!" Hattie exclaimed.

Loring shared her reaction. He wasn't sure he'd ask his wife to live there. "After this next bend we'll be going through the upper gateway and pulling into Crawford Station. You'll see the grand Crawford House hotel just past there. We'll be getting off at that station."

"Do we change trains again?"

"No, this is our destination for the afternoon."

After the train squeezed through the narrow gateway that really didn't seem wide enough, but just barely was, it pulled to a stop. As she stepped off the train into the bright midday light, Hattie did indeed see the grand hotel sitting close by, an immensity such as she'd never seen before. *My word! The hotels are almost as big as the mountains,* she thought, wondering briefly who could afford to stay in such a place.

Turning suddenly to Loring and losing the blanket off her lap in the process, Hattie threw her arms around his neck and exclaimed, "Oh, Loring! Can it be possible to be the luckiest woman in the world?"

"Probably. You're married to the luckiest man in the world."

Five

~ 1898 - 1903 ~
Summit Boomerang

"Thunderation!" Hattie exclaimed, nearly tripping on another rock. "This skirt will be the death of me. Why on earth didn't I wear a pair of your trousers to hike up this mountain?"

"Because you'd drown in them!" Loring laughed, seeing her plight. "Here, take my arm."

They had taken a trail that began opposite the station. Loring hadn't told her where they were going or that it might be steeper than she was used to. He hadn't thought about her long skirt making such climbing difficult. He was glad the fabric was dark at least, so mud wouldn't show so badly. Fortunately, the steeper portions of the trail were fewer than the more level ones. She enjoyed the swollen waterfalls of early spring along the path and the sound the water made as it slipped over the rocks. When they needed to cross over one of the brooks, she appreciated Loring's strong grip and steadying hand. At least he was carrying their food so she could use her other arm for balance.

After about another hour, the path opened to a bare granite ledge. They approached the edge of the enormous rock shelf with caution and there, from a height of nearly three thousand feet, was an expansive, breathtaking view of the valley below, known as Crawford Notch. Hattie could scarcely take it in and simply sat down on the rock, completely enthralled.

"This is the finest view in all of New Hampshire," Loring said without apology, feasting on the curving valley of velvet greens below. "In fact, guess who almost agrees with me? P.T. Barnum. The great circus man himself."

Hattie looked up at him wondering if he was telling a tale. "You're pulling my leg, right?"

"No, I'm not. But he wasn't here when he said it. He was on top of Mount Washington. He said, 'This is the second greatest show on earth!'" Hattie laughed.

The valley and its mountains rising majestically on either side looked like giant green waves in a tree-covered ocean. Loring didn't think he had to point out the tracks they'd just been on. There they were, in plain sight, the silver snake that cut a path through the middles of three mountains. Directly below them, about nine hundred feet down, was the house they'd passed, now looking much less striking from this height.

Neither said anything for a few minutes. Words seemed almost powerless before this view. When she was willing to break the silence, she asked, "Where *is* Mount Washington from here?" Loring pointed her northward and there it was, in the distance, still miles away, but so much closer than ever before. It was frosted with its recognizable snowy icing. It had not lost its mystique one bit. Hattie held both hands to her mouth in a feeling of sheer reverence for this place.

Yet, when she studied the ground where she was sitting, she noticed the dainty wildflowers sprouting here and there. Tiny, four-petaled flowers painted in pastel colors. Delicate blue. Almost pink. Lavender. Snowy white. They'd had to walk on them to get to the ledge, she realized. She hadn't seen them for the grander view in the distance. On several of the blossoms she noticed tiny bee-like insects, in search of nectar, she assumed. The world beneath her as well as the one beyond her were both spectacular in their own ways. She decided she'd choose her steps more carefully going back.

The peaceful silence was again broken, this time by Loring, who had to suggest they have their dinner. They'd need to head back down to catch the next train east. Hattie spread out the blanket and food and thought there could be no finer thing than to have a picnic dinner in such a perfect place. As she took in the expanse before her, she said, "You know, Loring, we're surrounded by 'w' mountains."

"By what?"

"'W' mountains. Willey, Willard, Webster, and Washington!"

"By golly, you're right," he said. He hadn't thought of it that way before.

After they ate and cleaned up, they stood and took one last, long look at the Notch. Loring stepped behind his wife and surrounded her with his arms, holding her close to him. Hattie said, "Thank you so much, Loring. I shall never, ever forget this. I can't wait to come back some day." Loring kissed his bride, and they started down the mountain.

Back inside Crawford Station, Loring told Hattie to have a seat. He said he would return in just a few moments. Then he disappeared through a doorway behind the ticket window. This station was small compared to Portland's grand one. *Quaint. That's what it is. Quaint,* Hattie thought. She became aware of rhythmic clicking sounds after which Loring was back. Before she could ask him what he was doing, their train pulled into the station, and they boarded along with the other passengers. This time Loring grabbed a seat on the downhill side of the train so that she could enjoy a different viewpoint, though for only a short time in the waning light. She hardly noticed the Monahans' house this time, so lost in her own thoughts.

When it was too dark to appreciate anything outside the train, Loring said, "I should probably tell you that the last passenger train for Lewiston left from Portland three hours ago." She gasped, turning abruptly to face him. He looked at her sheepishly. Loring could tell she was about to give him a piece of her mind, so he very quickly added, "But I'm arranging for another way home. Did you hear the clicking sounds coming from the station agent's room?" Hattie nodded, still clearly dubious. "I went into his office to wire Portland. I'm hoping we can take a freight back."

"A freight? Loring Evans, I will not ride with pigs or whatever they're carrying on that train!"

"I won't make you ride with pigs. I promise," he laughed.

"This isn't a laughing matter, Loring. Not to me, anyway. My feet are tired and I'd like to sit on a seat, not on a box *or* a pig!" she spat out.

"My love, would I fail you?" he said, tenderly.

"Well, you haven't yet, I guess," she admitted. She remained quiet, resting her head on Loring's shoulder in the darkness as she listened to the rhythm of the rails and thought about their day. Soon they pulled into Portland Union Station.

"I need to go into the agent's office here, too, and send another message. I won't be long."

While Hattie waited for Loring to return, she took a seat in the expansive lobby. It was quite beautiful, with white marble and gray slate checkerboard flooring and magnificent chandeliers hanging down from very high above. Two enormous fireplaces blazed at either end of the room.

Soon Loring returned. "Our train will be here in about an hour. It'll make a quick stop way out there on those far tracks," he said, pointing out the back windows of the station. "When it comes, we'll need to be ready for it. Meanwhile, we have a little time to look around the station if you want."

Although she would have been happy to wait where she was, she was curious what else occupied the enormous building. First things first, however. Loring steered her to the ladies' room. When she came out, she was eager to tell him all about the beautiful furnishings and decorations in there. She'd certainly never seen anything like it. *Fit for a queen*, Hattie thought. They strolled the massive hallways arm in arm and passed the fruit stand they'd stopped at that morning. It had been laden with fruits in picturesque arrangements. Hattie had hated to pull two luscious looking apples from one of the trays, but she was grateful she had as soon as she had bitten into hers at lunch. Loring had looked longingly at the cigars in the booth next to the fruit but had decided they were all too expensive. Now the stand was inside and closed for the evening.

Hattie was just thinking about how much walking they could do without going outside when Loring stopped her in front of the entrance to the dining room. It, too, was closed for the evening, but they could easily see into the beautiful room thanks to the nearly wall-to-wall windows. A dozen tables covered with white linens, each set for six, filled the room. Linen napkins sculpted like calla lilies filled each glass. A serving counter ran the length of the room, sporting China plates in piles, serving platters in wait, and high, glass-domed cake stands for tomorrow's dessert. Dish cabinets were placed along adjoining walls for easy access. Mounted deer and moose heads hung high off the floors and several more elaborate chandeliers completed the scene. Hattie could only wonder if the meals they served were as fine as the room itself.

Loring spied a clock and nudged Hattie away and back into the waiting area none too soon. A glaring headlight approached the station. The engine rolled slowly by on the track farthest from them. Loring stood and reached for Hattie's hand saying, "Our train's here. We need to hurry. Come with me." He led her outside, across the sizable platform, then helped her walk over several tracks.

"Step lightly, Evans! Old man Morrison isn't real happy about this stop," yelled someone from the caboose.

"Lightly? Me?" Loring laughed as they approached the car.

When he let Hattie's hand drop, he made a gallant sweeping gesture toward the steps as though she were to board a grand carriage. *My husband's full of surprises today. I can't believe I'm going home in a caboose! Better than a livestock car, I guess!*

"Thanks, Ed," Loring said, passing the conductor who leaned out against the rail and lifted his lantern straight up and then back down. Loring motioned to the seat, which Hattie took gratefully. She immediately heard two short toots from the distant engine before it came to life. Then, one by one, each car in front of them stretched out and lurched forward. Hattie took Loring's hand while she watched the world melt away. *This isn't a half bad way to travel,* she thought, *especially with this little potbelly stove taking the chill off.* As if hearing her thoughts, Loring turned to her and smiled.

Then, turning to the conductor, Loring said, "Ed, I want you to meet my wife, Hattie. Hattie, Ed Davis."

"How do you do?" Hattie said, nodding.

"Nice to meet you, ma'am. I heard Loring took a wife recently." Then, turning to Loring and ribbing him with an elbow, Ed said, "Didn't know she was a pretty thing, though." Loring beamed at Hattie as her cheeks colored and he sat down next to her. How he loved this woman.

The men chatted railroad business that Hattie only half listened to. They were headed for Lewiston, the last leg of this wonderful day. It would be late, and Loring would be tired in the morning, but she knew he was mighty happy with the way things turned out.

The next morning, after Hattie kissed Loring good-bye, she shared breakfast with Martha and the Reverend, telling them all about her day in the mountains. Martha was happy for the young couple, as she had sensed they'd had a falling out recently. Martha was well aware that even the closest couples don't always agree. It was where they landed after the spat that told the tale of their relationship. She had no worries for their young boarders.

As if Martha had shared her thoughts aloud, Hattie said, "Things seem so easy between the two of you. Has it always been that way?"

"No, dear," Martha said. "That has come with a lot of learning about how to read each other, listen well, offer a lot of forgiveness, and speak with compassion. It isn't easy to build a meaningful relationship with anyone. It's perhaps harder the more invested we are in the relationship, but both of us wanted to make it work and we stuck with it. Eventually we came to a peace the Bible speaks of, a peace that passes all understanding." Then she chuckled and glanced at her husband.

"Well, most of the time, anyway," Amos said with a smile and Hattie had no need to further the subject. She would, however, be thinking about what Martha had said and wonder if the kind of peace Martha spoke of was different than any other.

After Hattie was finished eating and helping with the dishes, she asked the Reverend if she might look at the newspaper, explaining that she wanted to look for job opportunities. The couple reacted with subtle surprise on their faces but said nothing. The Reverend pointed to the paper on the little table beside his chair, telling Hattie to help herself. She read that the job opportunities in the textile mills were plentiful, and she could walk to many of them. One of the closest was the Bates Manufacturing Company, which was hiring several starting positions. She could go right now. Grabbing her sweater, she headed to the factory, resolute in her mission, even if slightly anxious.

"The job's in the spinning room up ahead," the woman, a spinner herself, told Hattie as they walked a narrow hallway painted a drab green. The closer they came to the end of the hall, the louder things became. But when the woman opened the door to the cavernously large room into which she ushered Hattie, it wasn't the smell of industrialism that hit Hattie first—the smells weren't especially egregious. Nor was it the intensity of what she was seeing, despite the many massive and fascinating machines. It was the roar of moving machinery echoing off the expanse of hard surfaces that almost made Hattie run the other way. "You'd be called a piecer," the woman shouted, then motioned for Hattie to follow her out and around a corner to a still noisy, but much smaller, room. Once the door was shut, Hattie's ears rang as if to mock her for thinking she could get away from the roar. "As I said, you'd be called a piecer. And you'd be working ten hours a day starting at seven in the morning." Hattie struggled to single out this woman's voice from the overwhelming thoughts in her head. "Ya get three short breaks and clock out at five thirty. There's a half hour for dinner. Sundays are the day off. Yer pay would be eight fifty a week, nine dollars if you're a good worker and been here at least six months. But you'd only be paid five dollars for the first six weeks while ya learn. Ya want the job?"

Hattie suddenly felt rushed. She had to gather her wits to think as quickly as possible. *I would be gone about the same amount of time as Loring and have the same day off. I don't know how to be a piecer, but they'd teach me that. It's only about a twenty-minute walk to and from the factory. Yes, I think it'll do.* "Yes, ma'am, I'll take it."

"Fine. Be here tomorrow morning at seven. Report to me and don't be late." And just like that, Hattie was shown the door. As she walked back through the way they'd come, she realized she would once again be earning a weekly wage. She walked to the Boothby's lost in thought about what her day might be like tomorrow. *How fast can I learn? How tired will I get? Will I make any friends? And can I ever get used to the noise?* She entered Martha's home using the back door. Martha had said that friends came in the back door and insisted Hattie and Loring use it.

"Well, hello there," Martha said as she kneaded the bread with her stout fingers. "How did it go, dear?"

Sitting down, Hattie told Martha she accepted the job.

"So quickly, dear?"

"Yes, the hours are right and it's close by."

"Won't it be hot, dirty work? I've heard that it is. Wouldn't you rather work in the nice little millinery shop, over on Howe Street, I think it is?"

"That does sound nice, but I've worked in stores before. I think I'd like to learn about the cloth industry, and I'm not afraid of hard work," Hattie said, choosing to leave out the fact that the heat and dirt might pale in comparison to the noise, which she fervently hoped she'd get used to. "My feet might get sore at first. That happened when I started at the general store a few years back, but I got used to it soon enough. I start in the spinning room tomorrow, bright and early. I'll leave the house about six thirty."

"All right, dear. I'll see to some breakfast before you go. Six o'clock it'll be ready for you. You'll be needing a dinner pail, too. What time will you be home?"

"About six."

"That's fine, dear. The Reverend and I will eat at our usual time and leave you and Loring to yourselves for supper. If you would, please clean the dishes you two make dirty."

"Of course," Hattie said. She might have offered to help with Martha's bread, but instead she asked, "Do you mind if I play your organ? Would I be bothering you if I do?" She didn't want to impose on the natural kindness of the older woman, who would be napping soon.

"I'd love it, dear. Go right ahead. I love it when you play hymns."

Hattie's favorite music wasn't always hymns. She liked some of the popular music as well as some classics, but those she preferred to play on the piano and the Boothbys didn't have a piano. So, hymns would have to do. Just producing music brought her joy and calmed her. It would also afford her time to process the feelings she had about going to the factory tomorrow. She was always nervous until she understood a new job and what was expected of her, but she liked the idea of earning money to build a nest egg. *I hope Loring is still willing to let me work,* she thought as she played "I Surrender All," not catching the irony. *I'll have to be careful not to appear too tired out at supper tomorrow night, lest he tell me it was too much for me. I don't think he will, but we've never crossed this bridge before.*

Later, as they lay in bed, Hattie was finally willing to admit her anxiety about what was to come in the morning. But Loring was already asleep. She turned down the lamp, then snuggled into his side and closed her eyes.

Learning the task assigned to her the next day at the mill took some concentration. The work wasn't particularly difficult, but it needed to be done with speed and accuracy, and Hattie's head began to hurt with the grinding and banging of the machines. She was shown how to watch the many cotton threads for breaks and how to mend them quickly, tying the loose ends into knots. She managed to get through the first day, though both her head and feet ached, but she'd nonetheless done it and felt satisfied with her work. The next day was somewhat better. She noticed a few things she hadn't had the mind for the day before. Some of the workers were children and she wondered if they did this job before school, or if they didn't go to school at all. The other piecers were women, dressed in obvious work clothes. Long drab cotton skirts or dresses. Some wore what looked like homemade feed-bag dresses that could take abuse. She looked down at her skirt with chagrin. She'd wanted to look nice. Not fancy, but respectable. What she chose was a little *too* nice for this place. She'd have to see about finding at least a thick apron to wear over her skirts.

Her concentration on doing the job well prevented her from having any meaningful conversations with anyone until the end of that first week. On one of her breaks, she learned some first names and offered hers. To those bits of information, Hattie slowly learned more and more about her coworkers. Esther Tate introduced herself at dinner that first Friday and gave Hattie tips about the job as well as where she could find things in the enormous building. Esther also warned Hattie about one woman who continually found fault with everyone and everything. She suggested Hattie just smile at the woman and keep her distance if she wanted to have a nicer day. Gradually, over the weeks and months to follow, she became adept at the work and could chat easily with the others whenever they weren't in the spinning room. She and Esther shared almost every break, getting to know one another. Hattie enjoyed the ease of her new routine, and she especially liked the paycheck once she'd passed her learning phase and earned her raise.

Before they knew it, it was New Year's Eve at the turn of the century. The Boothbys didn't stay up to see in the new year, but Hattie and Loring did. Though they'd both have to be up for work at the usual time, they kissed at midnight. "Here's to a wonderful new year and century, Hattie, my love. May we be as richly blessed as we have been already." The couple had no reason to worry about their future. They were blessed with paying jobs, a warm place to stay, good health, and wonderful Sunday adventures together.

That winter, Loring thought that they had made enough money to rent something bigger than their one room. In case a child might be conceived, they should be ready with more space and a place of their own, he reasoned. But before they could settle on where to go, Martha fell ill and passed away.

Hattie would miss the dear woman who had become like a mother to her, but for Martha's husband this was an obvious shock. He was initially distraught, having been married to Martha for thirty-two years. In subsequent talks that the Reverend had with Hattie and Loring, it became obvious that the elderly man would need help with the house and meals. They decided together that Hattie would quit her factory job and work at the Boothby home in exchange for their room and board.

So it was, that her nearly two years working at the mill came to an end. In some ways, Hattie was sorry. She would miss her coworkers. Esther Tate had become an especially close friend. With very short dark hair, Esther had appeared rather harsh at first, as if she was trying to imitate a man, even sneaking an occasional smoke. Hattie came to appreciate Esther's abrupt yet sincere personality and marveled at her stamina after learning she had four boys. But when Hattie learned Esther's husband had left her with the children, the fate of their relationship was sealed with a respect Hattie hadn't known for anyone else quite that way. The two women promised to keep in touch when Hattie left the factory.

She would miss her regular paychecks. But now, free to stay at home, Hattie enjoyed the outdoors when she could. She listened to the birds sing and the squirrels chatter to her heart's content. The Reverend had been happy to let Hattie make a small garden out back in which she'd planted vegetables and some of her favorite flowers. Having her hands in dirt again and watching things grow brought her a rich sense of life.

One lovely autumn day, as Hattie walked home after a nice visit with Esther, she felt she was being followed. Turning around, however, she saw nothing. A few more steps and she sensed it again. Still nothing. Finally, the third time, she laid eyes on a kitten, light-gray and white with greenish-brown eyes. She stooped to pick it up and it meowed loudly. "I'll just bet you're hungry. I wonder where you live?" Hattie turned in all directions trying to see if a mother cat might be following close behind, but she saw nothing. The kitten looked to be several months old and scrawny from neglect. Hattie desperately wanted to take the little thing home but knew she couldn't. The cat likely belonged to someone else, and besides, the house was the Reverend's, not hers. She put the cat down and walked away briskly, hoping the cat would not follow her. It did, but for only a short time, then it turned and meowed itself in the opposite direction. *Can't be helped,* Hattie thought. *May the kitten find a home.*

The next spring, Hattie was outside checking the state of the garden. *The ground seems almost thawed enough,* she thought, as she bent to try her trowel in the dirt. Suddenly, her long skirt ruffled as if a stiff wind had just picked it up. *But it's not particularly windy,* she thought. She paid it no more mind until it happened again. Standing up and turning around she saw a fully-grown cat, though thin and ragged looking. "Well, for heaven's sake! Will ya look at that," Hattie crooned picking up the cat, which then began to purr. It looked like a coon cat mix. "You look a little like…no, you look a *lot* like the kitten that followed me half a year ago. How on earth did you find me?" After a while she put the cat down to finish her early spading without much luck. The ground was just too hard. Holding the trowel at her waist, she surveyed the plot of ground to think through this year's planting. What worked well last year, what she'd try new, and where it would all go. The cat never left her side.

When it was time to begin supper preparations, Hattie went inside to find the Reverend first and asked him to come out back. "Reverend, I have a story to tell you," she said, picking the cat up again.

After she'd finished, Reverend Boothby said, "And you wish to keep it?"

"If I may."

"As long as you take care of it, I have no objection. Martha had cats in the beginning of our marriage. She surely did love them. I could take them or leave them, myself. But that's fine." The old man turned toward the door, then turned again to face Hattie. "You know? Come to think of it, that cat of yours looks an awful lot like one of Martha's." And as he stepped into the house, Hattie heard him mumble, "Martha, that cat is like a boomerang."

And so, Boomerang became a welcome part of the household. He was sitting on Hattie's lap one Friday afternoon when Loring walked into the house after finishing his shift on the tracks. He had a look on his face that she knew meant that he had something important to tell her. "After supper," was all he said when she inquired.

As soon as Hattie had finished washing and putting the supper dishes away, they went upstairs to their room and sat down on the bed. Suddenly, she was worried about what was coming. Hattie loved to know the facts about things and not be surprised. Loring knew that and learned to be more careful over the years not to withhold important information from her. "Hattie, W. D. Sawyer, a Maine Central official, has recommended me for the position of section foreman for 129."

"That's in Crawford Notch, right? The one they offered you before?" she said.

"Ayuh. And I know how much you loved seeing the Notch years ago. But the section house there, the one the Monahans live in, that's where we'd live. It's considered a wilderness post. There's plenty of visitors, but not many people stay, so it could get lonely, and the weather can be harsh. Sawyer is offering me a dollar seventy-five a day. That's ten fifty a week, same as I get here, but we would have use of the house, too. So, we wouldn't have to pay rent. I won't take the job unless you want to move there. But, Hattie, before you say one way or the other, you need to know that you'd be expected to cook and do laundry for the four section men who live there. Essentially, you'd be running a boarding house. And the house is bigger than anything you've lived in, so it'll be a lot to keep up with. Please, Hattie, think it over before you answer. I'll be right back." Loring purposely left his wife alone to allow her time to think in private. He needed to be sure that if she agreed to go, she'd be doing it as much for herself as for him.

When Loring came back, Hattie said nothing right away. So many thoughts had crossed her mind like the many tracks at Portland Union Station. Finally, she said, "Well, since we don't have children to worry about, I don't see why not. I'm no stranger to hard work, as you know by now. But I want to know what you think, not just the job details."

"I think I'd love living in a bigger space with the mountains right out our back door. Well, front door *and* back door," he said with a chuckle, "but the main thing is that if you're willing, I am. It won't be easy up there. For either of us. But I've been a foreman long enough now that I think I can handle the harder section."

"And we both love nature," Hattie cut in, "and the Notch is nothing if not that. And we both know how to put in a long day's work. We wouldn't have to stay for the rest of our lives, either. If we give it our all for a few years and feel like moving on, we could, right? Loring, we both love an adventure. Let's do it," she finished, satisfied with her sensible reasoning.

"That's true. We wouldn't be locked in for the rest of our lives. Alright, then," Loring said, loving his ever-practical wife.

"How soon would we move, though?" Hattie asked. "We'll need to tell the Reverend so he can find someone else to help him. Oh, and I hope I can take Boomerang." At the sound of his name, the cat jumped onto her lap.

"The Monahans still live there," Loring said. "They had a baby last year and they wanted a less severe drop in the back of the house to raise her, I guess, so Joe took the foreman position the next section down. I think they'll move later this summer. We'll need to move at the same time so I can cover the job. We can tell Amos as soon as I let work know officially. And yes, I don't see why you couldn't take Boomerang. He'll certainly have a few things to learn, though, won't he? He won't be a city cat much longer!" Again, Hattie was quiet. Loring thought that perhaps she saw a roadblock in these plans. "What is it, Hattie?"

"Loring," she said quietly, "do you realize what day it is today?" She waited only a brief moment before saying, "It's May 8, exactly five years to the day since we climbed Mount Willard."

Six

~ 1903 ~
Changing Places

"Reverend," Hattie said, getting Amos's attention, "I'll keep the garden going through the summer. By August, when we leave, I'll have picked everything over for you. There will be things that will keep growing, of course, like the beets, carrots, and cabbage. If you can't eat it all, I'm sure you can find a neighbor or someone who can help you."

"Thank you, Hattie. You and Loring have been very good to me since Martha died. I'll be sorry to see you go."

"Likewise, Reverend. We've been happy here."

August arrived and with it a flurry of activity. The railroad company had arranged to have a boxcar sitting in the Rumford Junction siding just south of Lewiston to move their belongings. They would have two days to fill it. The boxcar would be added to a freight train that would be delivered to Crawford Station's siding. It would then be brought down to the Mount Willard House by helper engine to be unloaded.

There had been much to do since May. They visited Loring's family to tell them the news of their move and say their goodbyes, inviting them to visit the Notch. They also made sure to let his family know that they'd be down to visit when they could, and Hattie assured them she would write often. Hattie also made a point of visiting Esther once more.

After the majority of their goodbyes had been said, they gathered everything they thought they might need to set up the new household. They hadn't started their marriage with much and hadn't needed much while living with the Boothbys, but in the past two months they'd accumulated quite a lot for their new home. They were able to fill some furniture needs with hand-me-downs from Loring's generous family. Some things they bought used from different places around Lewiston. Some things seemed to have come from God Himself.

"You mean it, Reverend? Really?"

"Yes. You'll make better use of them than if they were to sit here gathering dust," he said, looking at Martha's sewing machine and organ with what Hattie thought was a mixture of love and grief. "Martha and me, we have no children to pass things along to, you know. Our niece's and nephew's homes are well established by now. May as well you and Loring have them as anyone. I think Martha would have given them to you herself if she were still here, God rest her soul."

When it was time to load the train car, Loring and some of his coworkers carried the organ out of the house first, with some difficulty. They were able to move the sewing machine and most of their things much more easily. When almost everything had been moved out, the Reverend handed Hattie a few of the kitchen utensils he knew he would never use. It was with mixed feelings that Hattie took these well-used items from his hands. Martha's love had made their food with these. She felt a debt of deep gratitude to both of the Boothbys, a debt she gladly bore but could never repay.

That night, with what little energy they still had, Loring and Hattie lay on their bed talking. Hattie said, "So, we'll leave early Sunday morning, right? The Reverend should be up in time for us to say goodbye. Then we'll get to the Notch in time to see Florence, I hope. I have so much to ask her!"

Loring yawned largely, "Joe said they'll have their things moved down to the Willey House by then, but they'll make sure to see both of us sometime during that day."

"Good. I'll make a list of the things I need to ask her on our way up to the Notch. Don't let me forget to take paper! And I need a box for Boomerang to ride in. I think he'll be happier to be contained. Did you remember to save me a box for him?"

"Ayuh. But, Hattie, I think it's time to let tomorrow take care of tomorrow and go to sleep. What is it you always say? 'Everything will work out for the best.' You've never been wrong, love. Good night." He leaned over to kiss her and hopefully seal shut not only her mouth but also her mind. He needed sleep and knew she did, too.

Rather than be silenced, she said, "When I was little and got all fussed up about something instead of going to sleep, my mother would say, 'Hattie Frances! Turn off that brain of yours and go to sleep!' I hated those words then, and you as much as said them now," she smiled and kissed him back.

"Understood," he said, trying to stifle another yawn.

The next day, packing and hauling the remainder of their items to the boxcar went well and soon that day, too, was over. Hattie dreaded the morning, though. Nevertheless, it came. And with it, feelings of more grief than she had ever felt. It wasn't going to be easy to say goodbye to the Reverend, whom she'd grown to love. If Martha had been a surrogate mother, Amos had been the father she'd never had. He'd been caring, yet firm, wise, yet not overbearing.

"Reverend," Hattie addressed the old man as she approached him, with Loring by her side. She reached in to hug him. She couldn't help her eyes misting over. She stepped back to let Loring in. He hugged Amos, too, mostly because Amos had held his arms out. Normally they would have shaken hands, but Loring accepted the older man's affection in that hug.

"Just one thing, Hattie," Amos said. "All this time, I've wondered why you always call me Reverend. You could as well have called me Amos."

After a moment's thought, Hattie said, "I guess because I saw something in you I've respected all these years. Reverend feels more respectful to me."

"Well, I thank you, then." Those were Amos's last words before the couple walked away from a place that had been so good for them as newlyweds. Calling back, Hattie added, "I'll write!"

Now they turned their faces to a new chapter in their lives and hoped it would be just as good as this one had been.

"And here's your pantry. Lots of space here, isn't there? I kept my pots and pans in here, but you can do what you like with yours, of course. There's a serving hatch between here and the dining room. I always loved that about this kitchen. It makes it so easy to serve the men in the dining room without having to walk all the way around. Someone had his head on straight when he laid out the plans for this place! And then there's the stove. It's coal burning, as you can tell, and you'll have no trouble having enough coal, thanks to the railroad! In fact, this place is always plenty warm enough even in the winter, with steam heat coming up from the cellar and through the radiators, thanks to the coal furnace down there. Your water is always fresh, too, because it will either come from the brook or, in the winter, from the trains. They'll fill your tank when it's needed. Any questions so far? I know it's a lot at first, but soon it will just be life at the Mount Willard House." Baby Gertrude, on Florence's hip, sucked on her thumb. She had her eye on Boomerang down by Hattie's feet.

"How old is Gertrude?"

"She's about a year and a half now. Joe and I were thinking we'd like to live closer to the school when Gertrude is old enough, so when the section foreman job down the hill came open recently, we decided to take it."

Hattie was grateful to have Florence's help. Even then, it was a bit overwhelming to think about setting up a household for herself and Loring and four section men. She hadn't felt this overwhelmed since the first day she'd walked into Bate's Mill. Routine, she kept telling herself. As soon as I get a good routine down, I'll be fine. She was suddenly grateful she didn't need to figure out how to add children to all of this.

Before Hattie could think of another question, Florence continued, "Now, I've made some food to get you started until you have all your things and get an order together."

"I really appreciate that, Florence." Then suddenly she realized she didn't know how to get the ingredients she'd need when Florence's food ran out. It had been so easy in Lewiston. She'd just walk to a grocer or a general store and get what she needed. That certainly wasn't going to work here. "How will I get supplies?"

"Just make a list and give it to one of the crewmen. I usually give mine to my husband and he passes it along. Most things will come from Bartlett. Sometimes I give my lists directly to Bobby Morse or whoever's on that day. He's one engineer who'll stop on the way down if you attach your order to the message pole out front. I'll show you that later. There's really any number of ways to get your list or mail or any kind of message sent. You'll figure out what works best for you. And by the way, I'll be the postmaster, or mistress, I guess, for Hart's Location. I'll also be the telegrapher."

"Where's Hart's Location? I thought you were moving just the next section down. Will you be working away from home, then?"

"You're standing in Hart's Location!" Florence said sweeping her hand in an arc in front of her. "There aren't many of us who live in this town. I think it's the smallest town in New Hampshire, actually. It stretches from the gateway up by Crawford Station down to almost Bartlett. It's long and very narrow, basically the tracks and a bit of land on either side. But we get to know each other here by way of this railroad mostly. My office will be in our home. That reminds me of something I need to show you, and then how about we sit on the front porch and talk? I need to feed this one," Florence said, giving the baby a kiss.

They walked into the dining room where Hattie noticed the beautiful wood floor with the Maine Central Railroad logo painted in the center. On the back side of the house was a bay window looking down over the valley. Florence stopped beside a desk and said, "Here's your telegraph key. Do you know how to send and receive messages yet? Do you know Morse code?" Hattie shook her head. "Well, you'll want to learn. You'll hear messages coming through a lot, but most won't be anything you'll need to worry about. You'll get used to hearing them enough to know what to pay attention to, though. You'll hear 'MW' for Mount Willard before messages for this house. 'WH' for Willey House is ours. 'CS' is Crawford Station. 'BS' is for Bartlett Station, and so on. So, the quicker you learn, the better. Loring can help you."

At that, they left the dining room and went through the parlor, which had a lovely, nearly wall-to-wall carpet over its hardwood floor. "I haven't left you much by the way of furniture, I'm afraid."

"That's alright," Hattie said, stepping onto the porch, "hopefully ours'll be here soon. So how do I get whatever I've ordered when it comes in? Will Bobby stop and drop it off?" Hattie was using a first name for a man she had no knowledge of, which felt strange.

"Not usually," Florence answered, discreetly lifting her blouse, and hiding Gertrude underneath. Hattie wondered briefly what that must be like to nurse a child. Florence continued, "Whenever your order comes to Crawford Station, the men will bring it down with the handcar or pushcart. Sometimes, if there's a light engine going down, they'll put your groceries on the little flat place over the cowcatcher. Trust me, those men want to eat. They'll be more than happy to see that you get your groceries!" Both women nodded knowingly to one another. Some things were the same no matter where a person lived.

Just then, Loring and Joe came walking up. "Hello, girls!" Loring said. He was obviously enjoying whatever he and Joe had talked about. He seemed jolly as usual and not a bit overwhelmed. *And why should he be?* Hattie thought. *His job will be about the same as usual, I suppose.*

"Hello," both women said at the same time. Hattie felt strangely protective of Florence nursing in front of Loring, but if Florence was disturbed by it, she didn't show it. Besides, Loring probably hadn't even noticed.

"Joe's been showin' me some of the peculiarities about this section. He showed me a great blueberry patch down there," Loring said pointing downhill toward Bartlett.

"I don't think that has anything to do with keeping the section in working order," Florence leaned toward Hattie as if to whisper, but looked straight at Joe and Loring and smiled. Hattie could see a friendship in Florence starting already.

After the men had retreated into the house, Hattie asked, "Did you like living here? Honestly?"

"Yes, I did, actually. Each of these section houses have their own distinctions. This one has views like no other. I'll miss that the most, I think. It's also quite large. You'll find that out soon enough when you have to clean all the soot and dust the trains kick up. I also liked being close to Crawfords, too. That's what locals call the Crawford House hotel up there. There are so many interesting people that stay there and sometimes they walk down here just to see how a house like this even exists."

"Did you feel safe here?" Hattie asked.

"Absolutely. The people from Crawfords are gentlefolk. I've yet to meet one I didn't like. That goes for the hotel guests as well as the hired staff. They're usually so amazed by this place, and they're fun to talk to."

"That's good to know, but I guess I was thinking more of safety from animals in these woods," Hattie said.

"Oh. You'll want to keep your eyes open. There are bears and lynxes around here, but they're more scared of us than we are of them. In fact, you aren't likely to see either out in the open here, but you might if you go climbing in the woods. And speaking of climbing in the woods, have you heard about English Jack yet?"

"No, who's that?"

"He's quite a character, that one. He's an old guy from England with a story or two or a hundred to tell," Florence smiled. "You'll meet him. No need to say more."

"Is the house safe? I mean, we aren't very far from the tracks sitting here. And the house is right on the edge of the mountain."

"You know, Hattie, I had that same question at first. I thought, Lord bless me, if I don't wake up at the bottom of the hill one of these days! Or if one of those trains doesn't come straight through the parlor! But you know, even though it's always windy here and there are occasional bad storms, I don't think this house will go anywhere. It's built on solid granite, my Joe told me. As for the house sitting nearly right on the tracks, well…Oh! Well, speak of the devil. A train's comin' from down there." Florence pointed past the bridge.

Hattie looked and realized the only time she'd been this close to railroad tracks was when she boarded trains at stations. *But those trains were standing still,* she thought. *And now, I'm sitting not twelve feet away from a moving train on my own front porch! Good heavens!* She noticed smoke from just beyond the rocks and heard the unmistakable chuff-chuff-chuff of the engine. When the train came into view, she thought she could feel a slight vibration. She saw the smokestack cough a gray cloud into the air and each rhythmic chuff kept the cloud inflated.

Florence stood up. "We can go inside if it feels like too much to you."

"No, that's all right." Hattie was determined to stay put, not wanting to miss anything about what was to become her whole world soon. As the black engine approached, it grew louder than Hattie could have imagined. She could see the slow but insistent progress it was making, working hard to climb the hill. Not only did smoke pour out of the stack above the engine, but steam also shot out from each side of the cowcatcher. It looked and sounded quite like a great dragon, snorting with terrifying anger. The enormous wheels held tight to the track and the side rods connecting them worked slowly, yet steadily. The noise was almost deafening as the engineer passed, sporting a big smile and waving heartily. Hattie was so engrossed, she forgot to wave back. The sheer size of such a beast commanded great respect. As it passed, Hattie felt something new, something she absolutely did not expect—from deep inside her she felt thrilled. Florence looked at Hattie's wide eyes and awed expression and smiled to herself. *This girl will do just fine here.*

Seven

~ 1903 ~
Up the Tracks to English Jack's

attie met the section men next. John Green, brothers Denny and Ed Meany, and Billy Powell all introduced themselves to her. John had apparently met Loring before. He'd been a switchman at Fabyan's, the next station west of Crawford, prior to joining Section 129 earlier that summer. He and Loring had crossed paths before Loring had met Hattie. He said he liked Loring and looked forward to working with him. Florence, still standing beside Hattie, said with a grin, "You'll get to know these boys pretty well after you've fed them and washed their clothes for a while." The men laughed and went into the house.

"They go inside looking like that?" Hattie remarked on the appearance of their blackened, sooty overalls, complete with black faces and hands. Loring never entered Martha's house until he'd shed off his overalls in their small out kitchen and washed up.

"They'll go right down to the cellar first to clean up. They won't usually come to your table dirty. 'Course today, there isn't a table for them to sit at, is there?" Florence pointed out with a laugh. Hattie liked Florence more and more. Her good nature was a pleasure.

Joe and Loring walked out of the house. Joe said, "Flo, we'll take this next train down." That was Florence's cue to ready herself and give Hattie any more bits of information she could. Hattie couldn't think of anything more to ask about, though she was absolutely certain something would occur to her the moment Florence left on the train. She watched the train stop and the conductor take Gertrude from Florence's arms with a familiarity that surprised her. Then he helped Florence up onto the train. Finally, Joe jumped aboard as the train began moving. Florence yelled out to Hattie, "Don't forget, I'm just the next house down!"

Loring put his arm around his wife as they watched the train leave. Hattie felt almost panicky to realize that she, not Florence, was now responsible for all these men. "I think the boxcar will get here day after tomorrow," Loring said, "so, we should have our things soon. I don't have to report to work until Wednesday. Joe will cover both sections, but this crew knows what needs to be done here for the next couple days. So, tomorrow, you and I are going exploring."

"That sounds wonderful to me!" Hattie said. "There isn't much I can do here. Florence left things in great shape, thank goodness. And I need to put some space between my anxious thoughts. Walking will do me good." Then, thinking of something, she asked, "But, if we go up to Crawfords, for instance, do we just walk on the tracks? Or wait for a train? Or do we have to pick our way down to the road through the trees?"

"We'll walk the tracks. It's a lot quicker."

"But what if a train comes?"

"Then we'll get off the tracks!" Loring smiled, loving his obvious answer. He knew he'd get a reaction from Hattie. He wasn't disappointed.

"Oh. Funny, Loring. Real funny." Hattie swatted his arm, playfully.

"There are places on either side where we can wait out the train," he said, giving her the answer she was looking for. "There are narrow spots, too, but we can't miss hearing a train coming. We'll find a safe place in plenty of time."

"Oh, and I watched Florence hand little Gertrude into the conductor's arms as if they were family. Gertrude went to him easily. Are they related or something?"

"No," Loring said, "but they may as well be. Everyone here gets to know each other like family. You will, too. You'll see."

The men and Hattie ate supper picnic-style on the porch that evening and began getting to know one another through light-hearted conversation. The porch roof shielded them from the light mist in the air. Boomerang made an appearance and stayed close to Hattie.

Before the men parted ways with Hattie and Loring, Hattie asked John about the slight accent she could hear when he used certain words. Somewhat modestly, Hattie thought, John said, "My parents were both born in Ireland. I suppose I picked up a bit of their brogue. Good evening, ma'am." With a nod, he followed the other men into the house.

When the rain cleared that evening, some of the brighter stars peeked around the corners of the clouds that were breaking up. Hattie and Loring picked out Jupiter, Sagittarius, and Ursa Major right away and marveled at their brilliance when suddenly everything around them took on an ethereal glow. Two clouds parted company and gave way to a full moon. An iridescent blue illuminated the Notch below with stunning clarity. "Isn't this just incredible?" Hattie whispered. "And then with the new moon, imagine how the sky will explode with stars!" Loring, who was standing behind her, pulled Hattie closer as they witnessed the miracle above them, a scene that would never grow old. As they walked back into the house and through the dining room, Hattie said, "I need to learn to use the telegraph key. You'll have to teach me. I know some of the code but not enough to do much good."

Later, after Hattie hurriedly wrote a letter to the Reverend, she and Loring retired for the night. It had been quite a day. With no bed of their own, John Green had offered his to Hattie, but she politely declined. She and Loring preferred to sleep together in their new bedroom, even though they'd be on the floor.

"We're home, Loring. Just think of it. We have our own home. I've never set up my own home before."

"We're not quite home yet," Loring said, teasingly. "There's one more thing I want to do before I can call this home."

"What's that?"

"Not telling you. Not yet."

"Oh, you tease, Loring Evans!" Hattie said, looking him square on to see the twinkle in those eyes and the grin on his face.

Loring kissed his bride passionately. They weren't newlyweds anymore in some respects, but here, in this "castle halfway to the sky" as he liked to call it, it felt like they were. The house was theirs. This room was theirs. The night was theirs.

Sometime toward morning a blinding light shone through their bedroom windows and a rumbling that grew in intensity startled Hattie awake. Loring very sleepily said, "It's okay. It's just a freight." He was snoring soundly a few moments later, but Hattie lay awake in the pre-dawn darkness thinking, *Welcome home, Hattie. This interruption is going to be a regular night's occurrence. Best get used to it.*

Though they were, admittedly, a bit stiff the next morning, they had a quick breakfast, packed a sandwich with the food Florence had left, and walked out into the brilliant day. Almost directly across from the house was a small building. "Now, here's what they call the carhouse, where the three-wheeled handcar is kept, among other things. See the grindstone? Next spring, new growth'll need to be cut back away from the tracks with a scythe. Every day the scythes have to be sharpened. One man turns the grindstone and another moves the scythe across it. Sharpens up right quick, Joe told me."

Across the tracks from the carhouse was another small building. "Over there is the icehouse for perishables, but Florence probably showed you that."

"Speaking of Florence," Hattie said, as they walked beyond the house, "were the Monahans the first family to live in this house?"

"No, it was built for the James Mitchell family in 1887. We'll pass by the place where the Mitchells lived before that. It's gone now, but that first section house was called the Foreman's Cottage. It was smaller than our house, but it held the Mitchell family and the section crew. It was built under the cliffs up there," Loring said, pointing up and ahead of where they were walking, "and I guess rockslides were common in that area, enough so that some of the rocks came straight through the house."

"Oh, dear! Do rockslides…"

"No," Loring broke in to answer Hattie's unspoken question. "That won't happen to our house because it's built in a safer location. You've noticed the iron grates over the downstairs, track-side windows, I assume. That's not for rockslides. That's for the smaller rocks that get kicked up, especially in the winter by the snowplows. The company doesn't want to replace windows all the time. Anyway, one night there was a pretty good storm with a lot of lightning and thunder and several rockslides hit their house. Mitchell quit right then and there. By that time, these tracks were being leased by the Maine Central company, who asked Mitchell if he'd stay on as foreman if they built a new house. He said he would, so they had our house built and the other one torn down. The Mitchells stayed until 1898 when he retired and the Monahans came."

They walked silently for a time. Hattie gazed down into the valley below. "It's so beautiful," she said, sighing. "It doesn't look like the forest fires this year came this far."

"No, I don't think they did. As far as I know, Mount Stickney, which isn't very far north of here, is the closest they came. But it's amazing the Notch didn't burn. Fires took so much of Maine and New Hampshire, it's just awful."

"I would feel so sad to see all this beauty taken away by fire."

"Well, those fires were mostly due to the awful dry spring we had, you know. It didn't take much to set them off. But several of the fires started because of a spark from a train. The fire that nearly took out Intervale down there by North Conway was from the noon express. Our job on this section is critical to make sure sparks don't set off the bridge or the ties the same way."

Goodness, Hattie thought, *that would be dreadful.*

"But eventually, hopefully soon, the company will replace the wood with steel. They're doing that now with the smaller bridges. Once they do that, I'll feel better. We'll still have to watch for sparks on the ties, of course."

Just before the gateway, they came to a small carved-out cave. Loring told her the men called this the blacksmith's shop. He said it had been dug out twenty years ago to forge rails but was no longer used. *If I were a child,* thought Hattie, *I'd love playing in there.* On second thought, she said, "There aren't animals that live in there now, are there?"

"I don't think it goes that deep, but I suppose I'd want to stomp and holler some before going in."

When they reached Crawford Station, they went inside to mail Hattie's letter. This gave them a chance to say hello to Herb Chase, the new agent who worked there now. After paying Herb their two cents postage, they walked on to the Crawford House through the railroad yard and waved at the two section men, Denny and Billy, working there. Then they set their sights on the huge hotel, watching it grow larger with every step. It was such a grand building. People leisurely crisscrossed the vast lawns, steering clear of a game of baseball being played in the hotel's front yard. Hattie noticed the fine clothing the women were wearing and felt embarrassingly unsophisticated but didn't say so. She'd never felt that way before and since she had no intentions of becoming suddenly refined, she decided not to think any more about it.

Behind the hotel they saw some cottages and other structures, some large, some smaller. As they walked among the buildings, a woman approached them and said, "Hello. How are you this fine day?"

"Very well, thank you, ma'am. I'm Loring Evans and this is my wife, Hattie. We're new to the section house down there."

"Ah," the woman said, holding out her hand for a shake, "so I've heard. Word gets around quickly in these parts. I'm Beth Peabody."

"Good to meet ya, Beth. Could you point out a few of the buildings back here and what they're for? This is a big place," Loring said.

"I sure can. My husband George and I live in this cottage here. He's the caretaker at the big house. The hotel, I mean.

We call it the big house. I cook for the help. After tourist season, when most of the help is gone, I run the Bretton Woods post office in my dining room. Most of the other cottages are lodging for the staff and the entertainment, like the orchestra. That building there is the icehouse, where the butcher's shop is. And that big one over there is the stable. There's cows in there, besides the horses and burros. And that's the garage for the big coach, to bring guests over from the station, you know, and wagons and other vehicles. That's mostly it." Changing the subject, Beth said, "When'd you get in?"

"Yesterday," Hattie offered.

Beth nodded her acknowledgment, then said to Hattie, "You're welcome to come visit any time. If I'm not here, I'm in the big house. Just come find me." Then to Loring Beth said, "I guess I'll be seeing you up here in the yard from time to time then."

"I'm sure you will. Well, thank you kindly, Beth," Loring said, smiling.

"Bye, now," Hattie said, "and thank you." She was grateful for the friendliness of those she'd met so far.

"Bye, neighbors!" Beth said, turning away.

"Next, I think we should go meet another neighbor of ours, this English Jack everyone talks about," Loring said, turning them toward the base of the mountain. It wasn't difficult to find Jack's trail. Down near the gateway they'd just walked through rested a large, handsome sign that read "THE HOUSE THAT JACK BUILT" in bold, white, capital letters. On the trail, Loring told Hattie that James Mitchell had been so enthralled by English Jack that he wrote an epic poem about the man. *Seems this English Jack is something of a legend around here,* she mused. *This should be interesting.*

After twisting and turning along the trail, they began hearing voices up ahead. The path opened to a clearing where a few people stood around a white-bearded, portly man sitting on a box. He wore a slouch hat and tattered, old clothing. They assumed they'd found English Jack. Behind him was a rough-looking cabin where it appeared the old man lived. The roof and sides of the several small buildings were haphazardly built of unpainted, flat boards of varying lengths. The dwellings together made a compound of sorts, complete with fencing.

He was telling a story while whittling a long, sturdy-looking limb of spruce. "Come on in, folks," Jack interrupted himself with a sweep of his hand in Hattie and Loring's direction. When he began talking again, he had an undeniably British accent mixed with an American one. It was charming, Hattie thought. Jack seemed to command a spellbinding presence with his voice alone. He was very practiced in front of an audience. And he looked so much like Saint Nicholas that Hattie and Loring both wondered if the small children had their eyes fixed on the old man for that very reason.

"Yes," he continued, "Mary, my little blue-eyed blondie, just as sweet as she could be, felt more lost than me, and that was saying something. She was so young to be so lost. She was only five years old. I took pity on her. 'What're ye doing down in these docks, little one?' I asked her. 'I'm looking fer m' daddy's ship,' she says and then doesn't she burst out crying for her mother. She says she's hungry. Well, being an orphan myself, no more than twelve, I knew what it meant to be hungry. So, I spent my last sixpence on a little cake for her. She ate it while we were walking along the docks, and we chatted the whole time. Got to know each other some. Then along came an omnibus with two right jolly sailors on top. And little Mary started jumping up and down, shouting, 'Oh! Me daddy! Me daddy! Daddy, here is *me!*' And don't ya know, it got me right here, in m' heart and didn't water leak right out of m' eyes."

Jack stopped to apologize for keeping his audience so long. He offered some of his homemade root beer, saying, "It won't hurt you and perhaps it'll do ya some good. It's made of hops and roots that grow right around here. It's mighty good to help digest your food." Jack patted his stomach and paused, holding out a jug and glass. Some stepped forward to try Jack's beer. Loring started to, but Hattie held him back with a look. Some other time, he wisely decided.

Jack began again, with tears in his eyes, telling about the grand reunion of the sailor father and his small daughter, Mary. In the story, Mary offered her father an explanation for young Jack's tears, telling him "'e lost 'is daddy, too." Jack explained that Mary pushed him to tell her father of his ambitions to be a sailor. At that, Mary's mother and father took young Jack in and, when it came time for the father to go back out to sea, he took young Jack with him as a cabin boy. "A young man's dream come true," Jack said.

"For the next eight years, I grew up at sea. I became an able seaman. Eventually, I realized Mary was growing up as well. She was the sweetest flower ever to come from heaven, she was," Jack said dreamily. "I decided right then 'n' there to take her as my wife one day." Hattie and Loring exchanged glances at this tale of budding romance.

"Then we took to sea in the *Nelson*, bound for the Indian Ocean." Jack described going around the Cape of Good Hope and sailing past Madagascar toward Ceylon. "All at once, one Sunday afternoon, we heard, 'All hands! 'All hands on deck! Tike in sail!' So great were the winds. Then we heard a bellowing voice call, 'Hard-a-port! Fer God's sake, hard-a-port! Land straight ahead!' Next thing I know, I'm flying into the sea, along with everyone else on that ship. Mary's father and me and ten others walked to shore," Jack's voice went quieter, and he said as he wiped away a tear. "But the rest washed ashore, lifeless."

There was not a peep from Jack's audience, as they waited to hear what happened next. "Those that survived the sea had yet to survive the land. We shared some soggy bread. That's all we had from the ship. So, we spread out to find anything we could on that island. Mussels, crabs, limpets. Within a week, all but four of us died. For nineteen long months this went on, if our figuring was correct. I learned to eat snails and snakes, anything to keep from starving." Jack stopped and, hooking a finger into his jug, he hoisted it up on the crook of his arm to get a good swig of his brew. He must have known that not a soul would leave the story now, even if he stopped talking for a time.

But he didn't keep his audience waiting for long. "Mary's daddy, God rest his soul, got weaker and weaker. His last words to me were, 'Jack, yer a good boy. Take care of me family fer me.' And then he died. Such bad luck we had. Then, believe it or not, a storm came up the week after that. If it wasn't a hurricane, it was nearly so. It shook that little island and those of us left thought it would do us in. But, lo and behold, if we didn't see a sail on the horizon when the rain stopped. And it was an American ship! I don't know where they were supposed to be going, but they headed for England to take us back and on the way the other two sailors gorged themselves on all the rich food and died. I was the only one left. Me. Just me," Jack said, putting his hand to his chest and looking into the eyes of his beholders.

"When we reached England, I went straight for London to see Mary and her mother. It wasn't an easy task to have to bear the dreadful news to those two women. But when I got to their home in London, they were gone. I saw an old woman who was selling fruit on the street and I asked if she knew the whereabouts of Mary and her mother. 'The work'ouse,' she told me. Oh, how my heart bled for Mary. She and her mother must've been so poor. A workhouse is a dreadful place. I found the right workhouse, but Mary's mother had died. Poor Mary was so thin and frail, I hardly knew it was her. I wanted to marry her right then 'n' there, but she was still too young. So, as her guardian now, they released Mary to me, and I put her in a boarding school. 'Mary,' I say, 'in two years, when you're of age, we'll marry.' I remember her looking at me with dull blue eyes, the spark of life hardly in 'em, when I kissed her cheek. She gave me a smile and I left for the sea.

"I was gone a year. But I knew my Mary would wait. As soon as we docked, I couldn't get to the boarding school fast enough. When I got there, the faces of the other students told me the grim news. My Mary had died a month before. My poor heart was broken. Nothing left to live for." Sniffles could be heard from Jack's audience now. "I couldn't pick myself up for nearly a month. But hunger'll do things to a man that nothing else will. I joined the navy and sailed for a few years, not caring where we went. Even fought in the Crimean War. Finally, one day, my resolve returned, to start my life afresh. I went back to England one last time to tell my country farewell and when my ship eventually docked in America, I decided to stay." Jack paused. "Well," he said, "you got the rest of the story at the beginning. So, now, I'm just waiting for death to sound my call."

Jack had finished his sad tale. His listeners stood silent for a time in honor of what they'd heard, but eventually a few left and a few others bought a postcard or two from him or one of a number of canes he'd whittled. Loring wanted to wait to be the last so that he could take his time meeting the old man. "Thank you for telling your story, Jack. I'm Loring, and this is my wife, Hattie. We're new to the Mount Willard section house, so we'll likely see you again," Loring said, extending a hand.

Shaking it, the old man stayed seated and said, "I'd like that. It can get lonely up here. Nice to meet you, ma'am," tipping his hat Hattie's way.

"Nice to meet you, too," Hattie smiled.

Jack got up then and walked them around his cluster of buildings, talking some about how he'd built them and how long it had taken him. Eventually, it seemed Jack was ready to retire into his house, so Loring said, "Well, take care." Jack tipped his hat once more, nodded, then stood and went inside his shack.

"Do you think Jack's story is true?" Hattie asked Loring on their way back down the tracks.

"I don't know, but he sure is a good storyteller!"

Eight

~ 1903 ~
Waitin' for the Boxcar

"So, you met English Jack, eh?" John Green said cheerily the next morning.

"What a character!" Loring said by way of an answer. "We missed part of the story, though. What happened to him after he sailed here to America? How'd he end up here?"

"He says he got off in Portland and signed up to work with the P&O," John said. "Apparently he was sent here, building this railroad until it was finished in '75. He says he saved wood scraps from his days working on the railroad to build his house with. You know he calls it his ship? His house, I mean. He calls it his ship."

"Ya don't say," Loring said. "Guess that's as good a name as any given his story. Say, John, our boxcar should be coming down today. You think you and the boys could help us unload?"

"Sure," John answered. "I'll watch for it and be back. Gotta go work. You know Joe, a real stickler." John winked and left.

"Do you have any idea when the boxcar will arrive down here, Loring?" Hattie asked. "If it's going to be a while, I think I'd like to see if I can follow the path to the road below."

"I think you have time. You'll hear the train if you're down there, I suspect. I'll stay here and keep a lookout for it. I want to see what the men are doing, anyway, you know, to be ready for work tomorrow. Be careful down there. I'll bet that slope is pretty steep."

"I will," Hattie chirped and kissed her husband. She loved being cared for. She also loved that Loring didn't hold on too tightly. She walked to the back of the house, past the double doors to the cellar that would grant access to the coal bin when it was time to be filled. She kept her distance from the wet rocks coming from about the middle of the house underneath the two-hole outhouse. Florence had said the outhouse was continuously flushed out all year with water from the brook, except in winter when the water froze. She was grateful that the toilets were built onto the house even though they wouldn't get much heat in the winter. *It'll get mighty cold in there, I'll bet,* she thought, clearing the rocks to find the trail. She didn't have to hunt long and began picking her way down the mountain carefully.

There's something about a trail that beckons a soul, she thought. *Maybe it's proof that we aren't alone. That others have gone before us.* Hattie heard a bird singing. *That could be a bluebird, I suppose. Then again, maybe it's a mockingbird.* With this guess, she began humming "Listen to the Mockingbird" as she happily managed the narrow trail. Other than having to unsnag her skirt now and then, she enjoyed being alone in the woods. When she was by herself in the woods, she never felt lonely. Not like she sometimes felt when she was in a crowd of people. The creatures in a forest and the very trees, ferns, and underbrush always felt like a host of wordless friends. Branches creaked, squirrels chattered, leaves rustled. The wind whistled around the trees, birds sang, insects hummed. The symphony of the forest was, to her, some of the finest music in the world.

Then, from the corner of her eye, Hattie saw something move. She stopped humming and stood motionless. She heard discreet footfalls. Out from behind a thicket walked a buck. The deer stopped. He and Hattie locked eyes. He had a nice-sized rack, so he wasn't young. Hattie sent it thoughts of admiration for its beauty and well-wishes for the day, even knowing it could soon be food for her larder. *It's just the way of things,* she thought.

Meanwhile, Loring saw Denny and Ed just beyond the bridge and headed that way. Loring walked across the bridge, being mindful of how far below him Willey Brook was, but he wasn't prepared for the stiff wind at his back which felt as though it might throw him over the edge. With no railing to hold on to, he might have been performing a balancing act across a circus tight rope. Finally, when he'd nearly crossed, he looked up to see Denny and Ed leaning on their shovels, laughing at him. "Come on, old man, you can do it."

Loring was glad they felt they could joke with him. It's what most railroad men did after they'd been together a while. John must have told them he could take the ribbing. "That there's a whopper of a bridge when it's windy," Loring said a little shakily.

"And that's nearly every day, too," Denny offered. "Ethan Allen Crawford, the guy they named this Notch after, used to say that the wind here is so bad it requires two men to hold one's hair on. Hey, ain't you supposed to be off today?"

"Waitin' for the boxcar. Got some ties to replace?" Loring replied looking down at the tracks.

"Yeah," Denny answered. "Today we're just preparing for the job. We're supposed to be helpin' unload yer things. We'll work on these three ties here tomorrow. Billy is walkin' the rails checkin' spikes and John's up to Crawfords."

"Say, boss," Ed said, "while you're on this side of the bridge, wanna make good use of all that hard work crossin' it, uh, ya know, before you have to go back across? Only way to get home."

"You can call me Loring. Sure, what do ya mean?"

"Come 'ere," Ed looked at Denny, and nodded for his brother and Loring to follow. Denny knew where they were taking their new boss.

Just past the bridge, out of sight of the house, they came upon a homemade contraption that looked like a still. "That what I think it is?" Loring said, without judgment.

"Some of the finest corn whiskey this side of…uh…the bridge!" Ed quipped. "What it lacks in smoothness, it makes up for in its kick!"

"You boys best not be up the pole around my wife, if ya know what I mean. She's a pretty good shot. She might just shoot ya," Loring warned with a quirky smile. His message, that as long as they were on their best behavior around Hattie and on the job, he didn't care what they did on their own time, was clear.

"We've had practice with other wives up here, boss...uh, Loring. We'll be good," Ed said, realizing how that might have sounded. Thankfully, neither man commented further.

Loring was glad to have this banter with his men. He hoped they'd make a good team.

While Loring was being shown the finer points of the still, Hattie made it to the bottom of the mountain and stood on the dirt road that ran along the valley floor. She had to walk backwards a bit to see clear of the birch stand right by the road. And there it was, their castle halfway to the sky. *It looks so small from down here*, she thought. *It would be hard to convince anyone that the house is big if this were the only view they had.* Then she heard a train whistle. She looked up and could just make out a puff of smoke coming from what she assumed was Crawford Station.

"Oh! I need to get back," Hattie said to no one. She found the entrance to the trail and started back up. *We should attach some boards or something to some of these trees to make this easier. I can't imagine doing this while carrying something! This is much steeper than English Jack's trail or even the one to the top of Mount Willard.* She made a mental note to mention her idea to Loring.

Denny, Loring, and Ed heard the train, too. It was time to cross back over the bridge. *At least we know the train will be stopping at the house and not coming across the bridge right away,* Loring thought as he followed the others across. Then he said, "Tell me, if that train was not stopping at the house, would you say we had time to cross this bridge?"

"That depends," Denny called back. "You get pretty good at judging that once you consider the speed the train's comin', how much head wind you're buckin', how slick it might be dependin' on weather, things like that. Today? Sure, we'd have plenty of time."

Indeed, they beat the train to the house with no problem, but Loring knew it would take a few more crossings to feel as comfortable as the other men felt. He walked into the house expecting to see Hattie, but she wasn't back yet. He wasn't concerned for her safety, but he knew she'd want to be here to direct every piece of furniture to what she would consider its rightful place. He walked down behind the house to look for her. Not seeing her, he called out. He heard nothing and wondered if he should go look for her. But the train couldn't stop on the tracks for long. They'd need to unload it as quickly as possible, so he went back up the hill.

Hattie was mad at herself for insisting on this little venture. *It might have waited.* Now she was hurrying. She knew that wasn't a good thing to do, but she couldn't help herself. *Just around this tree and that bend, and I'll see the house,* she told herself. But she didn't. She stopped just for a moment to catch her breath and inspect the tear in her hem. Suddenly, she felt a presence. It didn't feel the same as seeing the buck. A chill went up her spine. She looked around and saw nothing she hadn't seen on the way down. What she didn't hear was the train, because, she realized with chagrin, it had already stopped at the house. *Oh dear, oh dear!* She started up again and hadn't gone far when she felt the presence again. Florence had mentioned some of the wild animals that lived in these mountains that were much more adept at navigating these woods than she was. Bears, lynx, and deer. These were the big ones. Then there were the raccoons, porcupines, and foxes. This was their home, not hers. And if it wasn't an animal…well, she shuddered to think of the kind of person who might be following her.

"I can't understand why Hattie isn't up here yet," Loring muttered to himself. "Maybe I *am* a tiny bit anxious. But that girl can take care of herself. Put that box in the kitchen," he said more loudly so that John could hear him, "and that one can go in that room there." He was doing the best he could without her, but she'd done most of the packing and would know exactly where she'd want these things to go.

Hattie stood still again with all her senses heightened. Seeing nothing, she knew she had to keep climbing. Still, she watched for something she couldn't see. Unfortunately, what she wasn't watching for was footing and she tripped on an exposed tree root, falling hard on her side. "Ow!" She felt the pain in her ankle instantly. Assessing the damage, she decided it wasn't broken. Probably sprained. But she couldn't just sit there. She had to get up the hill. So, she hoisted herself up and gingerly tried stepping on her bad ankle. It held but was terribly painful. Hattie looked around for a fallen branch to use as a crutch. She'd manage the best she could.

Hobbling, taking much smaller steps than she would have preferred, she made slow progress. The woods were thinning, giving way to an opening up ahead, when she sensed the presence again. She stopped, looked around her, and still saw nothing. She didn't know if she was becoming paranoid or perturbed. She just wanted to get to the house.

She took another step and heard a loud yowl. "Oh, dear. I'm sorry Boomerang. I'm so sorry. I didn't mean to step on you. What are you doing down here, anyway? Ah, I'll bet it's the commotion at the house that scared you. Well, I'd pick you up and carry you but I'm afraid I can't. So, follow me." Soon, Hattie saw the house and was very relieved.

Shuffling up the last hill beside the house, Loring came into her sight. She could tell by his eyes that he was relieved to see her, then worried by her hobbling. Since he was carrying something heavy, all she did was smile at him to let him know she was okay. Once inside, she was ever so grateful that her favorite chair had been put in the parlor already. She sat and Boomerang immediately jumped into her lap.

Hattie took over directing the men to put things where she wanted them. If she'd been able, she'd have been much more precise. *Well, Hattie, ol' girl. You've done it good this time, haven't ya? Could've been worse. So much worse. It is what it is.* "That can go in the bedroom over there." She felt so silly to have fallen, but she felt so grateful to be home. Again, life in opposites. Then it hit her. She'd said to herself she was so grateful to be home. Home. What a wonderful realization!

When everything was off the train and the engine had left, everyone was hungry. Again, Hattie felt awful about being unable to do the very duties she was here to do—take care of everyone. Now that her kitchen items were here, she hoped to go through the boxes and put things away. Then she could concentrate on putting in an order for what food they'd need. Somehow, she'd have to manage so that she could begin her job in earnest. *I'll just have to be able to walk tomorrow*, she decided. *No more of the men waiting on me. But I may as well enjoy it for now.*

After supper, when the men were either in their rooms or outside somewhere, Loring and Hattie finally had a chance to talk about her mishap. "What happened to you?"

"Well, first of all, you have to see what this house looks like from the road below! It's a completely different experience. It really does look like a castle halfway to the sky! But, anyway, I made it down to the road all right and that's when I heard the train whistle. So, I knew I had to hurry back up. And you're right, it is steep. I was thinking it might be good to fix some boards to some of the trees as handholds for the way up. What do you think?"

"That should be easy enough to do. But what about your ankle?"

"Well, I feel so silly to have let that happen." Loring thought he could see color creep up Hattie's neck into her face. "I was in such a hurry and just wasn't looking where I was going, and I tripped on a tree root. That's all. But the reason I wasn't watching is what I really wanted to tell you about. I don't know if this will sound crazy or not, but about halfway up the trail I felt something, like I was being watched or followed. I stopped to look around, but I didn't see anything unusual. In fact, I stopped twice because the presence was so strong."

"Oh, Hattie, I'm just glad you're here, safe and sound."

"Oh, and then," Hattie began to laugh, "I made myself this make-shift crutch here and took a step right on top of Boomerang. He wasn't very appreciative of that, but you know, that cat stayed right beside me the rest of the way up the hill. You don't suppose Boomerang was the presence I felt, do you?"

"I don't know. There are wild animals around here, though. And hobos live in the woods, too. I think we need a dog, Hattie.

What would you think of that? A nice big dog that can go with you on your walks and alert you to any danger?"

"I've no objections. Boomerang might have some, though!"

"Boomerang will just have to handle it. I'll keep my ears open for where we might find a dog. But for now, do you think you could come outside for a moment? I'll help you." Hattie hobbled outside using Loring's shoulder to lean on. He led her just to the porch. Holding her close to him, he looked into her eyes. "Hattie, when we were married six years ago, I had no idea where our life together would lead us. And to tell you the truth, I didn't really care, as long as you were beside me to enjoy it with." Hattie's eyes misted. To be loved like this had been beyond anything she could even imagine. Loring continued, "When you were so long down there, and you weren't even here when the train pulled in, I got worried. I think that's the first time it's ever occurred to me that I might lose you some day. I can't imagine my life without you, and I don't want to." Tears fell down her face as he spoke. "I told you that there was one more thing I wanted to do before I could call this home."

He leaned down and lifted her off her feet. "I want to carry you over this threshold. I know I did that right after we were married, but this house feels like home in a way no other place has." With her eyes still fixed on his, Loring stepped over the threshold of their new home and carried her directly to their bedroom, laying her on their still-unmade bed. He sat beside her, looking adoringly at her, and said, "Welcome home, my love."

Nine

~ 1903 ~
No Matter What Season

The next few days were a blur of activity for both Hattie and Loring as each became familiar with their new responsibilities. Loring had served as foreman for enough years that he knew how to make the day's assignments, and he knew how to be assertive. Sometimes his men on other sections had called him fussy because of his tendencies toward perfectionism on the job, but that trait had continued to reward him with foreman positions and the pay that went with it. The work itself came naturally to him now, whether it was replacing old, battered ties, leveling and gauging the rails, or clearing tracks of debris. He knew what to look for and soon he'd know which man was best for a particular job. What was new to him, however, was how the trains wore down the inside rails on tight curves over time, and just how clean tracks had to be for a train to pull the steep grade in any weather. The bridge over such an expanse was also new, as was squeezing a train through the narrow gateway. Here, a good job done seemed to hinge on the work being perfectly executed. There was little room for sloppiness on this section.

Hattie, too, had both familiar and new aspects to her job. She was used to long days of hard work. She knew her way around the kitchen and washing clothes was a chore that didn't change much wherever she was. However, Florence had warned her that if she hung laundry outside, soot from the steam engines could ruin her hard work. Best to hang things outside in between trains. At least on bad weather days she could hang the wash in the cellar. The food Hattie cooked would essentially be the same as she was used to making, but here she'd cook for hard-working men who needed mealtimes to be ready on a stricter schedule.

She took her duties seriously and in earnest. Those first few days after she sprained her ankle were trying. She longed for her two normal legs again to get things done in good time. She was willing, however, to concede to a mandatory slower pace. She took time when she needed to rest her ankle to look out the back windows, letting the view afford her a peace of mind as few other things ever had. *The closest I've come to letting a view of nature speak to me like this was when I gazed at Mount Washington on White's Bridge as a child,* she thought. *And when Loring and I climbed Mount Willard years ago, this was the view of views. Who would have ever thought I'd be able to see it every single day?* She sighed at her good fortune.

Eventually, both ankles worked perfectly and she set up routines that made life hum like clockwork. Monday was laundry day, Tuesday was for ironing and mending, Wednesday brought midweek baking, Thursday was a thorough cleaning of most of the rooms, Friday was for tidying the kitchen and parlor, and Saturday was baking and bath day. Every day was a cooking day, of course. She'd quickly become familiar with the routine of ordering her staple items for the kitchen as well as things like yarn, needles, thread, and cloth. She learned which items would come right away and which would come when they were available. It took time to get used to not picking out all her own groceries and other items. She had to accept what she was given and, if a thing didn't suit her, she'd send word next time for something different. And she learned that the men were happiest when they could help themselves to a cookie or doughnut from the jar in the pantry, so she seldom let it become empty.

Other jobs, like cleaning the kerosene lamps, wiping down the incessant dust kicked up by the trains, and sweeping the hardwood floors, were also tasks that begged to be completed daily. Writing letters was something she did whenever she could fit it in. She'd received her first letters from friends and family almost right away, which made her feel nearer to Maine. Each day she could walk to the station for mail or wait until it was brought down by Loring or one of the others. A day that mail came was always a good day. So far, she'd received a letter from Esther, her friend at the mill, telling her that not much had changed there. The spinning room had a new boss, but this woman was much like the old one had been. She also said that her boys were doing well, save for a bout of coughing that they'd passed to one another and, unfortunately, to her. Hattie had also heard from Nell, whose son Earl was "growing like a weed." But one of her favorite letters was from the Reverend. He seemed to be doing well and had taken in a boarder who helped him much as Hattie had. Together they had harvested the rest of the vegetables. He said he missed Hattie's meals and the talks they had, and that he even missed Boomerang. She wondered if he might take in his own stray cat one day.

Sunday was everyone's day off. As much as she enjoyed her routines, she looked forward to Sundays most of all, when she and Loring could go exploring or fishing or hunting. The first few Sundays, however, she and Loring spent getting the house in order with pictures on walls, wildflowers in vases, and all the things that would make this a warm and cozy home.

One Sunday in October, when the fall colors were spectacular and going for a walk seemed the only reasonable thing to do, she and Loring decided to pay a visit to the Willey House, where the Monahans lived now. It would be Hattie's first time there and she looked forward to some female conversation for a change. Loring thought this was a good opportunity to have Hattie send a message to Florence by telegraph. Ordinarily, they wouldn't clog up the line with something so superficial, but Sundays were generally light workdays and she needed to learn.

He had Hattie write out what she wanted to say: *Hattie and Loring coming down for visit today if all right.* Loring told her to remember to keep the message as short as possible yet keep its meaning. She tried again: *Hattie and Loring coming for visit.* He reminded her to begin with the abbreviation for Willey House and end with just her name.

She made some adjustments and Loring said, "That's it!" She placed her finger lightly on the small, flat, round platform and slowly keyed in: *WH COMING FOR VISIT HATTIE*. In a short time, the telegraph key began clicking and Hattie was ready to transcribe the coded message: *MW WONERFUL FLORENCE*. Even though she'd missed the "d" in "wonderful," Hattie was pleased with her telegraph lesson. Loring said that she and Florence could make up their own code for their names and whatever else would help to keep the message short. Then they started on their way down the tracks.

Loring helped steady Hattie over the bridge and suggested she not look down, at least this first time. It wasn't the easiest thing she'd ever managed to do, but Loring told her it would get easier with practice. The rest of the way down the tracks was delightful. It was cool but not cold. The air was fresh. And, of course, the view was breathtaking.

Florence and Gertrude were waiting for them when they arrived. Joe was somewhere nearby but out of sight. As Florence had told her, the Willey House was not as large as the Mount Willard House was. When they went out for a walk, letting Gertrude set the slow pace of a toddler, Hattie could see how this house, too, was very close to the tracks. "How do you keep Gertrude from wandering onto the rails, Florence? I'd be scared to death to let her outside."

"We try to stay in the back yard, such as it is. But if we're out front, I tie her to a tall stake in the ground. I'm not going to tell you living here is easy, but you do the best you can, you know?" Hattie just couldn't imagine raising children beside these tracks.

"If I may change the subject, I don't understand something," Hattie said. "I get Mount Willard, Mount Willey, Willey Brook, and this Willey House all confused. Is your house named for the mountain?"

"Uh, guess you haven't heard this story yet. Well, nearly a hundred years ago, a settler named Samuel Willey moved here with his family. 'Course this railroad didn't exist then. Anyway, summer the next year, 1826, there was a drought which ended with a terrific storm. This whole valley was completely flooded. The Saco River rose twenty feet overnight, they say. I guess an avalanche started somewhere up there," Florence said, pointing to the top of the mountain behind the house. "It came straight for the house. After the storm, Samuel's brother and some other locals went to check out the damage and found the house in perfect condition. From what they could tell, the avalanche had been diverted by the rock ledge there just before it would have hit the house."

"Oh, my! How fortunate!" Hattie exclaimed.

"Well, it wasn't so fortunate, actually. When the men entered the house, they didn't find anyone in there. It was as if the family left in a mighty hurry. I mean, who wouldn't. The sound of the storm must have been very frightening. And they likely saw the river rising and maybe ran up to higher ground. I guess by leaving the house they were safe from the flooding, but they had actually gone into the path of the avalanche. Everything inside the house was just as they'd left it. There was an open Bible on the table and the dog was still there howling. When they searched the area they found the bodies of both parents, two of their daughters, and two hired hands. They never did find the bodies of the other three Willey children, though. It's just so sad. Nine people gone, just like that. Anyway, this mountain is named for them, and so is the house."

"Oh, goodness me. That's just awful. Loring told me about the rockslides that came through the foreman's cottage before the Mount Willard House was built. Now I learn of this. Are you sure you aren't afraid of living here?" Hattie asked her friend for the second time.

Florence measured her words before saying, "You know, Hattie, I *am* sure. I guess I just figure these things are few and far between. They're more the exceptions than the rule. I don't want to give in to my fears that easily or teach my daughter to be afraid unnecessarily."

"You're right, of course. I guess I've just taken in a number of exceptional stories lately as if they all happened at the same time. Spread out, I guess they really don't happen often."

Hattie thoroughly enjoyed her time with Florence. This was not only a simple friendship between women, but between people who understood what living by the tracks really meant. Too soon, Hattie and Loring needed to head home. It had been such a wonderful day. When it came time to say goodbye, Florence whispered, patting her stomach, "I think we're going to have another one." Hattie was about to congratulate Florence when Florence quickly put her finger to her mouth. Hattie understood. Florence wanted to be sure before announcing her news. But Hattie also understood that Florence had just included her in her inner circle and Hattie was pleased and grateful.

"Thanks, Joe," Loring said, shaking his fellow foreman's hand. Florence had picked up Gertrude and waved goodbye with Gertrude's hand, making the baby giggle. Hattie and Loring both waved as they started back up toward home. It would be another beautiful walk.

"Did you and Florence have a nice time talking?"

"We did, but she told me about the Willey family disaster of 1826. Awful thing, wasn't it? I assume you knew about it?"

"I did, yes. Not much point in telling you about it, though. I thought it might worry you needlessly. How did she come to tell you that story?"

"I asked her about all the names for things right here in this part of Hart's Location. I get confused when the names of the mountains sound so much alike, Willey and Willard. Then Willey Brook divides the two mountains but isn't close to the Willey House at all. Anyway, I think I have it now." Changing the subject, Hattie asked, "So, Mr. Evans, what shall we do about your birthday and our anniversary coming up soon? Do you want anything special? It is, after all, your thirtieth."

"All I want is you!" he said, playfully, coming at her as though to tackle her, but grabbing her waist instead.

"Oh, you!" she said, loving him so much.

His birthday and their anniversary came and went without much fanfare. They celebrated privately that evening and stayed up later than usual. The first Sunday in November they enjoyed a lovely hike into the woods that were nearly barren of leaves. The views were so different than they had been in May a few years ago, or even just this past August. Still, they both agreed it was the most beautiful view in the world no matter what season.

But they hadn't yet seen the Notch in winter and that first winter was a humdinger. Hattie hoped for a white Christmas this first year in the Mount Willard House. She was used to snow, and she was more than willing to be out in it if need be. Leading up to Christmas Day, however, they hadn't had any storms that amounted to much.

For Loring, who also enjoyed a Christmas Day in snowy splendor, the job of the section men would be much harder in heavy snow. So, he would welcome whichever way Mother Nature decided to play her hand this year. One of their main concerns would be to keep the switches in Crawford yard from freezing. If a switch was frozen in one position, it could be rendered useless to a train needing to use one of the other tracks in the train yard. Significant snow meant a tremendous amount of shoveling would be needed at Crawford Station, even after the enormous snowplow pushed equally enormous amounts of snow off the tracks. Delays in schedule were unwelcome at best, disastrous at worst. Loring and his crew took their job seriously and if working extra hard or long was necessary, so be it.

Since the ground was dry, although frozen solid, it didn't appear that all the men were needed over the holiday, so Loring decided to let all but one man take time off. John volunteered to stay in the Notch. He was quiet about his family, save for telling Hattie that his parents had been born in Ireland. Both Hattie and Loring suspected that John may not have been terribly close to his family, making staying at the house over the holiday preferable.

When Christmas Day broke, the first thing everyone noticed when they crawled out of bed was that the temperature had risen some. It was probably closer to freezing than in the teens. The second thing they noticed was the snow. The muffled sound of a heavy snow was unequaled. Hattie clasped her hands together with glee at the thought of a lovely white Christmas, a true winter wonderland and their first in the Notch. She could hardly wait for the day to brighten. With pine boughs adorning the windows, the food she had planned for their dinner, and tobacco in the men's pipes, it was sure to be a most delightful and aroma-filled day. "Merry Christmas, Loring!" She kissed him lightly, dressed quickly, and headed for the kitchen to stoke the fire. Boomerang followed her, expecting the bit of milk she gave him in the mornings.

In a few minutes, Loring came into the kitchen with his overalls on. All Hattie could do was stare for a moment, not quite able to comprehend Loring working on this day of all days. Loring knew he was about to break his wife's heart. He walked up close to Hattie and took her hands in his, "Hattie, love, I'm sorry, but John and I will need to go up to Crawfords to make sure the switches are clear. I'm not sure if there's any traffic scheduled at all for today, but John and I have to go and make sure things are clear no matter what. I hope not to have to spend more than a few hours there. Best not count on us for dinner. We'll take something in our pails and hope to be back by dark. And then, my dear," Loring said, dropping her hands and putting his arms around her small waist to draw her close, "then we'll have a wonderful Christmas supper and celebration." He kissed her nose. She smiled back, a smile he was grateful for. It might just keep him warm enough to complete their task ahead. Neither noticed that John had been standing in the doorway and had just witnessed all of this.

After they'd eaten breakfast and Hattie had filled both their pails, the men left for the station. Hattie saw how deep the snow really was as the men tried moving through it. Then she watched them retrieve their snowshoes from the carhouse. Even if they thought they could make it to Crawford Station without the snowshoes, they'd probably need them to return. The snow showed no sign of letting up. The sky was slate gray, not unlike the smoke from the steam engines when they worked so hard to pull the steep grade.

"Well, old girl, now you have plenty of time to cook up a feast," Hattie said to herself. The first thing she needed to do was retrieve the venison haunch from the icehouse. She'd need to thaw it out if it was frozen, although she hoped the thick wrapping had kept it cold, nearly frozen but not completely. John had shot the deer back in November. She hoped it was not the one she'd seen in August. *Can't be helped.*

She pulled on boots and wrapped herself in her coat, scarf, and hat and stepped outside. Lifting her knees high enough to get over the drifts was a workout, especially in a long skirt. She shivered when the snow touched her stockinged legs. Once she had reached the icehouse, she needed to shovel enough snow away from the door to get it open. Pulling hard, she cracked it open just enough to slip inside, retrieve the piece of meat, and walk back out. She closed the icehouse door again and turned around. When her eyes landed on the view before her, she was unable to move. As far as she could see, which wasn't as far as usual in this storm, everything was white. Pristine white. Only white shapes with rounded edges distinguished one object from another. The wind picked up the falling snow and danced with it in swirls. Save for that wind, everything was quiet. She heard no trains, no animals, no human beings, not even swaying trees. Just quiet. For some reason she thought of the Reverend, maybe because this silence had an almost holy quality to it. Or maybe because she hoped he was okay if Lewiston was getting this storm, too. Either way, she sent up a quick prayer for him as she retraced her footsteps on the way back to the kitchen.

How grateful she was for this warm house, and how worried she was for Loring and John out there in this storm. Another quick prayer. Then she rolled up her sleeves, donned her apron, and unwrapped the meat. It needed to be thawed some. She was suddenly glad for the extra time she had to cook. She now had enough time to make Loring's favorite molasses cookies, too. As she dropped the balls of dough onto her baking sheet and then prepared her turnips for later, she hummed Christmas songs. Maybe she could find a few minutes to play the organ. All the while she kept an eye out for the men, hoping to see them coming back. All she could see was white.

Soon it was time to prepare the venison for baking. She wiped it very dry, enclosed it in a covering of dough made of flour and water, then rubbed it with butter and savory herbs. While it baked, she'd need to baste it periodically with melted butter. After she'd washed and pricked the sweet potatoes to be ready for the oven later and basted the meat again, she realized there was nothing she needed to do for a time. Hattie felt conflicted, wanting to write a few letters but also to play the organ. Finally decided, she washed and dried her hands, applied some lanolin, and went into the parlor to Martha Boothby's well-loved organ. As Hattie settled on the seat where Martha had sat so often, she thought about the older woman, then laid her fingers on the same ivory keys that had once given way under Martha's hands. Hattie's eyes filled with tears for her dear friend as she began pumping air into the body of the organ, pushing the large rectangular plates with the balls of her feet until she could tell it was full of air. She would play the carols Martha had loved and began with "Away in a Manger." Then "O Little Town of Bethlehem." When she got to "Go Tell It on the Mountain," she thought about hearing it for the first time at Martha's house. At the time, given the way Martha played the song, Hattie had thought it peppy and fun. But this time she heard it in a whole new way, and she hoped Mount Willard heard this music flowing out of the very cracks of this house, a tribute to its grandeur.

When it was time to baste the meat, she checked again to see if the men were on their way back. Still seeing nothing, she was at least pleased with the wonderful aromas the men would be treated to upon their first steps into the house. She filled the rest of the afternoon with kitchen duties, organ music, letter writing, and finishing the scarf she was knitting for Loring's Christmas present.

It began to grow dusky and still the men were not in sight. She determined not to worry about them and kept humming. The meat was done and resting, the sweet potatoes could be pulled out of the oven and the turnips were softening nicely. She retrieved the mincemeat pie and rolls she'd made yesterday from the pantry. The pie was Loring's mother's recipe, and Hattie knew he would love it. She had just a few minutes to play another carol before she'd need to mash the turnips with butter and a bit of sugar. All she could do was hope the men would be back soon enough to eat a hot meal.

Since it was almost dark, she decided to play Martha's favorite carol, "Silent Night." Hattie pumped air into the beautiful instrument and pulled out the stops that would make the music sound gentle and then reverently laid her fingers on the keys and started to play. The tender, sweet notes seemed magically joyful, yet deeply touching as they wafted out into the room. *A fitting tribute to a beautiful soul*, she reflected with a touch of melancholy. *Sleep in heavenly peace, Martha. Sleep in heavenly peace.* The music stopped. She sat still for several moments. The last notes hung in her mind even after they disappeared from the room. It was serenely quiet in the house. Though it was dark beyond the windows, the lamplight was not unlike the light of Martha's memory burning in Hattie's heart. After a long moment, she turned to slip off the bench and there they were, Loring and John. Standing, dripping with wet snow from the bottoms of their overalls, looking at her with soft eyes. She hadn't heard them come in but was so grateful to see them. She walked to Loring's strong, open arms and let him embrace her in the quiet of the moment. He understood that her heart was with Martha.

Ten

~ Flood Week ~
Tuesday, November 1, 1927

When Hattie awoke, she felt uncharacteristically anxious. In fact, she hadn't slept as well as she usually did. Monday's laundry and other chores were always strenuous enough to be an elixir of sorts, making her sleep very soundly. She had even heard the freight train in the wee hours, which she almost never did anymore. As she reached for her calico housedress, she thought about yesterday's newspaper. It had said that a late season tropical depression was creeping up the eastern coast. Surely it wouldn't come this far, she reasoned. Yet, remembering the first year she and Loring had come to Crawford Notch with its unusual amount of precipitation, both in snow and rain, she couldn't deny that this area suffered unexpectedly harsh storms. Too often such storms unsettled rocks and boulders that careened down the side of the mountain, having their way with whatever crossed their paths. Some storms were strong enough to crack mature trees in two, sending their tops hurtling to the ground, changing the forest landscape. So far—and for this she was of course very grateful—her fourteen years in the Notch had seen no significant damage to either her house or the Monahans'.

These mountains had been through the remnants of tropical depressions and hurricanes before, but the heavier rain they brought never seemed to amount to more than any other strong storm. And storms didn't particularly bother Hattie, anyway. *In fact,* she thought, *I've always loved the extraordinary seasons here. I love to watch the storms roll down the valley and hear the thunder echo off the mountain walls.* If this was to be nothing more than a good old-fashioned thunderstorm, why was she feeling anxious? Mentally, she chastised herself. *Now Hattie, this just isn't like you. You never worry so.* She brushed out her hair and fixed it neatly, slipped into her shoes, then beckoned Laddie and picked up the lamp. *All is well,* she reminded herself as she began her day.

Hattie eagerly awaited the day's newspaper. She hoped to read that the storm had veered out to sea. Perhaps then she might be able to let go of her anxiety, if indeed that was the cause. It was late morning, and she was catching up on some of the darning. "I can always count on Raymond to wear through his stockings," Hattie mused aloud as she threaded her needle and shoved her wooden darning egg into the first heel. As she began weaving the cotton thread back and forth, she heard someone say, "Yoo-hoo!" and saw two people she did not recognize step onto the front porch. She put her darning down and walked briskly to the door, opening it.

"I hope we aren't disturbing you, ma'am. Hattie, is it?" the woman said. She stood next to a man dressed in a black suit with a maroon and black tie. Over that, he wore what looked like an expensive gray wool dress coat. The woman wore a stylish, elegant wool coat with a black fur collar. *It isn't really cold enough for such heavy coats,* Hattie thought, wondering why they were wearing them. *And dressed to the nines! I must look so simple. At least I'm still fairly clean.* Hattie glanced down quickly at the state of her apron.

"Of course not. Come right in. Yes, it's Hattie," she said, gesturing for the pair to step into the parlor. "May I take your coats?" Hattie said politely, though she wasn't sure she even wanted to be responsible for handling such expensive clothing. She decided to let Laddie outside while her guests were here. It wouldn't do to have him jump up on them, though he didn't usually do that. Hattie noticed the woman's roundish face and blue eyes roughly the color of a clear sky near the horizon. She also noticed the man's thick, dark hair that threatened to cover his glasses once he removed his fedora. She saw that he was carrying a feedsack full of something.

"We really can't stay," the woman said, as she and the gentleman stepped into the parlor. She made no move to give up her coat or take a seat. "I'm Muriel Kelly, and this is my husband, Adam. We've been staying at the Crawford House and we're leaving today. We have an afternoon train to catch." Hattie listened as the pretty blonde seemed to want to explain their presence, almost apologetically. "You see, we wouldn't have stayed here so long but for a delay in the building of our new home in Raymond, Maine." Hattie's breath caught just a little. "The hotel was ever so kind to let us stay up to closing, but we must move on now. What a fine view of the Notch you have," the woman suddenly digressed. "Anyway, we were all packed and there wasn't much left to do before our train leaves. And I overheard two of the other hotel guests talking about you living up here. I mean, we did see the house on our way up and I thought, 'Oh, my, I'm not certain I would like to live on the side of a mountain like this'," she said, sweeping her arm out toward the back of the house. "And I thought whoever lives there must be very brave. So, I entered the conversation the guests were having, and I asked them about this house. They told us a bit about you. And, well, I just decided I wanted to meet you myself and Adam thought we'd have the time to do so. It's a bit farther than we had thought, though."

Muriel caught her breath and was about to begin again when Adam spoke. "Ma'am..."

"Hattie, please."

"Yes, Hattie, we thank you for receiving us unannounced into your lovely home. Muriel believes you might make use of some of the clothing she doesn't care to take with her. I hope you can appreciate our gesture and not take offense."

"None taken, Mr. Kelly," Hattie smiled warmly taking the offered sack in her arms. She could make a number of things from the feedsack itself if the clothes didn't suit, but she wasn't about to mention as much to these two. She couldn't help noticing the proper etiquette of the couple, both in word and behavior. They probably had no idea that feedsacks could be turned into clothing, even if only simple work clothes. "Are you certain you won't have a seat? Maybe rest a bit before walking back?"

Muriel looked at Adam, raising her eyebrows slightly. "Okay, but only for a few minutes," Adam said softly, answering her with his eyes as much as his words. Then to Hattie he said, "We don't want to be late for our train." The young couple took a seat on the couch.

"Would you like something to drink?"

"Water would be nice, yes. Thank you," Muriel answered. "These coats are a little too warm for today, but we decided not to pack them."

Hattie set the sack down out of the way. She retreated to the kitchen and soon returned with two glasses of water and set them on the coffee table, along with a plate of oatmeal cookies. Then she took a seat opposite her guests. "Will Raymond be a new town for you?" Hattie suddenly missed Sebago Lake. Hearing about the area would be lovely. She secretly hoped the couple might pick up on her curiosity and ask if she knew the town.

"Not for me," Muriel said. "I come from there. Adam is from Portland. We met in Portland. Mutual friends put us together two years ago and now we're married," Muriel said brightly, extending her left hand to show off her rather large diamond-studded ring. This couple was young and something in the way Muriel looked at Adam made Hattie think this could quite possibly have been the couple's honeymoon, but she didn't ask. "This will be our first home. We've been staying with Adam's folks while our house is being built. I wanted to live on Sebago. I'm more a lake girl than an ocean girl."

Hattie's mind drifted momentarily to those wonderful times she'd spent on Loring's family farm in Raymond. It seemed like such a long time ago now. She hadn't been to the farm since most of the land was sold a few years ago. Muriel interrupted Hattie's thoughts, "What's it like living up here?"

"I love it," Hattie began slowly, not sure how much to say. "When my husband and I first came here, I couldn't imagine living right by the tracks. We started calling it 'home' right away, I think because we needed to believe that we were here to stay. But time has made it *feel* like home." *Time and many experiences*, Hattie thought. Not everything that happened here had been pleasant, but she had yet to allow any difficulty to get the best of her. One can always find a silver lining to any storm cloud, she believed. And once lived out or conquered, experiences became the building blocks of a home. She couldn't imagine living anywhere else, even back in Maine, although visiting was always wonderful.

The slight pause in Hattie's thinking allowed Adam a foothold into the conversation and he declared it time to head back up the tracks. He thanked Hattie again, rising to his feet, and after putting his hat on, offered Muriel a hand. They did seem to make a handsome couple. *I wonder if people thought that of Loring and me in our early years*, Hattie wondered.

Showing them to the door, she watched the couple step onto the porch. Laddie gratefully passed them to come back into the house. Muriel looked back at Hattie and said with child-like excitement, "Look for us on the two-thirty train. We'll be sure to get a window seat and wave!"

Trains are *exciting*, Hattie thought with a smile and then said as she waved goodbye, "Thank you for the sack of clothing."

Once back to her darning, she pondered the Kellys' quick visit and decided to look into the bag later that evening. She'd hoped to hear more about the lake, and perhaps more about Muriel's family—whom she might even know—but it wasn't to be. Maybe they'd be back next year.

That afternoon Hattie heard the low rumble of the midday passenger coming from Crawford Station. She stepped onto the porch to catch a glimpse of Muriel and Adam. As the engine approached, she self-consciously picked up the bottom of her apron which was now dirty from the day's work. As the engine went by, she saw that the engineer was someone new and waved. It was hard not to think of Bobby. Thunk! The newspaper smacked the ground where the news agent had tossed it with a smile. And soon after, sure enough, there was Muriel, in a window seat beaming from ear to ear and waving as if she'd known Hattie all her life. Hattie smiled and waved back, sincerely hoping the young couple might come again next season. Each time someone new enthused over the house's location and wanted to know what it was like to live on the side of a mountain, Hattie remembered again why she'd always loved living here. When the train had passed, she picked up the paper and retreated into the house.

The weather! She'd almost forgotten her concern as her day moved from the surprise visit of the morning to the afternoon's tasks. Forgotten, that is, until she saw the paper. Hattie was about to open it to the more detailed weather account when her eye caught something on the front page that made her heart flip. A large article there warned of hurricane-like wind and rain reaching upper New England by tomorrow night. The concern, it said, was saturated ground and swollen rivers from the rains of October. The ground just couldn't absorb more water.

That evening, the men, too, showed concern, which only added to her own. They sat in the parlor together with Hattie and told of rumors that had been passed along up and down the rails. People were becoming afraid of the potential for flooding. The men reasoned that since those rumors were coming from people who lived west of them, the coming storm could reasonably continue north and on into Canada without affecting New Hampshire. Still, Vermont and New Hampshire were not an enormous area even put together. Some of the men had relatives in Vermont, like Henry, and almost all of them knew someone in the upper part of that state. Finally, as if every soul in that parlor, Hattie included, had had enough worry, someone changed the subject and it wasn't long before each one stood to retire for the night, bidding a peaceful sleep. Hattie wondered if John's eyes really had averted her own. Perhaps not, she thought.

Hattie banked the stove for the night and tidied the kitchen. She let Laddie outside one more time and took the sack of clothes into her bedroom. She was eager now to see what, exactly, Muriel was willing to part with. The bag opened to a rainbow of colored material. Hattie fingered luxurious fabrics that she would never consider functional for the kind of daily work required of her, and in strong colors she felt were equally useless. Nevertheless, Hattie couldn't help holding the lovely dresses up to her and wondering if Loring would like them. Would he like the new look the flappers wore? *I'm sure Muriel looks keen*, Hattie thought, enjoying a word she'd heard the younger generation use. The word seemed so appropriate when she thought of the Kellys, especially Muriel. Only a small part of her wished to be someone other than the no-nonsense woman she was. These dresses awakened that small part, but not for long. She folded them up with a sigh, put them back in the bag and stored them in her closet.

After letting Laddie back in the house, Hattie began getting ready for bed. As she brushed and twisted her hair and put on her nightcap, Laddie settled in his usual spot in her room. Sneakers jumped up on her bed and plunked down purposefully there. She reached to turn down the lamp. She was ready to let this day go.

Eleven

~ 1904 ~
A Puppy, a Bear, and a Nephew

"He's gone, Hattie." She'd known by the look on her husband's face that the news was not going to be good. "The Reverend. He died a few days ago. Word came from his neighbors."

Hattie was stunned. The Reverend wasn't ill that she could tell from his recent letter. It was dated early January, not long ago. The Reverend, gone. The idea shocked her. "What did he die of?" she asked.

"Pneumonia."

"Oh, dear. Maybe he couldn't keep his house warm enough. It's been so dreadfully cold and snowy. Oh, dear me. I want to do something for him, but there's nothing more to be done, is there?"

"No. I'm sorry, Hattie. I know you loved him like the father you never really had."

Hattie took a moment to sit down. Boomerang hopped onto her lap. She couldn't bring the man back, so there was no need to waste time on what if, but she did need to imagine a world without the Reverend in it anymore. No more letters to or from him. No visiting him. The last time she saw him was the day they moved out; she so wished she'd had the chance to see him one more time. She sat in silence for several minutes, stroking the cat, and mentally said her goodbyes. Then she put Boomerang on the floor and stood up. *What's done is done. Couldn't be helped. Rest in peace, Reverend, with your beloved Martha.*

Since that first big storm over Christmas, which dumped about nineteen inches of snow, as Loring measured it, there had been several more storms that gave them another forty inches or so. What had been so delightful in December had become quite a burden for everyone's work week. They all did their best to complete their tasks on time, but Mother Nature was certainly making that difficult.

And yet, Mother Nature was also providing for them by making Saco Lake freeze over so thickly. One day, Hattie headed for Crawfords to pick up mail and send her letters. It had been quite a strenuous walk through the drifted snow, made at least doable in snowshoes. Still, she was ready to sit and talk with Beth a while and catch her breath. Mail service was in the caretaker's cottage now that it was off-season. After she and her friend had caught up, Hattie told Beth she wanted to watch the ice cutting on Saco Lake. She invited Beth to join her, but Beth declined. She suspected Beth could watch it any time she wanted to, but Hattie hadn't taken time yet to see it.

Watching the operation now reminded her of watching the ice cutting on Sebago Lake every year when she was a child. Although she knew it was a job fraught with danger, she always found it fascinating to see those heavy draft horses walking on the ice as though it were solid ground. She supposed they sensed the ice could hold them or they wouldn't set the first hoof on it. Today she watched as two, two-horse teams dragged their sleds onto the ice, stopping beside enormous blocks that had been cut out overnight when the ice was thickest. Then, using a lever, the men lifted each block onto the sled with big forks. *There is no end to man's ingenuity*, she thought, intrigued at the process. She'd be grateful for the ice that would be brought to them by train and put in the icehouse. The sawdust packing around it would make it last through summer, possibly through fall.

The next Sunday when Hattie and Loring were taking a short walk, Loring said, "Well, Hattie, now 'tis you who has a birthday coming up this Wednesday. Your first one here. Thirty-two years old. What would make you happiest that day?"

"Oh, now, you know me, I'm happiest when I'm with you. So, just sit with me after supper."

"We do that most nights. You want nothing more?"

"No, Loring. Really. What could you possibly get me that I don't have already?"

He knew the answer to that. After supper that Wednesday, Loring came into the kitchen where she was finishing up and said, "What about that 'sit' you suggested for your birthday?"

"Yes, dear. I'm coming. Just give me a few more minutes," she said.

Finally, she wiped her hands, took off her apron and hung it up. In the parlor, she sat in her chair across from Loring and sighed. "I think I'm getting old," she said to no one in particular. Boomerang took his usual seat on her lap.

Loring watched her and waited. When he thought she was settled, he said, "I have something for you. I'll go get it."

Hattie was never one to be doted on, but she knew Loring enjoyed pampering her when he could. So, she allowed for his surprises. Soon he was back with a medium-sized, whimpering box. Boomerang immediately jumped down and sat across the room, curious from a distance. "Loring Evans, just what have you done now?" she said with love and a touch of excitement in her eyes that she couldn't conceal.

"Open it," he beamed.

When she did, the cutest little, long-haired, brown-and-white puppy yipped and tried very hard to jump out of the box. Hattie put it on her lap. "Well, now, aren't you just the cutest little thing!"

"Hopefully, he'll make a good companion in the house and on walks. He might be a decent hunting dog, too. I got him from someone Denny knows. The puppy's sire is apparently a good hunting dog, so we can hope. We've kept him at Joe's for the past few days. I imagine by now little Gertrude is quite in love with him."

"The next time I take care of her, she'll enjoy seeing him again, won't she?" The question needed no answer, but the puppy licked her face as if trying to.

"Did you name him yet?" she asked Loring.

"No. Thought you should do that."

"Well, he's sort of the color of rust. How about Rusty?"

"Sounds like a good enough name to me."

So it was, Rusty became the newest member of the household. He grew quickly the rest of that winter and loved to play in the snow. *Good thing,* Hattie thought, *with all this snow we're getting. He's going to have to be out in it a lot.* Hattie enjoyed training him. *He'll have to learn about these tracks like Boomerang has.* And as long as Rusty didn't intentionally bother Boomerang, the two got along fine. But Boomerang wasn't a kitten anymore and didn't appreciate the antics of a young, rambunctious puppy chasing, pouncing, or flopping on him. Boomerang found new places to hide. So instead, Rusty chased people around the house, or really anything that moved. Shadows, Hattie's broom, even dust. Hattie was thoroughly entertained and smitten, when she wasn't tripping over him.

As it turned out, that winter gave them more than one hundred fifteen inches of snow all the way through April, and then, unbelievably, five inches of rain in May. It also brought Ethel Monahan, the second Monahan girl. Florence and the baby were fine. Hattie helped out as much as she could, having Gertrude to the house and taking her back along with food. Gertrude and Rusty were perfect companions, and the house was noisily happy.

Meanwhile, Loring and the section men battled the growth of brush beside the tracks that spring, which drove them nearly crazy trying to keep it cut back. The heavy winter had damaged a good number of ties and it took them most of the summer to feel like they were catching up. As the men worked the tracks, Hattie entertained visitors from Crawford House. The people who stayed at a place like Crawfords were usually quite well-to-do. Summer was a time to take a break from their high-powered, stressful jobs and enjoy life in the beautiful White Mountains. Sometimes a husband came to the hotel for only a short time before going home to work. His wife would stay on to visit with friends she'd made during previous summers. Golf, baseball, and poker were some of the men's favorites at Crawfords, while gatherings over tea, walks around the grounds, or sitting on the grand veranda out of the sun appealed to the women. Everyone enjoyed the dances to live music, orchestra concerts, and burro rides to the top of Mount Willard. Some Crawfords patrons took walks to visit English Jack or the Evanses down the tracks. Both Jack's house and Hattie's provided good conversation. Hattie's had the extra benefit of ice that provided cold drinks. She always enjoyed her visitors. They brought interesting, fresh perspectives from beyond the Notch.

By the end of summer, Rusty was probably half the size he would end up being and that was enough to know that he would be a good-sized dog. He was smart and already learning to be obedient. He was good at staying with Hattie when she went for walks, except for a quick detour when a squirrel chase was handy.

In early August, Hattie and Loring received a letter from Loring's sister-in-law, Cora Bell, his oldest brother's wife. She asked to come visit, saying that her seven-year-old was enamored with trains and she thought it might be a nice outing before school began. She asked if she might be able to come on a Saturday and stay until Monday, thereby having one whole day to visit in between travel days. Loring was especially thrilled to visit with his nephew, whom he hardly knew.

Cora and young Weston started their travels that Saturday in a horse and buggy to Sebago Lake Station. They waited there to board the train for Crawford. Weston was so excited he could hardly sit still. His mother let him sit by the window and he took in every detail. He loved hearing the train whistles and trying to figure out what the patterns meant. Waving to the people they passed was especially fun when the people waved back. He also loved the rhythmic clickety-clack the wheels made as the train traveled along the rails. But his biggest delight was crossing the long, tall Frankenstein Trestle. He could hardly imagine constructing such a thing and peppered his mother with question after question that she simply couldn't answer. *That boy*, she thought, *he'll go far if he can corral that mind of his and put it to good use.* Crossing the Willey Brook bridge, he was again awestruck by the idea that something other than just the ground was supporting the weight of their train. He never doubted it could, he just didn't understand how. Then they passed a house where a woman waved, and he waved back. His mother wasn't looking out that side of the train, but, seeing men working on the other side of the tracks, she quickly scanned them to see if her brother-in-law was one of them.

Loring hadn't been working. Instead, he met them at the station and gave Cora a big hug. It had been some time since they'd seen one another. The last time he'd seen Weston was when the boy was but a toddler. "Look at you now," he addressed his nephew, "what a grown-up lad you've turned out to be." Weston shook his uncle's outstretched hand like a little gentleman.

Looking straight at Crawford House, Weston asked, "Is that your house?"

"Heavens no," Loring laughed. "Cora, what did you do, tell him we live like royalty?"

"I didn't tell him much because I didn't really know. And besides, he didn't ask," Cora laughed. "But even I could have told him that grand place wasn't yours."

"That's a hotel," Loring informed them. "You passed our house just a little while ago, right after the railroad bridge you came across."

"We came across two really big bridges! Did you know that?" Weston asked excitedly.

"I did," Loring smiled, thoroughly enjoying his young nephew. "Let's go on down to the house. Your Aunt Hattie probably waved as you went by. Did you see her?"

"I saw a lady waving and I waved back. Was that Aunt Hattie?"

Loring nodded and Cora said, "Oh! I must have missed that."

"Here," Loring said, reaching down for their bags, "let me put these on this three-wheeled cart."

"I can carry my own bag," Weston replied proudly.

"All right then. I'll just put your mother's things on this cart." Loring grabbed Cora's bags and put them on the three-wheeler with great fanfare, watching Weston's eyes grow large. "Okay, let's go!" Loring started pushing the cart with Cora walking on one side of him and Weston on the other. Loring pretended to be in deep conversation with Cora, though he winked to let her know that he was aware of Weston's growing interest in the three-wheeler.

"So, Cora, how is Birney doing?" He was genuinely interested about his brother, but he sensed Weston wasn't long for carrying his own bag.

Sure enough, Weston sidled closer to the cart and said, "I like that cart real well."

Loring let him off the hook and asked, "Would you like to ride on it? You and that bag of yours?"

"I sure would!" Loring stopped the cart and let Weston climb aboard, bag and all.

Loring winked at Cora again and then asked after his brother in earnest this time.

"He's well. Busy as usual with the farming but doing well. He wishes he could have come with us. We'd love to have you and Hattie visit us this fall. Maybe around cider time?"

Loring nodded. "Ayuh. Hattie and I have talked about doing that. And how is Lena? What's she up to?" Referring to his niece, now fifteen years old, he could hardly imagine what she looked like.

"She's doing well. Children love her. She's caring for the children of a family near us. This one," nodding toward Weston, "loves her, too. She dotes on him. She's probably spoiling him."

As they walked to the house, the conversation felt easy, as though no time had passed since they were last together. Cora asked Loring how his job was going. When she asked him why he had taken the job up here, it was obvious she was much more interested in what it was like to live halfway up a mountain. Most people were, he admitted to himself.

When the three of them were close to the house, Rusty bounded over to greet them. Weston hopped down to meet the dog and was pushed right over by the dog's enthusiasm. Weston loved it, took falling in his stride, and the two played the rest of the way.

Hattie was on the porch to greet her sister-in-law with a warm hug. "Come right in out of this sun. You must be thirsty. I'll get you some cold tea and maybe some fresh cookies?" she said, looking at Weston.

"Oh, yes, ma'am! Thank you. But I'd like milk with mine, please."

"Of course. I think we can arrange that. And you, young man, may call me Aunt Hattie. How about you and I go get those cookies?"

Meanwhile, Loring showed Cora upstairs to the room she and her son would share. Hattie had put fresh flowers in a vase and water in the basin with a clean towel, in case Cora wished to freshen up. Loring gave Cora her privacy and went down to the kitchen. He needed to go back to work, but he asked Weston if tomorrow, perhaps, he might like to meet a hermit. "Oh, yes!" he said. Loring ruffled the boy's hair, kissed Hattie, and left for the rest of the day.

"How was your trip up here, Cora?" Hattie asked her sister-in-law a little later. She was looking at Hattie's pictures on top of the organ. When she turned to answer Hattie, her eye caught Weston outside playing with Rusty.

"Is Weston safe to play with the dog near the tracks?" Cora worriedly asked Hattie.

"Yes. If we hear a train, we'll call them inside."

"All right. To answer your question, it's a longer trip than I'd realized. It didn't help that that old horse of ours has only one speed. Slow," Cora said with a touch of exasperation. "But the view makes up for it. It's heavenly, isn't it? Do you like living this far from things, though?"

"So far, I do. It's not as lonely as it might seem," Hattie said, anticipating the reason for Cora's question. "The men are always nearby and, of course, they live here, too, so I see them every day. I have a friend just the next house down the tracks and another one up at the big hotel. Sometimes there are hobos on the trains or living in the woods in the summer that stop here for a bite to eat or a…"

"And you *serve* them?" Cora interrupted.

"They're usually very nice, actually," Hattie answered straightening the magazines and books on the table near her. "There are a couple that I don't trust. Just a feeling I get around them, I guess. I offer them a sandwich on the porch. But many of them come in and sit in the kitchen and tell me about their lives. It's always interesting. Sometimes they enjoyed good homes growing up, sometimes not. Some of them had decent jobs but, for one reason or another, decided to quit. I guess working everyday isn't for everyone. By the way, Loring is going to take Weston to visit the hermit of Mount Willard tomorrow. He'll enjoy that. You can go along if you like."

"Oh, well, we'll see." Cora gave Hattie the distinct impression that she might rather stay in the house.

The next day promised the possibility of light showers, for which Cora was grateful. She wasn't particularly enthusiastic about going hiking to find a hermit. She thought she'd go perhaps for Weston's sake but, after the night she'd had, a good rest indoors out of the rain was much more to her liking.

"How did you sleep?" Hattie asked Cora after Loring and Weston had headed off with two dinner pails to see English Jack.

"Oh, my goodness, Hattie! How on earth do you sleep at all, ever? I don't know if it was the light coming through the window, the noise from the train and the windows rattling, or everything vibrating that woke me up first!"

"Probably all of it," Hattie said in her dry, amused way. "I had to get used to it. I'm sorry you didn't sleep well, Cora. Feel free to spend your day as you need to and let me know if there is anything I can get for you."

"Thank you, Hattie."

The women spent their day visiting in between Cora's naps. Meanwhile, as they walked the tracks, Weston asked Loring about many things that were new to him.

"What's a hermit?" Weston asked his uncle. "Is it like the pet crab my friend has?"

"No," Loring said. "No, this is a man who does live a little like a hermit crab, though. He lives alone in a house he built by himself."

"Uncle Loring, how do those tall bridges hold the weight of a train?"

"Well, that's a matter for an engineer. Not a train engineer, but a person who specializes in building things. Those tall bridges are sometimes called trestles. Trestles are those structures built underneath the tracks that anchor the bridge to the ground. They have crisscrossing boards that engineers know exactly how to place so that they can hold a lot of weight. Tell you what, later today, let's walk over to the bridge by the house and I'll show you what it looks like up close. Don't tell your ma about it, though. It's a long way down and she might not think you're old enough to stay safe. But I think you are, right?"

"Right!" Weston said.

The time went fast and soon they were in front of English Jack's house. "Weston, meet English Jack. Jack, this is my nephew, Weston." Jack bent low and extended a hand, which Weston shook.

"Well, there, little man. How would you like to see my performing bear?"

Weston's eyes got big. "Yes, sir," he said. He'd seen a bear or two in the distance but never one that performed.

English Jack disappeared behind his shack and emerged, leading a small black bear wearing a collar. This was the first time Loring had seen the bear, so he was just as excited as his nephew. Jack had the bear stand on its hind legs, walk a few steps upright, then climb a pedestal with a small platform on top that Jack had made. Weston and Loring were entranced.

Before they left, Loring purchased a child-sized bow and arrow set from Jack. The enthusiasm Weston showed was all the thanks Loring needed, and probably English Jack as well. They said their goodbyes to Jack and then climbed Mount Willard to have their picnic dinner.

When they got back to the house, as promised, Loring took Weston to see the bridge up close. Weston was impressed but also distracted for want of using his new bow and arrow. Loring left him to practice shooting this and that with his bow. When a train came, Hattie and Cora held Weston safely to the side. He and his mother gawked at the sheer size and noise of the immense black machine that passed so close to the house. When it was gone, Weston resumed target practice and managed to shoot one of his arrows across the tracks and onto a ledge. He tried to climb up and get it but just couldn't quite hoist himself up there. Seeing Weston's predicament, Loring retrieved the wayward arrow for him. He was having as much fun as his nephew was, Hattie could see. It gripped her heart to think of him not having children of his own to love. *It is what it is,* she told herself for at least the hundredth time.

Early the next day, Loring, Hattie, and Rusty accompanied Cora and Weston to the station. It had been a short though fine visit, save for a loss of sleep on Cora's part. But it was obvious Cora loved hearing Weston's description of English Jack with his performing bear, and the view from way up over the house. If the boy had told his mother about seeing the bridge, Loring never knew about it.

When they were near the station, Loring stopped and crouched down before his nephew and said, "Weston, there's one more thing I want to show you. See way over there on the side of that mountain, there's a big rock sticking out? What does that rock remind you of?"

"Ummm, it sorta looks like the head of an elephant."

"Smart boy ya got here, Cora," he said to his sister-in-law. Then looking again at Weston, "You and a lot of other people have thought the very same thing, and that's why the rock's called Elephant Head."

Weston stared at the rock a while and then, without prompting from his mother, gave both Loring and Hattie a hug. Then he gave Rusty one, too. With Loring and Hattie's promises of a fall visit, Weston and Cora boarded their train and left for home.

Watching them leave, Hattie told her husband about Cora's reaction to the trains in the night. "Not much to be done about it," Loring said. "I guess you could offer our guests some cotton for their ears."

"Oh!" Hattie said, suddenly changing the subject, "Did you know that your sister-in-law is going to have another baby next year?" Loring knew how bittersweet it was for his wife when she learned of other women having babies and he thought she did awfully well to be excited for them. He took her hand and squeezed it. Then they parted company so that each could go back to work.

Twelve

~ 1904 - 1905 ~
Another Year of New Experiences

hings at our Mount Willard House are shaping up into a fine homestead, Hattie thought, with her hands on her hips, surveying the fruits of her labors. She was pleased. Rusty sniffed the yard. He was never far from her. *Trusty Rusty.* She was so glad Loring had insisted she have a dog by her side. At first, she'd thought her husband was being silly and overly concerned, but Rusty had proven to be an ever-faithful friend. When again she could have sworn there was something watching her on one of the trails, she studied the dog for signs that he might have picked up on something neither of them would want to encounter. He often stopped and sniffed out animals but never anything she worried about.

Hattie's heart-shaped flower garden was looking very nice. She was able to grow bachelor buttons, petunias, and sweet peas, along with some transplanted wildflowers she'd found on her hikes. Her bluebells delighted her. The sweet, yellow marigolds and violet blossoms gave her endless joy. And the window box of vibrantly red geraniums grew best on the bridge side of the house with its share of southeastern sun. She'd tried, oh, how she'd tried to grow her own vegetables, but the deer and rabbits left nothing of value, making her miss the little garden behind the Reverend's house that much more. She'd gotten a new flag for the pole to replace the old tattered one, and her daily ritual of putting it up and taking it down bookended her days. Between Rusty, the flag, and her garden, she had ample reason to go outside every day. But she didn't really need any of these reasons. The outdoors felt as much like home to her as the house did.

To help keep her larder full and give them all an alternative meat, Hattie started keeping chickens in a little coop behind the house. Mostly the hens would stay put but occasionally one would get out. Hattie was grateful when a train came by with Bobby Morse driving it. He knew the hen wasn't supposed to be there and he'd open the petcock valve and shoot a stream of steam out the front of the engine. That'd scare the hen right back to where she was supposed to be.

In the fall, when the first snows began to fly, the urge as well as the need to go deer hunting had hit them all. Rifles ready, one day in late October, with several inches of early snow on the ground to deaden the sound of their feet, Loring, John, and Denny set out. The bounty was good—two four-point bucks and one six-point. The men hauled them all back home, one at a time, which was no small task. They tied one deer's legs to a long, sturdy tree limb so that two men were able to walk it to the house with the pole on their shoulders. There they'd hang the deer to be bled, skinned, and butchered for some of the best meals any of them could imagine. Everyone especially loved Hattie's venison stew, complete with potatoes, onions, turnips, carrots, and, of course, fresh biscuits on the side.

That November, Hattie and Loring took a quick trip to visit the Evans family farm in Raymond. Everyone was there. Even Birney and Cora, and their children Lena, Weston, and new baby girl Ione were able to make it for a few hours. While Loring and Will went to buy cider from Will's neighbor, Hattie visited with Nell and the family matriarch, Sarah. Her sister-in-law's infectious enthusiasm for life and Sarah's maternal patience always made the visits delightful. Unfortunately, Loring felt he needed to get back to the Notch, so they weren't able to stay as long as the family wished them to. On the way home, Hattie remarked, "It's a wonder Cora didn't lose that baby when she stayed with us, as frightened as she was that first night. And isn't your mother doing well? She's a wonder to me. I don't know how I'd do after having had eight children!"

In the spring of 1905, as the weather became more favorable, Hattie and Loring once again had family and friends who came to visit. They had become accustomed to all the curious questions folks had about living in the Notch. Hattie was familiar with most of the questions by now, but every so often she'd get a new one. Once she was asked if she'd seen any bears. "Well, of course," she'd said matter-of-factly. "Once, when I was climbing the hill up from the road, I turned a sharp corner and nearly shook hands with one that was standing upright!" Visitors either thought she was kidding or were amazed that she would go out in the woods at all. She wasn't kidding.

Someone asked how she kept her valuables safe from hobos and vagrants that could snoop around when no one was at the house since the doors were never locked. She didn't want to give away her secret hiding place, a culvert near the house under the tracks that worked very nicely, so she just said, "I have faith in people's good character." It wasn't a lie, it just wasn't the answer the person was looking for. But even she knew that sometimes it wasn't bad character that led a person to steal. Sometimes it was raw need.

One day in early June, Loring found Hattie in their bedroom changing sheets. "You remember I said that the bridges were being worked on and that ours should be next? Well, they plan to start in a few weeks."

"How will that affect us?" Hattie asked. A pleasant breeze blew the sheer curtains toward her playfully. She breathed in the fresh scent of the new season. The work Loring spoke of would be just outside these windows.

"I don't think it will affect my crew so much. I suppose we may be asked to help, but I haven't heard about that yet. I *have* heard they will expect you to feed the men. And there will be a lot of them, Hattie, maybe as many as forty or fifty." Hattie's eyebrows shot up. "Some of the men will bring their own dinner pails, I suspect. I'm just not sure of the details yet. But if I know you, you'll have everything in order." He gave her a peck on the cheek before going back to work.

Well, this will be interesting now, won't it? she thought, the wheels in her head already spinning as to what she could make ahead of time and what she might want to have on hand. The next week she learned that most of the men would not need dinners. Also, they would eat with the Crawford House staff before retiring to their bunks in the work trains parked at Crawford yard. So, what was needed from her was not nearly as much as she'd thought. But Hattie was never one to tolerate a skimpy larder. She loved to cook, and serving good meals was half the reason. If only she could have a garden, she could provide more fresh vegetables. Instead, she was given or bought fresh vegetables from neighbors' gardens. She still had a few of those she'd put up last year as well. She made more bread than usual. And, of course, more doughnuts and cookies of all different kinds.

Once the job began, it was obvious the men who were hired from a Portland company had done this work many times. Loring and his crew were seldom needed, so when their own work didn't detain them, they watched the proceedings with fascination. They knew they were seeing something they'd probably never see the likes of again. Rusty was closely watched and often left in the house, which he didn't appreciate.

Not long after the bridge crew began working, Nell and Earl came for a visit. Nell had married her beau, Walter, the year after Loring and Hattie's wedding. It had been a glorious affair. Hattie had enjoyed playing a special organ piece at Nell's wedding. Not long after, Nell was with child, but it had ended in a miscarriage, for which Hattie felt a sincere pang of grief. The next year resulted in another miscarriage. Hattie had stayed by Nell's side for several days doing what she could to help the grieving woman. Then, miraculously in 1901, Nell and Walter welcomed their son, Earl. There had been much to rejoice.

This summer, when Nell came for a visit, Earl was four years old, and Hattie could hardly believe how much he'd grown just since the past November. The bridge work provided a fair bit of entertainment for the youngster. Loring enjoyed stealing moments from his own work to sit with his nephew at the edge of the ravine and watch. This afforded Hattie and Nell several opportunities for nice, long talks. Loring said he could never understand what on earth the two women had to talk about for that long. He was just glad he wasn't expected to join them. He'd been satisfied to learn all that he cared to know over mealtimes.

Then, not a week later, Hattie welcomed Millie, a friend from home. Millie lived in North Gorham up the hill from Forest Hall where Hattie had first danced with Loring. The two women had met at the home where Hattie had taken care of the five children until she was nearly twenty. Millie was friends with the oldest girl, and sometimes the two girls played at one or the other's homes. Since Millie lived on a farm and Lillian lived in town, the girls enjoyed the different things each home offered. Hattie lost touch with Millie after she finished working at that house, so she had been pleasantly surprised to get a letter from the now young woman asking to visit the Notch.

"Welcome to Crawford Notch, Millie!" Hattie said, as Millie stepped off the train. "This is Rusty here." Millie bent to greet him. Then hugging the younger woman warmly, they set off down the tracks. "So, how are you? I hope your trip was agreeable."

"Oh, yes! It was a lovely ride up here. Such views! I've always loved seeing Mount Washington from White's Bridge, but what a thrill to be right in these mountains!"

"I've said as much myself. Did you finish school?"

"I did. I graduated from North Gorham in '97. I thought I might work right away after that, but Papa insisted I continue my studies in Latin and English at Gorham for three more years. We graduated in 1900 and they called us the class of the double nothings! I always found that so funny. After that I was going to go to normal school."

"I assume you wanted to be a teacher. What happened?"

"I didn't end up going because I was the only one left to care for Papa by the time I graduated from North Gorham. Mama died in '96; I don't know if you knew that." Hattie shook her head. She certainly knew something about being without a mother at a young age. "Papa took another wife so she could help him at home while I went to high school in Gorham Center, where I boarded. But I could tell he wasn't happy with her. So, after graduation, I decided to stay home. When Papa's second wife left soon after I moved back, I knew she had only been there to fill in for me."

"I learned that you lost your sister and brother, but I didn't know you lost your mother, too. I'm so sorry your family suffered so many deaths, Millie."

"Thank you. It wasn't easy, that's true. Only one brother survived, and he moved to Massachusetts to teach. Papa and I fell into a rhythm together, though. I kept house and he worked the farm, such as it was by then, smaller by far without my brothers to help him. This spring I had a suitor who asked Papa for my hand, but it didn't work out. I think Papa didn't want me to marry a farmer, knowing how hard farm work is on a woman. And I didn't want to leave Papa alone. He's never been entirely well after being wounded in the Rebellion. So, I decided to turn down my suitor. I guess it wasn't meant to be."

Hearing Millie's subtle change of mood, Hattie asked her gently, "Was it difficult to say no to the man?"

"Surprisingly more difficult than I would have thought. I may never be asked to marry another."

"You're what, about twenty-five now? You're young. I should hope you'd have other suitors."

"Perhaps, but North Gorham isn't much of a town. And staying on the farm doesn't give me a lot of chances to meet people."

Once they reached the house, Hattie settled Millie into her room, then poured them both some lemonade. Boomerang and Millie met and were fast friends. Millie scratched Boomerang behind his ear and the cat showed his appreciation by jumping into her lap when she sat down, expecting the attention to continue as the two women talked.

Their visit went quickly. When Hattie put Millie on the train back home, she assured her she was welcome anytime. Hattie hoped the visit had been good for her friend who had apparently needed the boost of morale. For Hattie, the visit made her ponder the pain of waiting for something one longs for that seems out of reach, though she didn't mention her own longing for a child.

Thirteen

~ 1905 - 1906 ~
Wondrous Events

I t had been nearly seven weeks since the bridge crews had begun working. Two on the bridge itself, one stone crew, and a work-train crew had rebuilt most of the wooden and iron spans of the existing bridge using steel. Piece by piece the new bridge took shape. Loring wished his nephew Weston could see all this now. If he was fascinated before, this might just turn him into an engineer!

One day, while Hattie was standing outside with Loring watching the men work, he told her that he'd heard they'd be ready to switch out the old bridge with the new one the coming Sunday. And when that happened, he wanted her to be sure to see it. Hattie took in the beehive of activity. The sights of machinery she'd never seen, of framework meant to hold tons of weight, of men of all colors and cultures. The sounds of clanging metal pieces being tethered to one another, the thuds of wood tossed aside, the grunts and groans of men working in the August heat. She might have watched longer, but she needed to go back inside and took her leave.

When she turned to walk the short distance to the house, she saw that the porch door was standing open. *Tsk! We'll have every bug that flies in this house. I wonder why the door was open.* Hattie walked into the house, closing the door firmly behind her. As she entered the dining room, she heard strange sounds coming from the kitchen and quickened her pace. Scritch, scritch, chitter, chitter. When she got there, she couldn't believe what she saw. A squirrel was helping itself to some of her bread! "Scat! Scat!" she yelled, picking up her broom and swatting at it, making it run all over the kitchen to escape its tempest. Hattie realized then that the squirrel had no exit, so she opened the door and swept it out. When she did, Rusty came trotting in. "Oh, so you're the culprit, I'll bet! And where have you been?" Rusty looked up with guilty eyes. Hattie gave him a pat on the head which instantly changed his guilty look to his usual adoring one. Then she looked at the damage and determined it not to be so very bad. Shaking her head she said, "I love nature, but I'd rather it stay outside in most cases."

On August 13, 1905, there was excitement in the air as the Portland crew assembled to make the switch. Both bridges, the old wooden one and the new steel frame, were placed on continuous rolls, and heavy rope tackle connected the rolls with hand winches. There were four winches to each span and six men to each winch. When everyone was in place, a signal would be given for each man to turn his winch in exact unison to the movements of the man next to him. This would be repeated until the track was once more in place. Incredibly, the whole operation was to take no more than ten minutes if all went well. Hattie, Loring, and the section crew were outside watching.

When all the bridge men were ready, everything got quiet. Loring had purchased a used camera and had it ready to go. *I don't know if he's more excited about watching the operation or taking the pictures,* Hattie thought. She loved seeing Loring like this, almost childlike with excitement. Finally, at the sound of a large gong, the ratcheting began. Gong! Each man ratcheted one notch. Gong! Ratchet one notch. Gong! Ratchet. Those who had pocket watches had them out. No one could believe this could possibly take no more than ten minutes. In fact, Loring's crew had wagered bets as to how long this would actually take. The man closest to the half minute would take all. When the new track was in place, a cheer went up. It had taken nine minutes and thirty seconds. Ed Meany had the closest guess and slapped his fellow betters on their backs. "Told ya they'd do it in under ten, like they said!" The bridge crews had clean-up work to do, which would take several more days, but nothing could compare to seeing the track switched.

A few days later, Hattie found that same squirrel inside stealing food again. And again she swatted it out. And it continued to happen. No one was sure how the squirrel got in the house, but Hattie was now inclined to believe that Rusty may not have been the culprit the first time. Some days the dog had a go at the creature, never coming close enough to catch it. Eventually, Hattie sighed and decided that she had a pet squirrel on her hands. She could tell that particular squirrel by the small slice torn out of one ear. She called it Twitch, and Loring thought she was a bit silly to encourage a squirrel. *Only Hattie*, he thought, remembering how she'd held her hand out the kitchen window last winter with food in her palm to encourage chickadees to alight there. Sure enough, she'd had at least one taker. *Hattie could probably tell the birds apart enough to give each one a name*, Loring chuckled to himself.

Early that fall, Beth Peabody and her husband George, the Crawford House caretakers, decided to take another hotel job. Hattie was sad to see Beth go. Although she had friends in Hart's Location, there weren't many she was close to. Beth had been one that Hattie had come to enjoy a great deal. It wasn't that the two women saw one another especially often, more that they understood each other. They were able to catch up quickly whenever they did visit. Hattie relied on Beth for things like local news and the comings and goings at Crawfords. There was always someone exciting coming through the Crawford House's impressive front doors. Most recently, Wilbur Wright had stayed there. Didn't Hattie enjoy hearing all about the brothers who had conquered the great frontier of the air! It was extremely difficult to believe that anything big enough to carry the weight of a person could leave the ground. Beth said that Wilbur was every bit the gentleman. He was there to promote his and Orville's plans for further flying expeditions. The Crawford House was a good place to do that with all the notables walking its red carpets.

In the Peabodys' place, John and Elizabeth Jackson came to Crawfords. Hattie was just beginning to get to know the new caretakers by the time the snow started flying. They were younger than she was, but Hattie was hopeful they would be friends. Elizabeth had a cheerful warmth about her that drew people in and a lovely, caring nature it would be hard not to appreciate. She was shorter than Hattie, and more petite. She had the most beautiful wavy auburn hair Hattie had ever seen, and the freckles to go with it. Her eyes sparkled when she smiled, which was often.

Throughout the following winter and into spring, Hattie continued to learn the language of mountain weather. Thunderstorms, the likes of which she couldn't remember ever seeing, had their own magic and beauty as lightning bolt after lightning bolt struck the tops of the surrounding mountains. It was as though God wanted to point out each mountain summit one at a time with a fiery finger. Hattie was rarely afraid for their home in strong thunderstorms, but, as with heavy snowstorms, she wasn't especially happy when the men were out working in it. Still, she spent at least a few minutes every day taking stock of what nature had to say. The better she could read Mother Nature's mind, the better she could predict when and how to move about this mountain home.

In the blink of an eye, July was upon them. Remarkably, Hattie and Loring, and even the section men, remained relatively healthy. Maybe it was the mountain air. But that's why in August, when Hattie felt more tired than usual, she couldn't account for it. She blamed it on the heat and took short naps when she was able. When the men began to notice, she was worried about how obvious it was. She didn't want to be a burden.

John came into the kitchen one hot, sticky afternoon to get drinks for everyone. "Hello, Hattie. Just came in for some water." She was sitting at the table, working on a shopping list, and started to get up. "No, no," John said, "no need to get up. I'm perfectly able to get water." She allowed herself to feel grateful. "How're ya feeling today?" John asked her.

"Not bad," she said, hoping to sound convincing.

"Is there anything I can do for ya?"

"I was just going to ask her that." Loring had just come in. "I'll take care of her, John." John took the cue and went back to work. The exchange might not have been noticed by anyone else, but it made Hattie uneasy.

"Hattie, love," Loring said, standing by the table. "You just don't seem to be yourself lately. Should we send for Doc Shedd?" Doctor George Shedd lived in Bartlett and was well known in Hart's Location and probably much further. He had studied at Bowdoin College in Maine and was highly respected. They were lucky he was only an easy train ride down the mountain.

"Oh, pfft," Hattie replied, "I don't think it's anything all that bad. Probably just the heat."

"Stand up," he said. She did, and he pulled her into his arms. "You know something, Mrs. Evans? You are like that oak tree down there behind the house. Sturdy, healthy, dependable…I…well, we, the crew and I, count on you for a lot. But I don't want to take that for granted. All you need to do is say the word and we'll have the doc here in no time. There's no shame in feeling peaked once in a while."

"Thank you, Loring. Really. I'm all right. I'll let you know when a doctor is needed. But you know what you remind *me* of sometimes?"

His eyes crinkled as his face reflected amused curiosity. "What's that? A bear? No, a muffin!"

"You're much more than your ample tummy, you know," she said, rolling her eyes. "No, I think of you like an otter. You're playful and intelligent and curious. And…you like to fish!"

There was just nothing left to communicate that a kiss couldn't say.

By September, Hattie was no better. Worse, if anything. When she lost her breakfast one day, she said nothing but began to suspect what was ailing her. It would be so wonderful if she was right, but she didn't want to get her hopes up. After all, Nell had lost two babies before she had Earl. Hattie was still able to wear her regular clothes, so no one was the wiser.

Later that month, Loring decided it was time to go home for a visit soon. So, in early October they boarded the train at Crawfords and headed for Raymond. Loring had given the men a list of things to accomplish in his absence and put John in charge. Hattie had had time to make some food ahead, and the men would see to Rusty and Boomerang's care. They said they'd have nothing to do with feeding her squirrel, though.

"Happy?" Loring asked Hattie on their way down the mountain.

"Very," she answered, smiling inside at what she now knew for sure. She planned to make an announcement when they were with the family.

Hattie was grateful to be picked up at Sebago Lake Station by Nell. They talked all the way to Raymond while Loring handled the reins. Once at the farm, Loring took care of the horses while Nell showed Hattie to their room, and then it was just the two of them, left to catch up with each other. Nell suddenly became quiet, looking into Hattie's eyes in a peculiar way.

"What is it, Nell?"

"Well? Are you, you know, late? You look different, Hattie."

Hattie smiled. Nell would, as it turned out, be the first to know after all. "Yes." Nell almost screamed, but Hattie quickly put her finger on Nell's lips. "I'll announce it while we're here. I thought you all might like to see Loring's reaction. What do you think?"

"Oh, my heavens! Loring doesn't even know? Good thing I didn't blurt this out in the wagon! What fun to watch my brother! I can hardly wait! It always amazes me when men don't pick up on that. I'll just have to be good and not let your secret slip, but it will be very hard for me, you know." As if

Hattie didn't. She lovingly smiled at Nell. She did so like this sister of Loring's. "Most of the family is coming here Sunday afternoon. That might be a good time to tell everyone."

Hattie made a mental note, then changing the subject, asked, "Where is Earl?"

"Oh, he's probably out with his grandpa," Nell said as the two of them went into the kitchen. "He really can be quite helpful at five years old, believe it or not. Right, ma?"

"Right, indeed!" Sarah said coming toward them. Hattie hugged her mother-in-law and asked her how she was doing. Sarah, always quick to laugh but otherwise rather quiet, said she was doing well. She asked after Hattie and they exchanged the usual pleasantries, always under Nell's watchful eye, Hattie noticed. Hattie realized with sudden interest that watching how Sarah interacted with her large family, once they all arrived, might give her clues as to how to be a good mother. She knew she didn't want to pattern herself off her own mother's parenting, and she was suddenly curious about how Sarah had managed to bring up such a large, loving family.

The trip and the rest of that day wore Hattie out more than she liked, so she went to bed early that night, even before Loring and his parents were ready to part for bed. The next day, Loring's brothers, Charlie and Will, came to pick him up to get cider in Standish. They had six jugs to fill. Since Will and his wife, Harriet, had plenty of children, some of them had been loaned out to their neighbor to help in the orchard and in exchange he would supply them with a bit of cider from his press. On their way to get the cider, the three brothers enjoyed not only catching up, but also telling stories. Their laughter could be heard well beyond the wagon. The cider they got would make for a rollicking good time Sunday, too. Perhaps one of the best rewards for going to get cider, though, was the molasses cookies that always awaited them when they got back to their father's farm.

Sunday arrived, cloudy and cool. Hattie would need the wrap she brought when she was outside. Family began arriving mid-morning. The Evans family had grown over the years.

But, of course, with eight children to John and Sarah's credit, and more than ten grandchildren already, the family would continue growing quickly.

Many hands made quick work of their abundant dinner meal. Sarah and her daughters, Nell and Nora, finished the food dishes in the kitchen. Hattie and the other daughters-in-law, Cora, Harriet, and Leonora, arranged the food on the makeshift tables the men had fashioned, laying old doors on top of sawhorses. These were then covered with sheets and decorated with gaily colored mums, making the food look all the more appealing. *Loring will not lose any weight while we're here,* Hattie thought as she surveyed the bounty. *Then again, I won't either. But on me it will be hard to tell whether it's food or baby.* When the family had formed a circle around the tables, Nell eyed Hattie to let her know that her announcement had best be now. Hattie took a deep breath. She didn't particularly enjoy being the center of attention but, like it or not, she soon wouldn't be able to conceal her condition anyway. She and Loring had been married ten years already and no one thought the next new grandchild would come from them. She'd have to get used to drawing attention.

Hattie nodded to Nell who banged a serving spoon on the table. When the family quieted, she said, "Hattie has something she would like to say."

Loring turned quickly to Hattie with a shocked look on his face. This was new, Hattie speaking out in a crowd. Everyone saw Loring's expression and knew that whatever was coming would be news to him, as well. As Martha used to say, one could hear a pin drop. "Uh, first of all," Hattie began nervously, "I would like to thank you, John and Sarah, for making our stay so pleasant, as usual." She paused. Her parents-in-law murmured, "You're welcome," and gave her their winning smiles. Then it quieted quickly. "I, uh, I mean, well…Loring and I are going to have a baby in March, God willing."

The cacophony that erupted was, for Hattie, absolutely secondary to Loring's face. Tears welled in his eyes and then hers as they looked at each other. Only they knew fully what this meant to them. Others could only speculate. They had hoped for this moment for the past decade. God only knew why a child was so delayed for them, but it didn't matter anymore. Before he could say anything to his wife, he was slapped on the back and congratulated by the men. The women had to stand in line to hug Hattie, with Nell holding back until last. Hattie and Nell held each other long enough to convey what only a woman could say to another woman. Hattie knew that Nell would be there for her if needed.

Once the commotion died down and everyone began vying for a place in the dinner line, Loring grabbed Hattie and held her tight. He knew what this meant to her. As for him, it was just sinking in that he was hugging two people at once.

Fourteen

~ 1906 - 1907 ~
A New Addition to the Family

There could be no doubt of Rusty's primary loyalty the moment Hattie and Loring walked into their house. He galloped over to them and then raised his full body to Hattie's. Were it not for Loring's quick arm to steady her, the dog might have knocked her down. With an affectionate chuckle, she soothed, "Yes, yes, Rusty, I missed you, too."

Protectively, Loring was more inclined to speak sharply at the dog but thought better of it. Instead, he said to Hattie, "You're probably tired out. Why don't you go lie down a while?"

"Loring, I appreciate you trying to take care of me, but I'm not broken. I'll lie down when I need to. I promise. After all, I did that when neither you nor I knew my condition, didn't I?" She kissed him, then turned to put their things away.

That evening the two of them together broke their news to the crew. The men were thrilled for the couple, though Hattie sensed an unspoken question. Would Loring and Hattie stay on at Mount Willard once the baby came? The Monahans hadn't. So, Hattie broached the subject when she and Loring were alone. "Loring, when I wanted to work in Lewiston, we compromised. You were okay with me working as long as we revisited things if we had a baby. That was nearly ten years ago. What do you think now?"

Loring put the question back to her, "Do you think you can handle both working and taking care of a baby?"

"Of course, I won't know until we get that far, but I'd like to think I can."

"All right. If ever you can't manage, we'll figure out what to do. But I'll be watching you, Hattie. Sometimes I think you can be too stoic for your own good."

The next day, Loring got his camera out. He said, "I want to take your picture before this baby comes. Before you're a mother. And the light is good right now."

She honored his request, though she knew she already was a mother. But she didn't correct him. As she stood up, she scooped Boomerang into her arms before he could jump down and carried him outside with her. Loring quickly snapped the picture of both of them standing beside the tracks. Although Hattie had to squint in the bright sunlight, Loring thought she looked beautiful in her burgundy skirt and ruffled white blouse, her luxurious head of hair fixed to the top of her head. *How lovely this picture would be if her hair was down, blowing in the breeze,* he thought wistfully. But her untethered hair was something only he had ever seen behind closed doors. Nevertheless, he loved her hair, down or up. Her slender corseted waist would disappear soon and be replaced with another kind of beauty. The fact that they would be a family of three caught him off guard now and then.

Once Loring had taken the picture, he said, "I think this is going to be a beautiful picture. I can't wait to develop it."

"I think I should take *your* picture now, Loring Evans, before you're a father. Besides, I still can't get used to you without your mustache. I'd like to document your smooth face." Loring lovingly obliged before they both had to get back to their workdays. Hattie decided to get her work done as quickly as she could and then take Rusty for a walk to Florence's house. Her friend had given birth to her third baby in August. Hattie could take her some food and ask for some advice in return.

It was hard to tell who was more excited once they got to the Willey House, Rusty or the girls, Hattie or Florence. Hattie reached for the baby immediately. Florence was extremely excited for Hattie's new baby coming, and though it was obvious that Hattie was, too, Florence also detected that Hattie was nervous about something. "Is something bothering you?"

Hattie looked up from baby Hazel's dark, glossy eyes and said, "Well, it's all so new to me. I guess I'm afraid I won't know the right things to do. And I could write and ask my sister-in-law, Nell, but it's so much nicer to be able to talk in person."

"Anything in particular that you're concerned about?" Florence asked, keeping an eye on her girls and Rusty.

"Are there things I should or shouldn't eat right now?" Hattie began.

"Your baby will help you with that, trust me," Florence said with the authority of experience in her voice. "There are things you'll crave that you never did before and things you used to love that you won't want to come within smelling distance of. Some doctors will tell you not to give in to your cravings. I just did what my body told me to and as you can see, I did just fine. Anything else?"

"Loring is already hovering over me like I'm going to break. I usually tell him I'm fine, but maybe he's got a point. I mean, I know I won't break, but should I be more careful?"

"Again, Hattie, listen to your body. If you feel like you need rest, then rest. You can do that more easily than I can since you don't have other children pulling at you. But don't be afraid to ask for help when you need it," Florence gently advised her.

"What can I wear when I get bigger?" Hattie asked, beginning to feel a little less anxious.

"Oh, darlin', I can give you a few clothes for that. We're about the same size, I think. They've been spit up on plenty, but I've washed 'em good. I'd be happy to loan you all that I have right now, but I'll need to lose some of this belly of mine first!" Florence said un-self-consciously patting her stomach.

After more questions and answers and some catching up, Hattie said to four-year-old Gertrude and two-year-old Ethel, "Goodbye girls. Thank you for letting me hold your little sister." Hattie handed Hazel over to Florence and said, "Thank you.

You've been more help than you know. I need to be getting on home, but you'll hear from me again soon, I'm sure. And once the baby comes, I may as well move in with you! I know I'll have more questions then."

"You have more common sense than you give yourself credit for. Believe me, you'll do just fine. But I don't mind answering questions when it's about something I know as well as this."

The two women hugged, and Hattie headed home with Rusty trotting ahead of her.

On her way up to the house, it began to rain. She had to watch her step more carefully on the ties as they tended to get slick. *Maybe that's why Rusty is running ahead of me. He probably knew this rain was coming and wants to hurry me along.* She thought about the letters that needed to be written about the coming blessed event. Loring's family had been present in enough numbers that any who hadn't been there probably knew about the baby by now. She'd write to her Lewiston friend, Esther, of course. And, since reconnecting with Millie, she'd write and hope Millie would enjoy her news. Suddenly, a pang of grief went through Hattie's body when she realized the one letter she didn't need to write. *The Reverend would have been so happy for us. Martha, too.* It was a painful thought.

Over the next few days, Hattie had written her letters of announcement and a few more in answer to letters she'd recently received. She decided to go up to Crawfords to mail them herself rather than give them to one of the men. That way she could also visit Elizabeth. She really needed to get to know her neighbor better since their lives would inevitably cross paths. Then, depending on how she felt in Elizabeth's presence, she might disclose her news there, too.

"Come on, Rusty. Wanna go for a walk to Crawfords with me?" Hattie grabbed her sweater, not sure if she'd need it or not. These October days were fickle. A week or so ago, they'd had a heavy rain just before the temperature dropped drastically, leaving them with a lot of ice. Yet now it seemed more like early fall. One thing remained the same, though. Any day was a good day to walk as far as Rusty was concerned.

When Hattie and Rusty entered the station, Herb was behind the ticket window. He immediately came out to greet them. "Hi there, Rusty!" Herb said, giving the dog a friendly pat. "And how are you, Hattie?"

"I'm fine, thank you. I've got letters for you today. Six of them." She said, handing Herb her mail and the twelve cents to go with it. "How are you?"

"Doin' well. Not lookin' forward to winter, though. My legs ache so in the cold. But other than that, not complainin'."

"Well, it's always good to see you," Hattie said, turning to leave. "Come on, Rusty! Bye, Herb!"

"Bye, now," Herb said, and retreated into the office.

As Hattie headed on to the hotel, she began to whistle. It was then she realized how happy she was. She may be dealing with new physical issues now, but there was a spring to her step and color to her cheeks. "Hello!" Hattie called out when she reached what used to be Beth's cottage. "Elizabeth?"

"Oh, hi, Hattie! Come on in. How are you?"

"I'm fine. Loring and I are both fine. And you?"

"John and I are doing well. I think we're beginning to feel like we know what we're doing here. Maybe," Elizabeth said, screwing up her face. "What brings you up to Crawfords? Mail?"

"Yes," Hattie answered, "that and a quick visit if you have time?"

"I do. Have a seat."

"Any news from up this way?" Hattie asked.

"Well, let's see," Elizabeth mused. "We've had a few of the help quit and others get hired. Oh, and we're getting to know Asa Barron. Most of us feel he's a fair employer. He seems to care a lot about his visitors as well as his staff. His wife, well, she's a bit uppity, I think, but not unkind. You should see the dresses she wears. You always know what's in style when you look at her! Actually, come to think of it, I've heard a rumor. And that may be all there is to it, the way people talk, you know. But I've heard that the Barrons may pass the hotel over to their son. Who knows what the place will be like then, right?"

"I've seen Mrs. Barron, I think, but I've never met her," Hattie said.

"And I've also heard that English Jack is going to live with the Fahey family in Twin Mountain this winter," Elizabeth added.

"Oh, he is? Is he ill?" Hattie asked.

"I don't know about illness, but he *is* getting up in age. Maybe winters are just too much for him now."

"Poor man. That shack he lives in mustn't hold heat very well," Hattie said, with a quick prayer of gratitude that her house had no such problems. The cold had never really agreed with her and was one reason she kept active in the winter. She loved the season plenty if she was warm enough wherever she was. But she, unlike Jack, was still young. At his age, there'd be no good remedy for the cold.

Elizabeth had gone quiet. Hattie studied her face while she waited to see if the younger woman had anything to add. Elizabeth's warm, brownish-green eyes conveyed contentment, Hattie thought. She was just wondering if the Jacksons had any children when Elizabeth cleared her throat. "One other thing is new, but no one knows about it here yet. I'll tell you, though. John and I are going to have a baby this winter!"

Hattie gasped, "Oh! So are Loring and I!"

Before Hattie could say it, Elizabeth said, "Congratulations! When are you due?"

"We think mid-March. What about you?" Hattie said.

"Mid-February," Elizabeth said.

"My heavens, but those babies will be close in age, won't they?" Hattie couldn't help wondering if Elizabeth's baby would be born on her own birthday but didn't say so.

"They will! Winter babies and hopefully playmates one day. But I sure hope the weather doesn't make it hard to get the doctor. I don't want to have this baby alone! Are you having the doctor or a midwife?"

"Hopefully Doc Shedd down in Bartlett. And I've had the same thought, Elizabeth. I hope the doctor can come quickly. I don't mind living on the tracks, but I've never had to depend on them for something as big as this."

Elizabeth and Hattie had much to chat about, but their fates were sealed by this interesting pairing of events. On her way home, Hattie wondered how she might have received Elizabeth's news if she weren't having a baby herself. No matter. That wasn't the case, and she began to whistle again.

As the weeks went on, Hattie grew to love the child within her even though she didn't know anything about it yet. She'd soon be thirty-five years old. She and Loring had long ago assumed they were not able to conceive. Just when they were beginning to accept that they would not have children, here she was, near to giving birth. It had never occurred to her that she could actually love someone she'd never met. When the baby began to move within her, she learned its peculiarities. It truly amazed her that an unborn being seemed to have preferences and a schedule of its own.

Loring, too, grew more and more fascinated as the months went by, and he began dreaming of teaching his son to fish and hunt. Instead of a nephew, he'd be pushing his own child on the three-wheeler or taking him to meet English Jack. At night, he'd lie beside Hattie, falling asleep with his hand on her belly. When Hattie could feel movement, she wasn't the only one who was mesmerized. Loring, too, loved feeling the life of his child, his legacy. If they were blessed with more than one child, he realized he'd be ever so grateful, but if this was to be the only one, God help the child not to become spoiled by its father!

Rusty seemed even more attentive to Hattie, if that was possible. He insisted on being there to hoist the flag and take it down each day, help her do her daily chores, and even accompany her to the privy, *For Glory's sake*, she thought, rolling her eyes at the dog. Rusty had a new purpose and took his duties seriously. Boomerang, on the other hand, was more and more aloof. Hattie reasoned that he was probably perturbed that her lap was quickly becoming too small for him. And the fact that it bumped him now and then didn't help matters.

The crew acted like good brothers, curious from a distance, ready to assist, and proud, as if this baby was their own niece or nephew. Hattie noticed that John was especially watchful and wondered why. Did he have a favorite sister whose pregnancy he'd not been present for? Did he have a sister, perhaps, who had died in childbirth, God forbid? That did happen far too often, she knew.

One thing was becoming apparent. All the men assumed the baby was a boy. At least that was what their banter seemed to say. Hattie reminded them they'd best be prepared for either.

Loring's birthday and their anniversary came and went. Christmas, New Year's Day, and Hattie's birthday all passed with the usual fanfare. On the first of March, Hattie learned that Elizabeth had just had a baby boy they'd named Peter who had arrived on February 25, just the week after Hattie's birthday. She was very grateful that both Elizabeth and Peter were doing well and couldn't wait to meet the little one. But by this time, winter, along with her size, kept her closer to home, if not inside all day.

In the second week of March, Hattie felt some pains in her belly. She had no way of knowing if these were labor pains or the false ones that Florence had told her about. So, she waited them out and before long they disappeared. *Good thing,* she thought. *Let the snow come. I've no need for concern, at least not today.* She'd correctly assessed the floor of the dark gray clouds that had moved in earlier to be storm clouds. How much snow they'd get she had no way of knowing, but before long she could tell the storm meant business. The wind blew the tiny flakes of a telltale, heavy snowstorm in swirls outside her windows. She looked out over the valley. It rested serenely, accepting its new blanket of white.

The only difficulties for her this particular day had nothing to do with the storm. It was all about getting her work done with a barrel affixed to her abdomen. She had found alternate ways of bending over to pick things up and also found muscles she didn't know she had. Placing her large belly in a certain position allowed her enough arm's length to peel potatoes or iron clothes. If the snow was especially deep, she'd let one of the men gather the eggs. And she couldn't remember ever being more thankful for the chamber pot in their bedroom. All well and good for her, but she thought about the men out in storms like this. For the most part they took it in their stride as part of the job, but she'd heard them grumble from time to time when they trudged back into the house, covered in snow.

By late afternoon that day she heard the single, long blow of the whistle that meant the snowplow was coming, get off the tracks. You didn't have much time to move if that's where you were. The plows came through hard and fast. There was no train any louder than one with a plow. You'd have thought an earthquake was trying to open a brand-new valley in the Notch. Glad as she was for those immense machines clearing the only good way on or off the mountain in winter, she hoped she'd eventually get used to the pounding they gave the earth. And what a sight to behold when they blasted past the house! The plow created an instant wall of white while simultaneously hurling rocks, sticks, and whatever else it picked up, straight at the house. The onslaught of debris against the metal screening over the windows only lasted seconds. The impact of that much snow and rubble dumped at the front porch lasted much longer. Hattie was grateful to know that the men wouldn't tarry about clearing it out.

The next Thursday, Hattie felt something different, something new and not precisely like the pains she'd had the week before. It was the first full day of spring and snowing again. Her intuition told her that these pains were important. "Besides, I'm as big as a moose! This baby had better come soon," she muttered, mostly to herself, although Rusty assumed she was speaking to him and walked over to the side of her chair and sat down. "You're a good boy, Rusty. You've been taking good care of me, haven't ya, old boy?" She could almost see his chest puff out with pride. "If this pain is what I think it is, you might just have another body to guard around here pretty soon. I'd best get on with my chores just in case this baby decides to arrive today."

Her Thursday chores were mostly finished. She just needed to clean up her bedroom, which seemed appropriate, given where this birth would likely take place. Hattie tried not to imagine what would happen if things didn't go well. She looked out the windows at the storm, then busied herself. The more she swept or dusted, the more her abdomen hurt. And the pains were coming with regularity now. She sat a while. Then she got up and worked until it hurt too much and sat back down. At some point, from how she felt and from things Florence had told her, she realized she probably needed to alert the doctor. *Thankfully, Loring is near the end of his workday,* she thought anxiously, not knowing exactly where he was.

She went to the dining room and sent a message to Bartlett: *BS SEND DR HATTIE.* The return message said: *MW COMING ASAP BS.* Now she would wait until the doctor and Loring arrived. When Hattie was satisfied that her house looked as presentable as possible, she drew a pack of playing cards from a drawer in the parlor and began playing solitaire.

Hattie heard the back door open and felt the rush of cold air find its way throughout the house and straight to her feet. She heard voices and the stomping of boots. She had no idea how much snow had fallen so far. Loring walked into the parlor, calling her name uneasily. He was accustomed to seeing her in the kitchen when he walked in. "Are you all right?" he asked nervously when he saw her playing cards instead of finishing the supper meal.

"I'm fine, but the baby's coming," Hattie said in a matter-of-fact voice.

"It is? I'll message for Doc Shedd!" He headed to the dining room.

"I've already done that, Loring."

Turning back around he asked, "Do you need anything?"

She said, "I have all the food ready to go, but one of you boys will need to serve it and clean things up after you eat, I'm sorry to say. I'm comfortable in this chair and I don't want to do anything to disrupt that, at least until the doctor gets here."

"What about you, Hattie? Do you need to eat?" He felt so helpless. If he hadn't been second to youngest in his family, he might have remembered seeing his mother go through this. As it was, he was totally inexperienced. He marveled that his wife was so calm as to play cards.

"Not right now. I'm drinking this tea here and I have crackers to nibble on. I'm fine. I'll yell if I need you."

Reluctantly, Loring left her and tended to supper.

While the men ate, they all heard the long single whistle of the snowplow. After they'd eaten, they donned their outer clothes once more and shoveled out a path to the porch for the doctor. By the time they finished, it was dark. After they had cleaned up, they came and sat in the parlor with Hattie. She wondered if they were curious, excited, or nervous. Whatever they were, she very much felt that she was the center of attention, and how could she not be? Every time she felt the pains coming on, she had to stop playing her game to let the pain crest and subside. She knew the men saw this.

Finally, they heard a train coming up and hoped it was the doctor. When the light engine stopped in front of the house, they were relieved. Loring opened the door for Doc Shedd and waved to the engineer who happened to be Bobby Morse. The engine continued to Crawford Station where it would stay until the doctor needed it again. Removing his coat and scarf, the doctor shook hands with Loring and said, when he saw the small crowd before him, "Well, hello there, everyone." Then turning to Hattie, "So, we have a baby that wants to come, eh? Nice night for it," he chuckled at his sarcasm. Then he said, "By the looks of things, you aren't ready to deliver this baby quite yet. Can we go to the room where you want to deliver? I want to examine you and ask you some questions." He walked toward Hattie and helped her up.

Hattie led the doctor to her bedroom, giving Loring a little wave and a smile as she passed. The door shut behind them. Suddenly, Loring felt very anxious. He silently prayed that Hattie would have a successful delivery. He didn't want to think about her dying. Or his child not living past birth. Barring all that, he would soon be a father. He didn't know the first thing about how to be one. He knew how to replace old railroad ties and measure spikes. How to sharpen a scythe or fix a shovel. How to shoot and kill a deer, skin it, and cut it up for meat. How to develop the photographs he took. How to know by sound which train was coming and what engineer was probably driving it. But he didn't know how to take care of a baby. And he didn't like the feeling of being so ignorant.

The men could see the worry he wore and suggested they play a friendly game of poker. Before long, the doctor came back out to the parlor. Hearing the men in the dining room, he went in there to find Loring. "Hattie's pains are getting strong enough that I prefer she rest in bed. I'll go check on her from time to time but let nature take its course for now. She's got a magazine to read if she's so inclined. Mind if I cut in?"

Loring felt some relief to know that the doctor wasn't worried. When ten o'clock came, the men excused themselves for bed. They'd take over for Loring in the morning. The doctor and Loring sat in the parlor. Rusty planted himself by the door that was preventing him from being with Hattie. About two o'clock in the morning, after checking her again, the doctor asked Loring to boil some water and find some clean towels or sheets. He said things were progressing nicely and it shouldn't be much longer. Loring was happy to do something productive and left for the kitchen.

After delivering the water and a sheet, and at least seeing his wife, if only for a second, to know that she was all right, he sat near the bedroom door. He heard Hattie moan and then cry out. How he wished he could be there with her, yet he was so grateful she was in the doctor's care and not his. She cried out loudly and then there was a silent pause followed by the sweetest sound Loring thought he'd ever heard. Almost like the newborn lambs on his childhood farm, his new child bleated in protest to leaving the warmth of Hattie's belly.

Doc Shedd poked his head out the door and said, "Loring, you have a son!" Loring wept quietly. He had a *son*.

Fifteen

~ 1907 - 1909 ~
Another Addition

March 22 dawned brilliant and beautiful with new mounds of fresh snow covering everything. But this was one day Hattie was in no rush to admire the outside world. For her, the world was right here in her arms with Loring by her side. "What are we going to name him?" Loring asked dreamily, partly from lack of sleep and partly because he was so in awe.

"Why don't you pick a name for him first? If I don't approve, I'll let you know," she said, thinking that since she'd had the privilege of knowing their son for the past nine months, it should be Loring's privilege to name him.

"I'll think on it while I start breakfast for everyone. By the way, should I send a message to Elizabeth? Didn't you say she might be willing to make some extra food for the crew for a couple days at least?"

Hattie smiled to herself. For Loring, so much of the world revolved around his next meal. "Yes, that's a good idea. And please wire your mother and Nell, too, when you can. Now, there are beans in the pot and bread and pie in the larder. Bean sandwiches and pie should hold all of you 'til supper. If Elizabeth can help out, we won't need anything until this evening. If she can't, there are other things we can have. We won't starve."

Loring turned to go when Hattie said, "Oh, and Loring, if the men want to see the baby, tell them I hope to sit in the parlor for a short time tonight."

The day went by quickly for everyone. Hattie thought she heard the telegraph key clicking with a message for someone in their house. Loring appeared at the bedroom door to give her the message: *MW HOPE MOTHER AND BABY ARE FINE FLO.* It was then that Hattie realized Florence had likely heard Hattie's message to Bartlett and must have assumed that Hattie had gone into labor when the light engine went by her house going up into the Notch and then again, going back down. But Florence wouldn't necessarily know if all was well. Hattie wondered when she'd remember this was a party line! No matter. She'd have Loring message both Florence and Elizabeth. Then she thought, as her son ate noisily, *There's at least one thing I don't have to ask Florence about. This baby is a good eater!* She'd changed plenty of diapers over the years, but she knew Loring hadn't. She decided it would be good to have him do a diaper change just in case he ever needed to, but she had no intention of giving the job of taking care of this baby to anyone else. She'd waited too long for this pleasure to miss even so much as a minute.

By evening, after the lovely supper Elizabeth had sent down, everyone was in the parlor. "So, what's his name?" John asked Hattie as Loring put the baby in John's waiting arms.

"Ask Loring," she answered. "He's supposed to be coming up with the first suggestion."

"Well, Loring?" John said.

"I've thought about John, after my father, or George, after Hattie's. But John is too common, no offense, John, and Hattie isn't happy with George. So, I don't know yet."

Each of the men were offered a turn holding the baby, but only John and Denny wanted to. Hattie watched Loring's face as he shared his beautiful son with other people for the first time.

"I think he favors you, Loring," Denny said.

"I agree with you," Hattie said.

"Don't all babies have pudgy faces?" Loring asked the group.

"Yes, but he's got your nose and cheekbones, I think. And besides," Hattie said, "he's definitely got your appetite!" Loring produced a crooked smile as everyone laughed. When the baby let out a good burp in Denny's arms, everyone looked at Loring and laughed even harder.

It wasn't until later, when Hattie, Loring, and the baby were snuggled in bed, that Loring suddenly said, "What about Gordon? I have a cousin once or twice removed by that name."

"I like that. What would you put with it for a middle name?" Hattie asked.

"Can you think of a good middle name?" Loring returned the question.

"I've always liked Lyle myself," Hattie said, looking adoringly at the baby.

"Gordon Lyle Evans. I think that sounds strong and intelligent," Loring said.

Hattie smiled. "Then I think we have just named our son. Gordon Lyle Evans."

Adding Gordon's care into her schedule was a delight. What was a little harder was adding her mother-in-law into things when she insisted on helping the following week. While Hattie and Sarah got along well enough on the Evans farm, Hattie didn't feel especially close to her and was uncomfortable accepting help. As a child, it had been made clear to Hattie that if she asked her own mother for something, she would be expected to reciprocate. She came to think of a mother's love as being conditional and something to be wary of. Still, Hattie appreciated the extra hands around the house for those few days. It meant she was free to take her time feeding her baby and bonding with him face to face. She didn't think she had ever been happier. And by the end of that week, she and Sarah had also bonded just a wee bit better.

As spring slowly pushed winter out of the way, Hattie began taking short walks again. Over the winter she had sewn a sling in which to carry Gordon and it worked beautifully.

But whenever she put the sling on, Rusty was right there expecting to go for a walk. What Rusty didn't understand was that sometimes the sling came in handy just around the house. The dog would go back and forth between Hattie and the door waiting for her to pick up on his intentions. "Sorry, Rusty. I can't walk just now. Maybe later," she'd say. "Lie down now like a good boy." Whether he understood her words or not, he could usually be persuaded to do her bidding.

To Rusty's delight, Hattie's first longer outing was down to Florence's house. He'd run down the tracks ahead of her, then double back to check in. He'd repeat this until, finally, he was worn out enough to walk alongside her. The little girls couldn't get their hands on Gordon fast enough. It was both overwhelming and charming to Hattie. She was grateful that Florence reigned the girls in quickly, asking them to sit down, which they did at Hattie's feet like baby birds with their hands open instead of their mouths. Gordon was carefully passed back and forth. Gertrude was five years old and clearly capable of holding a baby. Ethel, too, was experienced, but with supervision. Hazel was crawling and grabbing anything her chubby little fingers came close to, including what little hair Gordon had. He yowled at having his hair yanked. Florence asked Gertrude to please watch Hazel while she took her turn holding Gordon and she was soon able to soothe the poor baby. It was wonderful to have some time to catch up with Florence, whose life was full to overflowing and happy.

The next time Hattie, Gordon, and Rusty went out for a walk, it was in the other direction, up to Crawfords. Hattie was bringing Elizabeth's now-empty dishes to return them while she carried Gordon in the sling. The day was delightfully sunny and the breeze was luscious. She could hardly wait to meet little Peter and have Elizabeth meet Gordon. Elizabeth was busy but not so much that she couldn't spend a short time visiting. The two women warmly hugged and then exchanged babies and a very easy conversation. It hadn't taken this relationship long to form and it promised to be a lifetime friendship.

Hattie had some extra time on her hands since Elizabeth couldn't visit for long, so she headed up English Jack's path.

But when she could just make out his "ship," she stopped, hoping he hadn't heard her. She suddenly realized that Loring would want to be the one to introduce Jack to Gordon. She quickly turned around and headed home. On the way, she passed Loring and John who were headed to the station. "And where have you been on this fine day?" Loring said, pulling his son from the sling. John indicated that he would continue to the station and meet Loring there.

"Gordon and Peter met for the first time today. Oh, Loring, you should have seen them together. So adorable! But Elizabeth was busy, so we didn't visit for very long. I started up the path to English Jack's since I had some time, but I turned around before I got there. I want you to introduce Jack to Gordon. Maybe this Sunday if the weather holds?"

"Thank you," Loring said. "I'd very much like to take Gordon to meet Jack. I assume, then, that Jack is back from his winter home in Twin Mountain?"

"Apparently, yes. Elizabeth thinks she saw him recently."

"Here you go, Gordon, into your little kangaroo pouch." Loring put Gordon back in the sling and gave Hattie a quick kiss. "I'll see you later, my love. Oh, and Hattie, there's a freight coming up. You can duck in the blacksmith's shop."

Goodness, that man is over the moon with happiness, Hattie beamed as they parted ways. She knew exactly how he felt.

As he'd said, she heard the train before she saw it. Once she cleared the gateway, she could see that it was just passing the house. She quickened her step to reach the small cave in plenty of time and stomped her presence. When nothing exited the cave, she sat on a rock, catching her breath.

"So, my little darling," she cooed, looking at Gordon's peaceful face as he slept contentedly in the sling, "meeting all these new people must be wearing you out." She gazed at his sweet face as the train approached. Roaring by, puffing like a dragon, the noise woke Gordon. She said, "Better get used to it. This is your life, too." When the train had passed, she walked on home.

Loring and Hattie took Gordon to meet Jack on a beautiful day in May. Jack was duly enamored with the baby and Loring was proud as a peacock. "I'll bring Gordon up here when he's old enough to appreciate one of those bow and arrow sets like I bought for my nephew a few years ago."

"I think that you'll be bringing him up here before that happens!" Hattie corrected her husband.

"She's right, of course, Jack."

After their visit, they decided to climb Mount Willard. Whenever they could get up there, especially in May, it brought back such sweet memories of Hattie's first visit to the summit. As they looked down over the edge of the cliff, Hattie saw the stones that outlined her heart-shaped garden. She couldn't wait to get it ready for her flowers. Then she eyed the house. The first time she'd seen it, that's all it was. Just a house. Now she saw not just a building, she saw their home. Her heart swelled. The meals they shared, the conversations, the laughter. Hattie said, "That first time we came up here—what year was that? '98? Nearly ten years!—anyway, I could never have imagined when I looked down at Joe and Florence's house that it would become ours. In fact, I'm not sure I would have wanted to know that then," she laughed, thinking of the work it took to make a house a home.

Loring put his arms around Hattie from behind her as he had that first time. Only this time he had to reach far enough to encompass Gordon, too. "No, I think things turned out just right the way they did."

In June, Nell came for a visit. Hattie was surprised it took her sister-in-law that long to come and meet her nephew, but when she saw six-year-old Earl, she realized that school kept Nell from traveling any time she wanted. Earl was delighted to know he had a little boy cousin to play with. It took some explaining to help him realize that it would be a few years before Gordon would be old enough to play. In the meantime, Rusty was always willing to be a playmate.

Nell and Earl stayed a few days and Nell enjoyed time with Loring as well as Hattie and Gordon. Others of Loring's family visited that summer, too. Hattie was also pleased that Esther and her sons made their way up to Mount Willard for a visit before school started. Millie had sent a letter expressing her congratulations along with the small bonnet she'd knitted.

By the end of September, Gordon was sitting up. He loved playing with Rusty, which essentially meant that when Rusty came near, Gordon swatted at him, which made Rusty run in circles, which caused Gordon to laugh so hard he'd fall over. Boomerang was less willing to play and just kept his distance. *He'd rather spend his energy finding mice*, Hattie thought, *and that is exactly what I need him to do.*

One warm Sunday, Loring, Hattie, and Gordon were fishing at the edge of Saco Lake. Mostly, it was Loring doing the fishing while Hattie kept an eye on the baby and served a wonderful picnic dinner. While they ate their sandwiches and potato salad, Hattie said, "Loring, it's time I let you in on a secret."

"Oh? And what's that?" Loring said absentmindedly, taking another bite.

"We're going to have another baby."

Poor Loring almost choked on his food. "What? When? So soon?"

Hattie laughed. "I thought you might react this way. It should come sometime around Gordon's birthday."

Loring was ecstatic. He all but tackled Hattie on the spot, being mindful that Gordon was next to her. He nonetheless kissed her passionately and said, "Oh, Mrs. Evans, you do know how to make me a happy, happy man."

Shortly after his first birthday, Gordon started walking and got into everything, which kept Hattie extra busy. The house was more than enough space for him to toddle around in and get the exercise a little one ought to have. At least he slept through the night, so they could all get their rest. He was still a very good eater, rivaling his father. Loring had a great time taking little Gordon everywhere, whenever he could, whether it was up the tracks or through the snowdrifts. Hattie's visits with both Florence and Elizabeth had been sparse over the past few months. Again, the combination of winter and her heaviness made it difficult. Having to take Gordon, who wanted to walk, made it even harder than it had been last year. So, they got out and played in the snow around the house, which Gordon loved. Especially when Rusty was involved.

Early morning on April 6, 1908, Hattie sent a message to Doc Shedd, same as she had last year about this time. Her pains had begun as twinges the night before. By late afternoon, the doctor poked his head out of the bedroom and said to Loring, "You have a daughter!" Loring could not believe his fortune. First a son and now a daughter. The men all slapped him on the back, then they broke out some cigars. When the doctor indicated that Hattie and the baby could be seen, Loring picked up Gordon and found Hattie sitting up in bed like a queen, holding their new princess.

They discussed names and decided to use the one they might have used if Gordon had been a girl, Mildred Elizabeth. Sarah came to help again and was especially pleased to learn that she and Mildred shared the same middle name. The bulk of her help this time was in chasing Gordon around. She loved hearing her grandson begin to babble the word "Grammy," which really sounded nothing at all like that word. But his attempts were delightful.

As with the year before, Hattie was outside as soon as she was able. It was spring and a lovelier time of year for being outside with two small children couldn't be had. The air smelled of newly formed leaves, sweet and fresh. Hattie had her hands full, though, so her visits to see her friends were usually on Sundays when Loring could go with her and manage Gordon. When Hattie needed to be home, and the day was sunny, she tied Gordon to the porch so that he wouldn't wander onto the tracks. She hated to tether his free spirit, but it couldn't be helped. There were things she still needed to accomplish and constantly chasing Gordon kept her from her work. At least tethering him like that didn't seem to dampen his happiness.

Hattie wrote to friends and family about the birth of their second child. She especially enjoyed writing Millie this time.

Hattie hadn't known for sure, but she assumed Millie's given name was Mildred. "To keep you and my daughter straight, I'll keep calling you Millie," she'd written.

Writing these letters made her think once more about Loring's need to know if she could manage both work and children. Loring hadn't brought it up, so she guessed he must think she was handling things all right. And she wasn't about to say anything, mostly because she *knew* she could handle things. Being a mother came as naturally to her as butter on bread. The truth was that she felt being a mother brought out the best in her. Even now with two little ones.

As Mildred grew, she needed more attention than Gordon had. Maybe it was just that Hattie's attention was more divided now and Mildred felt that. Loring thoroughly enjoyed giving both his children his attention when he could, so that helped. Hattie loved watching him come in from work and head straight for the children. He'd pretend to wrestle with Gordon, then he'd pick up Mildred and hold her way over his head, making her laugh. Never mind that the baby would sometimes spit up on her father, even on his face. To Loring it was all just glorious. Of course, Gordon would want the same kind of fun Loring had given his little sister, so Loring would hoist Gordon high up over his head and both father and son would laugh and laugh.

There was no keeping time from rushing on and soon it was already New Year's Day. In just a couple of months, Gordon would be two years old and Mildred one. The holidays had been ever so much fun with children in the house. But by the new year, Hattie had a familiar inkling. She kept it to herself for a while longer to be sure. Finally, one night after the children were down for the night and Hattie and Loring lay face to face on their bed, Hattie said, "Loring, I think I need to tell you something…"

Sixteen

~ 1909 ~
A Quiver Full?

Raymond Willard Evans arrived on August 24, 1909, a day the thermometer read ninety degrees. Named for Loring's hometown and their mountain, the newborn was instantly surrounded by a house full of love. Mildred, at one and a half, was curious about this new person in her mother's arms. She touched his face and watched his little hands and feet play with the air. When she was invited to give him a kiss, she planted the sweetest little peck on his cheek that Hattie had ever seen. She thought her heart would melt right then and there. Gordon, at two and a half, studied his little brother intensely. Every so often he'd proclaim Raymond's state of being in one or two words, presumably to be helpful. At least Hattie took it that way and usually thanked him. When Sarah came to help, she delighted in both Gordon and Mildred and they in her, practiced grandmother that she was. And Hattie was, by now, very grateful for Sarah's postnatal visits.

Hattie and Loring couldn't have been happier. As Hattie lay on her bed one evening shortly after Raymond's birth, staring into yet another brand-new face, she marveled at how this baby had similarities to both Gordon and Mildred and yet was completely unique at the very same time. Three utterly different human beings from the same two parents. *If we had twelve children, would they still each look as unique as this?* Hattie wondered. Then she suddenly remembered something she'd heard from the woman she had worked for when she was young. The woman could be quite outspoken about her faith sometimes. One day she read a passage from the Bible that was about children. Hattie remembered that it was in Psalms somewhere. She asked Loring for Martha's Bible that the Reverend had given her, and found the passage in chapter 127, verses 3 through 5:

> *Lo, children are an heritage of the LORD:*
> *and the fruit of the womb is his reward.*
> *As arrows are in the hand of a mighty man;*
> *so are children of the youth.*
> *Happy is the man that hath his quiver full of them.*

At the time, she hadn't understood what it meant. Now, she remembered that the woman had said her quiver was full with five children, which meant that she intended not to have any more. Hattie wondered if her own quiver was now full with three. And then she thought, *How can one know when their quiver is full?* She certainly didn't know, so perhaps it wasn't full yet.

What *was* full were her days. Sometimes she thought she was running a three-ring circus after Sarah's help was gone. The difference between two children and three seemed more than a simple addition problem. At least with two, she'd been able to hand one over to Loring while tending to the other. With three, sometimes she'd reluctantly ask one of the men to help. She just didn't want them to bear what was not their responsibility. And yet, there were many times when one man or another would entertain Gordon or Mildred while she was feeding Raymond. It seemed they did so from their own desire either to be helpful or to play with the child, or perhaps both. She really didn't know what their motives were but was always grateful for the extra pair of hands.

Most of the daytime she was the only adult in the house. Feeding, clothing, diapering, and getting children down for naps, as well as cooking, hauling hods of coal, doing laundry, making up beds, cleaning, caring for the animals, gathering the eggs, and tending the garden was all essentially up to her.

It isn't that she minded doing any of it. It was simply that there were only so many hours in a day and most of her duties were necessary. Much as she hated to, she had to concede some of the cleaning and gardening. It just worked out that way after everything else was done and her body craved a few hours of rest. Only once did Loring ask if she was too overwhelmed, but she told him that, truthfully, she'd be doing everything she was doing whether she was running a boarding house or not. He never brought it up again.

Florence came up to see the new baby. She brought the girls, who entertained Gordon and Mildred. Florence's newest baby was another girl they'd named Alice. She was eight and a half months old. Hazel was three and Ethel was five and a half. Gertrude was seven and a half, and she was a very big help. "Florence, how on earth did you manage when the children were so young? It's exhausting."

Reaching for the baby, Florence said, "I had two years between mine, which is easier than a year apart like yours. Gertrude could be a big help to you. How would you like to have her come up a few days before school starts?"

Thinking of herself years ago, beginning to work as a young girl, gave Hattie strangely mixed feelings—nostalgia, anxiety, anger, and a little sadness. She would be sensitive to Gertrude's young age and not ask more of her than a seven-year-old should deal with. But should she ask this of Gertrude at all?

Florence saw Hattie's reservation and said, "If you'd rather not, that's all right, too."

"It isn't that," Hattie said. "Remember I told you once that I was made to work long days as a twelve-year-old? It was a lot for me to handle at first. I don't want to put the burden of work on Gertrude's young shoulders unless she'd really like to do it."

"I understand," Florence said, and then, "Gertrude, honey, come here please."

When Gertrude was by her mother's side, Florence asked her, "Would you mind coming up here a couple hours to help Hattie out? Maybe two or three times before school begins? You can be truthful. It's okay to say no." Hattie nodded firmly.

"I don't mind. It would be different than looking after my sisters, that's for sure!" Hattie chuckled inwardly at Gertrude's answer.

"Then, I'd love it," Hattie said sincerely.

Florence didn't want to tire Hattie out too much, so she got up to leave. "Girls," she called out, "it's time to go home." Florence reluctantly gave Raymond back to his mother. "Your babies are so darling, Hattie. Congratulations. Come on, girls. Let's go. Ethel, get your dolly. Hazel! Put down Mildred's toy! That's not yours." Then Florence picked up Alice who was happily playing with her toes on the floor.

Truthfully, what was most tiring for Hattie was the general noise and confusion of seven children under eight years old all wanting something different at the same time. She could do little to help, but she tolerated a lot in exchange for seeing Florence. And she did have a lot of affection for all the Monahan children.

"I know that Gertrude wants to help me, but are you sure you can spare her?" Hattie asked.

"Well, I wouldn't want to give her up for too long, I'll be honest about that. But Ethel is a big help when her older sister is in school. So, we'll be fine." Florence turned to go, then suddenly swung around. "Oh! I almost forgot. We're going to have a baby at the end of the year!"

Hattie laughed, "You almost *forgot*? Well, congratulations! By then, I should be able to help *you* out. It's a good thing we aren't having these babies the same month!"

"Mom-m-m!" Gertrude called out. "Let's go-o-o!"

"Coming, girls. I'll see you later, Hattie. Rest when you can."

"Well, you, too!" Hattie called out. And the Monahans were gone, taking much of the noise with them. As promised, Gertrude came and watched Gordon and Mildred, who loved being with her.

At two and a half, Gordon fully understood the word "no." He would look directly into the eyes of whoever was being too demanding (in his opinion), put his hands on his hips, stomp his little foot, and say with confidence, "NO!" Hattie tried hard not to laugh. He was so cute and, by this time, looked so much like his father that it was like conversing with a miniature Loring.

One thing Gordon never said no to was an outing with Loring. One Sunday afternoon he took Gordon and Mildred on the three-wheeler to visit English Jack. Gordon could carry on his own conversation with the old man, even if most of what he told Jack had to be interpreted. And although Jack had met Mildred as a baby, she was now toddling around fairly well. She did fine on level ground, but when she tripped over a tree root next to him, Jack hoisted her onto his lap. Mildred took one look at the face of the white-whiskered stranger and let out a howl. Loring quickly grabbed her and apologized to Jack who waved him off in a way that Loring guessed correctly— Mildred was not Jack's first rejection.

When Loring needed to go home, Jack offered to walk back to the house with him and the children, seeing as he had no other visitors. "I can see the new little one, then, can't I?" Loring wondered how hard it had been for the old man to have never had children of his own. Certainly, Loring knew something about that.

When Loring walked into the house with the two children and the hermit, Hattie eagerly welcomed Jack, and he was just as eager to accept her invitation to a homemade meal. As they spent time together that day, Hattie thought Jack was showing his age, slowing down. He was, after all, eighty-two years old now. He would spend his fourth winter in Twin Mountain and she, well, the whole Notch, had grown to love their very own hermit of Mount Willard. But Hattie feared his days were numbered. So, she relished this visit, watching Jack fuss over Raymond and play with Gordon and Mildred until he had to leave.

Raymond was a more temperamental baby than either Gordon or Mildred had been. Hattie needed to tend to him more closely, not assuming he would be content for the longer periods of time away from her as the others had been. Hence, she kept him close to her side as she worked. Her small wicker basket was a perfect bassinet to carry around with her. She could lay it on the table in the kitchen, on the floor next to her chair in the parlor, or wherever she happened to be.

Mildred's little blonde ringlets bobbed playfully on her head as she chased after Gordon or Rusty. She didn't always get very far before tripping on one thing or another. Hattie would say, "Boom!" when she went down and soon Gordon began saying it. Mildred was more vocal than Gordon had been at this age, so most of the time, Hattie knew where the children were just by listening to them talk, laugh, or yell at each other. The tricky part of raising little ones in this house, besides needing to tie them to the front porch, was keeping the stairs to the bedrooms blocked so that she needn't watch them every second. Loring had saved the day when he brought home a piece of sanded wood that wasn't too heavy, but tall enough to keep Mildred from climbing. As she got older, the wood could be moved up a step or two to give her a safe way to practice going up and down.

Gordon was able to go down the stairs backwards safely now. So, Hattie moved him to the room directly above hers. She'd be able to hear him from her bedroom. When Raymond was old enough, he and Gordon could room together, and Mildred would be in the turret room upstairs. Hattie and Loring began teaching the little ones the difference between their side of the upstairs and the men's side. The children would not be allowed to go into the two men's rooms and the men, in turn, would not visit the Evans' side uninvited.

When their anniversary rolled around in October, about all Hattie and Loring could manage by way of celebration was to say, "Happy anniversary!" to one another and kiss each other good night. They were both exhausted.

Loring laughed, "To think we wanted children! We didn't know how good we had it before all these little mites came along!"

He was asleep in another minute. Hattie turned down the wick to extinguish the flame, and whispered, "Yes, but I know how grateful you are for each of our 'little mites.'"

Hattie was looking forward to cooking Thanksgiving favorites, knowing the men as well as she did and what they loved to eat. Ordinarily, the men ate first, and the Evans family ate afterward because there wasn't enough room for all of them around one table. But on Thanksgiving, they made it work. They'd fix up smaller tables for the extra numbers and move everything around until it all fit in one room. She'd decorate the tables to look special and set out more food than they could possibly eat. All the better for the men's dinner pails the next day. The atmosphere was always gaily joyous. It reminded Loring of his own family gatherings. For Hattie, it was a dream come true to have the big family she hadn't grown up with.

Christmas with the children was delightful. Gordon was going on three, and he knew Christmas was special. He tutored Mildred about which of the decorations she was allowed to touch. He especially loved telling her what she shouldn't touch, even though Hattie noticed that he made exceptions for himself. But she was just too happy to be overly concerned with Gordon's young parenting attempts. John and Denny had made a small wagon for the children, their gift to the family. Loring carved out a small wooden duck on wheels and added a string for Mildred to pull. Hattie had made a rag doll for Raymond, although it appeared that all he needed was his fist to chew on. For Gordon, Loring had made a toddler-sized wooden hammer and a piece of wood with pegs that Gordon could practice hitting. Though Hattie was concerned about what else Gordon might hit, Loring insisted it was good practice for when his son would work for the railroad one day, securing spikes. *If that's Loring's dream, so be it,* Hattie thought. *But my only hope for our children is that they find their own path and carve out a life they love one day.*

Seventeen

~ 1910 - 1911 ~
Alone

On New Year's Day 1910, Florence gave birth to her and Joe's fifth daughter, whom they named Doris, though they quickly gave her the nickname "Dot." Hattie bundled up baby Raymond, Mildred, and Gordon, and walked to the Monahans' house the next day to take them some food. Since it was a Sunday, Loring was able to go along. It was cold and blustery but clear. The snow crunched under their feet while the sun was warm on their faces. And their hearts were full.

Once they arrived, they could hardly see the baby for the crowd of young sisters around her, each one as proud as could be. When Hattie was finally able to hold Doris, she looked down at the baby's pudgy little cheeks. She was cute as a button. They stayed just long enough to get warmed up again with hot chocolate. Walking back, Loring and Hattie talked about how the little village of Hart's Location was gaining numbers rapidly thanks to only three households along the tracks. Nine new children in only seven years!

Early in February, Hattie came down with the same nasty cold Florence's household had just battled. She did her best to continue her work as usual, but, when six-month-old Raymond began sneezing and became cranky, she needed some help. Between Loring and the men, they did as much of the household chores as they were able, without completely ignoring their work on the tracks. But when Mildred and then Gordon also became sick, Loring basically took over Hattie's kitchen all day long, fixing tea, coffee, broth, milk toast, anything they could eat. He even made a mustard plaster for them all. But when he tried to wrap the plastered fabric around Mildred's chest, she said, "Ewww, that stinks!" Then she promptly ran in the other direction.

The first time Loring came into their bedroom, which was now the sick room, carrying a tray of hot liquids and crackers, Hattie burst into gales of laughter, mixed with bouts of coughing. Loring had put on Hattie's apron which barely covered his belly. He'd grabbed her nightcap when she wasn't looking and put that on, too. Gordon laughed to see his father being so silly. Mildred laughed because everyone else was laughing. And for those few moments, illness was forgotten and that was the best medicine they could have had. Loring left the room to go back to the kitchen and ran into Ed and Billy who had come looking for him to ask a question. Oh, didn't the men howl when they saw him! Loring did a little ballet twirl to add to the fun, then took off his stolen clothing and became their boss again.

Before Hattie was completely well, Elizabeth and Peter came down on the train to bring some chicken soup for which everyone was most grateful. Hattie and the children because it would be soothing on the throat, Loring because he didn't especially love to cook, and the crew because there was only so long they would want to tolerate Loring's culinary skills, or rather lack thereof. It isn't that Loring's cooking was bad, but it was simple and repetitive, and certainly not up to Hattie's standards.

Elizabeth appeared at Hattie's bedroom door where Hattie had her hand up to keep Elizabeth from coming closer. Peter toddled around looking for Gordon. "Thank you," Hattie rasped.

Elizabeth wasn't used to seeing Hattie sick. "I'm so sorry you don't feel well. I put the chicken soup on the back burner to warm. I also brought fixings for pea soup and bread. And some oatmeal cookies. And here's a couple magazines from Crawfords for you to look through if you're searching for something to keep from going stir crazy. No need to get them back to me," Elizabeth said.

Just then Peter came to the doorway and Elizabeth had to keep him from going into the room. "I think Peter is looking for Gordon. Is he sick, too?"

Hattie pointed and Elizabeth saw both Gordon and Mildred asleep on make-shift beds on the floor. When she explained to Peter that he couldn't play with Gordon, Peter began to cry, so Elizabeth picked him up.

"Looks like we'll be going now," the younger woman said rolling her eyes, "But maybe this will cheer you up some… we're expecting a baby in September."

"Congratulations!" Hattie managed to rasp and then cough. Elizabeth winced to hear her.

"Thank you," Elizabeth said, taking a step to leave. "Now, you rest, and I'll see you soon."

A week later, Hattie and the children were much better, almost normal save for their persistent coughs. She was back in her kitchen and grateful to be there. She whistled while kneading her bread dough, listening to the howling wind of a nor'easter. Gordon and Mildred were out in the parlor with their toys and Raymond was busy scooting around the kitchen floor, investigating anything he could put in his mouth. Hattie had long since taken anything he might choke on and set it up high, out of reach. She was lost in thought when she heard a series of small explosions, and then the sound of a train stopping. She hurried to the window to see what was happening. Hattie knew enough to know that the crew must have put torpedo explosives on the rails to warn the engineer of a problem up ahead. Apparently, the engineer must not have seen the warning flag they would have tried first.

The train was stopped right in front of the house. Looking the other way, up the tracks, she could just barely make out a huge boulder that had settled in between the rails, compliments of Mount Willard. *Must have come down during this storm,* she thought. *It doesn't look like anyone was hurt though. Only real problem could be getting the train started again once the tracks are clear.* She picked up Raymond and walked to the parlor. Gordon and Mildred were quietly mesmerized by the train sitting just outside the window. She helped them onto a chair so they could see it better and then turned to watch the crew using their heavy-duty pry bars and a block and tackle to work the boulder off the rails. It was no easy job to move rocks that big, and the crew didn't especially enjoy doing it during a snowstorm. But they had no choice.

Since Gordon and Mildred were so fascinated by the train, Hattie pointed out different cars and what they might be carrying. She saw an opportunity to quiz Gordon on the colors she was teaching him. "What color is that car?" "Red!" Gordon said. "Boo!" Mildred shouted at the same time. Hattie laughed at her daughter's enthusiasm. "Yes, Gordon, that one is red. Mildred, some of it *is* blue. Good for both of you!"

Sudden movement to their left made them all turn to see a man walking toward the house. He knocked on their door. Gordon was the first one there to greet him. The man stepped inside. "Well, hello there," he said to Gordon then turned to Hattie. "Afternoon, ma'am. I don't know if you remember me, but I heard you and Loring had taken on this section. I don't usually have a chance to stop here in front of your house. Ed Davis," he said, extending a cold hand. "I met you years ago when Morrison took you young'uns to Lewiston from Portland. Frankly, I was surprised Morrison agreed to pick you up that day. Once he gets going, he hates to stop. He's on today, too. And this unscheduled stop won't make him much of a sweetheart to be around!"

"I do remember you, Ed," Hattie said with the pleasure of reminiscence boosting her memory. "How nice to see you again. But it's more than ten years since then. We're hardly young anymore!" she laughed. "Children, this is Mr. Davis. Ed, I want you to meet Raymond, he's about six months old. This is Mildred, she'll be two in April. And Gordon, here, will be three in March."

Ed bent down and shook Gordon's hand saying, "It's nice to meet you, son."

"I not your son. I have a dad." Hattie and Ed exchanged amused glances.

Then Mildred stuck her hand out so that Ed wouldn't overlook her. "Miss Mildred," he said, with a flair that made Mildred beam.

"You and Loring have been some busy, it seems," Ed said, straightening back up. "You must have quite a household now, between your family and the crew."

"I do," Hattie smiled. Just then, she and Ed heard Morrison blow the whistle and saw that the boulder had been removed. The helper had probably reached the back of the train, so Ed turned to open the door.

"How about a doughnut before you have to go out again?"

Before Ed could say anything, Gordon was off to the kitchen and back with the dark brown confection. "Here," he said, handing it to Ed.

Mildred added, "It's chock-it!"

Then, seeing Gordon's up-turned face and raised eyebrows, Hattie conceded, "Yes. Go get one for you and Mildred to share. You two can eat it at the kitchen table." They were off like a pair of awkward jackrabbits. "But only one!" she called out after them.

"Thanks for this," he said, tipping his doughnut. "Nice to meet your family. And good to see you again. I'll wave to Loring on the way by but tell him I said hi."

"Good to see you, too, Ed," Hattie said. Ed stepped off the porch to wait for the caboose and Hattie closed the door. As she watched the train go by and Ed hop aboard, warm, fond memories flooded her mind. Walking to the kitchen she thought, *What a wonderful day that was so long ago!*

She opened the kitchen door. "Oh, my goodness! How many of those have you two had? You are a sight to behold." Both children looked up and grinned with chocolate smiles. Hattie knew she ought to discipline them. All she managed was to clean them up and shoo them off to play, knowing it would take a while for their tummies to growl again.

Quick as a wink, it was August and Raymond's first birthday. Hattie couldn't resist a small celebration with cake. She certainly got no resistance from anyone else in the house where cake was involved. That night, when they lay in bed, Hattie told Loring she was definitely expecting another baby, around Christmastime. Loring had suspected as much. Holding her tight, Loring said, "I can't think of a better present, can you? Oh, Hattie, I love you so much. What would I do without you? Who would we be without our children?" he sighed contentedly. "Our very own family. Can you believe it?"

Could she believe it? Yes, she could. She was already battling morning sickness and she was actively, *very* actively, raising three little people every day. Believing it was not a problem. But she knew what he meant—the astonishment that they'd be a family of six by the end of the year. "It will be a very merry Christmas," she said, quietly. "And I love you, too, Loring, very, very much."

On September twenty-third, Hattie got word via the Location's grapevine that Elizabeth had had a little girl they named Martha. One day soon after, Hattie took all the children to pay Elizabeth a visit and bring food. Rusty joyfully trotted along with everyone else. Hattie couldn't make great time with Raymond wanting to walk by himself. She managed to hold him part of the way by giving Gordon some of the food to carry, but he didn't like doing that for more than a few minutes at a time. About halfway to Crawfords she almost turned back. Raymond was heavy sitting on top of her blossoming belly. But she chuckled to herself, suddenly conscious of what they must look like, a circus parade of performers that toddled, skipped, jumped, twirled, threw stones, and barked. She decided she could manage with a healthy dose of patience because the children were having such a marvelous time.

When she got to Crawford yard and saw Loring, she motioned him over to ask if he could spare a few moments to help her the rest of the way. One look at his wife and her entourage and Loring could hardly say no. Once they reached Elizabeth's cottage, Loring knocked on the door, then went back to work. Peter opened the door for them all and Hattie went straight to Elizabeth's kitchen to put the food away. When she came back to where Elizabeth sat beside the wooden cradle, she saw Peter standing next to Martha, arms crossed over his puffed-out chest, feet slightly apart, like a sentry. Hattie wondered with amusement if Peter would even allow her to get close to his new sister.

"She's just so beautiful, Elizabeth," Hattie said truthfully, seeing the wisps of auburn fuzz on the top of her head. "She looks a bit like you, Peter."

He wrinkled his nose. "No, she doesn't! I'm a boy and she's a girl," he disclaimed indignantly, putting his fisted hands on his hips. Elizabeth rolled her eyes.

Hattie laughed. "Well, now that you say so, Peter, I believe I was mistaken. She does look like a girl and not like you." Peter indicated his just validation by nodding his head, then left the room to play with Gordon who followed close behind.

Hattie lifted Martha from her cradle and crouched down with the baby in her arms so that Mildred and Raymond could see her. "This is a little girl just like you, Mildred. What do you think of that?"

Mildred had no discernible expression that might give away whether she understood. Instead, she poked her little index finger straight into the baby's nostril. "No, no, honey! Don't do that. You'll hurt the baby." Hattie stood back up and Raymond wandered off to find his brother.

"How are you feeling?" Elizabeth asked when she could finally get a word in.

"Well enough to walk up here, anyway. I have my moments. But honestly, I forget sometimes that another one's coming. I'm too busy to notice the little things." Then realizing what she'd just said, she added, "You know, it just occurred to me that Florence said the same thing when her little Doris was on the way. I couldn't understand how Florence could forget something like knowing a baby was coming. I understand now, though."

Raymond was beginning to investigate things he shouldn't be into, and Mildred was becoming loud and bossy in her mothering of him. Raymond screeched at being ordered around by someone not that much taller than he. Hattie decided it was time to go and said her goodbyes over the protests of Gordon and Peter who wanted to keep playing together. Going back was easier without having to carry food and she was very glad to be back home again.

Christmas seemed to be upon them in the blink of an eye. Hattie felt like she was big as a barn, and standing on her feet for long periods of time was difficult. She wasn't one to complain overly much, so when she made one or two comments about her back or feet, Loring or one of the men were quick to ask if she needed help. They knew how busy she was every day. But she usually declined help. She thought that if she got used to sitting down on the job, she might never get back up again. She was, after all, nearly forty years old, she thought realistically, and didn't want to give in to her age.

She began to feel false contractions as she had with the others and knew it wouldn't be long before she'd need to send a message to the doctor again. But the new year came and went with no more contractions and no baby. Finally, on the morning of Wednesday, January 18, 1911, when she couldn't imagine existing one more day in her condition, she sent that message. Then she needed to find Loring. The first man she saw was John. "John!" she called out. He came as fast as he could through the snow.

"Everythin' all right?"

"Can you please let Loring know that this baby is coming? I've sent a message to Bartlett for the doctor. But someone needs to watch the other three for me."

"I'll tell him," John said, leaving quickly.

Hattie could feel this baby making rapid progress. Maybe too rapidly. Rusty stayed close to her while the children played with their usual enthusiasm in the same room. When their noise began to take its toll on her nerves, she was grateful to see Loring coming in the house and asked that he watch the children upstairs. Once they left the room she sat back in her chair and sighed. Now she could fully concentrate on this baby. When she felt settled, she pulled out her solitaire cards. "Ooh," Hattie said after she'd dealt herself the second hand, "I think I need to lie down a while." She disappeared into their bedroom. She could hardly believe that within the next hour, she felt the familiar need to push. She yelled for Loring. He immediately scooped up Raymond and Hattie heard them clambering down the stairs.

When she told Loring what was happening, he quickly summoned John who was shoveling near the house. "Things are happening fast, John. Watch the children!" Then he went back to Hattie.

"What can I do?" Loring asked anxiously. He fervently wished the doctor was the one sitting by Hattie. So did she, but she had no choice but to remain focused. Loring could see that Hattie was deeply concentrating and she was sweating, even though the temperature outside was below zero. He couldn't have been more grateful for the dependable heat in this house, but he, too, was sweating. He was a bundle of nerves and felt utterly powerless. He sat watching his wife and admiring her strength when she suddenly said with the force of nature, "Get some sheets and hot water! This baby is about to be born!"

Loring moved faster than he had ever moved in his life, gathered what Hattie had asked for, and then burst back into their room. His eyes met Hattie's, which were wide and joyous. She was pointing and when he followed her finger, he saw their beautiful newborn baby! A perfect little girl. They both stared at their new daughter, who was squawking loudly. They were in utter disbelief that a baby could come that fast. Yet, there she was. Loring wrapped her in the sheet and handed her to Hattie saying, "My dear woman, you have just given birth all alone!"

"I have, haven't I?" she said in wonder. "We have two boys and now two girls, Loring! What should we name this one?"

"Something unusual, the way she came, I should think," Loring said, amused now that the drama was over and they could manage until the doctor came.

"It's not the first time a woman has given birth without help. No offense, Loring. I mean without the help of a doctor or midwife. You were a great help with the children and getting me the sheet."

"I was *not* ready for this to happen!" he said, his heart rate returning to normal. "It's a good thing I hadn't known I might have to be the doctor, or I might have made sure I was out of calling distance!"

Hattie grew silent, thinking about possible names as she stared at their new daughter. The doctor arrived in the middle of her reverie, but they weren't prepared for the person who walked through their door. "Clever girl," Doctor Snow said.

"Who? Me or the baby?!" Hattie replied with quick wit. She'd forgotten it could be Doctor Snow who might come. He'd begun working with Doc Shedd not long ago. The older doctor was slowing down these days. But Doctor Snow was young. *Snow. Ironic name,* Hattie thought.

There wasn't much for the doctor to do, and he was gone before long. He could have let the light engine stay right there at the house had he known how quick he'd be.

Loring came back in the room with the other children. As they oohed and ahhed over their new baby sister, Hattie looked at Loring and said, "What about 'Enola'?"

"Enola? What's that?"

"Her name. Do you like it?" Hattie asked.

"I guess so. It's different. It qualifies as unusual, I guess."

"Loring...Enola is the word 'alone' spelled backwards!"

Eighteen

~ 1911 ~
Visiting

Mildred was ecstatic to have a sister, Gordon seemed ambivalent, and Raymond was no longer the baby. Hattie wasn't sure if her quiver was full yet or not, but since her heart was, that was all she cared about. She couldn't have been more grateful for Sarah's now yearly visit to watch the other children as Hattie cared for her newest child.

The house was always in a state of happy confusion, it seemed. By the summer of 1911, at any given moment one of the four children was yelling, laughing, crying, or had momentarily disappeared. Most often Gordon was yelling bossily, Mildred was laughing uncontrollably, and Raymond and Enola Mae might be crying or completely out of sight. But Hattie thrived on a happy household and loved making it so.

As fall of that year approached, Florence and the children came for a visit. While the children played or were bounced on a mother's knee, Hattie and Florence sipped their tea and had a considerably interrupted conversation about school. Since Florence had two children already in school, Hattie considered Florence something of a walking encyclopedia on the subject. Gordon would be going eventually, and Hattie had begun gathering information about the schools in the area.

"Remind me again, how old were Gertrude and Ethel when you started them in school?" Hattie asked, separating Raymond, Dot, and Enola, who were squabbling over possession of one toy.

"They were both six. Gertrude will start fourth year and Ethel will start second. Some children start when they're five, some when they're seven, depending on their birthdays and how ready for school they seem to be. If it was me, I'd start Gordon when he's six."

"That's what Loring and I were thinking. We've been talking about how Gordon will get to school. On the train, I assume. Is that what yours do?" Florence nodded, handing Dot a small piece of her cookie. "I just have a lot of questions about how it all works around here. Who the teachers are, how many scholars there are, what books and subjects they're prepared to teach. Things like that."

"Well, you know what, Hattie? Why don't you consider being on the school board? Then you could have a voice about the school. We usually meet once a month at my house since I have the biggest brood. There are only two of us on the board right now, me and Mrs. Morey. You'd be a welcome addition."

"Mrs. Morey? Charles's wife?"

"Yes."

"Yes, I'd like to consider that. I'd like to come to a meeting first before I decide, though."

"Absolutely," Florence said knowing that Hattie would make a sensible decision.

Hattie went to the next meeting, and it felt good to use her brain for something more than doubling a recipe or fixing the scrape on a child's knee. It wasn't that those things weren't important to her, but being a part of the decision-making for something as crucial as education meant a great deal to her. Before the evening was over, Hattie accepted the position. She and Loring had already discussed it in case she decided to say yes. Now Hattie would feel more essential to the town in an area she cared deeply about.

Before October's board meeting, Rusty began to falter. He stopped eating and often refused water. Hattie gathered her little ones to explain that Rusty was going to die soon, and that they could pet him gently and tell him they loved him. It wasn't long before the old dog passed, leaving his body beside the stove—his favorite spot. Hattie grieved the loss of her gentle friend. She wondered if she'd ever find a better canine companion but knew that she'd want to try.

The day of the next board meeting, Hattie brought the children to play with the Monahans, out of necessity but also because she knew it would brighten their spirits. Florence had an array of sweets out on her table to share and Hattie brought some of her own. Before Mrs. Morey arrived, Florence took Hattie aside to tell her that she was going to have baby number six in February or March.

"Oh, Florence! That's wonderful!" she said, then suddenly thought that Joe and Florence might not be so excited to have yet another mouth to feed. "You *are* happy about this, right?"

"Well, I have to admit, it was a bit of a shock. I thought maybe we were done. But I guess not! Joe wasn't terribly excited at first, but he's warming up to the idea of a women's baseball team if this one is a girl!" Florence said with a lopsided grin. "Frankly, I think he's given up on having a boy."

Mrs. Morey arrived and after some visiting the women got down to their business. Miss Ellen Small, the teacher, thought things were going as well as could be expected for the beginning of the school year. She was settling in at her boarding house. Florence could attest that the girls liked Miss Small. There may have been no more than a handful of scholars, but there was a desk that needed repair before one of the children sat down on the bench and ended up on the floor. And one of the windows stuck so badly it was impossible for Miss Small to open it for air flow. Florence volunteered her husband to look at both. Miss Small also said that she would like to begin teaching another level of arithmetic next term and needed new books. They determined there should be enough in the budget for that. There wasn't much else on the agenda, so the women visited a while longer and then adjourned.

"Congratulations again," Hattie said when she gave Florence a hug. Hattie's children said goodbye and they all started up the hill toward home.

The next day was excruciatingly beautiful, and Hattie could no more stay in her kitchen the whole day than sit on a hat pin. So, she took the children for a walk to Crawfords to visit Elizabeth and pick up any mail the Mount Willard household might have received. Elizabeth and Hattie stood outside chatting while all the children, save Enola, who rested on Hattie's hip most of the time, ran hither and yon around the wide expanse of yard. Now and then, when she came up to Crawfords, it bothered Hattie that her children didn't have the luxury of such a grand place to play as this. Sometimes she worried that they wouldn't develop properly without large, open spaces in which to run unhampered by train tracks or, worse, trains themselves. But Loring had assured her that they would find plenty of ways to exercise their young muscles and not to worry. Besides, there were always the long hikes in the woods and visits to Crawfords or the Monahans' to consider. Why, any child should be envious of the way the Evans children were growing up, Loring had told her more than once. So, she'd put her worries aside.

Hattie read her mail on the way home from her visit. She received a letter from Millie that was abnormally long. "Loring," Hattie said that evening as they sat in the parlor reading, "listen to this. Millie—you remember Millie from North Gorham, Maine?—she was engaged to marry this fellow named Lawrence Hanley at the end of this month. Loring, are you listening? Lo-o-ring! I think you'll appreciate what I'm going to tell you."

Feeling a bit sheepish, Loring said, "Oh, ayuh. Go on."

"Well, Millie was given a wedding shower recently and she sent the newspaper clipping of it. Here, read this," she said, handing the clipping to him.

"Pretty fancy affair for country folk, seems to me," Hattie said when Loring had finished reading it. "And to think, Millie thought she'd never have another suitor after she turned down the first one. Then this."

"I see what you mean," Loring said. "A 'silver shower' for one thing. And forty dollars! That's a lot of money."

"Right! Not to mention fifty to sixty guests, and then to have Professor MacMillan show up! I'm surprised Nell wasn't there! Seems like everyone from Windham to Standish attended."

"But you said Millie *was* engaged. See, I *was* listening!" Loring quipped. "She isn't anymore?"

"No. She was rather cryptic about the reason the engagement was broken off. All she said was that it didn't work out and she hoped it was all for the best. Good heavens. That girl really has had a rough start to life. Maybe she'll visit again over the summer and I'll learn more about what happened. I'm grateful she feels comfortable to write me of her troubles, though."

Hattie took out some paper and her fountain pen and decided Millie deserved a return letter as soon as possible, poor girl.

Meanwhile, before the snow started flying and English Jack would go live with a family in Twin Mountain for the winter, Loring took Gordon to see about getting a bow and arrow set. It felt sadly odd that Rusty wouldn't be accompanying them on their walk up the tracks. Once they came into Jack's clearing, Loring noticed that Jack wasn't sitting outside. They knocked on his thin door and heard Jack call them to come on in, followed by a series of coughs. The place was relatively clean, though cluttered. It was a bit dark, too, being in the middle of the woods. Loring immediately noticed the smell of illness in the small shack.

Jack had a braided rug at the doorway and a mat next to that with a picture of a hare sitting in a basket, which Gordon studied for a while. There were plenty of wooden straight-backed chairs for Jack's guests. He was sitting on one of them, his sailor's cap on his head and pipe in his teeth between his white mustache and beard. If Jack's hat had been a red stocking cap, Gordon might have asked to sit on the man's lap and tell him what he wanted for Christmas. On the walls were pictures he'd cut out of old calendars and magazines. He'd made poles to hang or prop up some of his wares and trinkets.

"Hi there, Jack. Good to see you. You remember Gordon here? He's all of four and a half now and he'd like one of your bow and arrow sets, if you have one."

"Yes, yes. Hello, Gordon. Nice to see you, m' boy." Jack coughed. "Well, now, let me just look and see what I have in my back room." He stood up slowly, coughing all the while, and ambled out of the living room, disappearing into another part of the house while Loring and Gordon waited. Before long, Jack returned with a small wooden bow and three arrows. Gordon's eyes grew wide with excitement. "Here ya go, m' boy." He coughed some more. "Be careful what you shoot at, though."

"More like *who* you shoot at," Loring said, laughing and looking directly at his son. "He has three younger siblings now and he'd best not take aim at one o' them!" Then he added, "Or the cat. You'll have your mother to answer to if you shoot at your brother and sisters or the cat. Right?" Gordon dutifully nodded but was much more interested in trying out the weapon than fearing his mother. "I'll let you use it on the way home." Turning to Jack again, Loring said, "How are ya, Jack?"

"I'm spry enough for an old fellow." He coughed. "It's these blasted cold winters that I can't take anymore. Makes m' bones ache. And this fox's cough just won't go away. It's this drafty place. I'm not complainin', mind you." He coughed some more. "You asked, and I told ya."

"Are you going to Twin again this winter?" Loring asked, assuming so.

"Yes. I'm goin' to the McGees' this time, though." Cough, cough. "Mrs. Fahey is ill and can't take me in this year." Cough, cough. Cough. "I'm sure the McGees will take good care o' me. I'm certainly grateful."

"Dad, can we go now?" Gordon asked. Both Loring and Jack were relieved to have a reason to part. Jack was tired, Loring could tell. And Loring wasn't entirely comfortable around Jack's constant cough.

Loring nodded to Gordon and then, reaching out his hand to the old man, he said, "Jack?" Jack excused it a moment with his finger up, to turn halfway around and cough. "Take care of yourself, Jack. We'll see ya next spring."

"I'll do my best to get back here," he sputtered through his coughing.

Loring turned toward the door, then spun around again, "Oh…what do I owe you for the bow and arrows?"

"I'll take…a twenty-five-cent piece for them, if ya got it."

Loring handed him the coin, thinking that was a fair price for four pieces of fine workmanship. "Gordon, tell Mr. Jack goodbye and thank you," Loring prompted.

"Goodbye, Mr. Jack. Thank you for the bow and arrow." But Jack probably hadn't heard Gordon's thin, young voice over his coughing fit.

English Jack closed his door and Loring and Gordon headed home.

"How did you find English Jack?" Hattie asked her husband when they'd returned.

"It was easy, mum, we just followed the trail right to his house," Gordon said with a hint of incredulity. He walked back outside to practice shooting his new bow.

Hattie and Loring looked at one another and burst out laughing.

Once they'd composed themselves, Loring said, "Not so good, I'm afraid. He's got a cough he can't seem to control. He called it a fox's cough. Ever hear of that?" Hattie shook her head. "Maybe it's an English term. Anyway, he said he's going to stay with the McGee family in Twin soon. I hope that cough will go away when he's in a home that's warmer, poor guy."

Nineteen

~ 1912 ~
Laughs, Losses, and Love

Hattie checked in on Florence as the days of February ticked off one by one, sometimes watching Hazel, Alice, and Dot during the day when the older girls were in school. She'd thought her fortieth birthday would slip by unnoticed, which was fine with her. But Loring had plans he hadn't told her about. He'd thrown her off by saying that he thought an outing with the children would be a nice way to celebrate her birthday the next day. Secretly, though, he'd arranged a party with the crew, Elizabeth and her family, and, of course, the Monahans. Loring didn't know if Florence would be able to make it, but she said that a good old party might get things started in the birth department, and, if it did, the doctor knew where the Evans house was just as well as hers. Loring had checked the schedule and arranged for the 786 to pick up the Monahans at noon and take them to Crawfords. There they visited with Elizabeth and Peter until the 787 departed eastbound just before three o'clock. They all arrived at the Evans home fifteen minutes later.

"Loring, why is the train stopped?" Hattie's answer came in the form of nine people who got out and walked into her parlor singing "Happy Birthday." Simultaneously, the crew came out of the dining room and joined in along with Loring. She was suddenly surrounded by people who loved her, and she could hardly keep her tears from flowing. Loring held her at his shoulder and beamed the smile of one who has pulled off a successful surprise. When the singing ended, Hattie was told to sit down and not lift a finger to serve anyone. Loring even made her take off her apron as a sign that she wasn't to be the hostess today. All the details had been taken care of.

After everyone had enjoyed cake and hot chocolate, Loring blindfolded Hattie. "Now what?" she asked. Everyone laughed. She felt like she was a schoolgirl again and it didn't feel bad.

"Just sit tight," Loring told her. He and the other men went outside and over to the carhouse where they had stored her surprise. Though it wasn't the best place for it, it was the only place they could think of where she wouldn't go. It had only been there since yesterday, though, so Loring hoped it would be all right. Hattie heard a great racket and felt cold air sweep across the room that smacked her whole body at once. She heard general, excited murmurs around the room and had no idea what was happening. Then suddenly Loring guided her to stand up, walk a few steps, and then sit back down on something small and cushioned. *What on earth?* she wondered. And then, with a grand gesture only Loring could make, he had Elizabeth whip off the blindfold so that Hattie could see him bowing grandly, pointing to her new upright piano!

She nearly fell off the stool. "Oh, my!" She put her hands reflexively on her cheeks, which were flushed with excitement and humility. "It's…it's so beautiful!" she said, running her fingers over the artistic flourishes and embellishments in the wood. "Where did you get this, Loring?" she asked, looking up at his face.

"Crawfords was replacing some of theirs, so I got it from them."

Everyone started clapping and asked her to play something. She appreciated the invitation, even if she wasn't prepared to perform. But she did want to see how the piano sounded, so she played a lively "Camptown Races" to which everyone burst into clapping and dance. If ever the house was going to come unhinged from its foundation, it would have been then.

As others took turns at the instrument, Loring put his arms around Hattie and said, "Happy birthday, my love. See?

Turning forty isn't so bad after all!" Loring kissed her cheek. All was happy mayhem until the party came to an end.

A week and a half later, about the time Florence thought her baby had decided to stay put in her belly forever, her pains started. Ivy Monahan was born on February 29, Leap Day. Clever Joe had decided that Ivy, or the Roman numeral "IV," was perfect for a baby whose birthday would technically come only once every four years. Mother and baby were fine. Hattie was much relieved for her friend. After talking to Florence about quivers, Florence was ready to say that hers was full enough with six and she'd do almost anything to keep it that way.

In late April, when the Notch was thinking about turning winter over to spring, the sad news came down the tracks that the hermit of Crawford Notch, English Jack, passed away while staying with the McGee family. In June, Crawfords held a memorial for him out on their front lawn, the one place that could hold everyone who would come. People shared memories of the old sailor and his "ship." His stories were perhaps most loved, but some talked about his willingness to eat a snake for twenty-five cents. Or about the root beer he brewed. Some came with the walking sticks he'd made them or the toys he'd carved. Some said they'd gone to visit his shack every summer they came to the Crawford House and would dearly miss his friendly presence on the mountain. A collection was taken up to have him buried in Straw Cemetery in Twin Mountain, with a suitable gravestone reading: THE HERMIT OF CRAWFORD NOTCH, JOHN VIALS, DIED APR 24, 1912, Æ 85 YEARS.

"I probably should have offered Jack a place to stay at least one of those winters," Hattie lamented on their way home. "He'd've been closer to his 'ship' here than in Twin."

"Yeah, mum! Then he could've made us toys all winter," Gordon observed.

"Don't fret yourself, Hattie," Loring said, "You know how the Faheys say he dressed nicely when he was with them and then made sure his clothes looked ragged and worn when he moved back home. I think he liked being closer to town for a few months, closer to stores and civilization. He did come from London, after all."

"Maybe so. Maybe his 'ship' was more his livelihood than anything," Hattie conceded. "I just know I'll miss the old guy."

"We all will," Loring agreed.

"Yes," Gordon chimed in.

"Yeth," Mildred echoed, nodding vigorously.

Time slipped by easily in the busyness of life, but one day in late June, Loring handed Hattie a telegram. His mother had passed away. Loring was clearly jolted; this was the first death in his immediate family. Hattie was crushed as well. For her, it was the death of someone she'd grown to love. She thought about Nell losing her mother and hoped to find her sister-in-law coping well enough. It was one thing to know that she herself would be able to move on, but quite another to watch Loring and Nell and not know how this would affect them. They needed to make a trip to Raymond right away and decided to take only Enola, leaving the other children with Florence.

Although she felt helpless in the face of the family sorrow, Hattie learned that her presence there had meant everything, especially to Loring and Nell. It was a new concept to Hattie that there were times when it was okay not to do anything but sit quietly beside a loved one, in a reverent, holy silence. Sometimes that was exactly what was needed.

Once they were back home, it was impossible to linger on thoughts of Sarah for very long with a house full of active children. Hattie could almost hear her mother-in-law say, "Life is for the living. Let the dead be." So, she felt no guilt in getting right back to her work. It was Enola's turn to be tethered to the porch while the other children romped around their small yard the rest of that summer. As September neared, Hattie and Loring decided to wait another year to send Gordon to school, though he probably could have gone that month. Next year Gordon would join nearly a dozen children in Hart's Location, or simply "the Location," as the locals called their town.

On the last day of October, Loring turned thirty-nine. Neither could believe that Loring would be forty next year, although Hattie had been forty for over eight months already. Since February, Loring had often teased her about being an old lady. *Just you wait till it's your turn, Mr. Evans,* she had thought, already trying to imagine how she could outdo the surprise party he'd pulled off. It was also hard to believe they'd been married fifteen years already. And what a wide-ranging fifteen it had been, from lowland to mountain and childless to quiver-full.

Each year, when their October celebrations were over, Hattie turned her thoughts to Thanksgiving and Christmas and how to make them special. There was nothing like the festive atmosphere of the holidays. She thought about the foods she wanted to make for Thanksgiving this year and the ingredients she'd need, especially if there was something new she wanted to try. She had learned years ago, the hard way, to double-check her lists before sending them off to town by train. It wouldn't do to leave out an important ingredient at holiday time.

Thanksgiving was grand, as usual, with a roasted chicken, mashed potatoes and turnips, creamed onions, beets, rolls, pumpkin pie, and bread pudding. Her favorite moment was when all the food was ready. She washed her hands, took off her apron, smoothed out her good dress, and served the meal with the satisfaction of any artist about to unveil their finished product.

Loring's favorite moment always had to do with a fork laden with good food. Watching him enjoy her cooking was her second favorite moment. The three older children all sat in "big people's" chairs while Enola was still in the wooden highchair. Hattie had taught the children to wait until everyone was seated with napkins in their laps and the hostess had lifted her fork. But on Thanksgiving it was particularly difficult to wait because words of gratitude were offered first. This year, they made sure to include Rusty, English Jack, and Sarah Evans in their list of thanks. Then, with sweet and savory smells filling the air and their noses, Hattie picked up her fork and the others gratefully did the same.

Later, while Loring took over bedtime reading with the children, Hattie sat and rocked in her chair, with Boomerang in her lap and hot tea in her hands, thinking over the wonderful day. Even though Gordon accidentally tipped his full glass of milk all over Raymond and Raymond retaliated by throwing a fistful of potatoes squarely in Gordon's face, the day had not been spoiled. After making sure her sons understood the folly of their misconduct, she laughed it all away and so did the others.

It had been easy to laugh because the afternoon had been filled with amusing stories. Hattie chuckled as she remembered something Ed Meany had shared. He had obviously told the story substituting familiar names, and, as she recalled, he had everyone's rapt attention from the start. "It was the edge of a precipice," Ed had begun, then paused for effect. "One prong of a pickaxe had a meager hold on the edge." He paused again. "To the handle of the pickaxe, dangling over space, desperately clung the adventurous mountain climber, John." Everyone looked at John who just shrugged. "To John's left foot clung another climber, equally adventurous and equally desperate. His name was Denny." Everyone looked at Denny, then burst out laughing. Ed let the room quiet down before delivering his final line, "Said John to Denny, 'Let go my foot, you, or I'll strike you with this pickaxe!'" After a short pause, the adults erupted in laughter. The children couldn't help but laugh, though Hattie knew they had no idea why. It was such fun and Hattie learned that Ed was a great storyteller.

With Thanksgiving Day past, Hattie turned her attention to Christmas. As December bore down on the big day, it was especially wonderful to play carols on the piano for the children, who danced and sang along with glee. Oh, how her heart was full! She and Loring made some decisions early in the month about gifts for the children so that they could begin crafting them. Hattie decorated the house with evergreen boughs, allowing the children to help as they could.

Her favorite moment on Christmas day was seeing the faces of their children when they entered the dining room to see a tree decorated with presents that had magically appeared overnight. After she made the family suffer through an obligatory breakfast and clean-up, it was time to open gifts. Hattie sat in her favorite chair with her feet up, smiling inside and out, drinking in the squeals of delight, sharing special moments with Loring when they lovingly exchanged glances.

That night, Loring and Hattie enjoyed their time alone after the children were in bed. They reminisced about their fifteen Christmases together. How very lean their first ones had been when they each wanted to give the other something that adequately spoke of their love. But even if they could have afforded expensive baubles, they would not have sufficed. Love couldn't be purchased.

"Those first Christmases remind me of the O. Henry story, 'The Gift of the Magi'," Hattie said. When Loring looked blank, she said, "You know, the one where the young wife secretly sells her hair to buy her husband a watch chain while he secretly sells his watch to buy her a set of beautiful combs for her long hair."

"I don't think I've heard that story," Loring admitted, "but that would be sad, or maybe just comical."

"I think it would be some of both, and maybe frustrating, but it would make a great story to tell their children, wouldn't it?" she asked, rhetorically. "But this, remembering our Christmases over the years, this fills my heart as nothing else can. No one else knows of our unspeakable joy those first Christmases or the Christmas I was expecting Gordon."

"I remember wanting to know if it was a girl or a boy at first, but then it was just fun to watch your belly grow," he said.

"I tried to think of my belly as expanding with promise, but it was hard sometimes not to just feel fat," Hattie said humbly. Then to circle back to their profound joys, she said, yawning,

"And who else but the two of us could know of the delight in seeing each of our children experience their first Christmas?" These memories were kept safely in their two hearts, two hearts that beat as one.

Loring turned down the lamp and whispered, "Good night, my love."

"Good night, Loring, and Merry Christmas," Hattie whispered back.

Twenty

~ 1912 - 1913 ~
A Decade in the Notch

Much had happened to the Evanses in those years, and the world had changed as well. Hattie enjoyed the National Geographic magazines that were passed from one house to another along the tracks. Usually, Crawfords acquired them and, when no one seemed to be looking at them anymore, Elizabeth passed them along. The daily newspaper came via the news agent who rode the train and usually tossed them to the porch as the train passed by. These and other publications gave her a more global sense than her small mountainside realm might suggest.

Just since she'd been born, the United States had grown by eleven new states, all west of the great Mississippi River. She assumed she'd never see the far west, let alone the middle west or even all the states in New England. So, she was fascinated by the articles she had read. Last year, New Mexico and Arizona were added to the list of states, bringing the total to forty-eight and warranting a new United States flag with a different star pattern.

A week and a half before English Jack died, there had been a great tragedy in the north Atlantic Ocean. More than fifteen hundred people drowned in icy waters as the enormous British passenger ship, the Titanic, scraped against an iceberg on its way to New York and sank. *Such a catastrophe,* Hattie thought. Then in late May of last year, Wilbur Wright passed away. *Too young,* she sighed. *Why, he was just a few years older than I am. And to think he had been right here in Crawford Notch not so very long ago.* After such tragedies, she thought that maybe people should stick to travel on the ground. A ship the size of that Titanic was bound to sink. And flying like birds, while it can be done, is quite a dangerous risk.

On the other hand, there had been things to celebrate. She'd read that a girl's counterpart to the Boy Scouts had been founded by a woman named Juliette Low from Savannah, Georgia. *Maybe my daughters, as well as Elizabeth's and Florence's, would benefit from such an organization if one came to New Hampshire,* she thought. And the United States elected a new president, Democrat Woodrow Wilson. She wasn't sure she agreed with everything Mr. Wilson stood for, but he did speak of breaking up business monopolies in favor of the middleman or the poor. She thought of working as a laborer in Lewiston. That experience had given Hattie a new perspective of the disparity between the large business owners and the less fortunate workers. *I'm not sure Loring could ever understand that like I do.*

And something else was beginning to arise in earnest in the United States—the determination of women to make a difference beyond their own kitchen sinks. Hattie had read many articles in the newspaper for and against women voting. She really couldn't understand the anti-suffragist arguments that women didn't have time to vote or stay up to date on politics, or that they lacked the mental capacity to offer a useful opinion on current affairs. The suffrage movement seemed only reasonable to Hattie. *I've worked as many hours as any man, at home and even punching time cards. I read at least as much as the men do to keep up with what's happening in our world. And as to lacking the mental capacity to offer a useful opinion? Maybe if I was asked for my opinion, I could give them a piece of my mind!* She recognized her resentment. As she continued reading about the strides women were making to earn the right to vote, Hattie realized that wanting her voice to be heard had been among the reasons she had chosen to be on the school board.

These things and many others filled her mind the rest of the winter as she kneaded bread dough, packed dinner pails, toilet trained Enola, cleaned her house, and took walks with the children. She sewed, she knitted, she played the piano and organ, she gardened, she plucked feathers off beheaded chickens for supper. She hunted, she fished, she read, she hummed and whistled. She let her children play with the other children up and down the tracks while she visited their mothers. She went to school board meetings. She even began raising pigs, which the men would slaughter in the fall for winter meals. And somewhere in between, she tried to make herself presentable for Loring. Hattie could not be accused of living half a life.

Loring, too, had his usual busy winter. Hart's Location was not a big town and the time required to fulfill his civic duties as selectman and constable usually fit in well with his job as foreman. As selectmen, Joe Monahan, Charles Morey, and Loring oversaw the workings of the town. It was their responsibility to call for town meetings and initiate the itinerary to be voted upon. They accounted for and published such things as taxes on machinery, horses, cows, hogs, and the four railroad section houses, along with the local homesteads and the land that came with them. Based on the previous year, with consideration for any upcoming changes, they proposed the budget for the monies needed for school buildings, tuition for scholars, tickets for pupils to be transported to and from school on the train, constable badges, office supplies, and the like.

As constables, Joe, Charles, George Murch, and Loring had policing authority of criminal or civil matters that arose in the Location. This never amounted to a lot of work, thankfully, but they were always to be on the ready. Loring never missed a town meeting or an election day. His civic pride was great, and he took his duties seriously.

The duty he took most seriously, though, was that of husband to the most wonderful woman in the world and father to four people who looked up to him as a role model. He cherished the limited time he had with the children and tried not to do things with them that Hattie wouldn't approve of, like teaching the boys a version of mumblety-peg that he and his brothers used to play. He conceded that to compete with another person to see who could throw a knife closer to his own foot was probably asking for trouble, but it sure was fun...until someone got stabbed, of course. Winter play with his children consisted of building snowmen or sliding down sections of the mountain. The boys in particular loved snowball fights, but the girls couldn't pass up a good time and would join in the fun. In the spring, Loring lived for the children's laughter when he put them all on the three-wheeler together and pushed them up and down the tracks. "More, dad! More!" or "Faster! Faster!" they'd shout.

He'd begun taking Gordon on photography excursions, showing him what made good subject matter and composition in a photograph. He explained how important good lighting was, which, in the mountains, could be tricky. Then he showed Gordon how to process the film. Loring hoped he'd pass down his love of photography to all his children.

He also hoped to teach his children the satisfaction of a job well done. It meant a lot to him that the engineers could count on a clean track every time they rolled through Section 129. It was physically demanding work, pounding spikes, lifting rails, replacing ties, shoveling ballast, or clearing the tracks of debris. It was also back-breaking work each spring to tame the new foliage along the tracks. But getting the job done didn't necessarily mean the work had to be drudgery. Loring and Joe had been talking about the upcoming battle of man versus spring vegetation. "Hey, what'd'ya say we have a contest to see which section can get the job done first?" Joe proposed one day in April. "My boys would be up for it, what about yours?"

"My boys will do almost anything if there's a wager involved!" Loring laughed, then said, "Just the vegetation or replacing ties, too?"

In spring, when new ties were unloaded, they were stacked so that the top layer slanted for the rain to run off. Then, one by one, the new ties replaced the most damaged or rotting ones. This job varied between the sections more than cutting back vegetation, meaning a tie-replacing competition might be unfair. "Let's just do the vegetation. What do you think would do for a prize?" Joe asked.

"How about the section that loses buys the other boys some of those fancy cigars I've seen at Crawfords?"

"You're on, Evans!" And they shook on it.

A couple weeks later, when the vegetation became too overgrown, Joe declared the start of the competition. Loring's men began at the top of their section, working down, and Joe's started at the bottom, working up. The first crew that made it to the line between the two sections would win. This job usually took at least a month to complete, but no one knew how much faster it might go when there were prize cigars involved. One stipulation was that the job still needed to be done right. There would be no cutting corners to win.

At the start of the competition, the children (all but Enola, who was still too young) eagerly awaited news each day about how far their father's crew had come. As the men made progress, the children could climb the back stairs and see them through the rainbow-shaped window. When the Monahan and Evans children played together during this time, there was a fair amount of bickering about whose father had the faster crew. One day, Gordon yelled, "I think they're at the blacksmith's shop!"

By mid-June, Loring's crew was past the carhouse. The children hopped about and cheered because there wasn't much farther to go. In fact, when Gordon and Mildred walked to the bridge, they could see Joe's crew coming. "There they are! There they are!" they shouted as they ran back to give their report to their father. Raymond desperately wanted to see what his sister and brother had just seen but was obliged to stay on the porch. He wasn't yet allowed to get too close to the bridge. But he shouted right along with his brother and sister as though he'd seen it, too. Enola was still tied to the porch column and was happily engaged in investigating the clover and pebbles where she sat. Hattie appeared on the porch when she heard all the yelling. She told herself she was just checking on the children, but truth to tell, the competitive fever had reached her as well.

When both sections could see one another, Joe and Loring agreed that if their wives were willing, Hattie and Florence should be at the finish line to witness and declare the winner. Then both sections, along with wives and children, could all have a picnic afterward. Hattie and Florence heartily agreed and started making plans. At that point, the men put every muscle they had into those scythes. A few days later, rather than arrive at the finish line so close to the end of the day, Loring and Joe called quitting time. They would make the finish by dinner the next day and then picnic in the afternoon. Both foremen agreed that their men had certainly earned an afternoon off. The children could hardly sleep that night and were up early the next day.

When it was time for the families to meet at the finish line, Hattie had to carefully cross the bridge with each child and all the food. Florence had an uphill climb with her brood and their dinner offerings. The very last yards of work to be done wouldn't begin until the families were all there. Once they were settled at the finish line, the women gave the signal to their respective crews to begin the home stretch. All the children jumped and shouted, waved and bellowed. In the end, the finish was very close, but Joe's crew hacked the very last piece of vegetation not two feet from Loring's crew. The hard work was finished. The men all shook hands, shared a few conciliatory remarks, as well as a few ribbings, like "See ya on the other end of my stogie!" Then everyone dove into the food. There was even a game of baseball on what could only be called the world's most squished baseball field right there by the tracks. Rain ended things prematurely, but everyone had plenty of fun.

That summer would mark ten years in the Notch and it was shaping up to be a fine summer, the last before Gordon would start school. Hattie took the children to find wild strawberries. On one of his days off, Loring took out his camera and asked Hattie to dress the children in their best clothes. Readying them for a picture was the easy part. Getting them all to stay in one place and look at the camera was harder. He had them all lined up against the house and ready to snap the photograph when Enola pointed at something. Raymond turned to look and so did Hattie. Loring sighed and took the picture anyway, not expecting much. But when it was developed, he stared at Hattie's captivating figure. She was beaming with a pride in their children and their home that matched his own.

Another Sunday, they all hiked up to Elephant Head, which was no small feat for little Enola. The view from there was never disappointing. It was especially fun to see Crawfords in the distance, looking like a dollhouse version of the original, complete with little people wandering around in the yard. Loring snapped another picture.

Nell and Earl came up for their usual summer visit. Twelve-year-old Earl loved being with the older two of his cousins and his Uncle Loring. Nell and Hattie took some strolls with Raymond and Enola. Nell expressed great concern about how Hattie would manage getting Gordon to school. "You're all so far from civilization up here with no horse and buggy or anything! Honestly, Hattie, I don't know how you handle all these children with no wide-open spaces for them to play." Hattie tried not to let Nell's words take root. The fact was, Hattie wasn't sure about how school was going to work either. And as for wide-open spaces for the children to play, well, that was just an ongoing, niggling concern of Hattie's anyway. But she didn't say as much to Nell.

It turned out that Nell's primary focus was not on Hattie's children, though, but on her father, John. He'd slowed down considerably, Nell worried. Some of the family had helped John plant his crops and were tending to the animals. Their father was grateful, but Nell could tell he was frustrated that his body seemed to be failing him lately. He was used to doing his own chores. Recently Nell had insisted that he call for his doctor and made a point of being at the farm when he came. The doctor checked the eighty-four-year-old man and said he didn't see or hear anything unusual for a man of John's age. John had admitted to some indigestion and constipation for which the doctor gave him a bottle of Morley's Liver and Kidney Cordial, told John to be reasonable about what he took on, and showed himself out. "I don't know, Hattie. Something just doesn't feel right," Nell concluded.

Two days after Nell returned from her visit with Hattie and Loring, she went to check on her father in the morning and found that he had passed in his sleep. Nell messaged that his service would be in three days, and could they please come? Hattie could tell that Nell wanted her there and Loring would be there regardless. Hattie packed them all for a three-day stay in Standish. She hoped the children would behave themselves.

For the most part they did behave. Funerals are not fun for anyone, and generally too long for children to bear, in Hattie's opinion. Enola had to be taken out twice to keep her from disturbing the solemnity of the service. Loring held up well and was a pall bearer for his father's coffin, along with his brothers Birney, Ed, Will, and Charlie, and his brother-in-law Walter. It was always difficult to see the end of a generation in one's family. But, despite the reason, it was nice to see family they didn't usually see.

Only after the service, when they were alone, did Loring open up about his grief. He had loved his father dearly, as he had loved his mother, Hattie knew. "What do I do with these holes in my heart, Hattie? First my mother, now my father. They were the foundation of the family. How do you handle times like this?"

"One day at a time, I suppose."

She wrapped her arms around Loring, comforting him as he had comforted her so many times.

Twenty-one

~ 1913 ~
Trains Give and Take

The rest of that summer, Hattie made new clothes for Gordon to wear to school. He was six and a half years old and hesitant about going. He knew he'd see some of the Monahan children, which was a comfort, Hattie knew. But, for now, he seemed uneasy about everything being so new. *That boy's a cut off my own cloth,* she thought as she sewed, not intending to make a joke, and smiled. Joking aside, they needed to come up with a system for his transportation. The town would pay for his train ticket if not for the fact that Loring's dependents already rode free, but it was up to them to figure out what train he'd take and how they'd get him on it. To further complicate matters, he might have to go to two different schools within the same school year. When there was a train traveling east, he could go to Bemis because the train could stop in front of the house to pick him up. It would then pick up the Monahans next and deliver them all to the station where they could easily walk to the school. But when the train schedule changed and there wasn't a train going east in the morning in time for school, she would need to send Gordon to Fabyans instead. He would just have to get used to being flexible and so would his teachers, Hattie realized. She needed to talk with both teachers about their situation, although she hoped they already knew at least something about it.

The most pressing issue was how to get him on a westbound train when necessary to go to Fabyans school. They couldn't just throw him onto the moving train as it passed the house, but taking him the mile and a half to Crawford Station wasn't ideal either. "Loring, I can't see a way to take Gordon to Crawfords every morning to catch the train, not with the others still so small and getting breakfast and dinner to you and the crew by seven."

"No. No, you're right. And I couldn't be counted on to get him up there every day, either. Ideally, it would be great if the train could pick him up in either direction, but obviously that won't work."

"Too bad the conductor or brakeman couldn't just hoop him up into the train," John said to Loring, who had brought up the subject of Gordon's getting to school.

"Yeah," Loring laughed, "he's not quite light enough, is he?" They both pictured Gordon skewered on a hooping stick like the train orders engineers sometimes got as they passed a station. "Hey, wait a minute," Loring suddenly said. "What if we could somehow pass Gordon up as the train went by? Pass him into the conductor's hands, maybe? Do you think the train is going too fast to safely do that?" Loring wondered aloud.

"I dunno," John shrugged.

"Guess I'd better run this by Hattie first, though. She might think it's too dangerous."

"Hmm. Seems dangerous, if not far-fetched," Hattie said after Loring expressed his idea. She was peeling potatoes and was about to say more when suddenly she laughed, "Oh! You're joking!" But when she turned around and saw that Loring wasn't smiling, she said, "Oh, no, I can't abide that option."

Loring knew enough to table the discussion for the time being. Meanwhile, Hattie continued sewing clothes for Gordon and thinking through what it would be like to have him gone during the daytime. "Come over here a moment, Gordon." He was playing checkers with Mildred indoors as it steadily rained outside. *Much as I want the children to have an education, I'm going to feel sad that first week or so, I'll bet,* she thought, keeping her feelings to herself. She didn't want Gordon to take on any of her emotions other than her excitement about him going to school. "Turn around back to me, please." She held up the shirt she was fashioning against his shoulders and pinned the collar in place. "Thank you, dear. You can go back to playing, but stay close a while. I'll need you again."

A few days after their short discussion about Loring's idea, he said, "I talked to Bobby today. He thinks it can work to pass Gordon off into the train. He said he'd talk with the conductor, too, and run it by him. But if we do try this, we're going to have to practice it before school starts."

Hattie was immediately angry with Loring. She thought she'd made her opinion quite clear, yet he'd gone on with his idea enough to discuss it with others. She wasn't prepared to discuss this civilly, and she said, "I can't talk about this right now." Loring knew she was upset and let it go for the time being, again. Maybe he should forget the idea altogether. Maybe Hattie was right.

But that night in bed Hattie said, "Oh, Loring. I don't know. I've been thinking about your idea a lot since you brought it up. I go back and forth on this thing. First, I think, absolutely not! It's just too dangerous to pass a child onto a moving train. But then I think, what else can we do other than not have him go to school at all? I could teach him myself, but then he'd miss out on learning with others, which I believe is valuable. Do you really think it would be safe enough to do that?"

"I think that if the engineers and conductors think it can work, we ought to trust them and give it a try."

"Well, I'd feel better if I could see it work. And what if Gordon is not willing to do it? He might not want to, you know," Hattie said, edging toward trying it.

"Ayuh. I've thought of that, too. If he's up for it, one of us can get him on the train and one of us can be waiting at Crawfords to see him off that first time. Actually, no, we could both get him on the first time and have one of the men meet him at the station. How does that sound?" Loring said.

"If we were both there to get him on, I'd feel much better. Then when September comes, I'll have to talk to his teacher about getting him back on the train after school. I'm just thankful that he'll be going to Bemis first. That's the easier trip," Hattie answered.

"I'm sure he'll manage if he isn't scared. Whenever you think he's ready to try it, let me know and I'll see when Bobby's on next. I'd just as soon have Bobby do this first. Gordon knows him the best," Loring concluded, pleased that his wife was just plucky enough to go along with something so unusual.

Then, after a pause, she added, "And Loring…when I said 'no' to your idea that first time, why did you go behind my back to investigate it further? That really hurt."

The color in his cheeks told her he felt trapped. So, she offered this, "Next time, please include me even if you know I don't agree. I still want to be a part of decisions as important as this one."

"I'm sorry. I guess I thought your reluctance was based on not seeing a good way forward. I thought if I could find a good solution, you'd be happy to hear it."

"Well, the issue is over now. Good night," Hattie said giving Loring a kiss and he turned down the lamp.

Now that the plan was in place, Hattie and Loring talked it over with Gordon. He still seemed hesitant but was warming to the idea gradually in the face of two parents who believed in him. But first, Hattie decided to take all the children down to Bemis Station to let Gordon walk the route from there to the school. She messaged Florence about going along and picnicking in the schoolyard. A date in late August was set, a particular train was determined, and when that day came, she attached the "stop" flag to the pole out front. None of them tired of a train ride or an adventure. After the Monahans boarded, the Evans children paired with one or another Monahan child and chattered the short way down to Bemis. There, they got off and walked to the school. Then they spread out a blanket and enjoyed their picnic while the children played. It was a delightful day, not only spending time with friends, but also completing a run-through for Gordon. Hattie knew it had accomplished what it was meant to when Gordon haughtily told Mildred, "This is gonna be *easy*."

The next thing Hattie did, when time permitted, was take Gordon to Fabyans and walk with him to that school. This time he seemed more comfortable tackling what would be required of him. Hattie marveled at his prowess. It was one thing to do something new herself for the first time, but quite another to entrust something brand new to her six-year-old child.

Finally, it was time to execute their plan for getting Gordon on the moving train and riding alone. This time Hattie couldn't go with him. She asked him if he felt ready. He said he did. He understood that his father would lift him up as the train steps passed by, and the conductor or brakeman—she wasn't sure which—would grab him from Loring's arms. Gordon knew he would travel alone up the tracks and meet John, who volunteered to be there at the station. Hattie was relieved that Gordon seemed excited. She felt quite certain that if he was afraid in any way, the whole plan would fall through. If they couldn't find a suitable way to get him to school, she'd just have to teach him at home. Not giving him at least some form of education was not an option.

Loring, Hattie, and the children waited outside for the train. When they heard the chuff-chuff-chuff of the steam engine climbing the hill, Hattie asked Gordon one last time if he was ready. He nodded. Mildred and Raymond watched with intense curiosity. Enola was tied to the porch, something she was used to by now and took in her stride, although Hattie had noticed lately that Enola wouldn't be tethered for long. When the train was almost at the house, Loring lifted Gordon up under his armpits and stepped as close to the tracks as he dared. Loring saw the conductor reach his arms out from where he stood on the steps, bracing himself against the rail, and was amazed to see that it was Ed Davis. Hattie could hardly believe their good fortune to be passing her child to someone who had actually met Gordon. In one swift movement that took no more than a blink of an eye, Loring thrust Gordon into Ed's arms where Gordon quickly found his footing. And just like that, he was on the train! They watched him wave until he disappeared around the bend.

That first trial run had gone well. Loring wanted to try it again, this time with Hattie passing Gordon off in case Loring wasn't able to for one reason or another. Hattie practiced lifting Gordon up by the armpits as Loring had, which was not an exercise Gordon had overly much patience for. But after all the preparation, Hattie was convinced it would work and Gordon was excited to start school.

On that first day, the whole family waited in the yard to see Gordon off to Bemis. He was the last to leave the house. When he appeared on the porch, Hattie clasped her hands over her heart. Gordon looked like a young man, a sight she wasn't entirely prepared for. There he stood in his neat white shirt and the tie she'd made from one of Loring's old ones. His navy-blue pants matched his tie and, with his dinner pail in hand, he looked like a small version of any businessman about to leave for work. When the train stopped, Gordon hopped aboard the caboose. When it crossed the bridge, Gordon waved happily as a tear rolled down his mother's cheek. Seeing him excited made sending her firstborn to his first day of school much easier for Hattie. *This is his time now,* she thought. Loring wiped the tear from her cheek and kissed her. Then with a knowing smile, he set off up the tracks toward Crawfords.

"Why did Gordon walk onto the train?" Mildred asked her mother. "I thought you were going to throw him to the conductor."

Hattie laughed. "We don't throw him on the train, or anywhere else, Mildred. We pass him to the conductor."

"That's what I said. Why didn't you?"

"Because this train can stop. It's only when the train goes the other direction that we need to pass him to the conductor."

"Oh. Well, what will Gordon do in school?"

"I'm not entirely sure," Hattie said, untying Enola. "But he'll have fun learning about letters and numbers. Now, can you be a big girl and help me carry this laundry basket, please? Raymond, will you help Enola up the steps?"

Mildred reached down and took one of the basket's handles and Raymond said, "Come on, 'Nola," and took his little sister's hand to lead her onto the porch and into the house.

That afternoon, when Gordon jumped down from the slowly moving train as it crept past the house, the whole family was there to greet him, even his father. Gordon received hugs and everyone wanted to hear all about his adventure.

"It was *real* good," Gordon said. "I like Miss Small real well. She's real nice. She had our names right there on our desks! We learned to raise our hands if we needed something or if we had a question. Otherwise, we were supposed to sit and be quiet." Hattie smiled at her little man and wished Nell could see how well her nephew did on his first day of school. She'd have to write Nell all about it.

"Did you learn about numbers and letters yet?" Mildred asked.

"Yeah! I'll show ya." He and Mildred started to the parlor for some paper and a pencil.

Hattie stopped them, "That's a good idea Gordon, *after* you change out of your school clothing, please."

"Yes, ma'am," he answered without enthusiasm.

Perhaps just this week I won't make him do his chores, Hattie thought.

It didn't take Mildred long to begin teaching her dolls and anything remotely like a person what she learned from Gordon each day. Sometimes Raymond and Enola sat in on her school lessons, but not often. They had other things to do that were much more fun than sitting still and being lectured by Mildred, who would have included Boomerang in her classroom if he'd stayed put for more than two seconds. But her dolls were very attentive for as long as Mildred wanted to educate them.

Raymond missed Gordon, who was his primary playmate, and was always delighted when the weekend came. Then they could go outdoors and play. Enola liked being in anyone's company, but her attention span wasn't long. She'd go from room to room searching for the next person willing to play with her. Hattie always kept an astute ear out for where her children were and what they were doing. Like most mothers, she could tell by their laughs and cries if she was needed and how urgently. Most days that fall, Mildred played with Enola, leaving Raymond to play alone until Gordon came home. Hattie felt sorry for Raymond, who looked so lost.

It was on one particularly trying day that she heard Mildred screaming something she knew meant trouble, and she quickly raced outside to see what was going on. She gasped to see Raymond part of the way across the bridge, on his hands and knees, looking over the edge. With her heart in her throat, she ran and scooped him up, setting him down on the grass.

"You aren't ever to cross that bridge alone, do you hear me, young man?"

"Yes, ma'am. But dad does it all the time."

"Your father is old enough to cross that bridge alone. *You…* are *not*! And that is the end of that! Now come inside and fetch me the switch."

Raymond was in no great hurry to have the switch applied to his back end, but there was no dodging it. As Hattie was about to tell him to pull down his britches, she sensed that Mildred and Enola were watching with curiosity. The switch was not often used and neither had had it used on them. But all their mother had to do was point to the door and Mildred knew enough to grab Enola's hand and lead them both out of the room. It didn't stop Mildred from cornering Raymond later, though, to ask him all about it, to which he said nothing and sulkily climbed the stairs to his room.

On the best weather days that fall, Hattie took her three younger children out for walks. One day, as she stood at her kitchen window drinking in the spectacular fall colors that draped the mountainsides, she decided she had time to let the children explore the steep hill behind the house to the road below. It would take time to allow Enola to walk and effort on Hattie's part to carry her when she tired. Going down was relatively easy. Occasionally Enola took a tumble. Mildred picked her way down carefully and Raymond hopped from rock to stump to fallen tree all the way to the road. It was slower on the way up for everyone but Raymond, who reversed his hopping, this time going upward. When the girls were too slow, he'd hop way ahead, then hop back down to meet them, then repeat the process until he was finally worn out. But halfway up, in approximately the same location as the first time she took this trail ten years ago, Hattie sensed a presence again. *Too bad Rusty isn't here,* she thought, realizing her anxiety wasn't as much for herself this time as for her three children. Hattie feigned fatigue, asking the children to stay still a moment and rest while she listened and watched intently. But once again, nothing materialized. The presence she felt remained strong until they had nearly reached the house. There, she was busy enough to forget the incident.

As Loring's fortieth birthday approached, Hattie determined to do something special for it as she'd promised herself since her own special day. The last day of October fell between workdays, so she decided to host a small party just for the family and the crew. She purchased a gift that she hoped Loring would consider appealing and useful. The children secretly worked on a treasure map that would take their father through the house and out into the yard to find his buried gift. Hattie was sure Loring would love it and the children couldn't wait for their father to come home.

When he and the crew finally came back and had cleaned up, and the children could wait no longer, Hattie let them present their map. Gordon handed his father the colorful paper they'd drawn while commentaries overlapped. "You start here, dad," Raymond said. At almost the same time, Mildred added, "I drew the trees. This one and this one, right here," pointing to each one. Gordon said that he had written the words because he was learning his letters at school. Enola sucked her thumb and positioned herself squarely in the middle of the mob. Loring beamed as he looked up at Hattie who was also grinning from ear to ear.

He studied his map and walked to the starting place in a corner of the kitchen. From there he walked through the dining room and parlor with the children following behind him like ducklings waddling to Saco Lake. When he reached the parlor, he deliberately turned the wrong way, to the squeals of corrections from the three oldest. Turning the right way, he headed out to the porch. Now his followers included all the adults who didn't want to miss the fun. Loring dutifully followed every dash on the paper even though he could clearly see how to cut straight to the "X." He passed the icehouse, then the carhouse, and back to the rock ledge. From there, he was to reverse direction again and pass the carhouse, but, this time, pick up the shovel one of the crew men had sneakily put there when Loring's back was turned. His map indicated that he was to walk twenty paces up the tracks, then cross over them and land just outside the boundary of Hattie's garden. But his footsteps were longer than the children's and he overshot the "X." The children were crestfallen, not knowing how to get him to the correct spot until Enola sat herself squarely on the burial place. When the others squawked at her to get up, Loring tried not to catch on. But Enola pointed down at the little patch of newly shoveled dirt and Gordon threw his hands up and said, "Nola!" Then, seeing his father's questioning look, Gordon said, with a defeated air, "Yes, dad, that's the place."

Loring acted excited enough that even Gordon couldn't stay dejected. It didn't take long for their father to find the treasure, wrapped in a piece of paper. He looked at the children quizzically, turning the treasure over and over until they all begged him to just open it. Inside he found a beautiful pipe with a black stem and cinnamon-brown bowl. The letter "E" was carved on the side. The children all waited for hugs, which Loring was quick to give. Then they ran back into the house while John picked up the abandoned shovel and took it back to the carhouse. Loring walked with his arm around Hattie's waist. "Thank you," was all he said. It was all she needed to hear. The rest of the evening involved supper and cake, and Loring's first draw of his new pipe with everyone watching. That night, in bed, Loring let Hattie know just how much he appreciated her.

It was time to begin thinking about Thanksgiving again. And again, Hattie planned to cook up a feast. This year a strong nor'easter had picked Thanksgiving Day as its target and wind began howling before Hattie and Loring had even gotten up. Hattie was in the kitchen feeding coal to the stove when a telegraph message began coming through. *MW*, it began. It was for them. *SWITCHES BURIED CS.* Loring had walked in before the message finished. "Guess we have to head out, my love. Hopefully we'll be back before dark. I'm sorry. I know this is a favorite day of yours. It is for me, too." Then, holding her around the waist, he said, "Just remember, I'll be hungry as a bear when I get back. So, keep everything warm!"

The crew dressed for the weather. Loring gave Hattie a quick kiss before leaving. It would be a difficult walk to Crawford Station in this storm and Hattie felt sorry for the men. The day dragged as Hattie took her time fixing all the favorites that always made Thanksgiving special. The children helped as they could, paring potatoes and apples, carrying up more coal, kneading the bread as long as their arms held out, and fetching eggs. Then she invited Gordon to make name tags for each person who would grace their Thanksgiving table and told him what letters to write. When their help was not needed, the children drew pictures and read some children's books Hattie had borrowed from Florence. Or they played with marbles or checkers or games they made up. Sometime in the afternoon, the scheduled freight came through later than usual, Hattie noticed. When it was almost dark, the children asked when their father would be back. "Any time now, I should think. Why don't you go sit on the steps and see if you can see the men coming." But it was impossible to see anything through the snow and darkening day. The children left the window to do other things.

Hattie had mixed feelings throughout the day, including sadness that Loring couldn't enjoy time with the family and irritation at the snowstorm's timing, which was useless, of course. When her feelings became mixed with anxiety, she told herself that Loring would send her a message if it got too much later. She poked her head out the door to see if the snow was still falling. *At least it's starting to subside a little,* she thought, and went back to the kitchen. Most everything was finished now. It was just a matter of keeping things from crusting over as they sat.

Hattie noticed that the afternoon passenger was also later than usual, and then she heard a knock on the porch door. One of the children opened it. *Who could that be on Thanksgiving in the middle of a storm?* she wondered, wiping her hands on her apron as she walked quickly to the parlor. *It can't be the men. They wouldn't knock.* It was Joe Monahan.

"Joe! Well, come in. Come in. Happy Thanksgiving!" Hattie said, closing the door behind him. "What brings..." She stopped when she saw Joe's expression and just stared at him.

"Hattie, can we talk privately a moment?"

"Sure, Joe," Hattie said, feeling anxiety rise from her stomach into her throat. Keeping her voice as calm as possible, she asked the children to please go upstairs to play. When they had left the room, Hattie spoke quietly, partly so they couldn't hear what was sure to be bad news and partly because her throat suddenly felt constricted. "What is it, Joe? Is Florence all right? The children?"

"Hattie, there's been an accident at Crawford."

Twenty-two

~ Flood Week ~
Wednesday, November 2, 1927

When Hattie awoke, still with her eyes closed, she realized she'd been dreaming. Trying to pull the dream back, she remembered it was something about a dance that she and Loring had attended. She wore the most beautiful, royal blue chiffon flapper dress adorned with rhinestones and topped off with a long strand of pearls gilding the front. Her hair was coiffed just so against her head and she wore a headband with an elegant peacock feather attached, its colors iridescent and dazzling. She wore matching pumps with two-inch heels that glittered when the light caught them just right. Loring looked dapper, indeed, as they strutted across the dance floor arm in arm. *Oh, he will love hearing about this dream*, Hattie thought, as she lazily allowed herself a few extra moments to relive that beautiful scene.

A sudden thump jolted her into the present and she quickly sat up. It was only Sneakers jumping down off her bed. But it was past time to dress for the day. As she did so, she wondered what had prompted her dream and suddenly remembered the bag of dresses the Kelly couple had dropped off yesterday. The dresses were all so beautiful, but she knew they were outrageously impractical for her, if they even fit at all. "I'll bet Mildred and Enola will love trying these on," Hattie murmured with pleasure. "I can see those two dancing the Charleston and trying to get the boys to join them." She laughed.

When the men arrived for breakfast, she overheard one of them, maybe Denny, talking about the rain coming. There it was again, the anxiety they all seemed to have by now. She'd been outside to hoist the flag and let Laddie out and noticed thickening cloud cover. Nothing unusual or spectacular, but, in her state of mind, ominous nonetheless. She smelled damp air, too warm for this time of year. Or was she imagining it?

Best get busy, Hattie thought after the men left. *After all, today is the tomorrow I worried about yesterday. How fitting that quote is! I've been foolish to worry so. I'll just send a telegram to Gordon and Mildred. If anything is brewing south of here, they will know.* With a new resolve to put her anxiety aside, she began mixing ingredients for the bread she could practically make in her sleep now. When the mixture was ready to sit and rise, she began making crusts for two mincemeat pies, something she'd be sure to make again this Christmas. In fact, she didn't usually make mincemeat this early in the season, but something told her a mincemeat pie might be nice to have on hand this weekend.

Hattie didn't bother with her sweater. She went out to get butter from the icehouse and eggs from the hens. Being in the icehouse made her wonder when the men would go deer hunting next. A rich venison stew would be especially nice when the weather turned more seasonably cool. Back in the house, she pulled out the flour and salt from the pantry and grabbed her bowl and measured her ingredients into it. As she cut in the butter, making floury crumbles, she thought, *If nothing else brings those children home, a good mincemeat pie will!* Hattie hummed softly to herself. She remembered teaching the girls how to make a flaky pie crust. The lesson had gone well until one of the girls flicked flour on the other which prompted a flour fight, all in good humor, until Hattie finally intervened. "Go outside and brush yourselves off!" Hattie had scolded. But the girls had seen right through to their mum's smile. The memory brought happiness mixed with a bit of sorrow at how fast the time was going. Now the girls' lives kept them apart too often.

By the time her crusts were finished, the butter she needed for the filling was nicely soft. She creamed her eggs and butter, added some sugar, a pinch of salt, a small amount of flour and her mincemeat, divided the mixture between the two crust-filled pie plates, and slid them into her oven. She added a bit more coal to bring it to the right temperature. She would leave it there to bake while she finished making the bread into loaves.

When the pies and bread were out and cooling, Hattie grabbed her sweater this time, called loudly to Laddie, who was losing more of his hearing now, and headed up the tracks for Crawfords. Laddie padded slowly beside her. He wasn't inclined to run along the tracks any more than she was these days. *Guess we're getting older, eh, Laddie?* For some reason, it felt right to wire the two older children, though she rarely did. On the way, she thought about what she would say to them while she made a mental note of the sky. *Lots of activity in those clouds. They seem to be pushing up so high. I wish they could speak. Maybe I'd know what to think about the weather we'll get this weekend.* She dearly loved having the children all home, but was it selfish of her to wish them here when the weather might be bad? Still, rain didn't stop the trains. Boulders did, and perhaps some flooding in the wrong places, but not rain. She passed the men working in Crawford yard and waved, then crossed the lawn and walked around the hotel to the caretaker's cottage where she hoped to find Elizabeth. She knew her friend might be in the hotel where the end-of-season cleaning would sound like a swarm of bees, but she decided to try the cottage first. Calling out a greeting when she reached the door, she heard her friend echo back and walked in. "How are you?"

"Hi Hattie. I'm fine. And you?"

"Good. I'm good. Thank the Good Lord for that. I came to wire Gordon and Mildred about this weekend."

"Really?" Elizabeth eyed her friend pensively, "It isn't like you to wire ahead. Are you wondering if the coming weather might discourage them?"

Hattie sighed, realizing that her anxiety must have subtly escaped before her words. "Well, yes, I guess I am. That's so selfish of me, isn't it? To expect them to come home every weekend. And even this weekend when they might have to travel through bad weather. To tell you the truth, Elizabeth," Hattie leaned forward as if about to divulge a secret, "I haven't known what to think about the children coming this weekend. I can't imagine Gordon and Mildred not coming home, but what if things really do get bad? What if the Saco floods? Who knows what might happen to the roads and trains. On one hand I know they'll come if they can. So, you're right, no encouragement is really necessary. On the other hand, what if they try to come home when it isn't safe, just to please me? Maybe what I should do is wire them not to come home? Maybe I shouldn't wire them at all." Hattie dropped her eyes to her lap.

Elizabeth paused, taking in her friend's unusual anxiety and the dreadful indecision in an otherwise decisive woman. Elizabeth genuinely hurt for Hattie and felt at a loss for words. With Peter working at Crawfords and Martha in Whitefield, her own children would not have trouble coming home this weekend and Elizabeth was confident the same would be true for Raymond and Enola. But it was more difficult to know what might be in store for the older two so far away. Then Elizabeth said the only thing she could think of, "Why don't you just sit there and think about it while I clean up the mess I've made. I'm cooking up supper for the girls who are cleaning over at the hotel. You caught me at a good time. I'm between fixings. This won't take me long."

Hattie rose to help her friend, but Elizabeth waved her back down. "Just sit. This will only take a moment."

So, Hattie closed her eyes and thought about what would bring her the most peace.

"There now," Elizabeth said, drying her hands and turning back around. She walked to the desk and sat down.

In those few moments, Hattie had been able to settle her mind and said, "I will send them each a wire. I think it will calm my nerves." Elizabeth took down the message: *DON'T COME HOME – STOP – WEATHER – STOP – MUM.* Elizabeth looked up at Hattie and smiled. She already looked much better than she had when she'd walked into the cottage.

After Hattie paid the twenty cents she owed, she told Elizabeth about her visit yesterday from the Kellys. Elizabeth knew who Hattie was talking about. "Muriel is a very nice-looking girl, isn't she? And she's sweet as well. Adam is a lucky young man, I think."

"I agree," Hattie said. "And you should see the dresses Muriel left me!" She laughed heartily. Then suddenly Hattie blushed. "Wait a minute. Muriel must have known about Mildred and Enola. Those dresses weren't for me at all, were they?" Both women enjoyed laughing together. It felt good not to think about the weather at all.

When Hattie composed herself, she said, "Lord, have mercy. Imagine an old woman like me wearing one of those beautiful dresses! I'm sure the girls will love them. But I tell you, Elizabeth, apparently the only way I could imagine wearing them myself was in a dream I had last night. If you have another few minutes, I'll tell you about it. It was so *keen!*" Hattie said with added emphasis on "keen," and both women laughed again as Hattie described her dream.

Time always went too fast when Hattie was with Elizabeth, and she couldn't let the day slip further away. Besides, she knew Elizabeth had given up precious time of her own. With a thoughtful hug of thanks, Hattie stepped outside. Laddie had stayed curled up outside near the cottage and was on his feet as soon as the door opened. Walking past the men once more, Hattie gave a quick wave while Laddie trotted over to them for a pat on the head. Then they both disappeared through the gateway and went on down the tracks.

Before they'd even reached home, it began to rain ever so softly.

Twenty-three

~ 1913 ~
A Staggering Truth

Joe instinctively reached out to steady Hattie. "What happened, Joe?" she asked, fearing the bottom line. "It's Loring, isn't it? Is he badly hurt?"

"Hattie, Loring's been killed." Joe could hardly get the words out. He led her to the nearest chair so that she could sit down. She couldn't think. Couldn't make sense of someone who had kissed her only hours ago never to kiss her again. Or eat the big meal she'd been making. It was surreal. Impossible, even. Joe sat near her and waited until she looked up at him. "What happened, Joe?" she said again, only this time she was looking for details.

"All I know is that a light engine backed up when Loring apparently thought it was going forward. The men will know more, but they're staying with him until the undertaker can get there. In this snow, I don't know how long it will take before they're back. I'm so sorry, Hattie. So, so sorry."

Hattie could see that Joe was shaken and near tears. His very close friend had just died. She reached out to lay her hand on his.

"Florence told me to come and stay with you as long as you need me," Joe said.

"I need to see him," Hattie said, beseechingly, looking directly at him. "If you could stay with the children, I can get up there myself."

Joe paused. This was all so difficult. "I don't think that's a good idea, Hattie," he said quietly, slowly shaking his head, hating to keep her from going to her husband. "It's bitter out there, and dangerous. And it's almost dark. And I don't know what shape Loring's..." Joe could go no further. He hung his head and wept silently.

Hattie was too stunned to cry. She wanted to do something. Anything. She thought she'd go crazy in this house without Loring, which was strange. Loring was often not in the house on workdays. Why did his absence feel so palpable now? She could only surmise that when a loved one is due to return, the expecting itself creates a presence.

Suddenly she became aware of the children upstairs prancing around, laughing. *The children. What do I say to the children? When should I tell them? And how?*

To Joe's admonition, she said, "All right. You're right, Joe, of course. I won't try to go to Crawfords. But I need to tell the children and I'd rather do that while you're here. I'm not asking you to be with me when I tell them, but I think they, no, *we* all need you in the house right now." Joe nodded. He knew Loring's offspring almost as well as he knew his own, and he couldn't imagine having to break such news to his girls. This whole thing was a nightmare from which he wondered if any of them would recover.

They sat in silence for a time, willing themselves to breathe the breath of the living, to prematurely accept what was about to be conveyed to the children. Then Hattie drew in a large breath, rose to her feet, and walked to the stairs. She took each step very slowly as if to gain more courage with each one. She walked into the boys' room and sat on Gordon's bed, then asked them all to come in because she needed to talk to them. Her demeanor conveyed the seriousness of her request and they responded immediately. The older three sat on Raymond's bed across from their mother. Enola wanted to sit on Hattie's lap. No one said anything for a moment.

"Children," Hattie began quietly with an awful lump in her throat, "I have something to tell you that is going to be very difficult for you to hear. There is no way to make this easy. I wish there was. So, you must be very brave now. Can you do that?" They nodded, eyes wide with fear. "There has been an accident at Crawford yard. That's why your father didn't come home." She paused. "Your father was killed this afternoon." Gordon instantly knew that his father was never coming back and began tearing up. Hattie couldn't tell yet what the others understood.

The hush that followed filled the room. It was as if the silence had inflated an enormous balloon that pressed each of them against the wall, leaving them to fight for air. Tears trickled down Gordon's cheeks. Mildred and Raymond studied their mother's face to find understanding. Enola stared at her siblings, then turned to look up at her mother. Hattie didn't want to break down in front of her children, so she chose not to look at Enola's sweet little face. Then suddenly, with a jolt that nearly threw her on the floor, it occurred to Hattie that Enola, and maybe Raymond and even Mildred, would probably not remember their father. History was repeating itself.

With an almost inhuman numbness, Hattie walked herself through that evening. She and Joe talked very little after she'd informed the children. There wasn't much to say yet. Or, if there was, they were both too stunned to think clearly. Hattie made sure the children had something to eat before putting them to bed. Then she walked to the kitchen intending to feed herself, as well as Joe. There certainly was plenty of food, but she found she had no appetite and Joe declined food, too. So, she did what she could to prepare the meal to sit overnight. Then she hung up her apron, walked into the parlor, and told Joe she was going to bed. Joe had not moved from the spot where he'd sat, and Hattie invited him to stay or take the next train back home. Then she turned for her bedroom.

Hattie couldn't bring herself to light the lamp, preferring the darkness to keep the reality of her loss at bay. That's what her world had suddenly become, dark and silent. She didn't even dress for bed. She knew she wouldn't sleep. The emptiness of their bed kept her awake. She never even cried. All she could do was breathe while memories flooded her mind, unbidden and unwelcome.

The men came back sometime in the middle of the night. Although Hattie heard them, she left them alone to get whatever rest they could after what she assumed had been a hellish day. The details could wait. She'd had enough for one day.

Very early the next morning, Hattie penned a note to Nell to be sent as a telegram. She'd have one of the men see to that today. Then she heard them coming downstairs.

They found Hattie in the dining room. She looked shriveled and ghostlike. She had robotically set the table and was laying some of the uneaten Thanksgiving food at its center. When she noticed their presence, she pointed to the table to have them sit and asked them to please eat. She knew they'd want to wait for her, but she also knew she couldn't eat. John spoke immediately as if he knew he was expected to. "Hattie, please have a seat with us." She sat as if it didn't matter whether she was there or in some other room, standing up or sitting. "First of all," John started, gently, "Joe decided to walk home once we were back. He said he needed to clear his head. He said Florence'll be up sometime today." Then, assuming Hattie wanted information, John got right to it, though it was the most difficult thing he hoped he would ever have to do the rest of his life. "We aren't sure exactly how the accident happened. All the trains were off schedule yesterday. Thanksgiving on top of the storm, I guess. So, the freight out of Bartlett was delayed."

"I heard it come through," Hattie said quietly, staring into space, realizing that very train was probably part of a horrifying story she was about to hear. John and the others noticed that Hattie was unconsciously folding and unfolding her napkin.

"The freight made it up to Crawfords and pulled through and sat there to get clearance," John continued. Hattie looked down at her napkin. "Dispatch had apparently instructed the helper to message for further instructions once he reached Crawford. We were all busy keeping the switches clear. That snow was coming so fast," he said, stating the obvious. "I had to go into the station and when I came out, I heard the three whistles for backing up. I assume the helper had uncoupled from the freight while I was in the station. Next thing I know the engineer of the helper comes running by me screaming, 'Man down! Man down!' That's when I found Loring," John paused, gathering courage. "Hattie," she looked up at John then, "he was gone instantly. He didn't suffer, from what I could tell. We carried him into the station and just sat with him. I thought about getting you up there to see him, but the storm was so bad and with the children to care for, there just wasn't any way you could get up there."

"Who was the engineer?" Hattie asked, her voice quivering.

"Someone new. I've only seen him once or twice."

"Where is Loring now?"

"Whitefield Funeral Parlor. They said they'll send his body down here first train on Sunday."

"But I don't understand something," Hattie said. "If the engineer whistled, why didn't Loring get out of the way?"

"We don't understand that either. Maybe he only heard two of them or maybe he didn't hear anything."

The silence that followed proved the futility of further conversation. "Thank you, John." Putting her written message on the table, she finally said, "Could one of you get this telegram sent for me today? And also tell Elizabeth what's going on. I don't want to convey that message by telegraph."

At this point, the children began to come downstairs. Mildred held Enola by one hand, while her other rubbed the sleep from her eyes. Hattie hugged them one by one as they came into the dining room. They weren't used to seeing the men linger after breakfast and, as their memories cleared a path through the fog of waking up, they understood and stayed in the room, standing close to their mother. Enola climbed into Hattie's lap.

"Well, ma'am, we need to be going out to work. Is there anything else we can do for now?"

"Your breakfast, John. You can't go out with nothing in your stomach." She'd noticed that he was the only one who hadn't touched the food. "Let me put something in your pails. I'll just be a minute." She quickly left the room with the girls following her.

Once she stepped into the kitchen, Hattie stopped as if she'd hit an invisible wall. The girls nearly ran into her. She looked around this place that was such a familiar domain, laying eyes on everything as if for the first time. The huge, black, cast-iron stove that was the center for warmth and hot meals, the heartbeat of the household, and the fulfillment of her love for everyone she fed, stood lifeless and looked harsh now, demanding. The table that was used for family meals and her paperwork now looked dreadfully forlorn. The cupboards and pantry she always kept full and organized seemed like a foreign country, too far away to reach. The counter that was always full of fruits and vegetables sat empty and waiting. The board on which loaves upon loaves of bread were kneaded while she gazed at the valley below beckoned her to come back. The sink, where she did so much of her thinking, looked cold and uninviting. Would this room ever feel the same again? It had always been a place she loved to be, a welcome beginning of a new day. Now it felt simply utilitarian. No, worse than that, it felt meaningless. Slowly, as if in a dream, she moved her body to answer the call for food. Mildred had taken it upon herself to sit and lift Enola onto her lap. They silently watched their mother while she performed the tasks they'd seen her do thousands of times before. The same. Yet different now.

As soon as Hattie and the girls had left the dining room, the men felt awkward alone with the boys. As if knowing they needed to attend to Gordon and Raymond more than going out to work, they lingered. But there was really only one subject on everyone's mind that no one would broach. So, John said, "Let's go to the parlor." Somehow it felt less awkward there. Then he asked Gordon about school.

"I think I'm supposed to be there today. I'll ask mum." Gordon turned to go to the kitchen.

"No, wait Gordon. I think your mum needs your help here at home today. I meant what are you learning in school?"

While Gordon and John talked, Denny and Ed reached out to Raymond. Billy, the quietest of the crew, said he would go see if Hattie needed help in the kitchen.

"Ma'am, can I do anything to help?" Billy asked.

"Thank you, but I don't think so," Hattie said. Then, "No, wait. Would you mind bringing up a hod of coal?"

"Sure thing, ma'am."

Hattie sliced meat off the chicken she'd so proudly roasted the day before and made sandwiches. Then she dished beans and corn into small jars and wrapped a hardboiled egg in waxed paper for each pail. Finally, she sliced some pie and put it on top of everything else. As Mildred watched, she wasn't sure whether to help or to sit quietly. Everything seemed so amiss today.

Billy was back with the coal, and, at Hattie's request, put some of it in the stove. Then she just stood for a few moments. No one moved or spoke. The children looked at their mother. Billy stared at the floor. When Hattie cleared her throat, they all looked at her. She realized, with great and terrible certainty, that she was now the head of this household. They would look to her for direction. It wasn't certain who would be foreman in Loring's place, but in the house, leadership was also needed. Beginning now. So, she said, "Come with me to the parlor, please." Hattie led the way and Billy ushered the girls out of the kitchen ahead of him. When Hattie had taken a seat, the others watched her, realizing she was going to say something.

She cleared her throat once more and said, "What's happened is for the best. We just don't know yet what the best is." Then she looked around the room at the children's little faces, so expectant, and the men's, so full of sorrow, and knew she needed to speak quickly, or she'd cry. "Thank you, John, Ed, Denny, Billy," nodding to each man as she spoke his name. Each nodded in return. "We'll get through this together, God willing." Then silence dominated the room again.

Hattie rose and called on Gordon and Mildred to wash the dishes. She asked Raymond to sweep the crumbs off the dining table and then sweep the floor. She didn't expect the children to do these things well, but the chores would keep them busy and, more importantly, give Hattie space to think.

Hattie turned to the men who were also standing now. She asked John where they needed to work today. "We'll start by shoveling a path to these doors. So, we'll be close by at first, then work our way up and down the tracks. Why do you ask? Do you need something?"

"No, I guess not. I just wondered." It felt so strange to have gotten her information about their day from someone other than Loring. It felt strange to have the men looking to her for instruction or normalcy or whatever they needed. It felt strange, period.

As the men started to leave, John hesitated. He guessed that Hattie was in need of an adult presence and hoped that Florence would come up soon. "We'll check in when we can," he said and turned to leave.

"Wait," she said, suddenly becoming clear about something else. "The undertaker will need clothing for Loring. If I get those to you, could you see that he gets them?"

"Of course," John said.

Good as done, Hattie thought. She would pick out his clothes when she mustered the courage. For now, she lifted Enola onto her hip, checked on the children's progress in the dining room and kitchen, then went back to the parlor to...do what? Hattie was so used to her routine that now she felt lost and couldn't find her rhythm. She honestly didn't know which way to turn. She put Enola down to play with the toys that had been left on the parlor floor the night before.

A coming train passed by and her stomach lurched. What was she to think about trains now? A boiler explosion had taken her father. A missed signal just took her husband. How many times had Loring told her that working the tracks was safer? Could she rely on trains in any capacity now? Yet trains carried their son to school. Was she to be anxious every time Gordon stepped aboard? Trains were also the family's lifeblood, bringing supplies, communication, visitors, and doctors. And then she allowed herself to wonder if she'd be able to stay at the Mount Willard House without Loring.

Hattie startled when she heard a knock on the door which brought the older children running to the parlor. It was Florence. Hattie fell into her friend's arms, saying nothing. Before Hattie had time to think about how it might affect the children, the tears that she hadn't allowed before now streamed down her face and sobs silently shook her body. Florence was crying, too. She had come alone. "Oh, Hattie," Florence sniffed. "Oh, dear, dear friend. How can this have happened?"

When the women parted, Florence removed her outer clothes and laid them on the nearest chair. She and Hattie both drew hankies from their pockets to blow their noses and dab at their tears. Then Florence scooped up Enola while Hattie asked the other children to go back to their tasks so the women could talk in private.

"Joe gave his crew their orders for the day, and he'll stay home with the girls for now. So, I'm here to help you. Cooking, cleaning, whatever you need from me. Have you heard anything from Whitefield?" Florence asked, not wanting to add, 'about Loring's coffin'.

"Yes, they will be here Sunday morning. I need to get this room rearranged."

"Then let's start there." Florence gave Enola a kiss on her little pink cheek and put her down. Then the two women began thinking through what space they'd need for the coffin.

A stomping on the porch brought Gordon flying to the parlor and he opened the door, this time to Elizabeth. Hattie gladly welcomed her friend. While Elizabeth took off her coat, Hattie excused Gordon. As he left the room, it occurred to her that maybe her son's need to answer the door was really a need to begin filling his father's shoes or perhaps just a need to stay close to his mother. Then Hattie told Elizabeth what she knew of the accident. Florence had yet to hear these details and came over to listen. When Hattie stopped talking, Elizabeth suddenly said, "Oh, this came for you," handing Hattie a telegram.

Florence summoned John inside and asked him to help them move the larger furniture while Hattie read the telegram:

COMING TODAY – STOP – ALL OF US – STOP – NELL.
Hattie teared up at the thought of Nell coming.

With the influx of people coming to the house, Hattie suddenly knew what she needed to do. There was food to prepare, beds to change, and housecleaning to do. The three women started down Hattie's list in earnest.

Twenty-four

~ 1913 ~
Final Goodbyes

I t was early evening when Nell, Walter, and Earl arrived. Florence and Elizabeth excused themselves, hugging Hattie with the promise of further help whenever it was needed. While Hattie's two friends stood outside waiting for the passenger train's return, Florence said, "Oh, Elizabeth, we've all suffered at one time or another but this…this seems unbearable."

"I know," said Elizabeth. "I keep wondering where Hattie will go once the funeral is over. Maybe she'll move closer to family in Maine. I'll sure miss her."

With little else to say, the two women hugged. Florence left on the train and Elizabeth headed out on foot in the opposite direction.

Meanwhile, Hattie turned her attention to Nell and her family, hugging each. Earl found his cousins and, at twelve years old, was a watchful eye as well as a needed friend. He helped them finish the chores Hattie had assigned them, then led them all upstairs to play, carrying Enola on his back.

Hattie filled Nell and Walter in on what she knew. Nell tried to be strong but had loved her brother too much not to break down in sobs. Finally, Nell said that Will and Charlie would come up tomorrow. There could be others, but Nell wasn't sure who. The one thing she did know was that Will wanted to have the funeral service at his home, which suited Hattie, who wished her husband's body to be buried near his family. Then Walter asked Hattie what he might do to help. It was difficult for Hattie to even think, but she finally told him to make himself comfortable for the time being. There would be things she might need later.

Hattie realized there was one thing she needed now, though. She turned to Nell and said, "I hate to ask this of you, but will you help me pick out some clothes to give the undertaker? I just can't do it alone." Nell nodded and they walked into Hattie's room. Hattie had no idea what Nell was feeling to have lost her brother, but she knew Nell was grieving deeply, too.

Hattie sorted through Loring's clothing. Even handling them was excruciating. "How formally does one dress the dead?" Hattie asked, realizing she'd never really given much thought to it even though she'd been to her share of funerals.

"Here," Nell answered, picking up what looked like the suit Loring had worn at their father's funeral. "This would do nicely. What do you think?"

"He hated formality. He'd probably rather be in his work clothes, really."

"I know," Nell said quietly. "But for this, I think he needs to be in his suit." Nell could see how her sister-in-law's grief was affecting Hattie's ability to think straight. It occurred to her that right now, their two brains weren't worth much combined.

Hattie agreed, and when that was finished, she asked to be alone for a moment. Nell wordlessly left the bedroom. Hattie gripped Loring's shirt and brought it to her face. Crying fresh tears and breathing deeply of his scent, she thought, *Oh, Loring, my dear, dear husband. We never conceived of having to part so young. This wasn't the way life was supposed to be. You and I were going to raise our children together. How will I do that alone? How will I do anything anymore without you?* Tears cascaded down her face while she caressed his shirt until his scent faded away. Then she folded it and the rest of the clothing neatly to be wrapped and sent away. She turned toward the bedroom door and set her mind to the remaining tasks for the day. She would work until there was nothing else to do but fall into bed.

Saturday dawned in Friday's place. Hattie realized that baths needed to happen early before family began arriving. She sought help from Nell and together they filled the galvanized tub, first with boiling water and then with cold. One by one, each older child took a turn bathing and then Nell washed little Enola. Hattie laid out suitable clothing for the children to wear, keeping in mind they'd need special clothes for the upcoming service. When she approached her own closet to fetch her dress for this first day of mourning, it saddened her to remember how recently she'd had to wear black.

As more family members arrived, it was a blessed relief to Hattie to have a houseful of people who needed her attention. She moved robotically, yet efficiently, getting things done. Nighttime finally came and, with it, fewer demands, but the solitude of her bedroom greeted her as a source of disquiet. She lay in the tomb-like darkness, feeling the heaviness of her uncertain future and thinking about Loring while shedding silent tears until she finally fell into an exhausted sleep.

On Sunday, an early eastbound freight stopped at the house, positioning the baggage car across from the porch. The door to the car opened, and the crew, along with the undertaker, carried Loring's coffin into the house, placing it against the far wall where space had been made for it. When the coffin was secure, the undertaker asked everyone but Hattie to leave the room. "Mrs. Evans, first let me say how very sorry I am for the loss of your husband." Hattie nodded. "I will open the coffin lid for you whenever you are ready. You may stay with your husband as long as you like and allow others to come in at your bidding. I will stay until the last train, after I have secured the coffin lid for the night. Where is the coffin to be buried?"

"Harding Cemetery in Standish Neck, Maine," Hattie said, grateful she and Nell had talked about these details.

"Will services be here or in Maine?" the undertaker asked.

"Maine," Hattie replied.

"What day will you want to hold your service?"

"This Tuesday," Hattie answered.

"Very good, Mrs. Evans. I will wire Standish and make the necessary arrangements for his burial. The coffin will need to be on a train tomorrow. Is there a minister you will have as officiant?"

"The Reverend Mr. Speirs in Standish Neck," Hattie said.

"I will wire him as well. Do you have any questions right now?" the undertaker finished.

"Will you make arrangements for a train to take his coffin, or must I do that?"

"I will do that, ma'am, and I will make sure you have those details. Anything else?"

"No."

"May I open the coffin, ma'am?"

Hattie said, "Yes, but may I first have our children in here to prepare them? I would like us to be together when you do that."

"Certainly."

When the children were in the parlor, Hattie sat down to be eye level with them as she spoke. "Children, you will see your father in this box here. It will look like him, but that is all we have of him now, just his body. You may touch him if you like, or talk to him, but he won't respond. Your father has gone on to Heaven and this box with his body will be buried in the ground Tuesday. Do you understand?"

Instead of answering his mother's question, Gordon asked, "Is dad happy in Heaven?"

"Yes, honey, I believe he is happy there," she said.

"Without us?" Gordon said, with an obvious heavy heart.

"I don't think he is happy to be without us, no. But I think the place where he has gone is a happy place, a good place." Gordon nodded. Hattie waited until she was sure the children were as ready as any of them could be, then she stood and picked up Enola. She nodded to the undertaker who lifted the coffin lid. Hattie's heart pounded in her chest as her eyes lay on Loring and her mind willed him to sit up. Those were the clothes she picked, but they somehow looked all wrong on his lifeless body. Gordon began crying. Mildred and Enola looked at their father with unreadable faces. She put Enola down and lifted Raymond up so he could see his father better. He, too, looked on vacantly. Then she put him down, telling him to please go tell the others they could come in to see his father and he scampered away.

In many ways, Hattie was suddenly grateful this moment would likely be forgotten by the younger children. She looked at her husband's face, so still and lifeless, none of his otter-like playful nature to be seen or felt. She touched his cold hand and spoke silently to him of her undying love, hoping that somewhere, somehow, he knew she was there. At Hattie's side, Gordon was clearly torn apart, and Hattie's heart broke for him.

Soon, family, friends, and crew came in and filed past the coffin. Some wept, others remained stony in the face of their grief for their fallen brother, uncle, friend, or foreman. Some hugged Hattie, others simply couldn't. Loring's family had just been together to honor their patriarch and now they gathered to honor Loring. It was a great deal to bear, and Hattie was grateful that Loring's father hadn't had to go through this. At the same time, she welcomed the closeness of Loring's family who lovingly included her.

Hattie couldn't keep her mind from drifting uncontrollably, first thinking of her poor husband being hit by a train and praying he didn't suffer, then wondering who would replace him, then thinking of a memory she hoped never to forget, then stressing over how she would manage parenting the children without their father. At one point, she gazed at Loring's face and realized he, or rather his body, was in this house, the place he'd been the happiest, the place where his children had been born.

Then her mind ran through all of it again…and again… and again.

Sunday came to an end. Most of the mourners had gone home on foot or by train. Nell, Walter, and Earl stayed, as well as the crewmen. They'd all leave tomorrow for Standish. Hattie had just one more night to be with Loring. When she put the children to bed that night, she stayed to listen to the grieving of their little hearts. It was almost more than she could bear, but death was a reality the living could not afford to deny. Most likely, her children would deal with death again and again, and she determined to be the first to help them through it. When they were quiet, she kissed each one twice, once for herself and once for their father. As she left them, she whispered something she'd known from her childhood but couldn't say where, "Sleep, my darlings, for tomorrow will come and with it the promise of another day's sun."

Then she went to the parlor to be with her husband of sixteen years. She sat in the chair beside him and decided that if sleep overtook her there, so be it. She quietly said to Loring, "Do you remember on our wedding night so long ago that I told you I knew I'd always feel safe with you by my side? Whatever will I do now to feel safe? And if I don't feel safe, the children won't. I have to find that feeling for the children's sake, don't I?" Silence was her only answer before she fell asleep in her chair.

The next day, the undertaker came riding in the freight that would take him and the coffin on to Maine. He spoke briefly to Hattie, then the men carried the coffin to the waiting boxcar. The space left by Loring's coffin suddenly felt unbearably empty. Hattie did not want to stay there any longer than she had to. She took the few small things she considered sacred now (Loring's pipe, for one) and stowed them in her hiding spot for safekeeping while they were gone. Then she and the children, along with Nell and Earl, boarded the next passenger train, leaving the others to finish tying up the loose ends in the house. Walter and the crew would leave early Tuesday morning for the service. They were to be pall bearers, a final act of devotion to a man they had respected and cared about.

At two o'clock Tuesday afternoon, Hattie and Nell made their way to the coffin in Will's parlor, with the children trailing behind and Earl carrying Enola. They each took one last look at Loring, then sat in the front row of chairs. The aroma of beautiful flowers perfumed the air, but Hattie was oblivious to them. The service was humbly sufficient with the Reverend Mr. Speirs from Standish Neck giving the eulogy and the Reverend Mr. Brown from Raymond giving the prayer. Will stood to offer a word on behalf of his family. John spoke for the crew. It was all very nice, and Hattie was grateful to all who had made it happen, but her heart wasn't there. It wasn't even with the coffin when it was lowered into the ground. It was back in Crawford Notch, she realized, in the home she'd made with Loring by her side. And suddenly, as much as she'd needed to leave the house yesterday, she now felt the need to return as soon as possible. The house would either be treasured for its good memories or too painful to live in. Either way, she needed to be where she felt closest to the love of her life to decide what to do next.

Twenty-five

~ 1913 ~
Maine Central General Office

When Hattie walked through the door to her parlor, the smells from the past few days still lingered and she had to will her knees not to buckle. One week ago, she'd been happily making a grand Thanksgiving meal. Today, the reality of what lay before her was daunting to say the least. And, like waking from any nightmare, a shroud of anxiety fell over the house once they were all back, as well as a tendency toward caution, particularly around Hattie. Everyone, save Enola, struggled to find firm footing again. Enola remained the one constant light in the house, chattering with anyone who looked her way. Raymond, while not especially affected by his father's death directly, had always looked to Gordon for brotherly direction and now found it faltering, both because his brother felt their father's death acutely and because Gordon would again be away at school. Mildred was the one Hattie wasn't sure about. Did she really understand her father's absence or was she also taking cues from her older brother? One thing *was* certain. Hattie observed the children playing together without their usual squabbles that first week.

In Loring's absence, the men picked up Enola more often, as if her light and energy could be infused directly into each of them. They also began talking more with the older children, taking deliberate note of what each was doing. But the men still had track work to do and did so, grateful to be away from Hattie's sad demeanor. Unfortunately, it also reminded them that they were without their foreman. John took over temporarily until a foreman could officially be named.

No one in the household wanted to put undue pressure on Hattie, which she sensed and appreciated. But she wondered when normalcy might return, if ever. Occasionally, Gordon or Mildred mentioned Loring by way of obtaining information they would normally get from him. When they did, their mother was quick to tear up. They interpreted her sadness as something they should not provoke by asking questions or even talking about their father anymore. Instead, they learned to avoid the subject.

As for Hattie, she just felt numb when they returned to the Notch. To her, Loring was everywhere in that house, especially their bedroom. She'd give his things away and adjust the house to his absence when she had the heart to, but she wouldn't give away his hat or new pipe, or the small frame with seashells on it, which sat on their bureau. It held a picture of the two of them taken one fall day after Loring had killed a six-point buck. As difficult as it was to see the picture every night, she knew she would never part with it. The only way she knew how to move on was to pick up her routine where she'd left off, as if nothing had happened. She couldn't help thinking about the Reverend going on without Martha. She hadn't understood what he must have been feeling. She did now, and she desperately wished she could talk to him.

Hattie sent Gordon to school the week after they returned from Maine, and that was when Mildred and Raymond were expected to do their chores as usual. They all accepted their mother's requirements because they didn't want to risk her tears or possible anger. And getting back into their normal schedules held comfort for them, too.

Routine was the crew's saving grace as well, though each day of that first week felt strange and awkward to them. For John to step into Loring's shoes was at least a natural shift because Loring had counted on John as second in command. Denny and Ed picked up where they'd left off with little trouble. But Billy Powell confided in John that he would stay only until his replacement could be found. He said that the accident shook him, and he decided it was time to seek other employment. John was in contact with the Maine Central office in Portland as they worked out the details.

One day, John approached Hattie and said that the office in Portland wanted to talk with them both and requested they come down to Portland the following Friday, if possible. Hattie asked Florence if she could watch the children. As a light snow fell, Hattie, John, and all the children boarded the eastbound passenger that Gordon normally rode alone. Hattie noticed that Gordon seemed excited and proud to share his school train with his siblings as far as the Willey House where Florence received them. After the train stopped to let Gordon off at Bemis, John and Hattie headed on to Portland, waving to Gordon as they passed.

"How're you doing?" John said, taking the opportunity to open the subject in case Hattie wanted or needed to talk about things.

"Well, I can honestly say I've been better," she said quietly as she pulled her black wool shawl more tightly around her shoulders.

"Can't we all," John replied, hoping Hattie would say more, but they sat in silence the rest of the way to Portland.

"Watch your step, Hattie," John said, helping her down the steps once the train stopped in Portland. They didn't have far to walk, but they did need to cross through the middle of the station and out along the front of the depot to reach the general offices next door. Hattie had always loved seeing Union Station in Portland. She always thought the stylish turrets and gables broke up the granite walls, giving the building the majestic grandeur of a fine hotel rather than a train depot. The clock tower, with its Roman numerals, was a separate wonder to behold. It had its own highly decorated gables on the pyramid roof. Even the lightning rod was ornate. The front lawn, though now covered in snow, she remembered as being well-manicured for those who walked through it in the summer months. The fountains weren't working this time of year, of course, but they, too, added to the splendor of this place. They passed several horses with carriages tied up, waiting for owners to return. Pedestrians were dressed warmly against the breeze coming off the ocean. A thin, briny smell wafted through the air.

When they reached the general office building, John held the door for Hattie through which they entered the lobby. Hattie brushed the snow off her dress before she was willing to venture past the doorway. As she studied the efficient-looking room, she realized, perhaps for the first time, that the Mount Willard House was painted to match the same Maine Central colors that were used here. If Loring had told her that, she'd forgotten. Gray and dark spruce could have been unspectacular colors were it not for the deep yellow accents that accompanied them. John went to the window to inquire as to where they should be and was told to have a seat, that someone would be with them soon.

"Do you know what they intend to say today?" Hattie asked John. She felt somewhat nervous, if she was truthful, fidgeting with her dress.

"I'm not sure, no. Could be about the accident, or maybe…"

"Mr. Green? Mrs. Evans? Right this way," a woman said, indicating they follow her down a narrow hallway with doors lining one side and windows the other.

The woman stopped at a door that read "Department of Personnel," and underneath that, "Joseph Abbott." She held the door open until Hattie and John walked through it and then shut the door behind them.

"Have a seat, please," the middle-aged, well-dressed man said, standing behind a wooden desk. Papers lay in small stacks neatly on top with pens and ink next to them. "I'm Joseph Abbott. Thank you both for coming in."

After Hattie and John were settled in luxurious leather chairs, the likes of which Hattie had never seen, Joe said, "First, Mrs. Evans, we all extend our sincerest and deepest condolences. We can't begin to know what you must be dealing with right now. But we want you to know that the company mourns the loss of a very good man and worker."

Hattie appreciated Joe's straightforward manner. "Thank you," she said.

"And John, may I call you that? I'm sure this isn't the best of times for you, either."

"You may, and no, it certainly isn't, sir," John said.

"It's Joe, please. We may as well be on a first name basis. We like to think of the people who work for us as family. Anyway, I'll get right down to brass tacks now if you don't mind," Joe said. "And I'll begin with you, John. Roadmaster Sawyer recommended you for the foreman position of Section 129. I believe you said you were acting in that position in the meantime, is that correct?"

"It is," John said with a formality Hattie had never heard.

"Well, then, if you're of a mind to continue, I'm authorized to pay you the same as Loring was getting this year, two fifteen a day. From all indications, you know how to be a foreman already. Will you take the job?"

"Yes, sir…Joe. I will."

"Alright then, if you'll sign these papers for us, it will be official immediately and I'll let W. D., uh, Mr. Sawyer know. Oh, and John, we're working on a replacement for William Powell. We'll let you know when we find someone. For now, you'll have to make do as a crew of four and we'll move as quickly as possible on this." John nodded as Joe turned some documents toward John and gave him a pen.

While Joe had been speaking with John, Hattie discreetly looked around Joe's office. A beautiful, large, roll top desk (made of oak, Hattie thought) stood open along one wall. Its slots were filled with letters or other paperwork. It had a dark-green blotter on the desktop with books, a stapler, and a magnifying glass scattered on it. And it was topped with photographs and a green plant of some kind. It looked as though Joe had several children and a nice-looking wife. An umbrella stand sat in the corner beside the desk. *All business, this room is,* Hattie thought.

When John finished signing the papers, Joe turned to Hattie and said, "Now, Mrs. Evans," he began. Hattie's thoughts turned immediately to the first name basis statement

Joe had made to John and the obvious difference in addressing her. She realized that only a few years ago she might not have noticed, given that Joe was using conventional formality. But Hattie's recent interest in the suffrage movement had her thinking of many things differently these days. "We have an offer for you, as well," Joe said. "You might need time to think about this, and if you do, that's fine. We are prepared to compensate you for your husband's loss, which should help if you move."

Hattie's mind exploded with two thoughts. *How could you ever compensate me for the loss of Loring?* And *did he just say 'if'? If I move? Did he assume I might stay?*

"But we'd rather have you stay on at the Mount Willard House and work. We're prepared to pay you two dollars a day to continue the fine job you're already doing there. We've heard good things about the meals you make and the house you keep for the crew." Hattie smiled modestly. "And for everyone's sake, it would be good to keep you on as continuity in a situation like this. But we know you have children, Mrs. Evans, and their welfares to consider as well as your own. We can give you until the first of the year to think about it. If you decide to leave Mount Willard, the railroad will, of course, move you wherever you decide to go. I don't expect an answer today, but do you have any questions?"

Hattie had already wondered if staying would be a possibility but hadn't given it any thought beyond that. If she felt that she could not stay, she'd need to figure out where to go with four children. Her first thought was to seek direction from Nell, which she'd planned to do soon. Perhaps there was a place she could stay near her sister-in-law until she got another job to support her family. She would never consider living on the railroad's compensation alone. But with Joe's proposal to consider, she did indeed need to think this through.

"I don't think I have questions as long as the work I'm currently doing is sufficient. If nothing needs to change, I will think over your offer and get back with you soon."

"I don't see why anything should change at all, Mrs. Evans. So, yes, please think it over. Should you decide to stay at

Mount Willard, I will mail the forms to you for your signature. You'd have no need to come back down to Portland. If you choose not to stay at the Mount Willard House, as soon as you let us know, we'll begin working out a plan to get you and your children moved." With that, Joe stood, indicating that the meeting was over. John and Hattie also stood.

"Sir…Joe," John said, reaching to shake Joe's outstretched hand, "does the Central Office know anything more about Loring's accident?" John wasn't sure it was all right with Hattie to bring this up. They hadn't talked about it. But he felt sure she'd want to know if there was anything new.

Joe walked around the desk to show them out, saying, "No, we don't. The investigation is still ongoing. We'll let you know if we have anything else to report. Thank you both again for coming in. Please take care, Mrs. Evans. And let us know if there is anything we can do to help."

"Thank you," John and Hattie both said and stepped out of the office.

Neither spoke as they walked back down the hall and through the lobby. The cold December air hit Hattie hard when the door opened. Somehow it felt colder now than when they'd arrived. It was still flurrying. She felt a shiver cascade down her body as she eyed the tiny white flakes against the black of her clothing.

When John and Hattie were seated again on the train to go home, both were lost in thought. John was mentally trying on the leadership role of foreman, that reality beginning to sink in. He knew he could do the job, but would the men be willing to see him as their boss rather than a section man working beside them as an equal? Loring had been a good leader, decisive and confident, yet fair and fun. Could he be another Loring? Should he even try? He didn't know who he would be as a boss. What if the men didn't like him in that role? What if they all quit in protest?

Hattie's offer didn't come with changes to her job, but being sole head of the household was change enough. The first thing she realized was that no matter whether she moved or stayed, she'd need to earn enough money to raise her children. But did she want to stay here to do that? There were benefits to staying on. The children were familiar with the house as the only place they'd ever called home. She knew the routine there and was comfortable with the men. She knew they'd watch out for her and the children, as would her neighbors on the tracks.

But she already felt the loneliness without her husband beside her. It was deep and felt claustrophobic. If she stayed on the mountain, would the loneliness be too much to bear? Would the sights and smells of the vestiges of Loring keep a stranglehold on her loneliness? She could move back to Maine and be around family, which would feel somewhat like being with Loring. The children would adapt to new surroundings that they were already familiar with. But this house was the only one she'd ever really considered her home. She loved the house. She adored the mountains. Would these reasons be enough to sustain her through the abyss of grief she felt? Or would the grief push her over an edge she had come up to for the first time in her life? She'd dealt with loss before but nothing so devastating as this.

Hattie might have spoken of this with John but didn't feel comfortable doing that. And John respected her silence as necessary. So, again, they rode quietly to Florence's house where the children were happy to see her. She hugged and kissed each one before they took a seat near her on the train. With Enola on her lap, she waved her thanks to Florence, sending a look that said much more to her friend than simply, "Thank you for watching the children."

How can life change so much in one, single defining moment? Hattie thought miserably.

Twenty-six

~ 1913 ~
Hattie Makes a Decision

Ready or not, adjustments were needed at the Mount Willard House and Section 129. Hattie preferred to believe that giving the children more chores after their father died would have happened regardless, or at least sooner or later. But the truth was that she needed their help right away. The crew was stretched thin with only four men. She absolutely could not ask any more of them.

Gordon was employed to dump ashes down the hill and return with a hod of coal each time. He helped crank the wringer on wash day and collected eggs from the henhouse daily. If he minded these things on top of his schoolwork, he didn't complain. At least not those first few weeks.

Mildred began cleaning the chimneys on the kerosene lamps. She would carefully remove the glass chimney to wipe it down, then refill the kerosene without spilling any. Once that was done, she would trim the wick just so, then reassemble all of the parts. There were lamps all over the house, so she understood that it was an important job. She was big enough to push the Bissell sweeper across the rugs, too, a chore she accepted with pride. Both Gordon and Mildred became accustomed to keeping an extra-vigilant eye on their younger siblings. While Enola loved the extra attention, Raymond saw this as an infringement on his independence, and often didn't make their job any easier. Hattie lost her patience more than once during this early adjustment to their new life. Everyone was stretched thin.

John asked for a fifth man not long after the meeting at the Maine Central office. So, they waited for two new crewmen. For Billy the wait was difficult. Every successive snow squall—and it didn't have to be much snow—he was a bundle of nerves around the trains, which was dangerous for all of them. John's nervous tendencies heightened those first few weeks, but he had watched Loring well and demanded the same high expectations Loring had. Since the men were used to achieving this level of work, continuing was not an issue. The only thing of concern on their parts was watching John have trouble relaxing into the foreman position and trusting his crew. They did what they could to help him cope, but they knew that John would have to manage things his own way for the most part.

Billy's relief came when Francis King was hired. Hattie would miss Billy and sent him off with a whole pie of his favorite kind. Before Christmas, Matthew McDunn was also hired on, which determined the need to add a third bed to one of the men's rooms. This wasn't ideal but couldn't be helped. No one complained to Hattie, although she bent an ear their way when she could. She wanted to be sure they were comfortable in her home and without Loring to learn things directly from the men while they worked, she had to find things out on her own. She wasn't ready to ask John for much information yet. She knew he would not be able to tell her the honest truth about some things. Maybe someday, if they worked together long enough, but not yet.

If anyone had told Hattie outright that she was handling Loring's absence superbly well, she would have begged to differ, if she'd been inclined to talk about it at all. To the outsider, it was as if she never skipped a beat in how the household was run, ever diligent and conscientious. She maintained her normal schedule, making sure Gordon was always dressed nicely for school each day. She didn't miss December's school board meeting and was never late with a meal. She even went hunting with the men. She was a marvel to many up and down the tracks as well as to those who knew her in Maine.

To the watchful eye of her closest women friends, however, she was different, even if only subtly so. The inner light to Hattie's soul seemed to be ever so slightly less bright. She still smiled and laughed, she still baked bread and made doughnuts and pie. Florence and Elizabeth saw her more than Hattie's other friends did. They talked frequently together about Hattie and what they might do for her, but Hattie was more likely to offer help than be helped. Her friends observed silently and remained ready to jump in when necessary. They didn't want to overstep their boundaries or their welcome with Hattie. They knew that to do so could weaken the bond they had, and they wanted to preserve that bond at all costs.

Hattie's spark was missing, and she knew it better than anyone. Loring had been the skip to her walk, the patience to her insistence, the play to her work. He brought her balance. He knew her, knew what she needed better than she did sometimes. He could read her mind, finish her sentences, and anticipate her questions. Without him, she felt as though her steps were misaligned, as though life was suddenly more precarious. It wasn't really fear on her part. She knew she could handle being without his physical protection. She knew she could ultimately come to her own decisions and be her own person without a husband by her side. She wasn't afraid to be a single woman in a man's world. She just felt unsteady, off balance.

Those who asked her how she was doing were likely to get a standard, "Fine," "Doing well, thank you," or "Managing as well as can be expected." Only she knew the truth buried deep in her heart. But every day that went by, the truth slipped deeper and deeper from a place of consciousness. To Hattie, the truth of her pain served no one any good. Not even her. It was easier to move away from her heart and into her head, pushing on through her daily life. Maybe one day, she reasoned, the pain would feel so distant as to be all but forgotten.

Nighttime was hardest, when there was nothing left to do but be alone with her thoughts. At first, she cried every night as silently as possible so as not to upset the children if they heard her. To cry seemed the only way to purge the pain enough to fall into a fitful slumber. Eventually, the tears stopped, and she was left with just the fitful slumber.

Some months later, her sleep came more naturally. And somewhere in the midst of all those nights with all those thoughts tumbling in her mind, she realized that the safety she had sought from Loring at the beginning of their relationship had been about needing him to define her existence, a safe place to reside in the world as his wife. Now that she no longer had him at her side, she was beginning to realize that she knew who she was aside from being Mrs. Evans. She saw she was much stronger than she had known, now that Loring's presence wasn't there to cast a shadow on her. It wasn't that she was grateful his shadow was gone, but that, even without it, she was a whole person. She cast her own shadow.

As important as all these thoughts were to parent their children effectively, Christmas was fast approaching, and Hattie had practical matters to attend to. She wanted to make this Christmas as meaningful and normal as it ever had been. She planned her meal with her usual careful consideration, only navigating around Loring's favorite pie and substituting another. She brought the outdoors in for decorations, letting the fresh scent of evergreen carry her into the woods each time she took a breath. The men took Mildred and Gordon to cut a tree and they all put it up. Hattie managed all of that very well. What was more difficult was bracing herself for the first time the children would ask her to play Christmas songs at the piano. The instrument itself reminded her of Loring so much that she all but ignored it. When Mildred asked her to play Christmas songs the day they decorated the tree, she didn't have the heart to say no. At the same time, moving to the seat she'd been led to blindfolded on her fortieth birthday felt like trying to walk through molasses.

But as soon as she began to play, the children sang along and danced, and a wondrous thing happened. Invisible to anyone else, Hattie realized that a happiness she'd tucked away suddenly made its presence known to her. It wasn't that she would never again mourn her loss. It was just that on top of the pain was a joy she could exist on, a joy that could lighten her steps, a joy that was hers whenever she chose to call upon it. That joy was her children. No...*their* children. She could raise their children for Loring's sake as well as her own. She could live from moment to moment, reveling in being with their children, hers and Loring's. Everything else could be taken away, but as long as she had Gordon, Mildred, Raymond, and Enola, she knew she would be just fine.

And something else became clear, ironically, while she played "It Came Upon a Midnight Clear." A tear stole its way down her cheek as she played the familiar Christmas carol. She took the words in as if she were hearing them for the first time. Was God speaking specifically to her? She played the final verse more slowly, more deliberately. The words "Oh, rest beside the weary road, and hear the angels sing!" may as well have read, "Oh, rest beside the weary track," because it was suddenly obvious, with exquisite clarity, that she and the children needed to stay right here in this house on the side of Mount Willard, where happiness had been born four miraculous times.

Twenty-seven

~ 1916 ~
Stutz Curve

It was 1916, two and a half years since Loring died, and the household hummed with regular work and growing children. John hadn't said as much to Hattie, but he had been grateful she had chosen to stay on. He hadn't even been completely sure why at the time, but at least that much hadn't changed when so many other things had, in so short a time.

He sat by the small lake with puffy white clouds parading a host of shapes across the sky, baiting his hook, keeping one eye on Gordon, who was patiently awaiting a nibble. Not far from the pond, Raymond played with Laddie. *Those two are both pups*, John thought, smiling as they tumbled over one another. The gift of a dog had been something John was especially proud of. Just a few months ago, John decided it had been long enough without a dog in the house. Apparently, the family had agreed because when he presented the little ball of brown and white fluff on Christmas Day, it appeared to be love at first sight for all of them. Even for Hattie, whom he hadn't told. He'd wanted to surprise her, too, and when she appeared to be pleased with the pup, he'd breathed an inner sigh of relief. The cocker spaniel mix puppy needed a name, and it was Raymond who said, "He's a little boy. Let's call him Little Laddie." So, Laddie it was.

Meanwhile, far enough away from the ruckus Raymond and Laddie were making, Mildred and Enola painstakingly picked wild clover, daisies, and dandelions close to the ground so as to have long enough stems with which to braid crowns. They proudly said they were making one for their mum, too. John could only hope the crown meant for Hattie would look somewhat like it was worthy of wearing by the time they got back. It was a fine Sunday in late May. Perfect, actually. John had hoped Hattie would come with them, too, but she was busy helping with a suffrage rally up in Littleton.

John had to admire Hattie. She had had a rough time after Loring died, but seemed rejuvenated when she'd made her decision to stay in the Notch. Her resolve was ironclad, and she never looked back, as far as he knew. She'd told John she welcomed him filling in for Loring with regard to the children. In the beginning, he was tentative about doing things for them for fear that he might be taking over too much. But by now, everyone seemed comfortable with him doing things for and with them, especially outdoor things. He actually liked being a big brother or father figure to them, whichever one they saw him as. They were great children.

He threw his baited line into the water, hoping for some nice-sized bass, perch, or pickerel that they could take back to Hattie. He hoped Gordon would be successful, too. He knew the boy would feel proud to contribute. Loring had started calling Gordon the section's mascot when he was about four years old. Gordon had had no idea at the time what a mascot was, but he knew it was a good thing and he wore the title with pride. Now, at nine, John could see the young man emerging in Gordon's sense of responsibility. In fact, often John tried to veer Gordon away from taking on more than a child his age should.

It was easy to see that Gordon missed his father greatly, and it seemed to John, although he was no psychologist, that Gordon was trying to step into his father's shoes. Gordon helped Hattie with heavier housework when he could, even beyond what she expected of him. He read to the younger children before bed and sometimes helped them with homework. None of this was particularly troublesome and was actually a great help to his mother. It was when Gordon asked to do certain jobs on the tracks that John had had to be cautious. If a job was too much for Gordon, John would tell him that one of these days Gordon would be old enough to work for the railroad. John wasn't sure how much consolation that was to Gordon, but the boy didn't argue. Today, John suspected that Gordon would love to tell his mother he'd brought home supper.

He'd decided to take the children to Bridgton, Maine, in the Model T Ford he had purchased last year. The children were always up for a ride in his automobile. They'd left early and it had only taken them two and a half hours to get to Woods Pond, a nice little sheltered body of water he'd found years ago. He might have argued that the fishing was just as good in Saco Lake, and that it was that much closer to home, but even he preferred a nice long drive over a shorter walk. There was just something about the wind in a man's hair with the world flying by that calmed the man and freed his soul.

He'd especially needed to get away from work lately. After Loring died, he had willingly moved into the foreman position. Denny had taken over as chief track assistant, second in command. They'd both worked long enough with Loring to manage the switch of positions well. Ed was content to continue as section man. Francis was coming along well, learning the job. It was Matthew who had made things difficult. He just didn't seem to want to be there. He was tense as a wound-up spring most of the time and the homemade brew they all had now and then only made him worse. There was tension everywhere Matthew was. It got so John was afraid to ask anything of the man. Correcting Matthew nearly gave John a stomachache leading up to having to confront him. John usually put it off until he simply had no more time to do it. One time Matthew looked ready to punch John, if it hadn't been that one of the children had come out of the house right then.

John talked to Hattie about the situation. She, too, had felt tense around Matthew, but she'd had no reason to confront him, for which she was grateful. She began telling John that he needed to deal with the situation definitively or it was going to eat a hole in his stomach from stewing so. Besides, she'd said, who knew when the man might take out his feelings on one of the children. He knew Hattie was right and if he'd thought Matthew was an immediate threat to her or the children, he'd have dealt with things right then and there. But Matthew had just enough good moments to make John think the situation would smooth out eventually.

Then Matthew crossed a line. He was on night duty, a responsibility that none of the crew particularly loved. But each of them had to take their turn patrolling the tracks for problems before the scheduled eastbound, night freight came through. If a section man took his job seriously, he would never slack on any of the assignments, let alone leave tracks riddled with debris in the middle of the night when sight was the worst for the engineers. Matthew had apparently taken the three-wheeler to inspect the track before the eastbound freight was scheduled to come through. Noticing that the gateway semaphore arm was down, he knew that the tracks ahead were clear. He finished inspecting the section, exactly as he should have done.

Then he rendezvoused with one of the girls working at Crawfords whom he'd met several weeks before. He had arranged to meet her that night, which was out of line. What he hadn't counted on was the short, intense thunderstorm that came up out of nowhere. In fact, he was so distracted with his date, he had barely noticed the storm and never rechecked the tracks. Unfortunately, lightning had dislodged a boulder from the mountain, which came to rest on the tracks between the house and the gateway. When the headlight of an unscheduled westbound freight rested on the rock, the engineer quickly applied full brakes. The awful screech of sliding metal wheels on steel rails and the thud of the engine striking the rock woke everyone in the house. John and the other men grabbed their pants and ran. After the rock was cleared and it was determined that neither the tracks nor the engine had suffered any damage, the train headed west once more.

John waited for the train to pass and then stormed toward the gateway expecting to see Matthew and the three-wheeler. Finding neither, he continued toward Crawfords until he finally found Matthew otherwise engaged with the young woman. Normally mild-mannered John was furious, and Matthew knew it. The section man was gone the next day of his own accord before John could fire him.

Matthew's replacement was a man by the name of Henry Hopper. Henry seemed a good enough chap. He had a good outlook on life, even if he was a bit young. John asked Ed to take him under his wing to show him the ropes, which Ed was happy to do. In fact, Ed was more than happy to pull out one of the oldest gags in the world for new track workers. The very first day, he told Henry to go to the carhouse and fetch some red kerosene for the lanterns. Denny and Francis knew Ed was going to pull that trick and feigned working close by to watch the fun. Henry spent a long time looking diligently for that red kerosene, in vain of course, while Denny and Francis had to turn their backs to keep from snickering. When poor Henry came to Ed, chagrined at not having been able to complete his first assignment on the job, Ed, Denny, and Francis doubled over, holding their sides, heaving in laughter. Then Ed picked up the lantern to show Henry the red-glassed sides, no red kerosene needed. Henry may not have passed the red kerosene test, but he did pass a much more important one in John's mind. Henry took the ribbing in his stride and laughed at himself off and on that day right along with the rest of the crew.

Being a foreman had its privileges, but it also came with responsibilities to do the jobs no one else wanted. And while John was willing to keep the position, a day off was necessary for body and soul.

"Look, John! Look what I caught!" Gordon yelled, running to John, his pail sloshing. He set the pail down beside John.

"Well, look at that! Ya got yourself a real nice perch. Good for you. You going to keep on fishing?"

"Maybe for a little while longer, if that's all right."

"Sure is. We probably want to eat soon, though. So, just a little while."

"Whoopee!" Gordon shouted and ran back to his lucky spot. His enthusiasm made John smile.

By now, Raymond had gone in swimming with Laddie, although John wondered how cold the pond was. Too cold for him, he knew. But a nearly-seven-year-old boy with energy like Raymond's could handle it, at least for a time. And the girls were still braiding. As John sat watching the four children, he counted himself fortunate to be trusted by Hattie. He wanted to do nothing to forfeit that trust.

Sudden splashing caused John to look to his left and Gordon to holler, "Hey! You're scarin' all my fish!" Raymond and Laddie were having the best time. While John empathized with Gordon, it was hard to be upset with a boy and his dog. The dog was yipping to Raymond's squeals and laughter. Raymond had been a tender four years old when Loring died. John wasn't sure how much the boy understood about all that, but it was clear he felt his mother's pain. In fact, it seemed almost instinctual in Raymond to know when his mother needed him. John had watched him go to his mum to give her a hug at precisely the right time. Hattie and Raymond shared an intense love of nature, too. Not that the other children didn't love a hike or being outside, but there was just something about Raymond that needed nature as much as nurture.

John laid a blanket on the ground and gathered the black dinner pails from his auto. He glanced at the girls trying on their flower crowns and skipping in wide circles to the music they hummed. Mildred was a second mother to Enola, who looked up to her big sister and imitated her often. It was Oscar Wilde, John knew, who said, "Imitation is the sincerest form of flattery." Mildred was the sort to love being imitated, mostly because she considered Enola a good student of her superb tutelage. The grief over losing their father was not as apparent in the girls, although they were more apt than the boys to ask John questions about Loring. He did his best to answer them, often wondering if the question they asked was only the tip of the iceberg of something much deeper. But if it was, he hoped Hattie would help them through their issues.

"Come and get it!" John yelled. Raymond and Laddie reached John first. John threw a towel at Raymond to dry off while Laddie shook water all over everything within five feet around him. The girls ran over and plopped onto the now-damp blanket with squeals of, "Ewww, Laddie!" Gordon wrestled with another fish and won the battle as he took another perch off his hook and threw it in the bucket with the others. He'd had a fine day fishing.

They all opened their pails to bean sandwiches and some of the pickles Hattie had put up early last fall. They ate and chatted, mostly the children with one another. John loved listening to their young minds sort out what they thought about their lives. The current subject had turned to school.

"Just wait till you're in third year, Mildred. Then you'll see. The arithmetic is a lot harder in third year than in second," Gordon said, boasting a bit. Then, seeing Mildred's face and the anxiety that had arisen there, he said, "But I'll help ya through it."

"Will ya help me through it, too?" Raymond asked with wide eyes, undoubtedly a little fearful of going to school for the first time in the fall.

"Oh, you won't need help, Raymond. It's easy in first year." Raymond was glad to hear the confidence in Gordon's words but didn't look altogether convinced.

"Don't worry, Raymond. I will help you with anything you need," said Mildred snootily, sticking out her tongue at Gordon, which he reciprocated.

"Well," Enola straightened up tall and proudly said, "I get to be with mum all alone while you're all gone to school!"

Gordon laughed, "All alone, eh, Nola? Well, that just fits you, doesn't it?" Enola nodded vigorously, understanding her brother's inference to the origin of her name, a distinction she took seriously.

"I have a surprise for you when we're all done here," John said, rescuing a potential sibling quarrel. He didn't see this often among them, although, admittedly, he was often off working. Still, the four of them were as apt to laugh together as fight. Typical, he assumed from things others had said about their families. He'd heard Loring talk about his big family and the capers they got into as well as the fierce way they each took care of one another. But John was an only child, so he didn't know from experience. Perhaps that was why he enjoyed being with the Evans children so much.

"And is the surprise for me, too?" Enola said, speaking from the reality that often something the others could do, she was still too young for.

"Yes, even you," John said grabbing Enola and making her giggle with delight at being singled out.

"What is it?" she asked.

"It wouldn't be a surprise if I told ya," John said, tickling Enola in the ribs before letting her go.

John didn't rush them through dinner. The longer it took, the drier Laddie would be in the Ford. Finally, when it was nearing midafternoon, everyone piled into the automobile surrounded by their gear, Gordon up front with John. "Gosh, you all probably don't even want the surprise anymore. We may's well head home now," John teased, heading toward the center of town. Cries of, "Yes, we *do!*" erupted as John smiled, enjoying himself.

One more bend in the road, the tight, ninety-degree turn just east of Bridgton, would bring them close to John's surprise destination. Just as he started the turn, a bright yellow Stutz Bearcat came roaring around the corner. In the nick of time, John swerved hard right to avoid the sporty car driven by a young man with a young woman as his passenger. John instinctively threw his right arm over Gordon's chest as if to save him from flying out the window, though he needn't have because the boy was nearly thrown onto John's lap instead.

"Wow!" Gordon cried. "That was close!"

"Yeah," John said, under his breath, pulling over to check on the children in the back seat. "Too close."

Everyone, including Laddie, seemed fine, if wide-eyed from shock. "Everyone all right back there?" John asked.

The three younger children all answered affirmatively. Laddie just panted, seemingly none the worse for the excitement. "Automobiles are dang'rous," Enola said plaintively.

"They sure can be," John said, "especially in the hands of a youngster who ought to know better." He looked back to see if the Stutz had pulled over to make sure everyone in John's car was all right. It hadn't. *Tsk!* John thought, *probably from a rich family and thinks he's beyond responsibility.* "Let this near miss be a lesson to you, boys. You'll be driving soon enough."

"I wanna drive, too," Mildred said.

"Me, too!" the five-year-old echoed her sister.

"Well, I guess you girls can if that's what you wanna do, but your mum may have to rob a bank to get cars for all of ya!" John laughed.

When Enola looked horrified, Mildred quickly explained what John had meant.

"You didn't actually think mum would go rob a bank, did ya, Nola? Now, *that'd* be somethin' to see!"

"Shush, Raymond!" Mildred mothered, protective of Enola.

"Okay, okay. But what about that surprise, John?" Raymond said.

"Let's go do it!" John said, still a bit shaky knowing how differently this day might have turned out. He tried to put the incident out of his mind and pulled back onto the road. He soon stopped in front of a small drugstore. "Here we are! Everybody out!"

Even Laddie exited the automobile and John tied the dog to the door handle with the short rope he'd brought. Laddie did not appreciate having to stay outside while everyone went into the store. Inside, John led them all to a counter near the door and told them to sit on the stools. Then he ordered five ice cream cones. One by one, the boy behind the counter handed each child a light-brown cone for them to hold. On top was a beautiful ball of bright white ice cream with a shiny red cherry to delight the eyes as well as the taste buds. Since the children had never had ice cream before, John had to tell them to lick it quickly before it dripped right down over their hands and onto the counter. He fervently wished he had Loring's camera right then. A row of children delightedly licking the sweet confections, with sounds of pleasure wafting from their throats, was a sight he would have a hard time explaining to their mother. But he knew the children would enjoy filling her in when they got back.

All the way up the Notch, talk from the children swung from ice cream to the Stutz and robbing banks. It was hard to tell which had had the bigger impact, frankly, but John didn't care because the day had been wonderful. Before it was over, after telling and retelling their stories, someone began calling the bend in the road at Bridgton "Stutz Curve." And it stuck.

Twenty-eight

~ 1917 - 1918 ~
Time Marches On

John had yet another test of his ability to lead a crew when the United States declared war on Germany. Francis King felt the call of duty and left the crew to fight in a war that threatened the whole world. It was rare to find someone not affected in some way by this cataclysm. John missed the respectful, steady work Francis gave him, the more so when Matthew McDunn begrudgingly filled in. There hadn't been a large pool of workers to draw from and Matthew could be spared from another section. If it had been up to John alone, he might have argued that the four men in his section could do the work of five rather than bring Matthew on again.

However, as providence would have it, there was another presence in the Notch at the same time. A man named Private L. Dudley Leavitt had been assigned to Section 129. The army hadn't wanted to take any risks in the Germans attacking the bridge, cutting off an important trade route for New England. For six weeks the young private patrolled the bridge alongside the crew as they worked. His presence, young though it was, commanded an extra respect that Matthew looked up to. Matthew was not as hard to handle after the private left, for which John was very grateful. He didn't think he and Matthew would ever be good friends, but working sufficiently well together was good enough. Hattie had gladly welcomed the private into her home for food and visits. He was a pleasant young man and Hattie was sorry to see him leave. On some level, she had felt she might be the mother the young man had left behind, a service to her country in her own small way.

In fact, Hattie learned of the need for balls of yarn to help the cause. She and her girls spent hours rolling yarn to be used for war victim's sweaters. It wasn't much, but Hattie felt that everyone should try to do something. She continued helping at suffrage rallies and going to their meetings, as well as serving on the school board. It gave her great satisfaction to help make decisions on behalf of all the women and children in the Notch.

It especially helped to have the telephone line that connected those on the tracks between Bartlett and Crawford Station. The line had taken some getting used to, hearing a specific ring rather than a set of clicks. But in the end, the telephone had made her work much easier. It was a thrill to be able to call down to Bartlett to place her weekly shopping orders and a relief not to bother the engineers and make them stop, although they never complained. When she learned how easy it was to convey the specifics of an order, for instance the precise hue of gingham or thread she wanted, she began placing smaller orders more frequently and having the shop owner put it on her tab. *You'd have loved the telephone, Loring. The way you liked to talk, I would have had to make an appointment to use it!* Hattie mused with a smile on her face.

"Here you go," Hattie said, handing Enola her dinner pail. It was 1918, Enola's second year of school. The leaden November skies and threat of snow didn't dampen Enola's enthusiasm to be going back to school after the weekend. Hattie was so happy that her youngest enjoyed school so much. As they waited for the train, Hattie looked at her children all lined up. The year after Loring died, she and John had determined that a space of forty feet between Gordon and Mildred was just about the right distance for the conductor to comfortably help each child up into the moving train. She was grateful to have learned years ago that it was easier for the conductor to take Gordon's outstretched hand than for her to lift him. Everyone was much happier with that arrangement. She'd put Gordon nearest the bridge to be picked up first so he could help Mildred with the process. When it was Raymond's turn to go to school, she'd simply added a new mark where he was to stand, forty feet from Mildred.

On her first day last year, Enola had been filled with excitement and nervous anticipation. "May I go to my spot now, mum?" Enola had asked well in advance of the train's arrival.

"Not quite yet. Soon." Hattie hadn't been ready to let the five-year-old fidget outside all by herself, waiting for the westbounder. Forty feet between her and Raymond was a considerable distance for him to help her out if Enola was doing something she shouldn't. He probably would go to her if that happened, but if he left his spot when the train came, the conductor might not be able to snatch both children. No, Hattie had stood with Enola until she was sure her youngest could manage by herself. After Hattie had first assigned a spot for Enola weeks early at the girl's insistence, Enola had practiced walking to the spot every day and standing on it in preparation for her big event. She had it in her head that being the farthest from the house was best because it meant she was entrusted to be farther from mum. When that first day came, Hattie had said to Enola, "You listen for the train and when you hear it, you come and tell me so we can all go outside." It wasn't that Hattie wouldn't hear the train approaching, but she knew that Enola had needed to feel grown up.

Hattie had been busy in the kitchen when she heard the train. Seconds later, Enola burst into the room saying, "Mum! Mum! Mum! It's comin'! It's comin'! Come on, mum, let's go outside!" Hattie's heart had all but burst with love for her youngest as she took Enola's outstretched hand in hers.

Once out the door, Enola had dropped her mother's hand and had run to her spot. When Hattie had walked up to Enola, who was standing feet together as if at attention, eyeing the train intensely, Enola had said, "I don't need your help, mum.

I know what to do." Hattie had thought, *No wonder. Enola's watched this procedure for several years.* So, Hattie had stood just far enough from Enola to make the youngster feel the independence she wanted. She'd watched as Theo Hanover, a new conductor, grabbed Gordon, then Mildred and Raymond. Enola had struggled to contain herself, but Theo had reached a hand down and pulled her aboard successfully, with Raymond ready to take her pail. When Hattie had heard Mildred and Raymond clap for their little sister, her eyes had welled up. Enola's happy little smile had beamed a mile wide even as the train was almost lost in the distance. Hattie had watched them all wave vigorously as they traveled toward Crawford Station where they would pick up Peter and Martha Jackson next. Hattie's eyes had overflowed as she watched them go. *This is just the beginning,* she thought.

Enola's excitement this day was only slightly less than it had been on that first day of school the previous year. She smoothed her skirt like a little lady and asked her mother how she looked. Hattie said, "Good enough to eat!" Then she bent down to kiss her youngest on the cheek. Enola gave her mother a winning smile. This year would be Gordon's last year of elementary school. Next year he would begin middle school in Twin Mountain. Hard as that was for Hattie to believe, it was harder to believe that Loring had been gone almost five years. She thought about him every time she made sure the children were in the right spots to be picked up by the westbounder. And today was one of those days, since Bemis was closed until a new teacher could be found.

Stepping down from the porch, Hattie paused with her hands on her hips, looking first one direction at Gordon and then the other, at the rest of the children all spaced out. Her pride was enormous. *Look at our children, Loring,* she said silently. *Aren't they growing up fine? I wish you were standing here beside me to watch them all get on the train today. I've finally learned to trust the trains with our children. I am managing. I'll never say it's been easy, though. Missing you has consumed much of my thoughts and energy, some days more than others.*

"Hey, Nola! You got your penny to buy candy from Charlie?" Raymond called out, referring to the boy who apparently sold candy on the train certain days.

"Yes!" Enola called back. "It's in my dinner pail!"

When the children were all on the train, Hattie waved and turned back to the house.

It had been easier to cope with her life when she and the children were contentedly busy. Mildred still found any opportunity to play school. Sometimes she and Enola took their dolls, Norah and Marguerite, to the blacksmith's shop to conduct school where there were no distractions other than the occasional train or a brother wanting to scare his sisters and their "students." Their friends, Alice and Dot Monahan and Martha Jackson, often attended Mildred's school as well.

Meanwhile, Gordon was growing in stature and maturity. This past summer, when he was just a few months past ten, he'd begun caddying at Crawfords, earning thirty-five cents for carrying one bag for nine holes and twice that for eighteen. Sometimes he got a nickel tip, which he found quite exciting. Some of the golfers were rich and could even afford a dollar tip, which made Gordon feel positively rich himself. Occasionally, Hattie walked with him to Crawfords or sometimes back home, giving mother and son precious time to talk. Hattie might hear what her son was learning about the game of golf and, more importantly, the game of life from his perspective. Sometimes Gordon shared how some of the golfers handled their frustration on the course. Once he told his mother exactly what one golfer said after playing badly and Hattie winced at what her son had heard. She made sure he knew with absolute certainty what words were never to be repeated.

Raymond happily stepped into Gordon's shoes as track mascot when Gordon was gone. But most of his time was spent learning the fine art of hunting and trapping animals. John and Denny loved teaching Raymond because he was a quick learner and thrived on being outdoors, the more time spent the better. Even now, at the tender age of nine, he was already hunting and trapping enough to save money from the pelts.

Deer, fox, raccoon, beaver, mink, and weasel were seldom a match for the boy.

So much was happening in her home, the Notch, and the world. To offset some of the more sobering elements of world events, Hattie enjoyed entertaining friends and family who visited that summer. Now that many had automobiles to take them where they wanted to go, they used the trains less often. Because the small parking space at the bottom of the trail was the closest anyone could get to the house, a system was devised to communicate a visitor's presence. Three automobile beeps from the visitor signaled arrival during the day. Only one beep was needed at night when the family could peer out the window and see headlights below. Then someone would head down the path with a flashlight to meet the visitor.

In August, Nell's husband, Walter, had dropped Nell off to spend the week. It had been so lovely to have her there for such a nice long time. The two women talked as if their lives depended on it. No subject was off limits or untouched. Nell helped cook, do laundry, and ball yarn as if she was part of the everyday family at Mount Willard. Her son, Earl, had graduated from high school and was working on his father's farm. He was interested in the strides being made in farming and agriculture. He wanted to be on the cutting edge of all things new, Nell told Hattie with obvious pride. "Earl told Walter that the new advances in farming would bring them into the twentieth century."

"New advances? Like what, for instance?" Hattie asked.

"Milking machines, tractors, better fertilization, crop rotation. I think there's more, but I can't remember now." Then laughing, she added, "Whenever those two are busy making advances in farming, I'm only visible when they're hungry." Nell saw Hattie's forehead compress in concern, and said, with a dismissive wave, "I cooked ahead for them. They'll be just fine without me for the week."

Nell had a chance to get to know Laddie and reacquaint herself with Boomerang, who was showing his age by now. During Nell's visit, Boomerang began to act strangely, not mousing, not even drinking regularly. One day, the cat went missing and didn't return. They all searched for him, but never did find him. What saddened them all even more than his disappearance was the way he probably had died, at the hands of a predator who sensed the cat's weakened condition. "Can't be helped," Hattie said to the children, who by now could have voiced their mother's well-worn adage themselves.

At the end of a very quick week, the women heard the three beeps that told them Walter was down below in his automobile. Hattie said, "I'll walk you down the hill and help carry things." Laddie heard the word "walk" and bolted to the door.

"So," Nell said in the heartfelt way of a sister as they started down the path, "you really are doing all right?"

"If you mean without Loring, yes, I think so. We all miss him, of course, but learning to do without has its benefits, too, you know?" No, Nell didn't know. She couldn't imagine how Loring's absence could be a benefit. "I think I'm growing in ways I might not have, or at least not so rapidly, without him. You can only know what you have when you're missing what you don't have. I've had to be mother and father sometimes, although John certainly has done an amazing job with the children."

"Yes, I've noticed," Nell said, meaning more than the simple statement suggested. Hattie picked up on it.

"What aren't you saying, Nell Burnell?"

At Hattie's formal use of her name, Nell smiled, knowing Hattie intended to get a satisfactory answer, "Well, sometimes it seems like John wants more than just being a father figure."

"More? In what way?"

"Oh, Hattie, I don't mean to open something up that wasn't opened before. Never mind. Silly me."

"No, Nell, tell me what you're thinking. Please."

Nell sighed. "Do you think John wants a relationship with you as well as the children?"

"Oh, heavens no!" Hattie uttered the first thing that came to her mind. Nell let the question stand for a few moments.

It didn't take long for Hattie to be concerned that she might have missed something right under her nose. "Well, maybe you're a better judge than me, an objective viewpoint, I guess. What makes you think so?"

"Just a feeling I get when he's around you. Nothing specific. But does the man ever seek the companionship of another woman that you know of? Does he even get out of the Notch on his day off?"

Hattie thought about that while she picked her way down the last of the trail. On one hand, Hattie didn't pry into the men's business. They were her clients, not her family. She mostly knew what she knew from conversations the men had in her presence after work or at the table. On the other hand, John had stayed closer to the children than the other men did. He'd made a point to talk with them, play with them, and teach them things he thought they ought to know. And because he was close to them, he was closer to her. She'd often used him as a sounding board when she was working through something about the children. They talked together easily, and she appreciated his help. She'd always thought it was his way of respecting Loring's absence in the same way he did when he took over as foreman.

Hattie stopped just shy of being seen by Walter and turned to Nell. "You know, I don't know much about the man, actually. I think I heard him say once that he's an only child, but I don't even know if he has family somewhere that he visits or writes to. He doesn't often go places without us, now that I think of it. I guess I've been so consumed by my own life, I haven't really taken the time to notice his." She stopped talking suddenly, then gasped, "Oh, Nell, if he does want more than to be a father to the children, what should I do?"

"Maybe nothing. At least not unless he should make his desires more obvious. I'm sorry I mentioned it, Hattie. Really, I am. I just figured you felt it, too. Forget I said anything."

Though Hattie said it was forgotten, she did so for Nell's sake. She knew Nell would never have said something that would make Hattie's life harder. That was just Nell being Nell—quick thinking and even quicker to speak. But the truth was that Hattie couldn't unthink the thoughts Nell's words had placed in her mind.

"We'd best get to Walter. He'll be wanting to get on home," Nell said.

"Yes, yes, of course," Hattie said quickly, turning back to what was left of the trail.

When they reached the automobile, the women hugged warmly, thanking each other for the blessings each had bestowed during the week. Hattie watched and waved at them until she couldn't see them anymore, then headed back up the mountain. She was so grateful for the boards Loring had attached at strategic intervals along the path. They truly made all the difference.

As Hattie climbed, her mind swirled with Nell's question. *Did* John want something more from her? How could she address something like that? Deep in thought, she was suddenly jolted by Laddie's low growl. "What is it, boy?" She stopped to look around her. Suddenly she sensed it, too. The presence. The presence that had been haunting her for years, ever since she came to the mountain. But she saw nothing, and Laddie had stayed by her side. "It's okay, Laddie," she said, giving him a scratch beneath his white muzzle while she looked into his eyes. "Let's just keep going. We aren't very far from the house." But now, not only was she having trouble letting go of Nell's question, she also couldn't shake the unmistakable presence she felt on that path yet again.

At the house, she busied herself starting supper, taking into account where the children were. Gordon was at Crawfords. Raymond was out…somewhere…doing…something in nature, she couldn't be sure exactly what. The girls were playing down at the Monahans'. John came into the kitchen, heading for the doughnut crock. *That man is skinny as a beanpole. I think he could eat a dozen doughnuts and all that would show is his hand on his aching belly*, she thought. Then Nell's question surfaced. And with it The Presence. She may as well name whatever this was. She'd certainly been sensing it long enough. "I felt The Presence again just now, climbing up the hill," Hattie said, suddenly glad she had something to say that wasn't about John's personal life. He'd heard her talk about The Presence before.

"Oh?" he said. "Was Laddie with you?"

"He was. He's the one who alerted me. He growled low and quiet, as though his warning was meant to alert only me, not The Presence. But then he didn't move away from me. He didn't go after anything. And when I looked around, I couldn't see anything untoward, so I just let it be."

"Would you feel better if me and the men did some scoutin' down there?"

"I guess, but I feel so silly sensing something I never see. If it weren't for Laddie's validation, I'd really think I was over the edge."

"I don't mind, Hattie, and I doubt the others would, either. Not if it gives you peace of mind. Great doughnuts as usual, by the way. We'll go looking after supper. All right if the boys go, too?"

"Yes," she sighed. "Wild horses probably couldn't stop Gordon and Raymond from going anyway."

"That's fine, then. I'll be goin' back to work now. See ya at supper." And he left with a little wave.

The search was fruitless, but Hattie had other things on her mind. Would she now always scrutinize everything John said for hidden meanings? She shook her head as if to loosen thoughts that threatened to stick to the walls of her brain. Tall-comb had wandered inside when the door behind John hadn't closed properly. Hawks were especially aggravating this year, flying low as if to pick the perfect chicken before diving down to close the deal. If the chickens knew they were in danger of being a hawk's supper, she'd be surprised, addle-brained as they were. Still, Tall-comb, as Enola had named her, sought out the kitchen whenever she could. She hopped right up onto the chair beside the pantry door and waited for Hattie to feed her some bread or other scraps. Hattie had stopped always shooing her outside. Tall-comb wasn't a problem in the kitchen as long as someone was there to win any arguments over the food Hattie would rather the chicken not eat.

Hattie hadn't felt The Presence throughout autumn. She'd had other things to think about anyway. The war was bad enough, but then, two months ago, at the end of September, the schools had had to shut down for the rest of the month and all of October. The school board learned of a powerful illness doctors said was a form of influenza. After meeting with two local doctors—one of which was not Doc Shedd, God rest his soul—everyone thought it best to cease classes before the sickness spread any further. It was striking not only in the United States but the whole world as well. Those who were infected risked pneumonia and other complications. While school-age children tended not to die from the disease, their parents might, making it extremely risky to hold large group gatherings of any kind. It had been easy to make the decision to shut the schools down until things got better.

Hattie's family could easily stay close to home because that was normal anyway. *But how on earth does one fight a war and influenza at the same time?* Hattie wondered, thinking of Francis and others she knew who were fighting in Europe. Many had fallen ill, Hattie read in the newspaper. None of her own children became sick, thank goodness, but Hattie had tacked schoolteacher onto her list of duties while they couldn't attend classes. She didn't want the children to fall behind, even though most of the children in the area would have stalled their schoolwork during this time.

Then, on November 11, Hattie saw for herself proof of rumors she'd heard recently. The front page of the Boston Herald Extra said, in the biggest, boldest letters Hattie had ever seen: *GERMAN SURRENDER MOST COMPLETE EVER KNOWN – President in Address to Congress Reveals Drastic and Far-Reaching Terms to Which Defeated Adversary Has Subscribed.* And in the next box down: *Huge Crowds in Boston Wildly Celebrate Victory and Peace.* As she walked back into the house, Hattie thought, *So, it's really over. This great and terrible war is over and now, may the world find peace at last.* The children had just started back to school after the closures, or she might have hugged them all right then and there, even though they probably wouldn't share the same intensity of excitement.

The crew emerged shortly after that, all shouting an end to the war. "I wonder if Francis will return to work?" John said aloud, not noticing the expression on Matthew's face. But Hattie saw the young man's pain knowing that if Francis returned, Matthew would lose his position.

Twenty-nine

~ Flood Week ~
Thursday Morning and Afternoon,
November 3, 1927

Waking to rain never caused Hattie concern. In fact, she rather liked it, as long as it wasn't sure to cause insurmountable problems for anyone in the household. And it almost never did. Perhaps an inconvenience now and then, but nothing more than that. Today's rain didn't change the tasks she intended to accomplish, but it did change the thoughts that would accompany her as she did them.

In fact, thoughts of the rain, the possibility of flood damage, and whether or not the children could come home this weekend were not the only thoughts on her mind as she set to doing a thorough cleaning of the rooms upstairs. After supper last evening, John had sat in the parlor where she was writing letters. He was the only one of the men to do so. It seemed obvious to Hattie that he wanted to say something in private to her, but he looked uncomfortable. She put down her pen.

"Was supper all right?" she began, certain it had been, but coaxing the man to relax into conversation.

"Yes, ma'am, it was very good, thank you." Pause. *Stilted,* Hattie thought. *Not using my first name.* She waited.

"Ma'am, uh, Hattie, I just wanted you to know that I am concerned about the weather myself."

Hattie had sensed this the past couple days in all the men. "Thank you, John," she said, trying to sound truly appreciative. It wasn't that she wasn't grateful. She couldn't imagine living with more respectful men. But she badly wanted and maybe needed to talk about her own fear. Instead, she said, "It helps to know I'm not the only one feeling something troubling about this weather."

Another pause. Finally, John spoke, "Yes, and where it isn't mine to pry, I wondered if your concern is with the children. When I saw you yesterday up to Crawfords, I wondered if everything was all right where it concerns them."

Ah, Hattie thought. *This is what was behind John's need for this exchange.* "John," she began softly, "I hope you know by now that if there was something seriously wrong with the children, I would tell you and the others. No, nothing's wrong that I know of, except my anxiety about how the weather might be affecting them. I've been feeling so helpless. I'm not used to feeling anxiety like this, at least not for days at a time. In the beginning I simply thought I was being a silly old woman, but something's been nagging at me and it got the better of me yesterday. So, I decided to wire Gordon and Mildred. I wasn't sure what to say, let alone whether it was the best idea to send a telegram at all. I didn't want to scare them half to death. I knew the walk to Crawfords might be good for me, to clear my head. It usually is, you know. I also knew Elizabeth would understand my anxiety from a mother's perspective."

"Was she? Helpful, I mean," he asked.

"Yes, she was. By the time I got to her cottage, I was all set to send a wire to encourage the children to come home, despite the weather. But...I don't know...when I was with Elizabeth, something told me to say the opposite. I know they know how to use good judgment. I guess it just made me feel better to say it. My hope is that they'll wire back letting me know they'll stay put. And Elizabeth said she isn't worried about Martha coming home from Whitefield. So, I guess I'm not concerned about Raymond and Enola at this point."

That conversation with John happened last night before the rain had really taken purchase in the Notch. Now it was midafternoon, and the rain was steady and falling harder. She let Laddie in. He'd asked to go out only moments before. *He must've done what he needed to very quickly,* she thought. *Can't say's I blame him.* Hattie sighed as he shook the rain off his coat, sending water every which way, all over everything.

She wiped down what she could, including his paws, then she walked to the back windows to have a look down the Notch. The sky was dark and not just because the sun was low, although with clouds as thick as these, who could tell there was a sun up there at all? No, these clouds were very thick and menacing. Each cloud looked agitated as if it was vying for some coveted position in the sky. The rain, too, looked angry to Hattie. Some rains felt like stubborn little cloud bursts that had their say and moved on. Some were playful drizzles as if the clouds were making up their minds whether to downpour or dry up. But not this. This rain was coming steadily and significantly, and the wind was beginning to ripple the rain drops like it did her sheets on a blustery day. It was hard to make out Mount Webster as she cast her eyes further than her own mountain. Yet, the little she could see looked dreamlike through the rain and mist. Hattie had to concede that even this rain looked beautiful, hitting the rocks and trees, cascading downhill, making gullies of water seeking a low point to settle into. *Nothing on God's earth or His sky is meant to harm, yet when nature is imbalanced,* she thought, *damage can occur.* How well she understood that. *Nature got out of hand, that day, didn't it? We are no match for the strength of Mother Nature when she brings on her worst. Oh, Loring, I'm scared about this storm. I'm scared the children will get hurt or perish. I know all too well what that feels like and I'm not sure I can go through that again.* She realized that had she spoken these words aloud, they would have sounded like a prayer. Maybe that's exactly what they were.

She needed to boil potatoes for supper. She shook off her musings and stoked the stove, set a pot of water on top, then went to the pantry to retrieve several potatoes. As she began to peel them, she heard the men come in and head for the cellar. To dry off, she presumed. They were quitting early today, and she wondered why. Working in steady rain can't be much fun, but she knew they wouldn't quit early solely for that reason.

When the oven was hot enough, she slid a pan of sliced ham and leftover vegetables into its yawning mouth to warm, then began mixing dough for raisin cookies. She'd no more than cracked the eggs into the bowl when all the men appeared in the kitchen. John asked her if she could leave her cooking for a few moments and come to the parlor. She saw in their eyes something she couldn't read. Hattie wiped her hands on her apron and headed toward the kitchen door. The men stepped back to let her go first, and she led them to the sitting room.

In some ways that short walk felt miles long as she realized they needed to tell her something difficult. Suddenly she was past anxiety and into real fear. Did they know something about the children? Knowing he would most likely speak for them all, she said, "John," trying to speak very calmly so as not to reveal her rising alarm. Maybe even to herself. "What is it?" she asked before she'd even had a seat.

"We've heard news coming in from Vermont and it isn't good. We only know a few specific details, but so far as we know, the children are safe where they are." John wanted to be sure to tell her that much right off. "This seems to be a storm aggravated by these mountains. The Winooski Valley is flooding. Badly. Railroad tracks and bridges are being swept away in parts of Vermont. All the mountains in Vermont and these here in New Hampshire are being hammered with rain. Shipments coming from the west aren't getting through. Maine seems to be doing better from what we hear. So, Gordon probably isn't seeing rain like this. Not sure about Keene, but we think that since it's flatter there, Mildred probably isn't in danger, either. It's these mountains that are making things bad, like I say. So far as we can tell, the rails are still open to Whitefield, so Raymond and Enola are likely fine where they are, too. We thought you'd want to know."

There was a tenderness underlying the obvious concern. Hattie said nothing except, "Thank you." So many thoughts ran through her mind. The fact that her week-long anxiety had been justified paled beside the picture John had just laid out before her. She was grateful she'd wired the children not to come home. She knew John was worried for them, too. All the men were. But these were her children. Her flesh and blood. They were her reason to live, to work, to be content. And they were Loring's children, too. She couldn't let anything happen to them. She just couldn't. *But what if what happens to them is beyond my control?*

"Supper will be ready after I finish the cookies," she finally said and walked back to the kitchen.

The men had had no more critical work they needed to do that afternoon. They'd just have to keep an eye on the tracks as much as possible. They had walked together to the house, discussing the information they'd heard from their coworkers to the west. John had said that he needed to tell Hattie what they'd heard and before supper if possible. Denny had suggested they not tell her everything right now. The news was starting to sound devastating. John agreed and said he would tell her only what he thought she needed to know, but asked that they all be there. He wanted Hattie to know that they were all in this together, for better or worse, whatever was coming their way.

In the end, John wondered if they should have told her any of the information. He had not seen Hattie this rattled since Loring's death. But, of course, yes, they had to. He knew she wanted them to be upfront and honest.

Thirty

~ 1919 ~
Seems the Right Thing to Do

It was Tuesday, January 14, an anniversary everyone remembered but which the adults would rather have forgotten. Even the children, who hadn't remembered the precise day, added their own thoughts to those of the crew, sitting in the parlor after supper. They were discussing the terrible accident that had happened in the Notch exactly a year ago. Francis had heard something about it and had brought up the subject at supper.

"What actually did happen?" Francis had asked during the meal. He'd recently returned to the crew after the war. If he was glad to have missed that accident, his relief was short-lived thinking about where he was last January instead of the Notch. Somewhere deep in a trench in France, he'd been exposed to mustard gas about that time. Though this and other gases were technically illegal, the enemy saw no shame in using them. Francis knew the Allies were using gases, too, but didn't care. He just considered himself lucky to have survived. The human destruction he witnessed in that war was worse than having suffered a few bad burns on himself which eventually healed well enough. He'd lost many a friend during that horrible time. Yet, devastating as it had been, he'd never regretted serving his country. It was just that now that he was back and working, it wasn't the exposure to gas that was still difficult. It was his nerves. Much as Francis wished it were different, fear didn't quickly leave a man's body when he'd had to be vigilant for his very life, moment upon awful moment, for months at a time. He couldn't be expected to forget that the enemy could be only one step away in any direction. He couldn't just get over loud noises, as people seemed to think he could, when for months explosions meant the difference between life and death, his or the man's next to him. The fact that he jumped every time he heard a door slam or a gun shot was just an involuntary move to protect himself. Even though he was very familiar with the sound trains made when they ran over the little torpedoes full of dynamite, knowing they provided fair and necessary warning to the engineers, he still flinched every single time. He just couldn't help it. And not everyone understood that. Raymond liked to scare him by jumping out from behind the dining room door when the men came down for supper. Who could blame a child who didn't know how difficult sudden noises and movements were for him? It was just child's play. But he hoped, for everyone's sake, that given enough time, his nerves would calm down and repair themselves.

"A train raced past the house going lickety split! *That's* what happened!" Raymond answered Francis's question with obvious excitement.

"Yeah," Gordon said, "it was not long after we got home from school that day, 'cause I remember thinking our train coulda been run into if it happened any earlier."

That caught Hattie's attention, and she turned to look at Gordon, thinking of a disaster averted. Her stomach clenched at the thought of what might have been. *But it wasn't, Hattie. It was what it was,* she reminded herself. *No point in borrowing trouble.* She decided to excuse herself to the kitchen, pretending she had work to do there. That wasn't exactly a lie. She could always find something that could be done. She just needed some time to herself. She had no need to revisit that day last year.

Hattie had been the only one who had yet to enter the conversation. It wasn't that she had forgotten the accident. It wasn't even that she hadn't wanted to hear it retold, although she'd rather not. But her mind was elsewhere. So, as the others reminisced, she'd sat staring out the window, letter in hand and lost in thought. Until Gordon's comment had made her decide to leave the room.

Denny puffed on his pipe, and said, "It was sure bitter cold that day. That's what I was thinking just before the train roared through. What was it, something like thirty-five below? Not fit for man nor beast."

"The engineer blew three long whistles to warn us, too! Good thing those ol' chickens weren't on the tracks," Mildred said, brushing Enola's thick hair for the night, an act Mildred did out of pleasure and Enola let her do.

"True enough," Henry added. "Engine 374 was picking up thirty-four loads and one empty out of Crawfords. Clemons says they checked the brakes like usual and didn't find anything wrong. But then coming outta the gateway they started pickin' up speed and wasn't nothin' they could do about it."

"Did I hear right that they were clocked going half the time as usual down past Willey Station?" Francis asked.

"Worse'n that," John said. "Florence down there, she clocked that thing as takin' only four minutes from the time it passed her to when it left the rails."

"Lord! What's the company's rules about the number of minutes through there?"

"No less than twenty-four!" Gordon said, proud that he knew the answer.

"Okay, so where did it derail?" Francis asked.

"Somewhere past the Bemis curve," Denny said, between puffs. "Joe says they heard an open whistle just blastin' away and knew that whatever was comin' was out of control. All they could do was wait for the crash. The cars were all bunched up and completely filled the Nancy Brook cut there at Bemis. The engineer and fireman were crushed to death. It's a miracle the two brakemen were okay. But one of them, Clemons, he switched jobs. Guess he figured he shoulda died that day. He's a fireman now. He says firemen are usually safer than brakemen. I don't know about that, myself."

Hattie could just make out where they were in the story and tried hard not to listen. It had been bad enough when it happened, but to hear how close her children, or Florence and Joe and their children, or God only knew who else, had come to perishing was more than she was willing to hear again. It was bad enough to lose an engineer and fireman. She tuned out their conversation and took out her dumpling recipe to make sure she had what she needed for tomorrow's chicken and dumpling soup.

"But John, tell him about the cleanup," Denny said.

"Yeah!" Raymond added, "tell him about Joe's pants!"

"Well," John said, subconsciously rubbing his leg, "the crew had no choice but to go help down there. Wasn't gonna be a single train through there until it was cleaned up, ya know. So, all five of us went down there. Matthew acted like it was a circus we were goin' to."

"Wait, Matthew? He came back? Boy, you're a glutton for punishment, ain't ya, John?" Francis suddenly realized that maybe he shouldn't have spoken that way in front of the children and started to apologize.

"They know Matthew wasn't an easy fella, don't ya?" John said looking around at the children nodding. Truthfully, he wasn't sure Enola understood, but it didn't appear that she cared, either.

"It wasn't up to me, Francis. They put Matthew on when you left. There wasn't exactly an abundance o' men to choose from. Anyway, we went down there and me and Joe worked a hundred and eight hours straight."

Francis whistled to show his astonishment at having to work four and a half days without sleep, although when he got to thinking about that later, he realized he'd had to do the same at times during the war.

John chuckled then and continued, "Joe was so tired he fell asleep huddled up next to the stove 'til someone shouted, 'Joe! Your pants are on fire!' Didn't we see ol' Joe hoppin' then!"

Everyone laughed. Not because it was truly funny, but somehow, with the danger behind them, and Joe all right, it felt okay to laugh about it.

"Even after all those hours, there was a lot more to do. That just got the trains rolling again, was all," John said.

"Sounds like a right mess. Does anyone know how fast that train was going when it left the rails?" Francis asked.

"Maybe six times what it shoulda been goin'?" John answered, shrugging to indicate that no one was able to determine the exact speed. "She was an awful heavy train, though."

"Are all trains called 'she'?" Enola asked. "Aren't there any 'he' trains?"

When Hattie had heard the laughter, she knew the story was about over and that it was time for the children to go to bed. She had heard Enola as she neared the parlor. "Little one," she said, "such big questions that only eight-year-olds ought to be asking."

"But I'm almost eight, mum! Just four more days! An' then I'll get *eight* pennies for my birthday!"

"Oh, mercy me, I do believe you're right!" Hattie said. "But even nearly eight-year-olds...*and* her brothers and sister," she said with emphasis, looking at the others, "need to be in bed. Thank Mildred for brushing your hair and then scoot, all of you. I'll be up to read you a story soon, but only to those who are completely ready for bed."

"Wait! I have a riddle for everyone," Gordon blurted out, disregarding his mother's order. "What month has twenty-eight days?"

"February!" Mildred shouted.

"Yes, but that's not the right answer," Gordon said, pleased that Mildred had given the answer he hoped someone would give. Mildred scowled. She didn't believe her brother one bit.

No one spoke for a minute. Then Hattie said, "If I give you the right answer, Gordon, then no more stalling."

"All right, but what if you give me the wrong answer?"

"Then I'll let you stay a few more moments while someone else tries to guess. Deal?"

"Deal!" he said.

"All of the months have twenty-eight days, at least," Hattie said, smiling at Gordon who was both happy to have produced a good riddle and sad that mum had gotten the answer so fast.

Everyone else was either puzzled at the answer or groaned at not having gotten it sooner. But all mum had to say was, "A deal's a deal," looking straight at Gordon who got to his feet.

The other children sighed as they stood, wishing mum had gotten the answer wrong. They all started for the stairs. Then Gordon turned and said, "Oh, mum…"

"What now, Gordon?"

"I need to have you read over my paragraph before school tomorrow."

"We'll do that in the morning. If I tried to be sensible right now, I might just as well feed it to Laddie as read it. I'll be up soon."

Hattie sat down heavily on her chair. The crew had left when the children had, but John remained.

"Ma'am," he said. He was always more formal addressing Hattie when he thought the children might hear him. "Seems you have something else on your mind tonight. Is everything all right?"

Hattie was always amazed at how well that man read her body language, something she assumed she was good at hiding. She honored him with the truth. "Not really. Well, yes. Well, I don't know," she stammered. "I got a letter from my stepbrother saying his father is ailing. It sounds serious."

"Oh. I'm sorry."

"Well, it just took me by surprise, I guess. Not that my stepfather is ill—that's been the case a long time. But to get a letter from my stepbrother surprises me. We've never been close. This is the first letter I've ever received from him. I guess it makes me wonder if he wants me to come see his father, although he didn't explicitly say that. And frankly, I'd rather not."

"Is there anything I can do?" John asked, uncomfortable that Hattie was once again in obvious distress.

"There's a suffrage rally in Portland next week that I had thought I might join, but then decided not to. I'm thinking now that maybe I should go after all. I could go a day early and stop to see my stepfather. It seems the right thing to do.

Florence has already said she's going to the rally. Maybe she'd be willing to go with me the extra day. If I do that, could you see that the children get on and off the train? I'll have their clothing laid out and ready for them and cook ahead enough for everyone. I should only be gone the two days, so Mildred can help Enola, and Gordon and Raymond can help each other. Do you mind?"

"No, ma'am, not at all. I'm happy to help out."

"Thank you so much. I'll leave a week from today. Now, to read to the children. Good night, John."

"Night, ma'am." And they parted company, Hattie picking up a pair of socks that had left Raymond's feet at some point during the day and stuffed them in her pockets to add to the laundry.

When Hattie reached the children, they were snug in their beds, waiting for her. On the way up the stairs, she had decided she should let the children know about her trip to see her stepfather, although they'd never heard about him. She called them together much as she had when their father had died. They must have remembered because their eyes were wide with anticipation, if not anxiety. She quickly dispelled their fears with facts they could handle and told them she would be gone for two days the next week. Then she read another few pages in *Rebecca of Sunnybrook Farm* to them, tucked them in, turned down the wick, and left them with a heartfelt, "Good night, my sweet children."

Then, at last, she was alone to think. How did she really feel about her stepfather dying? Who had he been to her? Though she had longed for a closer relationship with her mother, Hattie couldn't say the same about her stepfather. What was there to accomplish by going to Standish? Perhaps talking things over with Florence would help. She needed to make arrangements for them both if Florence was willing to accompany her the extra day.

As she finished her bedtime routine, she also thought about John's ability to see through her, pinpointing truths she wasn't even ready to divulge to herself sometimes. John was certainly a curiosity to Hattie, several men wrapped up into one. He was persnickety as a crew leader, which wasn't a bad thing. He had been able to lead as well as Loring had. Yet, he was gentle and patient with the children, a fact Hattie was beyond grateful for. And then there was his reticence to talk about his personal life, yet his sixth sense in drawing out hers. Did he have ulterior motives for befriending her children? Surely not. She would have felt that in him, and she was quite sure the children would, too. The children had adopted John as a father figure in ways she could never have predicted. It pleased her no end to watch them warm up to John. She could only hope that his motives were genuine and that he would stay on the job until they were older. It would be hard to tolerate watching her children suffer the pain of another father leaving them, no matter the reason. Life lessons along the way were one thing but seeing them hurt by a surrogate father would be unacceptable after they'd lost their own. *Oh, how life repeats itself*, she thought, closing her eyes and her mind.

Thirty-one

~ 1919 - 1920 ~
Winter Days

If Hattie had hoped the rest of her life would be without
incident, she would have been disappointed. But she was
a practical and sensible woman and she tried, at least, to
take life as it came to her. She'd returned home from the rally
in Portland more tired than she realized she could be. Going
to her childhood home had taken a lot out of her, and she was
very grateful that Florence had accompanied her there. Hattie
had found her stepfather to be a sick, old man who refused
help. She could tell that it hadn't been her stepfather who had
asked his son to write a letter. The flimsy relationships she'd
had with them when she was growing up were all but severed
now. If her stepfather wanted to preserve what little affection—
if one could call it that—there was between them, he didn't
give any indication of it. And if her stepbrother wanted her
help, he didn't say so. She was left to wonder exactly why he'd
written and why she was even there. But she did feel sorry for
both of them. They seemed to be two unhappy, hollow men.

She and Florence had talked far too late that night, lying
in Hattie's old room. Hattie told Florence details about her
childhood that Florence hadn't known, but talking about
it, particularly in that room, had been cathartic for Hattie.
Florence was grateful to be able to listen. Hattie had been
able to give her stepfather a hug before she left. She was fairly
certain she wouldn't see the man again and, as it turned out,
she didn't. He died not long after their visit. That was a door
in her life she could close for good.

For all the difficulty of her visit back home, she'd thoroughly enjoyed the rally. They heard speakers whose battle cries insisted that women understand that the right to vote would make them better wives and mothers. "Voting women would bring their moral superiority and domestic expertise to issues of public concern," one presenter had said. They also heard what the anti-suffragists had to say—that women would eventually be transformed into a masculine gender if they were allowed to vote. A gender inversion, some said. Neither Hattie nor Florence could imagine a gender inversion. They just couldn't see a negative side to women gaining the right to vote. One woman spoke for Susan B. Anthony and Elizabeth Cady Stanton when she quoted the women as saying, "Men their rights and nothing more; women their rights and nothing less." Just before Hattie and Florence needed to leave to catch the train home, they heard that there was to be a rally in Boston in February. The issue was heating up and coming to a head. The women had much to think and talk about on their way back to the Notch.

Hattie had never been more grateful to walk through the front door of her Mount Willard home. The children had all come running to hug her. That was the best medicine she could have had. That night she went to bed tired but with peace in her heart.

The following winter days were quiet ones, thankfully. New snow had fallen, and John had taken the children skiing down a path he and the men had made, beginning above the house and ending at the tracks. All bundled up with scarves, hats, and mittens, running and playing hard, they barely noticed the cold. Even the girls with only thick wool stockings under their jumpers were warm enough to stay out just past dark, having the time of their lives. They'd come into the house looking like a family of snowmen. Their winter clothes were put over the radiators to dry and a hot meal of baked beans and brown bread filled their stomachs. And as she watched, Hattie's heart was filled with joy.

One day in early February, a gorgeous blue-sky day when the sun made the temperature tolerable, Hattie sat with her hand out the kitchen window, palm up, loaded with feed for the chickadees she knew would come. She was thinking about her birthday coming up. She'd be forty-seven already. Her children were growing up faster than she liked to admit. Gordon would be off to middle school in the fall and the others really weren't far behind. She thought about the rallies she cared about and the school board meetings coming up, and all the different things her children were either doing or wanting to do. Life was going by more quickly these days it seemed. She wasn't the only one with a full schedule anymore.

A chickadee landed on her hand and pecked at the seed, lightly tickling her palm. She watched the small gray and white bird with its matching black cap and chin. *How free you are,* she thought, *so unencumbered, so beautiful. What is it like to fly, little bird, untethered, seeing sights I'll never see? What is it like to be so unburdened by anything but what keeps you alive? Is that why you fly? Because nothing ties you down?* She hummed quietly to herself, entranced by the tiny creature so perfectly made. Then suddenly she stopped humming and just like that, she'd made a decision to lighten her load. She will have been on the school board eight years come fall. There had been a number of new members lately who could well decide the fate of her children's last elementary years in Hart's Location. It was time to step down as soon as her year was over. Already she felt lighter. *Thank you, little bird. You have helped me more than you know.*

The blue sky began to fill in with clouds. Snow clouds. Then very quickly, the blue was gone. They'd get another storm overnight, Hattie thought as she closed the window and resumed her work, feeling the happiness of a decision made. The next morning, the snow was piled high. Hattie knew the children would have to wait until the snowplow came through to clear the tracks before they could take the train. Their teachers knew that the Evans children were dependent on trains to get to school on time and allowed for it. The children had eaten breakfast and were lined up in the parlor windows on their knees looking at the white wall of snow before them. They knew their wait would be rewarded by the snowplow that would come barreling up the tracks with a roar like a metal beast against nature. It would likely be Bobby Morse driving because he knew how to drive an engine hard and fast, and that's exactly what these tracks would need if other trains were to come through.

From a distance they all heard it—a low rumble almost like the thunder that bounced around the Notch in the summer. Hattie could hear the children peppering the air with their chatter, indistinct to her from the kitchen. The rumble quickly turned into a roar, which meant the plow was very close. As the wedge forced a deep groove through the snow, a white wall of ice and debris was hurled indiscriminately at the house. The sound of rocks hitting the grates over the windows was loud but didn't last long. It created a sort of game for the children to see who could stay near the window the longest. The natural reaction was to duck or run from such an intense spray coming straight at them, but the grating always held, and the windows stayed intact. Whoever stayed near the windows the longest won whatever prize they had all decided upon. The snowplow passed and one of the boys was cheering.

Just as the children broke into the kitchen to give Hattie the results of their game, they all heard a terrible sound come from just past the house. The children quickly climbed up the back stairs to look out the rainbow window. Gordon ran back down to Hattie as she walked to the back door. "Mum! The wedge is completely off the tracks!"

Hattie stepped out of the door to have a look, and her hands flew up to her cheeks. "Oh, dear me!" she exclaimed. "Oh, I hope no one has gotten hurt. Dear, dear me!"

She saw someone climb out of the engine. The children saw him, too. They all tumbled into the kitchen, shouting over each other, "It's Bobby Morse!"

Oh, thank goodness he's all right, Hattie thought.

"Can I go see what happened, mum? Can I?" Gordon said.

"Yeah, me, too! Me, too!" the others echoed.

"Absolutely not," Hattie said. "That wedge may not be settled in place yet and Bobby needs to assess the damage for himself without your help. Now go find something to do until we know if your train can get through. Scat!" she said lovingly. Three of them headed for the parlor, but when Gordon wasn't one of them, they turned around and found him up the back stairs again. That's where the best view was.

Hattie kept busy in the kitchen doing things that could wait, but she, too, was curious and concerned about the state of things outside. And to make sure none of the children tried to sneak out, she wanted to stay close by.

"Mum! Bobby's backing up!" Gordon shouted.

The engine stopped at the house and Bobby jumped down. Hattie opened the door for him. "Well," Bobby said with a sigh. "This is a sorry state of affairs, I guess."

"But you're all right, thank goodness," Hattie returned.

"Yes, I guess that is a good thing. But the company isn't going to like this mess. I hit a patch of ice just past your house and since I was pushing the plow hard, it derailed, and the coupling came loose. That plow plunged right off the rails and into the snowbank! At least the rails are clear. So, I'm going to go on up to Crawfords to make a report. Not sure what time or even if the children's usual train will come through, though. They'll have to get the wrecker up here to pull the wedge back on the tracks. That'll be something to see!"

"Could someone call to let me know what the amended train schedule will be today?" Hattie asked.

"I'll see what I can do," Bobby said.

"Thanks, Bobby," Hattie said as the man tipped his hat and turned to go back to the engine. Hattie felt for Bobby. He did push his engines hard, which had its place, but sometimes, like now, it could get him into trouble.

The whole thing created an air of excitement for the children, who had never seen anything like this happen. And to think they could see it right from home. They clearly hoped they couldn't go to school so they could stay and watch the wrecker.

"All right, children, we'll just have to wait to see if your train comes. Best get busy doing something or it's going to be a long day. And don't ask to go out to the wedge. I won't let you. You know where the switch is. Don't make me use it."

Four pairs of eyes looked across the kitchen to the pine bough switch resting in wait beside the stove. She'd not had to use it often, thank goodness, but they knew she meant business when they heard that tone of voice, let alone when she mentioned the dreaded switch. They scampered out of the kitchen and busied themselves as they'd been told to.

About then the crew came in, their workday having changed with the derailed wedge. The children heard them and ran back into the kitchen, hoping for exciting news.

"Bobby's pulled away now and we're waiting for the wrecker. In the meantime," John said, looking at Hattie, "can the children come out to look at the plow up close?" John suddenly noticed a resolute look on Hattie's face, and knew he'd have to convince her to let them go. He added, "I'll be right there with them. I won't let them get into any trouble."

Like a cat watching a swinging ball, the children had looked first to John while he spoke and then to their mother, expectantly. They knew enough not to beg and waited for her to speak.

After a few moments she finally said with a sigh, "Oh, all right."

The children all whooped and scrambled to get their winter coats. "But mind John!" Hattie said, knowing both that they hadn't really heard her and that they would mind him regardless.

A call told Hattie the children would get their day off school and that they'd have a ring-side view of the wrecker when it came, which provided them all with a first-hand demonstration of just how difficult and time consuming it could be to clean up an accident on the rails, something they would never forget.

From time to time, especially during winter storms, the wedge story slipped into conversations, mostly because John had taken his camera and snapped a shot of Gordon atop the wedge, a picture John didn't share with Hattie right away.

In March, one of the snows was a perfect packing snow, the makings of a snowman lay all around. "Come on!" Raymond yelled into the house when he learned what kind of snow had fallen the night before. "Come on! Let's make a snowman!"

The first response was from his mother, who came quickly from the kitchen. "For pity's sake. Stop yelling and close the door! I'll go find them. Stay where you are."

The invitation to build a snowman was alluring and soon all the children had coats and mittens on and were outside. The sky was blue and the temperature was just right to build a snowman without their hard work melting too soon. At the same time, it was warm enough to make a person feel they could work without a coat. Mum would never have allowed that, so they sweated underneath the wool.

Building a snowman at the Mount Willard House was an exercise in proportion. There was only so much level ground on which to roll snow. If most of it was used for the bottom, the top two sections would look emaciated. The children had learned by now how to build the perfect snowman. But though each one was proportioned well, the unique characteristics of each snowman were born from their imaginations. Sometimes it was a snowwoman rather than a man. Other times it was a snowchild, made to resemble one of them. This snowman was John—each ball about the same size to depict John's lankiness, a fourth ball added for the desired effect. They found one of John's old hats and borrowed a pipe. Stick arms were affixed with mittens and one arm angled up to appear as if it were permanently waving at trains coming by. One engineer gave a very short toot to say, "Hi." The children were thrilled, a reward for their painstaking perfection along with smiles and waves from the passengers on the train.

Thirty-two

~ 1920 - 1921 ~
A Landslide Win and
a Snowslide to Remember

The following August was thrilling for Hattie. After decades of fellow women working hard to gain the right to vote. After protests, lectures, lobbying, marches, and even civil disobedience. After her own interest and efforts to the cause. Congress passed the Nineteenth Amendment in June of the previous year, and it was ratified on August 18, just in time to vote in this year's presidential election. Hattie couldn't have been happier to have been a part of this historic event. She vowed to be one of the first to vote come Tuesday, November 2.

They'd gone to the Sawyer River Station early that day. There'd been no snow, but it was cold. Hattie, though, was warmed by her mission. She entered the building and walked toward the ballot box. She'd only seen it surrounded by men. Now, she nodded, hugged, or spoke to the other women who were there to cast their ballots for the president of the United States. She had taken her girls with her so they could watch this moment she was so proud to be part of. Mildred and Enola knew full well that their mother was proud and they, in turn, were proud of her, even at only nine and twelve years old. They were also curious and watched every detail. They watched their mother be given a piece of paper and pencil. They watched her read, then pause, and then begin what looked to them like scribbling. They watched her look again at the paper for a short moment and then stick it down into the slot in the wooden box. Their mother had cast her first federal ballot to vote for whom she hoped would become the country's twenty-ninth president and vice president. She'd enjoyed the thrill of knowing that her vote counted among the men's. It had been an astoundingly brief moment that had had such important ramifications.

After this momentous occasion, Hattie put Mildred on a westbounder that would meet up with Gordon waiting at Crawford Station. This was Mildred's first year in middle school, the only one she would share with Gordon in Twin Mountain. Mildred still loved school. Her only lament in leaving the one-room elementary schools was that she loved it when her teachers used her to tutor the younger scholars.

Once Mildred was gone, Hattie and Enola walked to the Bemis school to wait for Raymond, who would come down alone on the train. Hattie wondered if she ought to have brought Raymond and Gordon along to see her vote, but somehow witnessing this historic event for women seemed like it might be lost on the boys, who had accompanied John on occasion before anyone knew that voting wouldn't always be a man's privilege only. With Raymond and Enola both at school, Hattie headed back up toward home alone with a smile on her face and a glow in her heart.

This year, for the first time in history, election results would be broadcast by radio as they happened. As luck would have it, the Crawford House had recently acquired a radio. Hattie would be able to hear the news almost as soon as it took place, which was astounding. She had talked to Elizabeth that morning about bringing the family to Crawfords after school to listen for at least a little while. The hotel was in the process of their end-of-season cleaning and all of the summer guests were gone, so it was a perfect time to have an election party around the radio. She would meet Raymond and Enola at Crawford Station instead of their house and they would walk over to Crawfords together. Gordon and Mildred, coming the other direction from Twin Mountain, would meet them there. She would bring food to combine with Elizabeth's. Everyone was excited—the adults for the election results and the children for a night of fun.

As she walked up to the station, Hattie switched her heavy basket of food to her left arm, then used the other to pull her coat in close against the wind that chilled her legs and threatened to chill the rest of her. *Good thing this old coat is so warm. What* was *I thinking when I listened to my girls tell me I was out of style in my long skirts?* Then switching gears in her head, she thought of the man she had just voted for, Warren G. Harding. He'd built his campaign promising a return to normalcy after the war. *Who wouldn't want that?* Hattie asked herself, hoping he would win the election. Besides his campaign focus, she liked what she'd heard about the man. He was painted as genial in nature, impressive in stature, and unremarkable in his message, which felt calming to a lot of the angry and grieving country. Yet, Hattie knew some thought the man was horribly vague. One journalist, H. L. Mencken, said of a typical Harding speech, "It is so bad that a kind of grandeur creeps into it." Nevertheless, in a way, Hattie didn't care who won, so exciting was the whole event from voting to results.

When the whole family reached Crawfords, there was the usual mayhem of children and adults greeting one another, amplified by everyone's general excitement of the special evening. Supper was a joyous occasion, broken up by the shushing of one adult or another to listen to a new report coming in from KDKA radio in Pittsburgh. It wasn't always easy to make out what was being said, but among them they pieced together enough to hear news they all liked. As the state-by-state results came in, it was easy to see that this election was heading for a landslide win. Warren G. Harding was seemingly undefeated in the east, and then the Midwest, although not in the south. But before they would officially know who the president would be, it was time for everyone to go home.

The next day, Elizabeth called Hattie as soon as she heard that Warren G. Harding and Calvin Coolidge had won thirty-seven of the forty-eight states with some eight million more popular votes than James Cox, his Democrat opponent. And even better, in Elizabeth's mind, most of those were a result of women voters. "Thank you, Elizabeth! Oh, this *is* good news, isn't it?" Hattie said. She rode the high of her mountaintop experience all day long. Hattie wasn't sure when she'd finally put the election and its results aside, so foremost in her thoughts it had all been for so many months. *And to think, we women had that much impact in putting a new man in power!* Truly, women all over the country felt just a bit more empowered than they ever had before.

But Hattie couldn't live in her election fever forever. She had a much fuller life to live. Every day this year she'd seen her younger two off to Bemis and the older two to Twin Mountain. They'd all done well, but she was particularly interested in how Mildred was doing in her new level of school. So far as she could tell, Mildred enjoyed her middle school teachers and had made friends with other scholars from a wide variety of places, just as Gordon had last year. In the elementary years, their friends were mostly track friends who lived the same kind of life they did. Now, both Mildred and Gordon had begun asking if new friends could come home with them almost from the start. That told Hattie a lot, that her children were not ashamed of their mother or of the unusual life they lived on the mountain.

Gordon occasionally stayed with friends in their homes and could see for himself that his life was very similar in some ways and very different in others. Gordon remarked one time after having stayed overnight with a friend that he doubted his friend was expected to cut the heads off chickens to drain the blood. They had all laughed at the truth of Gordon's observation. Overall, Hattie was thankful for the things that taught her children about the world beyond this mountain, wonderful and fearful as it was. She knew the education they got just from living here was priceless, yet she also knew that it wasn't the only world she wanted for them. They needed the broader education that the Crawford House and the schools beyond Harts Location were giving them. As she watched Gordon blossom into a young version of the man he would be one day, and Mildred the young woman, she hoped Raymond and Enola would do as well.

Just after President Harding was sworn in and before Gordon's fourteenth birthday in March, there was a big snowstorm. Big enough that the children would be delayed getting to school. It wasn't unusual for the Notch to see significant snow in March, but big storms always played havoc with the train schedules.

"Mum! Can we go out and play in the snow?" Mildred asked. "Just until the plow comes through?"

Hattie's heart still skipped a beat during heavy snows, knowing that trains were harder to see and hear. She tried not to let memories of the past inhabit the present, not to pass her fear on to the children as her mother had to her. Sometimes that was so difficult. Like now. *Oh, Loring, it's so hard to let them play by the tracks in snowstorms like this. What should I do?* She looked out the dining room window and saw the crew beginning to shovel out the door by the kitchen.

"All right, as long as the crew is out there. But not for long. As soon as the snowplow comes through, the trains will roll, and you'll have to be ready for school."

"Thanks, mum!" she chirped.

All four donned their snow wear and stepped out into the storm through the only doorway that was shoveled out. She watched Gordon say something to John, and John give Gordon his shovel. Gordon walked past her window and toward the front porch. Hattie was happy and proud of Gordon for helping out without having to be asked first. The others tried to walk in the heavy snow up past their knees and higher in the drifts. Laddie had joined them, and Hattie watched them all frolic, laughing, throwing snow at each other, and having a wonderful time. She let her fears drift aside and her love for the children overtake her heart.

Hattie went into the kitchen to make some hot cocoa and hoped they'd have time to drink some before the train came for school. She hadn't gotten far when the children and the dog came back inside, the four children looking bright-eyed and cherry-cheeked. Laddie made sure the kitchen was covered with the snow he shook off himself.

The crew followed them in. "The snowplow's coming down from Crawford," John said.

"Oh. From that direction, huh? I think of the plow as coming from Bartlett. Well, anyway, let me get you all some hot cocoa. You children can sit and watch after you take your wet things off. Is Bobby driving?" she asked, knowing they probably didn't know. "If he is, I hope he doesn't push the wedge off the tracks again," she said with a little chuckle. If Bobby had been standing there, he would have laughed with everyone else. He'd been a pretty good sport about that day.

The children each took a mug of chocolate with them up the back stairway to watch for the plow out the rainbow window, taking turns at the best view and chattering all the while. Then, once the snowplow rounded the bend and was headed for the house, they'd run to the parlor to play their "chicken" game as it passed by. Hattie marveled at the things her children thought up. She hadn't had siblings to play creative games with. It was such fun listening to them now.

The crew sat in the dining room, sipping on steaming hot cocoa, enjoying their few moments of relaxation. Henry was talking to John. "Say, do you know anything about the south? Like Florida? Good beaches? I'm thinking I'd like to take a trip down there some day. I'm so blasted sick of these winters, you know?"

"I know what ya mean. I've had a mind to do the same from time to time. I've heard…"

Suddenly, from outside came a roar like thunder that was too close and went on for too long.

"Avalanche!" Denny yelled abruptly, realizing what was happening. He ran to the window, the others right behind him. The children all ran past Hattie to go up the back stairs, but she stopped them. It felt better to have them all right there with her even though it probably wouldn't matter where any of them were if the slide was big enough to push the house off the edge, God forbid.

She suddenly remembered the story of the killer avalanche of 1826 that took out nine people at the Willey House. They'd assumed the avalanche would destroy the house in its path, so they left it and walked directly into the slide and perished. *It must have felt like they were sitting ducks because that's what I feel like right now.* She shuddered. But Loring had always told her this house was very sturdy and safe and the men had no intentions of leaving, so she wasn't about to go outside the shelter of the house. Still, it was hard to sit and wait for whatever was going to happen. There was nothing any of them could do because there was no stopping what was coming from above them. There was no way to know how big the slide was, how long it would last, or where it would finally stop. A sudden extra-loud crash made Enola run over to Hattie and stand next to her mother for comfort, grabbing handfuls of Hattie's dress. Hattie felt powerless and of no real use to her daughter, or anyone else, for that matter. There just wasn't any predicting a snow or ice slide let alone a full-blown avalanche. And it could be any of these or a bit of all of them in March. What made this one different was its thunderous noise. This was no small slide. Very few things on that mountain could stop Hattie in her tracks as this did.

The roar of sliding snow and debris continued and soon the leading edge of the avalanche falling from the granite ledges above them nearly filled their view out the kitchen windows. No one moved while the roar and pummeling continued. But when it began to weaken and the adults realized the initial danger was probably over, everyone went to the girls' room in the turret upstairs to see what had just happened. The cries of, "Oh, my!" and "I don't believe it!" echoed around the room. The snow had filled up the cut of the track as far as they could see. It was as if the mountain was retaliating for the deep gash that had been carved out of her side so long ago. It would have been hard to say how long the slide had lasted. On one hand, the avalanche seemed to be going in slow motion, tumbling freely in somersaults down the mountain. On the other hand, once it did stop, Hattie realized how any of them might have been standing vulnerably in its path, as quickly as it had overtaken the land. There would have been no way to outrun it. The snow didn't care who was in its way and Hattie knew that with a chill.

"I can't see the plow anymore!" Raymond yelled.

No one could, they realized with a jolt. Raymond had been the first one to look beyond the snow and see that there was not only no track visible, but no engine either.

"I'm going out to look for the plow!" Raymond said excitedly, already turning to run downstairs.

"No, you aren't!" John said sharply. Raymond stopped and turned to him suddenly, not used to John's forceful tone. "It isn't safe yet. There could be more snow coming off that mountain."

"We won't have school today, will we mum?" Enola asked.

"Not likely, little one," Hattie said, moving away from the window to go back to the kitchen. "Come on down, everyone, and have some more hot cocoa and a doughnut. Heaven knows whoever goes outside next will need it."

Hurriedly the children raced back downstairs, fueled with the excitement of understanding that what they were seeing was unprecedented. John tried to phone Crawford Station, but the line was dead. The crew gulped down the warm, sweet cocoa and doughnuts and appreciated their full bellies as they geared up to go outside. Their first obstacle was to get through the back door which was held firmly shut by heavy, unyielding snow. Even at that, the back door would be easier to get to than the front porch which had already been blocked before the slide. Ever so slowly, together, they were able to push the door an inch without breaking it. They clawed at the snow with some of Hattie's cooking utensils but made little progress.

Then John had an idea and whispered something to Hattie, who nodded her consent. "Gordon. Raymond. Come upstairs with me," John said, "and bring your coats and things with you."

The boys looked at their mother and were surprised to see her nod toward the kitchen door. They grabbed their outerwear and ran to catch up to John. Hattie detained the girls, and the crew simply shrugged and went back to their pitifully slow progress. Several minutes later, they all heard a yell and a thud coming from over the front porch. They tried looking through the very top of the kitchen window, the only part not blocked with snow, but saw nothing. Then suddenly they heard both boys holler Tarzan-style, and right after that there were two sets of boots that magically appeared in the window!

Suddenly Raymond and Gordon's upside-down heads popped into view, and Raymond yelled, "John sent us through the upstairs window! And we jumped onto the porch roof!"

"Yeah," Gordon added, "then we walked over here on top of the snow! We're gonna see if we can dig out the door from out here!" Another ape-man yell, and their heads and boots disappeared. Soon they could hear the boys scraping at the snow on the other side of the door.

When John came back into the kitchen, he said with a grin, "Well, ma'am, even if it doesn't work, they're enjoying themselves. I might've been able to get myself out that window and still will if the boys can't help enough with the door. But they had so much fun jumping down into that snow and hoping they could save the day, I thought I'd just let them go at it. Did ya hear them yelling like Tarzan?"

Hattie laughed out loud. "I guess Gordon's getting *some*thing out of that Tarzan book, isn't he!"

Eventually, between the men and the boys, a narrow pathway out the door appeared. The men tied on their snowshoes and began the long, difficult trek up the tracks. This workday would now be another one they hadn't foreseen. The girls put on their winter clothing, called Laddie, and went outside with strict instructions not to go beyond the house and its buildings. Gordon and Raymond took the shovels and began making a dent in the wall of snow that used to be their front porch. And Hattie just shook her head and laughed at it all, grateful that this house and everyone in it were still in one piece.

Sometime later, John came in to report to the family, "You wouldn't believe how much snow fell off that mountain! All ya can see is the tops of the telephone poles now. Morrison's in the engine and he's all right. Shook a little, is all. He says he figured there was no way he'd make it through with the plow, but you know Morrison. He said he had to try. He figures that snowbank is at least twenty feet deep, and who knows how much of the tracks it's swallowed up. Sent Denny up to Crawford to tell them to get another engine down here from Lancaster."

That afternoon, the family got another report. When the second engine had arrived, the two engines together had fought valiantly with the plow as their only weapon against the snow fortress nature had unleashed. But all they managed to do was create a tunnel into the bank that completely buried the plow and both the engines. And then they were firmly stuck.

"Oh, good heavens," Hattie had said. "Well, take something for all of you to eat when you go back out. I'll put in extra for the engineers."

Later, they learned that a third engine was sent to the scene. Not to push through as the others had, at least not at first, but to pull the stuck engines out. The crew dug into the snow until they found the coupler on the nearest engine so that it could be pulled out. Then those two engines hauled out Morrison's engine, and finally the snowplow. For the next three days, fifty men, hired from all over the area, shoveled what they could by hand, then let the plow try to ram the pile of snow again. Every time the plow and engines didn't get clear through, the men shoveled some more, and the plow rammed the pile again. And again. And again. Of course, the engines needed water to function, so the shoveled snow went right into the water tender to melt it. If they didn't know already, they learned just how much snow it takes to make enough water for steam! All the while the children watched, sometimes outside, sometimes in, and always reluctant to leave their vigil, even to eat. But all those men plus the family had to be fed throughout what would end up being a three-day ordeal. Since no groceries could get through, Hattie had to creatively make food stretch. Having to serve meals that were less than her standard fare felt akin to failure to Hattie. But in this case, no one could fault her. Not even she could expect more than filling bellies with whatever was palatable. Toward the end, she was heard to say, "We're pretty near the bottom of the barrel for eating."

After three days of constant, back-breaking work, the tracks were open again. Hattie was especially happy to see the red nose plow, mostly white with snow now, go past the house. She could just barely make out a gleeful "Whoop!" from one of the men going by as he waved. She certainly wasn't the only one who was happy they finally made it through the avalanche.

Somehow everyone lived to talk about the great storm of '21. The snowbank was officially measured at twenty-one feet high and about two hundred feet long. No wonder the plow hadn't been able to make it through! To the children, it was sensational, and, with no school, it was the perfect winter holiday with one of the best sledding hills they'd ever been on, beginning right out their bedroom window.

Thirty-three

~ 1921 ~
A Mother's Pride

That year, when winter seemed never ending, it finally let go of its grasp on the Notch, and spring was especially appreciated. The children were in school, and Hattie had been hanging a load of wash outside in the luxurious sunshine when she became aware of a little dark-gray striped kitten that had wandered into the yard. It wound itself in and out of her legs, making a figure eight. She nearly tripped over it before picking it up and looking into its unblinking, honey-gold eyes. "Well, if you aren't precious. You remind me of another cat that found me years ago. I wonder where you have come from?" She couldn't imagine how it had safely made it this far but didn't want to risk its being found by a wild animal if she let it go. And besides needing another mouser, she knew the children would be ecstatic. She hoped Laddie would tolerate the kitten.

Hattie brought the cat inside and introduced it to Laddie, who seemed irritated only because the cat had woken him from his nap. She then went about her busy day, all but forgetting about the kitten. When the children came home, they changed clothes and then went to the kitchen for a cookie, as they usually did right after school, and Hattie said, "Children, I have a surprise for you today."

Expectant eyes looked up at their mother. "A kitten somehow made its way here and I brought it inside."

Hattie knew she'd just made their day, as they all started talking at once. "Where is it?" "What color is it?" "Is it a boy or a girl?" "Can we keep it?" "Ple-e-e-ase?"

"You'll have to go look for it. I haven't seen it in a little while. It could be anywhere down here."

It didn't take any more prompting for the search to begin, each child looking high and low all over the house.

"I don't think it's in *there*," Hattie laughed when Mildred pulled out a drawer.

"But mum, we can't find it anywhere!" Mildred said, exasperated.

"Keep looking. It has to be in here somewhere."

Finally, she heard whoops and hollers from them all as they came running into the kitchen. Enola was holding the small ball of gray fur. "Guess where it was, mum!" she said.

"I have no idea," Hattie said with her hands on her hips. "Tell me."

"It was in one of Gordon's sneakers! And I'm the one who found it," Enola said proudly.

"How on earth did that little thing get up all those stairs?" Hattie said rhetorically, realizing that no one had seen it climbing.

"It didn't!" Mildred took over the story with glee. "Gordon's shoe was downstairs behind a chair in the parlor. It was in there!"

"Well, now, that should show you something Gordon," Hattie said lightly. "Next time put your shoes where they belong."

"I found it. I should get to name it," Enola reasoned.

"Sneakers! I think we should name it Sneakers!" Gordon blurted out suddenly, the name having just dawned on him. "And look, it has two white back paws, like it's wearing white sneakers in the back." Even Enola couldn't argue with that.

Sneakers was now the newest member of the Evans household. By summer he had become the mouser Hattie needed and a solid friend to everyone, save Laddie. He was beloved by the younger Monahan girls and Martha

Jackson, who came to play with Enola sometimes. The only disconcerting thing about the cat was that he lived up to his name in another way, once he outgrew Gordon's shoes. How many times had Hattie almost tripped over the light-footed animal because he'd sneak into the room behind her? She'd sigh, picking up the cat once she steadied herself and say, "I guess I can't ask you to be a good mouser and then not expect you to know how to do your job."

As Sneakers grew, the younger children up and down the Notch were being left behind by the older ones who were working in the summers. Gordon and Peter Jackson from up at Crawfords were caddies again this summer. This year, Raymond had joined them in the caddy business. After "the war to end all wars" (as people were calling it), golf enjoyed something of an upswing, so to speak. This was good news to the boys, as they earned even more money caddying. When the Crawford House held their annual golf championship for male guests, the boys were sure to secure a good view of the action. That year, the well-known champion golfer Walter Hagen from New York won the Open, while Massachusetts-born Mike Brady came in second. For Gordon and Raymond, it was all terribly exciting.

Earning money while learning the game of golf and meeting famous people was secondary, however, to Hattie's practical need for the children to begin earning wages and setting aside money for a boarding house during their high school years. Crawfords had hiring opportunities for both the boys and the girls and became something of a second home to them once they started working there.

Mildred and Alice Monahan began working as two of about fifty waitresses who served the employees at Crawfords. They didn't need the fancy uniforms that the girls from Boston or Maine had to wear when serving the hotel guests. Mildred served a table of twenty chambermaids and made friends with many of them. She and Alice shared a room in the Jackson's cottage since they waitressed three meals a day, seven days a week. During their time off between meals, they learned how to press the chauffeur's uniforms to earn extra money. Sometimes they would thumb a ride down to nearby Bretton Woods for ice cream cones or candy bars. On very hot days they would go to the lower pond behind the hotel and splash around.

Sometimes they could watch an intramural baseball game on the hotel grounds. By now, Raymond and Gordon played with the team sometimes, though they played with real baseball bats rather than the pickaxes they used when they played at the house.

On special nights, the dining room tables were pushed back to show movies just for employees. And when magicians came up on the train from Boston, the employees were invited to the main ballroom to watch the show. There was a classical music concert every afternoon, attended mostly by the older guests. And every afternoon at four o'clock, a parlor maid would carry a silver urn into the lobby and serve fancy cookies made by the hotel's pastry chef.

Once in a while, Crawford House guests would take a burro ride up to Mount Willard, and one or two of the family would be able to accompany them. The burros needed a lot of prodding, so a hired man rode a horse behind them that would give the burros a nip whenever they stopped. The trail was wide enough to ride two abreast, which afforded good conversation or the chance to listen in on one during the two-hour ride to the top. Once there, the view of the house below or trains traveling the Notch paled only in comparison to the grander view of all the White Mountains in the distance.

In the evenings, employees were not allowed to walk around the front of the hotel, but, youngsters being youngsters, they often broke that rule when the orchestra played for dancing. They'd creep along the veranda and peer through the windows, watching the ladies in their gorgeous, long gowns and the men in their classy tuxedos. The orchestra that the hotel owner arranged for was the Boston Symphony Players, who came every summer and were housed in their own building. Dutch bassoonist Boaz Piller, who had charge of the orchestra, was friendly with Mildred. He kept in touch with her during the off-season and once sent her a postcard from Austria.

The boys, who were able to come back home at the end of their workdays, had stories of their own to tell. Sometimes their stories were gruesome, such as the hikers who ventured too far out on the summits of Elephant Head or Mount Willard and fell to their deaths. Or hikers in early spring who got lost and thought they could stay the night in the woods and then froze to death because they hadn't any idea how cold the mountains could be. Other stories were about golfers and their mishaps on the course. Raymond enjoyed golf enough to hit balls after work, down the tracks. He lost many a ball that bounced wildly off the rocks or rails. When he drove golf balls off the summit of Mount Willard to see if he could hit the house, Hattie had had to intervene and put her foot down before a window was broken or someone was conked out cold.

Perhaps the best thing Mildred did many days during her downtime between meals was to walk down to the house and visit her mum and Enola. She often brought new friends and occasionally even Boaz came. There was always the promise of a nice chat with mum, and maybe a tasty morsel or two to snack on. Enola always enjoyed catching Mildred up on family happenings that her sister missed, even being only a mile and a half up the tracks.

One time Enola could hardly contain her excitement waiting for Mildred to visit. "Guess what?" Enola said. "Sneakers got lost the other day. I couldn't find him anywhere 'n' I was gettin' nervous that he wasn't gonna come back, like Boomerang."

"Well, he's right here, so obviously, you found him," Mildred said as she stroked the cat in her lap. "So, where was he?"

"Well…a freight came down and stopped because mum had a message for Bobby. Then when the train started again and had gone by, there was Sneakers, lying between the rails! He wasn't moving at all at first. I thought he was dead! But he was just stunned, I guess."

"That'll teach ya, Sneakers!" Mildred said to the cat who was purring contentedly. "Don't use up all your nine lives too fast, okay?"

During another of Mildred's visits, Enola again was bursting with excitement. She said, "Hey, Mildred, come 'ere! I wanna show ya somethin'."

"What is it, Nola? I need to wash out a few things before I go back to work."

Enola called to Laddie and led Mildred and the dog to the back pathway. "Now, you sit down right here and just wait."

Before Mildred could object, Enola and Laddie were almost out of sight down the path to the road. Mildred sighed, wishing she had held Enola off a bit, but it was a beautiful summer day and some time off her feet was actually a welcome relief. Just as she was getting used to the idea that Enola was going to take her time with whatever it was she wanted Mildred to see, Laddie came bounding up the path and dropped the daily newspaper squarely in front of her feet. Mildred laughed, petting the dog fondly. "Good boy, Laddie! Now to teach you how to do that without getting it all slobbery."

Soon Enola appeared, smiling broadly. "Pretty good trick, huh? He learned that really quick, too. He's such a smart dog!"

"Quick-*ly*," Mildred corrected.

"Yeah," Enola said, happy that Mildred had understood.

Mildred rolled her eyes and changed the subject. "How does mum like her paper wet around the middle?" Mildred laughed as the two walked back into the house.

Not answering her sister's question and not yet ready to stop boasting about the dog, Enola beamed, "Since the paper is sometimes left at the bottom of the hill by a car when it isn't raining, the paperman honks three times and leaves the paper behind. Then we just send Laddie down to get it!"

"Right," Hattie chimed in from her seat in the parlor, "and I can usually read everything but the front page! But who needs that page anyway?" When her sarcasm was mixed with a twinkle in her eye, the children loved it. "Mildred," she said then, holding out one of Mildred's blouses, "I've taken this collar off and trimmed the frayed parts, then turned it around and stitched the bad edge back onto the shirt. I hope that's okay. It just looked poorly, and I didn't think you'd want it to look that way for work."

Mildred went to her mother and gave her a kiss on the cheek, "Thanks, mum. You're the best!"

Times were not getting any easier as far as finances went. It was expensive to board the children for high school and Gordon would be in his ninth year in Whitefield this September. She'd been setting aside money and Gordon had been working for the past few years to help out, too. But until she lived into the fall to see how much his room and board cost in reality, she was anxious. She'd found ways to economize. If she cut worn-out sheets in half and sewed the outside edges together, the middle was strong again and warm. And if she kept all the breadcrumbs as meatloaf filler, she could effectively stretch her meals. Mildred would also be boarding the next year. Hattie hoped she could manage the cost of both.

One Saturday that summer, when the roads could be counted on to not swallow the tires in mud, Hattie approached John with a suggestion. "I've a favor to ask. If tomorrow is as nice a day as it appears it might be, would you be willing to take us all in your Ford to Whitefield? It's time Gordon see the high school there, and I think it would be good to acquaint him with the town. We could picnic somewhere nice, too."

"You sure it isn't you who needs to acquaint yourself?" John winked.

"Well, yes, I guess Gordon *and me*, and it would do the others good to see what's coming, too."

"Would ya like to go there on our way to somewhere else?"

"What did you have in mind?" Hattie asked, curious as to where the day might ultimately lead them.

"I've been wanting to go up to see The Balsams in Dixville Notch, but it's about seventy-three miles north into the tip of New Hampshire. It would be a long day. What do ya think?"

"Let's do it. I'll make sure to put oatmeal on tonight and make up picnic dinners for everyone. I think it will be fun. Thank you."

Early the next morning, John said he was going up to Crawfords to get the automobile ready and Raymond asked to go along. He enjoyed watching John pamper his vehicle. Each spring, he would watch John take the head off the engine and clean the carburetor and valves and scrape the previous year's mud from beneath the fenders. This morning, John even let Raymond help put a quick coat of wax on the auto, which he really enjoyed.

It turned out to be a long and wonderful day with lots of laughter, wind in their hair, and Laddie lying on the floorboard in the back while four pairs of feet played with his fur. Hattie had gotten a sense of how far Whitefield was going to be for Gordon and the others. She hadn't wanted to think about how long a week without Gordon was going to feel, but there was no denying they'd need to find him a place to board. Time was beginning to feel like a devouring beast, claiming more of her children than she liked. But it couldn't be helped. She wouldn't concede to keeping them home in lieu of furthering their education, even though her children needn't stay in school past the age of fourteen. Hattie had been happy to have the Whitefield part of their outing over with first so that she could enjoy the rest of the day. The Balsams Hotel was certainly worth seeing, grand as it was, and it was fun to see another notch not so very different than their own. And no picnic outing with John was ever complete without a family picture. In this one, John was sure to position his automobile behind the family but clearly visible in the center background.

August came and with it a very memorable occasion. Raymond and Gordon burst into the house one day, out of breath, having raced each other home. "Mum!" Raymond said, just ahead of Gordon. "Guess what?"

"Sit down, catch your breath, then tell me," Hattie said, as she swept the floor. Enola was close by, cleaning a sooty lamp chimney with the rag her mother had given her. She looked up and waited to hear what the boys had found so exciting.

"Guess who's coming to Crawfords next week?" Gordon managed.

"Santa Claus?" Hattie teased.

"No! President Harding!" Raymond said, not able to contain his news any longer.

Hattie stopped and looked at the boys, "Really?" She could hardly believe it could be true, especially coming from Raymond, who liked a good joke.

"Yes, mum, really! Next Wednesday, the third, he's coming here. You gotta see him, mum! You gotta!"

"If the public is invited, then I surely shall try," Hattie said, containing her own excitement. *I must call Florence,* she thought.

The weather held that Wednesday, at least for the time the President was there. In the morning, Mr. Harding played a round of golf. Gordon caddied for him, and Raymond was the forecaddie, going on ahead to keep an eye on the president's ball at all times.

"Mum, President Harding was quite the jolly fellow and very talkative, too," Gordon told Hattie that afternoon when she was at Crawfords. She had to pinch herself to settle the idea in her bones that her boys really had caddied for the president of the United States, the very man she had helped vote into office.

Hattie couldn't believe the number of people who were there. And the number of women! She joined Florence and Elizabeth, and when the three women caught their first glimpse of the president, they agreed that he was a most handsome man. He was wearing a nicely fitted suit with a white shirt and bow tie. He really was "impressive of stature," as the newspapers had said. Here she was, seeing the very man himself, not a photograph, and she could hardly believe it. With all the stunningly stylish clothing and hats the women were wearing in honor of this visitor, Hattie felt embarrassed in her tired clothing, even though she'd worn one of her better dresses. But so did Elizabeth and Florence, and it helped to be together in their shame. Soon they forgot about what they were wearing when their attention was solely on President Harding pinning a small bunch of flowers on his lapel that a young girl had picked for him. The three women were impressed by his seemingly caring nature.

Soon, Elizabeth and Mildred had to excuse themselves to go back to work. Florence, Hattie, the boys, and Enola walked back down the tracks together. "I can't believe it," Hattie said. "You boys caddied for Mr. Harding! The president of the United States! And he actually joked with my girls. *My* girls! I just can't believe it. He even held Enola!"

"Yeah, and mum, he was so tall, and he laughed when he picked me up," Enola said. "A good kind of laugh. He was like a real person!" Enola had just spoken the words neither woman had thought to say out loud, but which both had felt and understood.

As Hattie walked through the back door, she couldn't help going over and over the events of the day. For a few moments, she let her thoughts drift away from the present. *If ever there was a time I wished you were here, Loring, it was today. You'd have been so proud of our children.*

Thirty-four

~ 1921 - 1923 ~
Where *Had* the Time Gone?

Hattie's emotional high the day of President Harding's visit to the Notch gradually gave way to the ebb and flow of her normal life, which necessarily included her children and the crew. In the fall, Francis King and Ed Meany both quit for different reasons. Francis no longer felt that he could do his job and the crew justice. His nerves after the war had not improved by the time the avalanche fell. The fact that such random devastation could happen, taking out lives, put Francis over the edge of tolerance. He promised to stay until fall. Ed made the same promise but only disclosed his reasons to his brother Denny and John. Hattie never knew why Ed left but she hugged both men warmly and wished them well. It was never easy when a valued member of the crew left. They were like family.

Henry Hopper and Freddy Harrison were hired to take their places. John was grateful to learn that both Henry and Freddy were known to be good workers and steady fellows. He hoped this crew of five would enjoy the sort of longevity and accompanying stability it had seen in the years before Loring died. Hattie could see the toll it had taken on John when his crew changed too much. She was thankful Loring had not had to deal with that. Only Denny had remained constant in John's crews. It took time to teach new crewmen, and longer still for the crew to work as a trusted team.

The children's worlds were changing, too. Gordon began boarding at the home of Reverend and Mrs. Templeton when he started ninth year in Whitefield. The middle-aged couple had two sons who had moved out of the house and were living on their own. Hattie often found herself comparing Gordon's experience with hers at the home of the Reverend and Martha. But instead of inside chores, he earned some of his room and board working outside, like shoveling snow or cutting wood. He left on the Monday noon train for his week of school, then returned home Friday evening. Hattie dearly missed Gordon and she was not the only one to miss him throughout the week. His load of chores was divided among his siblings, with Raymond taking on most of the extra work. One day Hattie overheard Raymond and Mildred quibbling about who had done the most work for the day so as to divide Gordon's job of cleaning out the hen house fairly.

Hattie had heard quite enough outside her kitchen window and wiped her hands of the biscuit dough she was making. She stepped through the kitchen door and stood on the top of the stoop, arms folded across her middle, and waited until the children noticed her presence, which wasn't long. When they looked up at their mother, they could tell she was none too happy. Until then, they hadn't even known she was listening to them.

"Children, I want you to hear me and hear me well. I read something that may come in mighty handy as you grow up. And I want you to think about it as you decide *quietly* how to come to a decision, because I want to hear no more of this pettiness. Do you understand me?"

"Yes, mum," they said in unison.

"All right then. This is what I want you to hear: 'To succeed, split more wood and fewer hairs.'" Then Hattie turned and walked back into the kitchen. For a time, she stood just inside the doorway. Hearing no more arguing, she returned to her biscuits.

Hattie was fair with her children. Her sincerest desire was to see that they grew in wisdom to be the keeper of their own futures. She knew of some mothers who seemed to desire first and foremost that their children were almost militantly obedient, but that was just not the kind of person she was. No, to her it was more important to teach her children lessons for a lifetime, not just for the moment.

The next year, on the first of July, more than four hundred thousand railroad shop workers went on strike due to a new round of wage cuts during a recession after the war. Locomotive repair shops, including Maine Central's chief location in Waterville, Maine, fought for better conditions. And they weren't the only ones. Coal miners, textile workers, and many more across the country went on strike, demanding better treatment and pay. Although the strikes didn't affect Section 129 directly, the crew certainly understood that millions of workers were generally poorly paid doing work that was often dangerous. Tensions around the country were high and the crew talked about the situation, often with disparaging or sympathetic remarks. But Hattie also heard them say that they were grateful to be section men who stayed in one place. And this particular place, with its warm house and plentiful food, was hard to beat.

Hattie contacted her friend, Esther, from the textile mill to see how she and her family were faring. In a letter from Esther, Hattie read, "It's so hard here. So many of us are holding out for better wages, but food is scarcer than ever. As you know, my hair was quite long when I saw you last. I was able to sell it for a few extra cents. Two of my sons and their wives and children asked to come back home to help us all make ends meet. I've made so many concessions that my grandchildren know enough not to ask for a solitary thing, save for a morsel of food." Hattie's heart broke for Esther's situation. It was so hard to know how to be helpful from a distance in a situation like that.

Then late that August, just before Mildred was to begin boarding in Whitefield for her ninth year of school, John walked into the house one day, breathless. "Engine 380 left the iron just west of the Bemis grade! We're going down there to see if they need us," John said, halfway out the door already. Hattie was busy as always, but Enola begged to see the derailment. Truth to tell, Hattie herself wanted to see what had happened. So, she and Enola followed the men, with Laddie beside them. It would be a good hike down there.

"The boys'll sure miss being able to see this one!" Enola stated in her excitement as they walked.

"Yes, I suppose so," Hattie said. "Things like this don't get resolved very quickly, though. Maybe they can go down after work if it's still a problem. I just hope no one was hurt. John didn't say as much, but maybe no one knows yet."

Indeed, they found the engine lying on its side beside the tracks. Amazingly, no one had been badly injured. The episode was mostly an embarrassing predicament for Clemons, the engineer. Hattie spotted Florence in the growing crowd and approached her.

"My goodness," Florence said. "These train accidents are no small matters, are they? I heard this one all right."

"What happened?" Hattie asked.

"Apparently, it pushed a freight up to Crawfords and was on its way back down. Something went wrong with the tender and caused the engine to jackknife. Poor Clemons! He'll take a ribbing after the company is through with him, I'll bet. Well, anyway, how are you, Hattie? We don't get to see each other as often these days, do we? I assume you're as busy as I am. Just can't keep our youngsters from growing up no matter how hard we try!"

"Don't I know it!" Hattie agreed. "To answer your question, though, I'm fine and so are the children. I'm more concerned about what this recession is doing to the shop and mill workers, though. Morale is pretty low all over from what I read. President Harding has his work cut out for him, doesn't he?"

"I should think so. I surely wouldn't want to trade places with him!" Florence said.

"And my friend, Esther, from Lewiston—you know who I mean, right?—well she's just in an awful situation with hardly any food for her family. Sometimes I wonder what would have happened to me and the children if I'd decided to move away when Loring died, you know? Shop work, mill work, factory work…that's likely what I'd be doing now. How can I feel so grateful for what I have and so awful for my friend at the same time?"

There really wasn't much Florence could say. She felt the same way, though.

"Anyway, how are you and your girls?"

"Doing well. Gertrude is still enjoying her job in Bridgton. She's apparently been courting a young man in town. I don't know if anything will come of it, though. I guess you know most everything else about us. Not much has changed since the last time Alice and Mildred talked, which was probably about ten minutes ago, if I know them!"

Hattie smiled in acknowledgment, then said, "Speaking of Mildred, she'll be boarding in another week or so as you know, and I can hardly believe she's old enough. But she was just telling me she couldn't imagine not seeing me for a whole five days in a row every week. I wonder if she's anxious about leaving. Does it sound like that to you?"

"Well, I don't know, but she could be. After all, girls get pretty close to their mothers. Most just want to grow up to be mothers themselves. They don't need a lot of education to get married and have babies. Maybe she just wants to stay home until she finds a man to marry," Florence said reasonably.

"I don't know. She's never even talked about getting married someday."

"Maybe she doesn't think you'd listen to anything but staying in school."

Hattie just shrugged her shoulders. The truth was, she was suddenly irritated with Florence's candor. She had always admired her friend for speaking so frankly, but now Florence's words bit into her heart and wouldn't let go. "Well, I should get home," Hattie said, looking around the gathering crowd for Enola and Laddie. "I really had no business coming down here like this. I have a lot to do today. But Enola wanted to come, so I decided the walk would do us both good. I'll see ya later, Florence."

"Yes. Let's do get together soon for tea," Florence said giving Hattie a hug.

Hattie beckoned Enola, who wanted to stay longer. "Don't get in the way!" she said, taking Laddie and walking back up the hill. As she walked, Hattie thought about what Florence had said and why her words had irked her so. Was it because there might be a thread of truth in them? Maybe Mildred really didn't feel ready to leave home. What would she do about it if that was so? Was she really that stubborn about seeing that the children got a good education? And if so, wasn't that a good thing to be stubborn about? Her irritation turned the corner toward real anger when she thought about having to make these sorts of decisions without Loring. Her footfalls hit the ties just a bit harder as she pounded out her feelings.

The next time Mildred came home on her work break, Hattie suggested they walk back to Crawfords together.

"Mildred, let me ask you something. Do you feel ready to board all the way in Whitefield this year?"

"Sure, mum. Why? Gordon does just fine," Mildred answered, revealing to Hattie that while her daughter may not want to be parted from home, she also wasn't about to leave school behind. But Hattie saw an opportunity to probe a bit further.

"Well, Gordon's a boy and he's learning to step into his future as a man. He'll go find a job pretty soon so he can support a wife and family someday, I hope."

"But I want to have a job teaching someday. Don't you think I should?" Mildred asked.

"I guess it isn't about should. Would you rather teach than have a family?"

"I'd rather do both," Mildred stated, totally oblivious to the idea that a school might not allow her to teach after marriage. Hattie just smiled at her adventurous daughter and decided to let the discussion end there. She was satisfied that she was doing the right thing sending Mildred on to Whitefield.

After supper that day, the boys ended up going down to the wreck and staying late into the night to watch the fallen engine be righted. That situation was resolved on the same day as the railroad strike. It had been a trying summer, after which it was time again for school.

Mildred began boarding with the Doctor Wilder family, doing housework and cleaning in exchange for room and board. This was all well and good, she reported to her mother in a letter, but occasionally she was asked to make oyster stew. Hattie knew that Mildred had no fondness for oysters at all and could see the face her daughter would make in her disgust. Mildred also told her mother that when Mrs. Wilder stepped into a cold bath, yelling at the shock to her body, Mildred just nestled closer to the fireplace for warmth, thinking how spoiled she'd always been in the luxury of a warm house. Hattie smiled to herself, knowing that her daughter was growing up.

Another school year passed in relative likeness to the others. The children had finished tenth, ninth, seventh, and sixth years, which meant that in the fall, the only major change would be Enola moving on to middle school with Raymond. Then Hattie would have no more children in the lower years anymore. Where *had* the time gone? Their years had been divided into two major parts, the school year and the summer, with two different sorts of schedules. Essentially, the three working children were hardly home in the summer and the older two were only home on weekends once school started. So, weekends during the school year usually felt special to all of them, like short holidays.

That August of 1923, Laddie came bounding up the hill with a newspaper in his mouth. He'd shown enough signs of his age lately to make it doubtful he could climb the steep hill well enough, but today his enthusiasm was that of his younger self. "Thank you, Laddie," Hattie said. "You can drop it now." *Before the front page can't be read*, she added to herself. Then she unfurled it and saw the headline: *PRESIDENT HARDING DEAD*! Shocked, Hattie read the article. She could hardly believe this wonderful man had just died of a heart attack while still in office. Calvin Coolidge would step into the role now. *Can't be helped, but dear me*, she thought as she walked back into the house with Laddie at her heels. *Dear, dear me. I hope Mr. Coolidge is as good a leader.*

Thirty-five

~ 1924 ~
The Gifts of Christmas

The next summer, all the children worked at Crawfords. The boys still came home in the evenings to sleep but were sometimes gone until quite late. The girls both stayed in the Jackson cottage all week and came home now and then as their time permitted. At least the four saw each other up to Crawfords, which Hattie knew they loved. It brought her a measure of comfort as well, though she missed them all terribly.

That fall, Gordon began his last year of school in Whitefield. Mildred, her second to last. Raymond began boarding with Gordon at the Templeton's, and Enola started her eighth and last year in middle school. In November, Hattie yet again exercised her right to vote and was pleased that President Harding's previous running mate, Calvin Coolidge, was elected to a full term. Enola had asked to go with her mother to vote, which Hattie allowed. Enola would miss school that day, but Hattie thought watching her mother vote was an important enough reason. Enola loved being the only one at home with mum during the week. She helped Hattie with kitchen duties, as well as other chores in the house. She enjoyed not sharing Sneakers and Laddie with anyone but mum. Sometimes she felt the burden of household chores when most of them fell to her, but the heartfelt talks and fun she had with her mother were well worth it. Then, each Friday, she could ride on the coattails of her mother's growing excitement to have everyone back at home. The happy chaos of the children enjoying each other's company was never too much for Hattie.

With the dynamics of the household shifting so quickly, Hattie often wished for more power over the passage of time. But she wouldn't trade her children's blossoming personalities just to keep them young. So, she accepted the advance of time and rejoiced in the moments that were given to her. And that year gave them a Christmas they would all remember.

It began in early December, just after Thanksgiving, the time of the year that always weighed heavily on Hattie's heart. Once she made it through Loring's birthday and their wedding anniversary, as well as his death anniversary, she felt the weight lift enough to genuinely enjoy the Christmas holiday. That's when her mind completely shifted off her darker memories and onto Christmas with the children. This year, she knew the girls would both love new scrapbooks. They enjoyed documenting highlights of home, local, and national events with pictures and news articles. And both girls found stories and poems they liked and pasted those into their scrapbooks as well. But Hattie knew the real gift would be the flapper clothing she would make for them. However, they may not like that along with the clothing would come Hattie's necessary stipulations about where she would allow the girls to wear such things.

The boys would get new clothes, too, though they wouldn't be particularly excited. For them, clothing was more a necessity than fun because they'd outgrown their things so quickly. She simply would not let them look anything but their best, so she planned to make them vests and ties and order new shoes. She'd also order them each a book. For Gordon, *A Christmas Carol* by Charles Dickens. He'd love the story for its commerce as well as its humanitarian aspects. For Raymond, with help from John, she'd order the *Hand Book of Automobiles* put out by the National Automobile Chamber of Commerce. The details of every car would keep him occupied for some time.

It was one thing to find something she knew each child would love, but she also wanted to give the men a little something, too. Finding things for them was much more difficult. Usually, she made them each a special food they liked, and she'd do that again, but she'd been made aware of something she could do for John that would be appropriate as well as fun for the whole household.

Beginning that past January, a new magazine had been published called the *Maine Central Employees Magazine,* or the MCEM. Each month it carried stories submitted by employees as well as railroad news. When the magazine appeared at the house, everyone wanted a turn reading it. Often the first person to read it became the deliverer of the best stories and jokes it had to offer. One time, John read the following story after supper:

> *A milkman tied his reins to the cart, put his feet up, and read the newspaper while the horse walked steadily on. Because the man was not paying attention, the horse walked straight into the third car of a moving train and was killed. The milkman subsequently blamed the engineer.*

This sparked laughter as well as a discussion of how human it is not to want to take responsibility for oneself.

Another story made Mildred laugh so heartily while reading the publication that the men persuaded her to tell them why. She read:

> *Why This Engagement Was Wrecked: A man informed his sweetheart, who was 24 years old, that he was sending her one rose for every year of her age. To the florist he gave the order to send the young woman two dozen of the finest red roses he could procure. "He is a very good customer," remarked the florist to the assistant who was packing the bouquet, "so I put in an extra dozen."*

Freddy once read a true account from an engineer:

> *My most terrible experience wasn't due to any ordinary carelessness. I was coming around Basin Mills on No. 96 when I saw a baby squarely between the rails. I put on the brakes and, just about that time, out came the frantic mother. Her foot slipped and she fell in the path of the train. I don't take any credit for what happened then. It was just luck, or the hand of Providence, perhaps. But we stopped within four feet of the helpless forms. Nobody in the world knows*

what an engineer and a fireman sometimes live through. Talk about a man's heart being in his mouth! There've been times when I could taste mine.

One issue made John remark, "Now here's a quote I think Hattie would like. In fact," he said, looking at her, "maybe you sent it in!"

"A man who has never gone to school may steal from a freight car; but if he has a university education, he may steal the whole railroad." -Theodore Roosevelt

They all nodded, looking at Hattie, who flatly denied having submitted the quote. "But you're right, John. If I'd found it first, I might have."

When the November issue arrived, Denny approached Hattie when they were alone. "Did you see this in the magazine?" He handed her the MCEM, open to the right page.

Hattie tried to read what Denny pointed to, but she gave it back to him saying, "My arms are about at the end of the extension I need to be able to read. You read it for me, please." *I've got to get some glasses*, she conceded.

So, he read, "The Maine Central Employees Magazine will give a prize of ten dollars for the most striking or unique picture submitted in time for publication in the December issue. It is open to all employees. Mail the picture to the Portland office at 222 Saint John Street. The photograph will be sent back in good condition."

"What are you thinking, Denny?" Hattie asked.

"Well, we all know John takes a mighty lot of pictures. What do ya think if we take one of them and send it in? Maybe he'd win. Be a nice Christmas surprise, don't ya think?"

"Oh, that's a splendid idea! Do you think you can take one without him noticing, though?"

"Should be able to. He leaves them scattered all over the bureau. If I find one, could you send it in?"

"Sure, Denny. I just hope it wins."

Now, in December, they waited for the magazine so that they could hide it from John if his picture won the prize.

Meanwhile, while the children were gone, Hattie sewed the best she could without being able to see as clearly these days. She ordered shoes for each of them, necklaces for the girls, and the game of Flinch for the household. Two new jigsaw puzzles were on order from Montgomery Ward as well. One was of a painting of three horses and the other a very sensible map of the United States. Hattie was pleased with all her choices.

On the Sunday before Christmas, when the children were all home for the holidays, Hattie declared that it was time to bundle up so they could all go to Crawfords to cut the perfect Christmas tree. Much cheering accompanied the frenzy of donning coats, mittens, scarves, and boots to make the yearly trek they all loved so much. John went with them, and Raymond carried the saw.

"You know, John, I haven't felt The Presence down the hill in a long time," Hattie said, as they walked the ties and looked out over the snowy expanse of creamy white. John was just about to assume she was stating a blessing when Hattie continued, "And then, just this week, I sensed it again, but this time it wasn't down the hill. It was close to the house. I felt it when I put up the flag Tuesday morning. I just don't understand it. I never see anything, but I sense something, you know?"

"I don't know what to tell ya, ma'am," John answered succinctly.

"Oh, I know. I wasn't really looking for an answer. It's just so curious. It's probably nothing anyway." She let the subject drop and listened instead to the crunch beneath their feet and the children's banter. Sometimes her children seemed not to have aged at all. They talked together as if no time had passed and they had their own sort of language, an understanding among them that excluded her and the rest of the world, which was just fine. More than fine, actually. One day she'd be gone, but they'd still have each other and that was how it should be. They were each wonderful people in their own right. There was only so much a parent could give a child and then the child had to decide on his own whether or not to fly. And she could already see her children's wings. This line of thought made her suddenly think of something. "Have you heard about Oscar and Margaret Clemons' newest baby?"

"It's their fifth, I think," John replied. And from there, the two chatted about friends the rest of the mile and a half up the tracks. Hattie intended to poke her head into Elizabeth's cottage at least to say Merry Christmas and give her the fruitcake she'd made this year. She'd given one to Florence when she and her girls had paid Hattie a visit the day before.

It was a wonderful day cutting the perfect tree. It was ten feet tall and would fit the dining room bay window perfectly. They cut extra boughs to use as swags for the windows and doors throughout the downstairs. These would make the house smell like the deep of the forest once again. There was plenty for everyone to do when they got back. While the swags were attached, the tree was decorated with clip-on candles (which were never lit, for safety's sake) and adorned with ornaments and strings of tinsel. This year they decided to string popcorn and cranberries for the tree. More and more popcorn was needed, as most of the first batches were consumed by hungry teenagers and one grateful pup.

On Christmas Eve, everyone helped make the sweets that were, by now, traditional favorites. Fondant, coffee creams, and potato coconut candy. And, of course, Christmas Eve candies wouldn't be complete without a peck of laughter, a bushel of healthy teasing, and a pinch of shenanigans, all wrapped in a whole lot of love. As they were finishing the last of the dirty dishes, one of the children cried out, "Music, mum! We need music!"

"Only if Mildred will join me on her ukulele," Hattie said, smiling and washing her sugary hands.

Then all the Christmas favorites were played and sung, and everybody danced. Hattie was glad she could play mostly from memory with her eyesight getting so much worse. Even John, who always stayed for Christmas, was coerced to join in. That night, before bed, Hattie reached for the Reverend's bible to read the Christmas story to everyone. Reading it had been a tradition Hattie had kept ever since the Reverend had passed away. When the children were small, the story was too long. They'd often fallen asleep before she finished. Now, they listened attentively while the kerosene lamps cast a golden glow around the room.

Every Christmas morning, her heart was filled with the expectant joy of watching her children open their presents. It had always been something she and Loring looked forward to all of December. Sometimes the buildup throughout that month was barely tolerable. This Christmas morning was no different than those of years ago, even though the children were so much older. The door to the dining room was closed and the children lined up, Enola first. When the door opened, the tree that had been empty the night before was now loaded with gifts. Hattie and John looked on with delight, knowing the children would be thrilled with their presents. And they were. The boys disappeared with their books and the girls left to dress up as flappers. The children gave Hattie presents, even though she'd told them not to get her anything. She got a beautiful lace handkerchief from the girls and a pen and some writing paper from the boys. She chuckled to herself about the writing paper and pen because she suspected the boys hoped they'd receive a lot of letters from her throughout their school weeks in Whitefield. She was always more than happy to comply.

When the train came through that day, the children were ready to retrieve the burlap bag filled with hard candy and different kinds of nuts that Maine Central provided for its employees each year. Even her tall teenagers reverted to young children in their excitement to experience this tradition. But they weren't prepared for John to come outside, too. Hattie busied herself getting their supper together when she noticed the train had stopped for too long and went to the front door to see what was happening. John and the conductor were carrying something very large and heavy up the steps to the porch and Hattie quickly opened the door for them. The item could not be concealed nor could the thorough excitement of the children. John had used hard-earned money, a lot of it, to purchase a Victrola from the Victor Talking Machine Company. It was four feet tall and made of beautiful mahogany wood that took Hattie's breath away. It had a wind-up motor to play its 78 RPM records. The children knew exactly what the machine was for and opened its front doors to see if there were any records in it. Finding none, they turned to Hattie and asked if they could use some of their summer money to buy a record or two.

She was about to tell them they could when John reappeared in the parlor from which he had slipped away after the train left. He was holding something conspicuously behind his back. When he loudly cleared his throat, everyone turned his way.

"John! What do you have behind your back?" Raymond yelled out, approaching John with a sinister look.

"Come on, John! Show us! Show us!" Enola and Mildred shouted.

Finally, John produced several records, which were eagerly grabbed by young hands. "Careful," John warned. "Hold them at the edge if you want them to sound good for a long time."

Everyone crowded around the amazing machine to watch John line up the center hole for the record "Dapper Dan" with the short post in the center of the turntable. Then he cranked the machine to start the record spinning and carefully laid the stylus at the outer edge of the record. In seconds, the loveliest sounds escaped from the front of the machine. Everyone stood transfixed around the Victrola, listening to the song of Dapper Dan, the trainman in the south looking for love. But it was the next one that created a stir, for when "Last Night on the Back Porch" cranked out a lively foxtrot, the girls, who were still dressed in their flapper attire, started dancing. They pulled Raymond and Gordon into the center of the room, who obliged the girls by joining in all the fun and laughter. But it was when they pulled Hattie and John in that the real fun began. All six danced and danced until Hattie and John sat down, weary but satisfied to watch the children.

"You really shouldn't have," Hattie spoke quietly so as not to embarrass John in the presence of the children. "I'm sure that cost you a few paychecks."

"Ma'am," John said, "I don't have anyone else to spend money on but myself, and I have all I need. It brings me great pleasure to see the family enjoy something this much. And I knew it would be the perfect gift."

Hattie let the matter drop. She didn't want anything to spoil the moment.

But John quietly continued, "I have something just for you." He handed her an envelope. Hattie slid her thumb under its loosely closed flap to produce a piece of paper. In very large letters, it read: "Go to the eye doctor! I'll pay for your first pair of glasses." Hattie looked at John, first with embarrassment for not having taken care of this herself long ago, then with gratitude, and finally, realizing the clever way he had made his point, she laughed and said, "I'll go. Soon. I promise."

Just then, she remembered something. "Oh!" she cried, jumping up from her seat and excusing herself. In her bedroom, beneath her mattress, she'd completely forgotten that the MCEM had come the week before. She'd been so busy she'd hidden it and forgotten all about it. She put the magazine behind her back and walked back out to the parlor. When the music stopped, she said, "I have one more gift and this one is for John." She handed him the magazine as the children all gathered around his chair. They were as intrigued as he was.

John looked at her curiously and then at the magazine. "I wondered why the December issue hadn't come yet. I just figured it'd come the week after Christmas, I guess. But why is this a gift?"

"Turn to page twenty-one," Hattie said with a smile she couldn't hide.

He turned to the right page and looked at a photo he knew all too well. So did Gordon. "Hey! That's me on top of the snowplow from when it came off Bobby's train!"

Thirty-six

~ 1926 - 1927 ~
Life, and Death as Its Inevitable Partner

Time and tide wait for no man, Hattie thought as she fanned herself with Mildred's 1926 high school commencement program. It was hot for early June, not unprecedented but unusual all the same. She sat with her other children and John, marveling at how quickly time had gotten them to the second family graduation already. These graduations also made her think of her own lacking education and how grateful she was that her children's formal training had not been cut short as hers had. She swelled with pride at their achievements. But proud as she was, she also felt a bit melancholy. Raymond had just finished his tenth year so the family would all be back here in two years for his graduation. Enola would have to wait another three years to finish school, but those years, Hattie knew, would go by in the blink of an eye. And then she'd truly have a home as empty of children as when they'd first come to the Mount Willard House.

She shook her sad thoughts away and said to herself, *But today is a day to celebrate. It's about their accomplishments, not my loss.* Gordon had finished his first year of business college and had brought all his belongings home for the summer when John retrieved him for Mildred's graduation. After the ceremony, Hattie watched him greet teachers he'd had in high school. She supposed Gordon was telling them all about what he had been doing this past year.

After that, the summer passed quietly but not insignificantly. Gordon was hired as a bellhop for his second summer at Crawfords, a significant step up from caddying in both responsibility and pay. Last summer he had met "Big Bill" Tilden, so named because he towered over most people at six feet two inches. But Gordon saw him as a big man in a different sense. William Tilden had held the title of world champion of amateur men's tennis for six consecutive years. His ace serves and powerful backhand drives had become legendary. He participated regularly at the New Hampshire regional championships of the U.S. Lawn Tennis Association at Crawford House. The tennis courts there had defied the naysayers' predictions that the surface could not hold up through the frigid mountain winters, being one of the first courts built at this altitude. However, its solid foundation remained firm due to the crushed railroad cinders beneath a layer of clay.

Tilden was back again this summer and, as if holding all those honors was not enough to gain Gordon's esteem of the man, Tilden would occasionally come down to the courts in the morning when Gordon and a friend played tennis and help them with their swing. When Tilden challenged Gordon to a few singles matches and proved to be a nice man on and off the court, he gained Gordon's admiration for life.

Mildred waitressed for the sixth year. It was always such fun for her to renew friendships with coworkers. She also applied and was accepted to Keene Normal School in the far southwestern corner of New Hampshire.

Raymond continued to caddy and earned the title of "special caddy," a distinction that allowed him to work for recurring golf parties. He caddied for one of the Johnson brothers of Johnson & Johnson, who took him along to other courses as well. His most regular customer was Charles Merrill, co-founder of Merrill Lynch investment company, who wrote letters to Raymond regularly during the off season. Raymond also played baseball for Crawfords and, at nearly sixteen, was often put in as pitcher. This appealed to him greatly as he had been following the rising star, George Herman "Babe" Ruth, Jr. since he was a little boy, when "The Great Bambino" had played for the Boston Red Sox. Already Babe Ruth had been a world series champion, an American League most valuable player, and RBI leader. He'd been the American League batting champion just two years ago and the fact that he now played for the New York Yankees didn't bother Raymond enough not to root for his favorite baseball hero.

Enola waitressed alongside her sister. She and Mildred now shared many of the same friends. But being able to work with one of her best friends, Martha Jackson, and even stay in her home for the summer was simply wonderful, even though occasionally the two of them needed a break from one another. But that was no different, really, than if they'd been biological sisters.

With the children's time so occupied, Hattie especially enjoyed visitors who came from a distance. That summer, Nell came for another extended visit. It was so easy to have her around. The two women felt just as close when they were chatting as they did when they were sitting in the parlor quietly passing the time reading. But when the children's schedule allowed them to be together, Nell and Hattie reveled in the fun they all had.

One special evening, in honor of their auntie's visit, the girls were able to take off work and come down to the house. Gordon and Raymond were already there. They pulled out the new records they especially loved singing and dancing to, such as "Listen to the Mockingbird," "Ta-Ra-Ra-Boom-De-Ay," and "The Entertainer." They avoided the ones they considered to be quite dreary, even though they were their mother's favorites. The one they liked best was "Who Threw the Overalls in Mrs. Murphy's Chowder?" They'd played it so many times that they not only knew all the words but could mime the actions, to the delight of all who were willing to be their audience.

Hattie and Nell howled with laughter along with the crew when Enola, as Mrs. Murphy, fainted, and Raymond, as McGinty, wanted to know who put the overalls in her chowder, all the while Gordon and Mildred sang their hearts out in mock disbelief and fury in keeping with their part of the song. Hattie marveled at the joy her children expressed when they were together. There was something very wholesome and heartwarming about her children's affection that Hattie had felt on the Evans family farm. She wondered if Nell saw the similarity or if it never occurred to her that family relationships could be anything else.

With autumn that year came what felt like a mass exodus to Hattie, at least as far as her heart was concerned. She, Mildred, and Enola went by train to Keene so that Hattie could see which trains Mildred would take and help her settle into her room at the school. At the same time, John drove Gordon to Portland for his second year of business school. Raymond went along for the ride. A couple weeks later, Hattie and John put Enola and Raymond on the train to Whitefield. Both children were going to boarding houses they were already familiar with, but Hattie knew that Raymond would watch out for his younger sister if any issues arose. It gave Hattie much comfort to know that Enola could always lean on her brother.

When all the children were gone, and she stood in her kitchen thinking about how the week's work could be adjusted with no helpers around, Hattie felt alone in a way she hadn't before. At least she'd been able to ease into this stage of having an empty nest. She sat at her kitchen window as she had so often done and stuck her seed-laden palm outside, waiting for birds to visit her. They each had mothers with literal empty nests, she thought. Maybe if birds found their way to her palm to be cared for, her own "little birds" would find their way to someone else's "open palm." She wouldn't hold her children back from the lives they needed to live, but she wasn't ready to feel completely happy about it either. That would take time.

Letters back and forth conveyed how happy Mildred and Gordon were. Both enjoyed classes and the freedom of building their own lives. She let them know that life by the tracks went on as usual. She told them about things they could well imagine, hopefully giving them a sense of home as they read her letters.

Raymond and Enola returned each weekend with stories of their own. Raymond was leaning toward any sort of work that kept him outside, especially if it was anywhere near or around nature. Enola simply seemed to love life and people. *She would make a fine nurse,* Hattie thought, remembering the natural care Enola would effortlessly give to any person or animal in need. But Enola had plenty of time to decide what she wanted to do with her life.

Each holiday that came was a grand celebration just to be together. Hattie could think of nothing better than to cook the children's favorite foods and then watch them eat voraciously. The occasional, "Gosh, mum, this is good!" could keep her going for the rest of her life. And of course, the crew didn't mind having the children home. Not just because the food suddenly had the sparkle of Hattie's joy in it, but because they genuinely enjoyed each child and loved hearing about the life of a scholar. None of them had chosen such a life. In fact, none went to school beyond his eighth year. But if they were jealous or envious of the children, they didn't show it in any other way than to razz them about being bluestockings or bookworms. The children were used to being teased by the crew and not only considered it normal but enjoyed it enough to tease right back. It was obvious to Hattie that Denny and John loved her children almost as much as she did.

One day in late January, John walked into the kitchen while Hattie was doing laundry. When she looked up at him, she immediately braced herself. He had a way of walking or standing that Hattie knew well. He obviously had something difficult to tell her. "What is it, John? Please tell me it isn't something about the children."

"Not yours, no. But Margaret Clemons died giving birth to their eighth child. Their oldest is only twelve and the missus wasn't more than thirty herself. Guess her body just wore out."

"Oh, no!" Hattie said, sitting down. "Did the child survive?"

"I guess so. I didn't hear otherwise."

"Well, that much is a blessing. But poor Margaret. And Oscar. Whatever will he do now? Eight children, and one a newborn. Oh, dear me," she said, shaking her head gently back and forth. "I don't believe I know where they live, but I'd like to help out if I can."

"I'm not sure myself, but I can find out if you like," John offered.

"No, that's all right," Hattie said. "Well, if you hear it come up in conversation, let me know. But I'll talk to Florence and see if she knows. Oh, dear. Those poor children and that poor, poor man. What's to become of them all?" Hattie was suddenly grateful that if she died, her children, for the most part, would be able to take care of themselves. It never occurred to her to compare the Clemons children losing a parent to her own children experiencing such a loss.

The railroad community stepped in to help one of its own. They were there for each other because they understood one another's lives and the built-in risks that came with working for the railroad and living in the Notch. Not many outside of this Notch could understand this particular kind of grandeur and toil, dedication and loss. She'd lived here nearly twenty-five years now and, while most days had become normal to her, there were those times, like now, when "normal" fell apart, exposing life's underbelly of vulnerability. The community rallied and did what it could to get Oscar back on his feet with a system that allowed for proper care for his eight children so that he could get back to work to provide for them. And life returned to the sort of normal people had grown to accept—life, with death as its inevitable partner.

Soon, another school year ended. Gordon graduated from business school and planned to begin a new job in Portland in the fall. Mildred finished her first year of normal school with flying colors, while Raymond and Enola would advance to another year of high school in the fall. As soon as they finished their respective studies, they went to Crawfords to check on their work assignments. Crawfords had been good for her family. Hattie assumed her family had been good for

Crawfords as well or the children wouldn't be welcomed back each summer with open arms.

The day before Independence Day, Hattie decided to walk to work with Raymond. They were chatting about the upcoming celebration that Crawfords was going to have. "Will they have fireworks again this year?" Hattie asked.

"Sure. Right by the pond, as usual," Raymond said.

"Oh, that's nice," Hattie said. "I'm getting a bit concerned about the state of the country these days. People seem so unsettled. Something like the fireworks always pulls people together. But everything is so expensive, I wasn't sure if they'd be able to buy them this year or not."

"They did and they have 'em already. I've seen 'em. In fact…"

Suddenly they heard an explosion from down the tracks and they both instantly turned back toward the house. They saw a plume of smoke come up from somewhere near Bemis. They looked at one another quizzically.

"You go on to work. I'm going back to the house," Hattie said, giving her son a quick hug.

When she got to the house, there was no one else there. She'd hoped perhaps one of the men could shed light on the explosion. She wasn't inclined to go look for the source herself, so she decided to do the dusting she had abandoned before walking with Raymond. But she couldn't get the explosion and smoke she'd seen off her mind. She set the items she'd lifted from the table back in place and walked to the phone. She was just dialing Florence when John came running back into the house. He was doubled over trying to catch his breath but when he finally straightened up, he had tears in his eyes, which startled Hattie terribly. "Hattie…" he stopped to breathe. "Hattie, the 505 just blew up. It was Oscar and Bobby in there. They're gone, Hattie. Gone. Oscar's eight children have no parents at all now. Bobby's seven have no father. Fifteen children have lost their father today. Fifteen. If Oscar hadn't changed jobs from being a brakeman when he was in that awful train wreck years ago to being a fireman, he wouldn't have died, Hattie.

The brakeman didn't die. I need to get down there." And he left.

In the moments that followed John's words, a thought began to form in Hattie's mind. She had to sit down. The burden of this information was too heavy, and she needed to think. Something was stirring inside her, something that had needed to be understood for many years. It was about her mother. And it was linked to this accident. Then, suddenly, she knew what it was. Hattie now understood something she couldn't have known before. She saw her mother's fear and her reticence to talk about it in a whole new light. Hattie's father had been part of the crew on an engine when it blew up and killed him. Hattie's mother never wanted to talk about what had happened to her husband. When Hattie was young and curious about her biological father, her mother always seemed embarrassed, an emotion Hattie never understood. Why be embarrassed about an accident? Now she realized that her mother thought the accident that had killed her husband and several other people had been her husband's fault.

What Hattie understood now, having worked for the railroad and seen many situations and accidents, was that something like this has no warning. If the water level in the engine gets too low and the remaining water becomes super-heated, it can convert to steam so fast it causes an explosion. And it isn't always the engine crew's error. Sometimes debris or chemicals in the water skewed the gauge that told the fireman the water level. He can think there's plenty of water, when in actuality the engine is about to blow up.

With a startling anguish, Hattie wished more than anything that she could talk to her mother. She could explain that what had happened all those years ago was just an accident; it was nobody's fault. And perhaps this reassurance could have mended a relationship that had gone nowhere all Hattie's life. Her mother's stagnation, Hattie realized now, was part of the cause of their relationship's decay. Hattie felt an overwhelming grief as she sat unraveling the past, not just for her mother but also for these fifteen children.

She could not bring herself to go to the accident site. Once it was cleared a few days later, she and the other residents of Hart's Location rallied again. This time, Hattie realized that part of her help would be her empathy. She knew what it was like for a spouse to die and leave a wife and children to carry on. She knew it would be months before a new sense of normalcy would settle in, and she understood how much these families would need the help of their community. Yet, she also knew that no amount of help could replace what they'd lost. No one here was immune from the deeply troubled feelings that drew them together once again.

As horrific as all of this was to wade through, the beauty of the valley around and beneath her reminded Hattie that there was a Creator more powerful than even the most tragic of accidents. One Monday a couple weeks later, as she checked the clothes she'd hung out to dry, she marveled at how the sky could be so iridescently blue and the Notch so passionately green. It renewed her faith to be cradled between the two as if between God's hands.

Unexpectedly, as she bent to pull a stocking from her basket, she felt The Presence more powerfully than ever before, as if someone, or something, was very, *very* close. She felt a chill ripple through her body as she slowly stood and let her eyes sweep the area around her. When her scan approached the area directly behind her, she knew it was there before she actually laid eyes on it. A Canadian lynx sat crouched on the ledge where little Weston had lost his arrow so long ago. The sleek animal with beautiful fur in mottled light browns with spots of black, scowled at her. Its intensely concentrating yellow eyes pierced an arrow-like track through the air directly to her own.

For a brief moment she was captivated by the animal's magnificence. *Why are you not afraid of me? Why are you even here and not hunting for a smaller animal than me?* Then, her senses alert again, she realized she and the cat were locked in a battle for their very lives. She slowly backed toward the house, the lynx's eyes and hers never parting company. The thought of hiding in the house never occurred to her. At any moment, one of the children could be coming home from work. She slowly grabbed John's rifle just inside the door, then raised it up gently so as not to startle the big cat into taking sudden action. She took aim and squeezed the trigger. She missed, but the cat remained, unflustered. *That cat must be very hungry*, Hattie thought. *I shan't miss again, or Laddie could come to see what the noise is about. Good thing his hearing isn't so great.* She reloaded and aimed again. Again, she missed. Now the cat shifted on its wide, padded feet, planting them just so and rising slightly on its haunches to use its powerful back legs effectively. *Good,* Hattie thought, *it's making itself a larger target.* She was never so grateful *not* to see Laddie. Once more she pulled the trigger. This time, the cat toppled and fell beneath the ledge.

Hattie let out the breath she'd been holding, but didn't move, partly to be sure the animal was dead and partly in awe. Suddenly, she knew with perfect clarity that this…this had been The Presence all along for all these years. Well, not this particular cat until recently. But a lynx. *Why me?* Hattie silently queried the beautiful animal. *Why me when your prey is more likely rabbits or rodents? Do you think I take pleasure in killing you? Maybe you're a mother with kits. If you are, then I understand completely that you would do anything to protect your young. But so would I.* Her gun, still warm, was a testament to the mother bear within her.

When she was sufficiently satisfied that the lynx posed no more threat, she walked across the tracks to where it lay. She reached down to grab a handful of skin at the nape of its neck as its mother would have when it was a cub and dragged it back to the porch. The cat was heavy for Hattie but not as much as she would have thought. It looked and felt thin.

With nothing else to do about it, she finished checking her wash, now and then stealing a look at the stunningly lovely animal. Even if the wash wasn't completely down when the next train came through, she'd enjoy holding up her rifle and showing off her kill. Just then, John showed up. He kept looking from the cat to Hattie and back.

"Well, I'll be," he said. "Good for you. But I don't wanna think about what I might've found if that cat'd won. Good thing you had your glasses on!" Hattie smirked and John continued, "You get a bounty of twenty dollars, I believe. Unless Raymond skins it first." Then suddenly, John put up a finger and raced into the house. He came back out with his camera. "Let's hang the thing on the clothesline here and I'll take your picture!"

"Let me just get these old socks off the line," Hattie said, sensibly, turning around. "We don't need *those* in the picture!"

"Aw, no one will even see them. Now, hold your gun in one hand and the cat's head up with the other. Yeah, like that. Perfect! You may just be the first woman in the state to get credit for killing a lynx! And I'll be the first one to take her picture!"

Thirty-seven

**~ Flood Week ~
Thursday, November 3 -
Friday, November 4, 1927**

Added to what John and the others had just told her about the damage reports coming in from the west was the fact that Hattie had not heard from either Gordon or Mildred. She chose not to tell the men that. She'd assumed at least Gordon would wire her back and now felt somewhat embarrassed that he hadn't. She was afraid some of the men would think her silly to have wired them in the first place. But why *hadn't* either one of them communicated with her?

Supper had been a solemn affair indeed. Hattie had served the men in stony silence, as if they were little boys being punished. But it wasn't like her to do that, even with the children. Again, John secretly chastised himself for having told Hattie some of the grim details he'd heard from up the line. He had spared her some of what he knew about the devastation in Vermont, and the many lives feared gone, but he'd had to give her enough information to keep her informed.

This deep silence from Hattie was something the men had never seen before. When she went to bed she managed a forced smile, but that was all. The only thing that made sense to the men was that her demeanor was born from fear. Fear for herself? Maybe. But fear for her children, most certainly. They understood because they each privately held their own fear. Thoughts of Loring's death, or really any of the disasters they had experienced, came back to haunt them with a cold terror that something very, very dreadful may have happened that could not be changed. As far as they knew, nothing had happened to Hattie's children, but a delay in communication meant something could have, and they wouldn't know about it. This storm was yet another monster. Blizzards, record snowfalls, deep freezes, avalanches, constant gales of wind. Now, unrelenting rain. These mountains could be so vitalizing, yet so brutal. And there was no denying that train work and life itself could be equally ruthless.

Hattie had let Laddie and Sneakers into her room before shutting the door. She needed to be present to any thoughts that might come from somewhere beyond this house, this mountain, this storm. She had no idea what there was to hear other than her own heartbeat, which was drumming its persistent reminder that she was alive. Then, as if to prove that her heartbeat was not her only company, a sudden gust of wind drove the rain savagely against the house.

She was alive, yes. But she felt alone. Utterly alone. She'd never felt lonely here, not like this. She'd felt lonely when the children were all in school, but that was a loneliness every mother expects to feel. This loneliness was about feeling isolated. Again, not something she'd ever felt on this mountain, though she'd been asked countless times and answered honestly. Yes, that was what she felt now, raw and alone, in some kind of intense pain. A suffering. Even the presence of her animals, the men, her friends, her relatives, the children, and even this exquisite, blasted mountain could not help her because none of them understood her pain. She wasn't sure *she* even understood this pain. She'd experienced times when her grief sought the comfort of shared experience, such as when Bobby Morse and Oscar Clemons died. The community had all needed one another then. But the pain of this loneliness felt different, as if sharing it might light the fuse on a stick of dynamite. Why did she feel as if she might explode?

Then slowly, like the sunrise creeping over the mountain, clarity began to dawn. And she suddenly knew the source of her raw pain. She wanted Loring. She wanted him here, right now, to wait out this ugly storm of fear she felt for their children's lives. He alone would feel exactly like she did. He alone would understand her fear of losing one of their children. Another gust of savagery hit the house. *What a howling tempest this is.*

She shivered. Not only did she feel fear and loneliness unlike any she'd ever known, but she was missing the courage she'd had so readily available through all her other challenges. She couldn't feel any of that right now. If she were asked to muster it, she wouldn't know how. It had always just been part of who she was. Had she lost her courage? If so, how would she go on without it? Who would she be?

Where, indeed, was that indomitable courage that had kept her going when her mother and stepfather could be so distant? The courage that had helped her overcome the panic of being hired out as a child. That had said yes to living on the side of a mountain and right beside railroad tracks. The courage of knowing deep within her bones that she could birth her babies on this mountain, and even all alone. That had helped her stoically accept that the weather had taken her husband. Where was the courage that had accepted the task of raising their children without their father?

Then, unexpectedly, as if her thoughts had opened a new door inside her, she felt anger as she had never let herself feel it before. As she railed against all that had been taken from her, she felt anger move down into her body. It coursed through her, taking over as savagely as the storm outside her home. She could no longer feel the loneliness or even the fear. All she felt was white-hot, ferocious anger. Honest, raw, justified fury. It began as a seedling in her mind that grew with each breath she took.

Not knowing what else to do, Hattie grabbed her pillow and, taking a deep breath, held it to her face and screamed into it for as long as she could. It was the scream of pent-up pain. Anger, heartbreak, mandatory submission to the elements, and then, finally, her fear. Not the mental fear of the rational mind. No. This was gut-wrenching, all-encompassing, knee-bending dread. Not for her own life, which she would willingly give up for her children, but fear that they would never see a full life as she had. She didn't think she could bear to see her children leave this world before her.

With the pillow still held fast to her face, she felt her spent anger give way to the tears she'd held inside for too long. Was her heart breaking? Or was it finally healing? She sobbed, letting her tears flow unimpeded, like the swollen waters of the Saco River. Her sobs shook her body while the tears washed through years of keeping her back straight and her nose to the grindstone, as she'd been taught to do. She sensed these tears were beneficial in a way she didn't know was even possible. Finally, when she was purged dry, she put the pillow, now soaked with her anguish, back on the bed. Then she put on her nightgown and nightcap. She nestled down under the covers and realized for the first time that both Sneakers and Laddie had come up onto the bed and were sitting on either side of her, silent and faithful. Then Hattie drifted into a deeply healing sleep, allowing both animals to stay beside her.

The next morning, as she readied herself for the new day, Hattie could tell just by listening that the worst of the rain was over. But she knew that didn't mean the worst of the damage was. Similarly, she could tell that the worst of her anger and fear had been spent, but she realized that she would have to learn a new way to live with the reasonable angers and worries of life. Hattie hoped, no, she was *sure*, that the emotional wrestling she'd done last night had been life changing. There was only so much steeling herself against the harshness of life she could do before becoming a person she didn't want to be. Rather than trying to control life before it controlled her, she wanted to live life before it took her.

As she brushed out her hair, she stared at the picture on her dresser and suddenly realized it didn't hurt to look at it the way it had before. Instead, she felt a profound joy in having known Loring all the wonderful years they'd had together. And in the midst of that joy, and because she had known him so well, she realized he *was* here. He lived in her thoughts, her sorrows, her joys, and most of all, in the love she had for their children. When she looked at it this way, she realized she wasn't all alone to bear this fear. Loring wasn't here physically, but he was with her, nonetheless.

As her thoughts drifted to all the other losses in her life, they, too, seemed to be framed differently. She hoped this meant that she was letting go of her deepest wounds and allowing life's tragedies to reside in the past where they belonged. Life may have taken a lot from her, but it had also given her a wealth of blessings. For the first time, Hattie knew that the mantras she'd meant as ways to move on wouldn't just be words she said, but words that reflected deep, honestly held beliefs from within her.

Without her locked-up pain, she felt herself expanding inside, giving her space to feel something much more joyous. And with it, she felt a serenity that was not dependent on anything outside of herself. *It's that peace that passes all understanding that Martha used to talk about,* she realized. She felt this new, very deep peace like a quiet river close to her heart. She opened her arms wide and took a deep breath, letting in the fresh air of a weight being lifted off her shoulders. It was as if the "have to's" of life had suddenly become the "want to's." Then she let the breath out. It was time to walk into this new day.

Hattie was relatively certain that most people would never see the difference in her. She would do the same things and say the same things which, to those around her, would effectively leave her unchanged. If her children or anyone else noticed a difference and asked her about it, she might be able to discuss the past with an openness she hadn't been able to before. But if they never did, that was okay, too.

Suddenly, a thought occurred to Hattie. She remembered the conversation she'd just had with John on Sunday. She had told him that wallowing in the past didn't do anyone any good. While she still believed that, she realized now that by not fully facing her own past, she had unconsciously been wallowing in it just as she'd insinuated John had. She still believed in moving on after loss, but moving on with a bucket of pain still stuck inside had caused her an additional kind of emotional heaviness that had actually tethered her to the source of her pain rather than liberating her.

Breakfast was just about ready when Hattie heard the men approaching and she suddenly felt anxious. She was essentially on the other side of old pain and felt very different than last night, and she didn't know how she would be received. Fortunately, she was quickly relieved when the men acted normal around her. *Probably they're just grateful to see me smiling and talking to them again,* Hattie thought sheepishly.

But I think I owe them an apology, for my own peace of mind if not theirs. "I'm sorry I was unable to speak with you last night. Please accept my apologies."

Again, John spoke for them all when he replied, "None needed, ma'am. We all know you fear for the children. So do we." Quickly moving on to business, he added, "We aim to go up the tracks to see what's happened overnight. Already a westbound freight we expected hasn't come through. The lake was looking swollen last night. Could be the Saco has flooded the road down below. We just don't know yet."

When the men were finished eating, all but John grabbed their jackets and headed out into the rain. John held back. "Hattie, I can see how rough all this has been on you. We all admire your strength. We'll do everything we can to see the children are all right."

What he hadn't said with words, he was saying with his eyes. *John is a decent and honorable man,* Hattie thought. She was grateful to him. "I know you will, John. I know it." She smiled and after he left another thought came to her. She'd thought it was courage that had always gotten her through her rough times. Maybe it was, but John had just said that the men admired her strength. He hadn't used the word "courage." *Was* she strong? Was that what this was? Were courage and strength one and the same? She'd never thought of herself as strong.

As she cleaned the breakfast dishes and started to tidy the parts of the house she hadn't gotten to yesterday, it dawned on her that part of her strength, if that's what it was, had always come in knowing that life goes on and there is solace in routine. Like a rainbow after a storm promises blue skies again, life would always have its devastations as well as its celebrations. It was just the way things were. She'd lost sight of the inevitable rainbows. She had been swallowed up by the storm within her. It wasn't that she felt completely calm as she dusted now, but she felt like she was in a place that would allow her troubles to coexist with her joys, side by side. She sincerely tried not to blame herself for not having dealt with her most difficult feelings until now. She couldn't have done anything different before. And, similarly, she tried not to chastise herself for allowing those feelings to finally surface. Having done so, she knew, had made her feel better.

Sometime after she'd eaten a bit of dinner, she let Laddie outside and, when she did, she saw two of the men emerge from the far curve, walking back. Her stomach lurched a bit and by sheer force of habit she instinctively folded her arms across her waist as if posturing against more bad news. *But maybe they're simply coming back for equipment. Or maybe they have a job on this end of the section to attend to. Maybe there's just nothing more they can do today. I'm probably reading more into this than there is.* She might have walked to meet them if it hadn't still been raining so hard. Instead, she went back inside to quiet herself with early supper preparations. Ordinarily, being a Friday, Raymond and Enola would be home for supper, arriving late afternoon. Today, though, Hattie couldn't be sure when her high schoolers would make it. They could be delayed until tomorrow. So, she wasn't sure how much food to fix. *I haven't been sure about a great many things these past few days,* she thought. *Even the trains aren't running as scheduled today and trains are one thing I can usually count on.*

Scraping carrots over the sink, she heard the door open behind her. With a carrot in one hand and a knife in the other, she turned to see whether the men's faces indicated what they might say. It took her a second to realize what she was seeing.

Thirty-eight

~ 1927 ~
John Bares His Soul

On Sunday, October 30, Hattie and Laddie walked to Crawford Station with Raymond and Enola and waited with them for the afternoon train. They'd both had reasons to leave for school today rather than tomorrow as they usually did, although Enola's reason was a bit flimsy, Hattie thought. *Likely, she prefers to take the train with Raymond. And that's perfectly all right. But I dare not say anything to her lest she take it as an insult.* Hattie waved goodbye and turned for home with Laddie by her side.

Now that Raymond and Enola were headed back to Whitefield and Gordon and Mildred had left for Portland and Keene, she followed the tracks toward home, feeling the familiar sadness of a coming week's quiet. *Yet sometimes I can't find solitude when all the children* are *around,* she thought. *I guess it's about finding serenity with or without the noises of life.*

She turned to look at the western sky, something she particularly loved because she couldn't see it from the house. Here, in the open space of the station, the western view was often a source of tranquility. *Proof that something bigger than me or my problems is in charge.* Low feathery clouds were beginning to take on the yellow and hints of orange from the sun sinking toward sunset, but the sky overhead was still brilliantly blue, almost purple. *What gifts this earth provides!*

She needed to move on. It would be time for supper before long. The meal would only be for her and John tonight. The other men had all left for the day and wouldn't be back until later in the evening. She would enjoy John's company. They nearly always talked about the children, laughing at their ingenuity and creative ideas. The adventures they had here in the Notch would one day, Hattie hoped, be a source of stories and laughter when they got together as grownups. As she passed the blacksmith's shop, she thought about the games they played using the small cave as any number of settings for whatever situation they had invented. In their younger years, they were outlaws hiding from the constables or constables waiting to ambush the outlaws. When the girls had the cave to themselves, it most often became a schoolhouse and occasionally something like a beauty parlor, dance studio, or shoe shop.

This, Hattie thought, *is half the reason I wanted to have several children. Loring, you may have come from a big, close family, but I was deprived of those ready-made playmates. And to think we were so convinced we'd never have one, let alone four! I remember how much you loved teaching the children and playing with them when they were so young.* It was hard for Hattie not to become overly melancholy when she thought about those bygone days. Half of their children were finished with high school now, and Gordon had graduated from business college and was working in Portland. He'd no doubt find a suitable woman to marry one day. Mildred wasn't far behind him. At least Gordon was free on weekends and still wanted to come back to the Notch. Eventually, they would all leave her nest. *Either You are cruel,* she thought, peering up at the sky, *or very wise, to design relationships the way You have—give and take, lose and gain. It seems we can't have one without the other the way You designed things. But I can't say I'd do it that way if it were up to me.*

Closer to home, she noticed Sneakers coming up the tracks and stooped to pick him up once they met. "What have you been up to today, Sneakers? Catch any mice…I hope?" There were a couple of mice that had come through the kitchen lately. She stroked the cat's silky fur which immediately started his little internal motor going and she could feel him purring against her body. Hattie finished walking the railroad ties as easily as she would a sidewalk through town. When she entered the house, John was at the desk in the dining room, writing. He looked up at her and said, "Hattie, there's something I want to discuss with you. Maybe after supper?"

"Certainly. Supper should be ready soon." Hattie walked into the kitchen and reached for her apron. She stoked the fire to warm some leftover pea soup and cornbread. Then she set the table and placed their simple meal down at their places. Though the morning had started out chilly, it was getting warmer the longer the day went on. Even so, she hoped the soup would taste good.

She and John enjoyed their usual light banter over the meal. "How about a bit of dessert and coffee in the parlor as soon as I clean things up?" John nodded, taking his dishes to the serving hatch. He was waiting for her in the parlor when she came in with a tray of the last of the apple pie and two steaming cups of coffee. She set the tray down so that John could take what he liked. Then they ate quietly. She noticed a hawk flying, or rather soaring, then dipping, then floating over the valley below. Hattie wasn't bothered by this silence between them, but she sensed that John seemed a bit nervous, more so than usual. She didn't push him.

Finally, he set his coffee cup on the tray and cleared his throat. "What I have to say, Hattie, is something I've been thinking about a long time now." Hattie couldn't help wondering what was coming. She suddenly had the urge to scrutinize the past. Had she missed something important? "I think you know how much I've admired you for carrying on without Loring all this time. What's it been now? Nearly fourteen years? You've raised your children to be fine young men and women, giving them as normal a childhood as any youngster in town, with as many or more opportunities to be well-rounded and experienced. You might've sheltered them, fearing the worst this mountain can do to a body. Can't imagine how difficult it must have been to live through Loring's death and not fear for your children's lives every single day. If you've been fearful all this time, not one of us would know it," John paused to sip his coffee which she knew was getting cold, but he gave no indication that he wanted her to warm it up.

Spoken compliments weren't usual for John. These made her a tiny bit uncomfortable, but she stayed quiet. She realized that for John to be so eloquent, he must have thought his words out thoroughly. But she still didn't know where he was going with them. She followed them in her mind as he spoke, first to Loring's death, then to her children's lives.

"From the start, after Loring's death, I've watched for opportunities to be helpful to you and the children," he took a breath to go on, but Hattie broke her silence.

"And you have been!"

"Thank you, Hattie. But there's something I need to get off my chest about the day he died."

Now John paused, bent at the waist, elbows on the arms of the chair and fingers laced in his lap. He was looking down. Hattie realized with a mixture of alarm and compassion that what followed might be something she'd have to think about. She took great care not to let her growing anxiety show. She knew he needed to finish what he'd started.

John finally looked up and began again, "I haven't wanted to talk about this for your sake, but I believe I need to, especially since there never was a report that gave us more information. That day, Loring's death happened so suddenly it was hard to understand what really took place. It'd been snowing so hard it was nearly impossible to see very far and the wind was howling so, it was hard to think, let alone to hear." This much Hattie knew.

"The engineer of that helper engine blew three short whistles to indicate backing rather than going on to Fabyans that day. I heard those whistles, but Loring must not've." Again, this was nothing new to Hattie. She waited and watched John's face contort in mental pain.

"Hattie…Loring and I were both working to clear the switch behind the helper. I had to go into the station for a moment, like I told you so long ago. When I came back out, I heard those three whistles. I assumed Loring and the others heard them, too. And because of that, I assumed Loring wasn't anywhere near that switch. In fact, I never gave it more thought than that. Loring would never be behind a train intending to back up. None of us would. But it was so hard to hear over the wind and it was impossible to see that Loring was still at the switch. I would've been there, too, if I hadn't had to go into the station just then. And if I had been with Loring, I might not've heard those three whistles, either. Or maybe between the two of us, we'd've heard all three. But if I'd been quicker getting back out there, I'd've been close enough to see him and push him out of the way." John stopped. He was looking into Hattie's eyes now. He had had the courage to say the words he'd been holding inside for fourteen years. He needed to meet her eyes with what he was saying. And maybe not saying.

Hattie waited to see if John had more to say, then she said softly, "John, are you saying you think this was your fault?"

"It's felt that way ever since that day and Lord knows how many times that day has gone through my mind."

He looked spent, Hattie thought, as if seeing John for the first time. *The weight of the world on one man's shoulders can make them sag.*

"John, now listen to me," she began quietly yet assertively, intent on being heard yet not scolding. She felt as she had each time she helped the children move through their own struggles. "This was an accident, pure and simple, and I believe that whatever happened was somehow for the best. There are any number of things that might have happened that day to give us a different outcome. You might have gone to the station at a different moment. Or it might have been Loring who'd had to leave for a few minutes. It might have been even worse, too. What if both of you had been at that switch and neither of you had heard those whistles? But none of those things are the way it happened. And going on is the only thing that makes sense. Anything else is wallowing in the past. And we all know that wallowing is good for fattening up pigs, but not much else."

It wasn't that John hadn't thought those same thoughts, but to hear it from her seemed to make a difference. "Thank you, Hattie."

A thought had formed in Hattie's mind. "Is that why you've been so attentive to me and the children? You feel guilty?" She didn't say it accusingly, but truly wondered.

"Well, maybe at first," John said honestly. "But after a while, it came so natural, being like a father to them. I'll probably never have children of my own, but yours were so young, it's been almost as though they *were* my own. They are great people, Hattie. I can see you and Loring in all of them."

"You've made a difference in their lives, John. You really have. All of you men have. But you, especially. I know the boys have thought of you as a role model for how to be young men. And the girls…well, I'll be the first to say how grateful I am that you have treated them respectfully. Their father knew how to honor and respect women. Loring never put me down. I think that was actually my first thought when it sunk in that Loring was gone—that the children wouldn't have a father to raise them, let alone raise them well. But you can be proud of the way you've stepped into Loring's shoes to help me parent them. You should be as proud as I am grateful. My children will always know they had a good father even though their own left them about as early as mine left me."

Inwardly, John winced, realizing suddenly how Hattie was reliving her past. He hadn't wanted to bring any more on her than he already knew he had to. Hoping not to further complicate things, he nevertheless felt compelled to be totally honest about something more.

"Hattie, you asked me if I've been attentive to you and the children because of guilt. Where it concerns you, it's been my pleasure to make things as easy for you as possible, although you don't really seem to count on being helped, I don't think," John's crooked smile was the first indication that he was feeling some better. "But I must confess, there've been times when I've hoped for something more between us." He was suddenly blushing, and Hattie saw it. "That's been purely selfish on my part. But since I'm clearing the air, I figure I may's well clear it up altogether. I hope you understand what I'm about to say. Loring was a great man to work for. He was willing to do the work of overseeing everything while working right along with us. He earned our respect. But I used to watch him with you and your children and was a mite envious. It's pretty hard to meet young women when you work up here. And even the ones I have gotten to know, I couldn't be with them enough to sustain much of a relationship. But Loring, he was fortunate to be able to bring his woman here with him. And it was obvious how much you two cared for each other. I wanted that. What man doesn't? So, selfishly, after a respectable time, that is, I began to hope that maybe there could be something between us." Hattie was beginning to look uncomfortable, so John was quick to wrap up his talking. "But Hattie, I came to understand that you are a one-man woman, that Loring was all you'd ever wanted. And I accept that."

If this speech had been delivered by anyone but John, good and faithful John, she couldn't imagine how she would feel or handle things from here. But she knew John was a man who would keep his word. He wasn't asking for anything now, just her continued friendship. Hattie had been aware that John felt their close relationship and she tried very consciously to keep her signals clear, especially after Nell had called their relationship into question. She didn't want to send any message other than that of deep gratitude for John's care for the children and friendship toward her. *But relationships can be so tricky.* She thought of Martha's answer about how it was that their marriage seemed so easy. *Men reading women's thoughts, women reading men's. We communicate very differently sometimes. Most of the time, truth to tell.*

When a woman happened to meet a man like Loring, a man who was a good soul, whom she had feelings for, she could count herself fortunate. She and Loring seemed like two halves of some whole that, without the other, made no sense. John was right about her—that she was a one-man woman. Besides, with John caring for the children and the railroad paying her to work for them, she really had everything she needed. *In fact,* she suddenly wondered, *does John think that I've been the one being selfish, allowing him to do as much as he does for us?* But she had never asked much of him in that respect. He'd seemed to fall into a parenting role very naturally. She let that question go.

When some time had gone by, Hattie said, "John, what do you need from me?"

After a moment, he said, "Nothing more, Hattie. If we can continue in the manner we have been, being friends, that'll be enough for me. Now that I've cleared my conscience about the day Loring died, I feel much better and I thank you for listening."

"You're welcome, John. If that's all, I think I'll tidy the kitchen and head to bed if you don't mind. Tomorrow starts a new week." She realized the kindest thing might be to give John a way to exit the conversation before it became too uncomfortable between them. This had been very difficult for John, she knew.

"Of course," John said. He knew she would never bring the subject up again and that she would take his deepest thoughts and secrets with her to the grave.

Thirty-nine

~ Flood Week ~
Friday, November 4 -
Saturday, November 5, 1927

Hattie turned to see whether the men's faces indicated what they might say. It took her a second to realize what she was seeing. "Raymond! Enola!" Hattie quickly crossed the kitchen and hugged each child tightly, still with a carrot in one hand and a knife in the other. She didn't care a whit about how wet her children were.

"Whoa-a-a!" Raymond said, taking the knife from his mother, laughing. "Some greeting! Get hugged and stabbed at the same time!" Enola had immediately crouched to greet Laddie and Sneakers with just as much enthusiasm.

Hattie put her free hand on her son's face affectionately, looking at him tenderly, still in amazement and gratitude that he and Enola were actually standing in her kitchen, that the "two men" walking the tracks hadn't been section men at all. When she could breathe again, she reached for her paring knife and said, "You two go put your things in your rooms and change out of those wet clothes while I finish the last of these carrots. Then meet me in the parlor. We have things to talk about."

Hattie rinsed and wiped her hands, walked to the parlor, and situated herself in her favorite chair with Sneakers, not far behind, jumping into his favorite lap. Not long after that, Raymond and Enola plopped themselves down on the couch. Sneakers jumped off Hattie's lap to take the opportunity to fill Enola's instead. Enola stroked the cat affectionately. They could all hear his purring. Hattie just watched Raymond and

Enola as if seeing ghosts. Very welcomed ghosts, to be sure. "First of all, why are you here early?"

"They let school out just after dinner," Raymond began. "We caught the 156. We had to walk here from Crawfords because the train stopped there to go back."

"Raymond came and got me from my class. He said we should grab what we needed from our boarding houses and run to catch the train. We got soaked," Enola said, as if Hattie couldn't see that much for herself. "Mum, the Saco is flooding. The water's up across the road! I've never seen it do that before." Then, with her mind obviously as flooded with thoughts as what she'd just seen, Enola asked, "Have you heard anything from Gordon and Mildred? Are they gonna try and come home? Oh, I hope they're all right. This rain is something, isn't it?"

Seeing how concerned these two were, Hattie picked her words carefully. "I wired them both two days ago not to try to come home. I haven't heard anything yet, but they're very busy, I'm sure. And I'm sure they're just fine." Her calm tone was what the two needed. They relaxed into the couch some. "So, tell me about school this week and about that stray cat, Enola," Hattie continued, asking a typical question to normalize things.

But just then, the men's door opened and shut. Hattie and the children went to see who it was and found John standing in the entranceway. Hattie stood closest to the kitchen door with Raymond and Enola just behind her. She felt her children's anticipation, waiting for news. It crossed Hattie's mind fleetingly to ask them to wait in the other room in case what John had to say was bad news. But Raymond and Enola were not really children anymore, she reminded herself. They were her young man and young woman now. She let them stay.

"Hi again," John peered around Hattie to speak to Raymond and Enola. Hattie surmised correctly that the men had seen the children get off the train at Crawfords. Then turning to Hattie, he said, "You won't hear from Gordon and Mildred. The lines are down. And there're mudslides everywhere and washouts down below us, so the trains can't get past North Conway. We've got a mess of rocks coming down off the ledges here. I suspect you two had to pick your way through them just to get here," he said, looking again at Raymond and Enola who nodded vigorously.

"McCann's section this side of Bartlett Station had a washout and there's a mudslide on Webster, too.

"But I suspect about the worst is Monahan's section," John continued, which caused Hattie to draw in a sharp breath remembering the Willey family and the landslide of 1826. Reading Hattie's mind, John quickly said, "Everyone is safe there. It's just that he's got a washout twenty feet deep to wrestle with. Oh," he said, suddenly remembering something else, "and a huge boulder came down in his section and struck freight Number 376 about in the middle of the train. It broke a loaded boxcar in two, derailing the two cars on either side." John saw his chance for a moment of levity and took it. "Guess what it was loaded with?"

"What?" Raymond and Enola said in unison, completely enwrapped in what John was saying.

"Envelopes and chamber pots! Now won't that be something to tell about!" They all laughed.

But Hattie was thinking about Gordon and Mildred and how surely any stubborn thoughts they might have had about trying to get home would be squelched if they heard about the conditions in the Notch. Besides, she reminded herself, she'd wired them to stay put. That wire went through before the lines went down so she knew they'd have gotten it. They'd listen to her.

Sometime in the late afternoon, the cold front finally came through that changed the rain to wet snow, more fitting for the time of year. Supper came and went. It was nice to have the children home to liven things up in such a sober situation as this. She almost hated to see bedtime come around. Then she would be alone with her thoughts instead of distracted by constant chatter. But bedtime did come around and the house silenced, save for the sloppy patter of diminishing wet snow. As she readied herself for bed, she thought about how grateful she was that two of her children were home and safe. She thought about the other two and hoped they were also safe where they were. And with this latter thought she suddenly realized that the peace she'd come to feel yesterday was still with her. It lay inside her like a firm foundation that even anxiety couldn't completely push away. She smiled. Like a constant companion, she prayed this peaceful foundation would never leave her.

Then her thoughts changed again. The mountain had seemed lonely without the trains coming through today. And there would be none tonight. Hattie wondered how long it would take before things got back to normal. She knew the miles of track below her very well and could picture where the damage was, as described by John. But visualizing what was happening west and south of her was something she knew less about. The unsettling thing was that it was precisely west and south that involved Mildred's travels home each week. As she brushed out her hair, then twisted it and put it up under her nightcap as she'd done so many times, she reminded herself that she'd made the unprecedented decision to tell them not to come home and then, pulling the covers up under her chin, she soon fell asleep.

Saturday dawned chilly, but, if she was not mistaken, Hattie did not hear rain or snow. That made her heart feel lighter than it had been all week. For a moment she smiled, thinking that all her children were in their rooms above, sleeping late as young ones tended to do. But sadly, reality came back to her. Laddie heard her door open and came slowly down the stairs. He had no doubt slept with Enola. Now he wanted to go outside, and she opened the door for him. *No precipitation,* Hattie confirmed silently. Then she surveyed the tracks. Even in the pre-dawn light she could see that where there were usually two unbroken, parallel silver threads, that stretched as far as her eye could see, the sheen was now broken up by the litter of rocks and mud. Her heart caught in her throat. She was so used to seeing the rails in perfect condition that to see them like this was similar to watching Laddie walk through her cleaned house with muddy paws, shaking filth all over everything. But the section men would take most of this in their stride as another day's work, albeit probably longer and more strenuous than usual. And she knew they'd work wherever they were needed over the next week or however long it took to clean up the mess and get the trains running again. That was their job, after all.

The trains, Hattie thought, alone with her memories, which now came more easily and ever so slightly more joyously. *How our lives have revolved around the trains all these years, for better or worse, like any serious commitment.* She began her work in the kitchen. *The men will need extra-hearty meals today and Raymond will work with them, I expect. I'm glad Enola's home. She can help me in here while we talk.* Hattie supposed she could also say that their lives revolved around the kitchen as much as the tracks. It sure did seem that way. Not that she minded. Quite the opposite. Food was a way of taking care of those she loved. Hattie decided to make eggs and bacon this morning, along with oatmeal. *They'll need the extra sustenance.*

As she worked, she continued her reverie on both trains and her kitchen. *I remember first meeting you, Loring. You were right that since I'd lived up to that point knowing how dangerous railroad work could be, I might not want to be involved with a train man. But you convinced me that working the rails would be much safer than working on engines. Oh, Loring. I'm glad we didn't know our future because look what we'd have missed if we'd walked away from this job. And I'd do everything all over again to have spent those sixteen years with you. They were some of the best of my life. The rails brought us such a rich life, didn't they? I remember when you carried me over the threshold of this house.* Hattie grinned. *Lordy, I thought you so silly for that. After all, you'd done that already six years before. But not in* this *house, you'd said.*

Remember when the children named the hens? She chuckled out loud as she whipped the eggs to scramble this morning, something she'd done countless times. *Those silly hens. And oh, the children! Birthing our babies up here, waiting for Doc Shedd. Or not waiting! I think the whole line from North Conway to Fabyans, maybe further, was waiting for these babies. I remember when your sister was so concerned about the children's education way up here. Well, the trains helped us make that work quite well, and they still do,* she thought defensively, on behalf of the trains.

Hattie began hearing the noises of awakening men. *These tracks and the people we know because of them have always been a part of our family, haven't they? And thank goodness for that. From dear John taking over for you to English Jack making toys for the children. And all the people we would never have met were it not for the trains bringing them into the Notch.* Her eyes misted over when she thought about the very close friendships she had with Beth, Florence, and Elizabeth. *We are all custodians of the beauty here and its power to heal. Somehow, I think that's what draws people back to these mountains—to re-experience the effect of its magnificence, which is as good as any tonic. In fact, that's the third thing life revolves around, isn't it? The trains, the kitchen, and these mountains.*

Hattie began slicing bread and had a sudden idea. *Since the children are here, I'll make this into French toast. They'll love that. So would I!* As she dipped the bread in the egg and waited for the skillet to heat up, she thought about how tenaciously the local families accepted the blessings as well as the difficulties in living here. Then she remembered the two families who left after the big snowstorm of '21. *Not all of us feel we can stay here, I guess. The Notch can be so harsh and unforgiving. But it gives as much as it takes,* she thought defensively again, this time on behalf of the mountains. *I can't imagine wanting to live anywhere else.*

Just then, as if they'd agreed to meet at the same time, the men and the children were all in her kitchen. There was an air of joy in the room. The children always seemed to do that, bring joy wherever they were. *Well, to be honest, not always, I guess.* She remembered some of the mischief and near misses they'd had growing up that taught her a thing or two about how to raise them. *Thank goodness for John and the crew stepping in so many times. I know the children especially love John, as well they should. I only wish it was Loring they first thought of as their father.*

"Off to the table with you. All of you, except you, Enola. Will you help me finish things?"

Enola shot her mother a do-I-have-to look. But, seeing her mother's return look of yes-you-do, she said, "Sure, mum." And Enola moved right into step with what needed to be done.

John made sure to let Hattie and Enola know the men would be working on the tracks right by the house and would come in for dinner. After breakfast, he said he'd be sure to let her know if he heard anything more about the storm damage. Then he and the men and Raymond went to clean the tracks while Enola helped her mother clean up the kitchen. "Mum? Do you suppose we won't have school next week?"

"Can't imagine you will," Hattie said, keeping her eyes on her work.

"Good! 'Cuz I like being home. I like school, too," she said quickly, "and living with the Wilders. But I like it here better."

Hattie smiled warmly at her youngest. She loved having Enola around, of course. But she hoped the girl would want to leave when she was a bit older. That was only right.

"Besides," Enola added, "I want to be here with all..." Enola's words stopped there, but Hattie knew what the rest of the sentence was.

"Oh, Enola, I know it won't be the same without Gordon and Mildred, but we wouldn't want them to try to get home."

"They could make it, mum. I *know* they could!"

"They may not realize just how much damage there is up here, dear. From what John says, it's pretty bad. If they tried to get home, they could get stuck part way. I'd rather they stayed put."

"Oh," Enola said, disappointed. Then brightening, she added, "Maybe we could go down to see them this week, if we don't have school anyway," she said with growing enthusiasm.

"Perhaps," Hattie said. "We'll just have to wait and see." Hattie couldn't imagine how on earth they'd be able to leave this place. And if the tracks were clean enough to run the trains, then school would start up again. But Hattie didn't have the heart to throw cold water on Enola's eagerness.

When the kitchen work was settled for the time being, Enola asked to leave and was granted permission. Hattie watched her go and felt tendrils of fear trying to creep out of their familiar hiding places inside her. Just how bad *were* things up the line? And south. Especially south. If only she could get word from Gordon and Mildred.

She was sitting at the kitchen table, working out how long their food supply would last without trains to freshen the pantry when Raymond and John stepped inside. They were a mess with mud. "Mum, John has some more information." Hattie tried to stay calm, especially for Raymond's sake. Instinctively, she covered her mouth with her hands, elbows resting on the table, as though to squelch any screams that might slip out like Thursday night.

"Well, ma'am," John said, addressing her more formally around Raymond, "we are hearing about deaths in Vermont. We've heard that the Lieutenant Governor there was killed. Now, that could be hearsay, I suppose. You know how rumors start. But they say whole towns are under water. And the covered bridge in St. Johnsbury was seen floating down river. That whole bridge. People are homeless. A lot of livestock can't be saved. And there's places where the tracks are just completely washed out, destroyed. They're saying this is the worst flood damage Vermont's ever seen." John stopped. Hattie waited for him to continue but he didn't. He hadn't said anything about Gordon or Mildred. Yet. She held her breath.

"Well, that's about all we know. We'll be going back out now." Hattie slowly released her breath as John turned to go. Raymond followed, after giving his mother a knowing look, one that said, "It'll be fine." How she loved that boy!

That afternoon, Hattie, Enola, and the animals were sitting in the parlor, listening to a stray rain shower mixed with wet snow that was a stubborn leftover as the storm moved east. It was strange not having to do some of the things she normally needed to, but with the trains not running and nowhere to go, there'd be no stray visitors, no need to make special food for a Sunday outing. She supposed she'd end up doing more than usual laundry, as dirty as the men were getting, but for now, that could wait. It was as if the whole world had stopped. Hers had, in any case.

"What's that?" Enola said. Laddie suddenly sat up and faced the noise.

"What's what?" Hattie answered, mostly engrossed in what she was reading.

"That pinging noise on the window. There! There it is again."

"The men must be shoveling rocks and probably a few stray ones hit the window."

"No, mum. I don't think so. I'm going out to look." Laddie followed. Enola wasn't gone long before coming back in and asking Hattie to come see.

Hattie put down her book, grabbed her sweater, and walked to the door. She looked the direction of the pinging noise. And there, to her utter disbelief, utter joy, and utter relief, was Gordon, throwing little pebbles against the window to get their attention and smiling from ear to ear, all while trying to be attentive to Laddie. Hattie ran, jumping over debris, and nearly falling into Gordon's arms. Enola went to Raymond and, arm in arm, they watched their mum's love surround their older brother. Enola began crying quietly. The men all stopped working to stare at Hattie and Gordon. They might have given Hattie a private moment with Gordon, but they, too, had been stunned as if seeing a ghost come walking up the tracks and across the bridge. They were, quite frankly, shocked, knowing how much damage there was for miles east of them. None of the men thought Gordon could make it home. Leaning on their shovels, they were almost embarrassed by Hattie's rare show of emotion. Almost. But had they been asked, they might have had to admit how much Gordon's return affected them, too.

"You made it," was all Hattie could manage to say, looking into her son's eyes.

"Of course I did. Couldn't miss a family weekend, could I?" Gordon winked in the direction of everyone watching.

"I don't know how you did it. I'm just grateful you're here in one piece. You can tell me the whole story later. Come inside and put your things down. There's some mincemeat pie if you're hungry. Of *course* you are! Here," she said, grabbing a smaller bag from one of his hands. "I'll take this in." And she headed for the house, looking over at the others and beaming, her happiness oozing from her whole being.

Suddenly, she stopped. "Wait. This is *Mildred's* bag!" She swung around and there, standing beside Gordon as if magically conjured out of thin air, was the last of her four children. She dropped the bag and she and Mildred ran to one another. Hattie caught Gordon's eye and waved him over. Then she looked over at Raymond and Enola, and they, too, stepped into the circle. They all felt the power of being there, together. Complete. No more anxiety, no more fear. Whatever was to come, they'd face it together as a family. For at least this one moment, the only world that really mattered to Hattie was right there in her arms. Hattie couldn't stop the tears this time.

As they all walked into the house, they failed to notice the enormous double rainbow arching over Crawford Notch behind them.

Epilogue

1941

Hattie stood on the hill by the house, taking in the same view she'd seen and loved hundreds of times. *I'm seventy years old and feel it in my bones*, Hattie thought, as if apologizing for her decision to retire. *I've served tens of thousands of meals. I've been broken and healed over and over again. Some of those I've loved here have died. But I'm a blessed woman indeed to have all my children. I've seen them marry and begin their families, settle into lives they love. My dear Loring, it's time for me to go. But, oh, how I have loved being in this house and on this mountain. It was your job that brought us here, but it was my heart that wouldn't let me leave. Now I'm tired. I'm ready to go.*

She looked up at John beside her, who was also surveying the place he called home. "How does one part company we've kept for almost forty years?" Hattie said. "You've been so good to me and my children. I certainly can't ever thank you enough."

"No thanks necessary, Hattie. I've received as much as I've given. Are you ready to bury Sunshine?"

"Yes," Hattie said, gazing at the little yellow bird she cradled in her hand. She'd had him for nearly ten years and found him dead at the bottom of his cage when she'd gotten up this morning. It was as if he didn't want to move from this place. *I understand*, she'd said to the canary. She watched John dig a small hole and then she gently lay the bird in its final resting place. They both stood quietly for a time.

"Where will you go now?" she asked John, breaking the silence. She'd heard him muse about traveling some, perhaps down south to enjoy warmer weather. And she'd heard him talk about other possibilities, but he'd never said where he would go today.

"I'm going to head south. I need to stop in Hanover to take care of a bit of business there first. Then I think I'd like to see Florida or Louisiana, maybe. Anywhere it's warm and stays that way for more than a month or two," he quipped. "You ready to make this walk one more time?"

She nodded, grabbed her purse and small satchel, which she insisted she could carry, and they turned toward Crawford Station.

"Did you know that Loring used to call this house 'the castle halfway to the sky'?" Hattie asked John.

"No," he answered.

"Yeah. I think he was truly and completely happy here. When I think of him leaving us when he did, I can either be selfish and sad that he wasn't with me all of my years here, or I can remember that the years he had were good ones and that he was happy," Hattie said thoughtfully. Neither spoke for some time. All was quiet, save for the ever-present wind and the sound of their footfalls against the ties.

Then Hattie said, "Remember when we went to Portland together? That one decision on both our parts was a good one."

"The best," he murmured. He couldn't help noticing a spike that looked too high on one of the ties. He'd mention that up at Crawfords. Then he chuckled to himself, realizing it was hard to break old habits. The spikes weren't his business anymore.

They chatted with the ease of old friends, sometimes with large pauses for introspective thoughts. It was a lot to take in, walking the mile and a half one more time. Seeing the blacksmith's shop, the curve up ahead that would narrow into the gateway.

Hattie stopped. She turned toward the view. *Thank you, Loring, my dear, dear husband. What a life I've had here.*

Then she turned again, this time toward her future. And she never looked back.

Loring Evans
(Craig Robinson Collection)

Hattie Evans
(Raymond Evans Collection)

Mount Willard Section House and Willey Brook Bridge
(Craig Robinson Collection)

Entering the Gateway
(Craig Robinson Collection)

Bird's-eye View of the Notch
(Craig Robinson Collection)

Crawford House Hotel and Crawford Station
(Craig Robinson Collection)

English Jack and His Performing Bear
(Raymond Evans Collection)

English Jack and His "Ship"
(Raymond Evans Collection)

Burro Riders atop Mount Willard
(Credit: *Life By the Tracks*, pg. 98)

Crawford Station circa 1910
(Bartlett Historical Society Collection)

Mount Willard Section House
(Craig Robinson Collection)

Carhouse and Crew with the Three-wheeler
L-R: Francis King, Dan Murphy, John Green, Denny Meany
(Craig Robinson Collection)

Loring (Left) and Crew
(Craig Robinson Collection)

Willey Brook Bridge Replacement, 1905
(Raymond Evans Collection)

John, Hattie, and Loring with a Doe
(Craig Robinson Collection)

Engine No. 380 Leaves the Rails, August 1922
(Raymond Evans Collection)

Gordon Ready for School
(Raymond Evans Collection)

Mount Willard House Rainbow Window
(Mary Anne Evans)

Previous Page (Top to Bottom): Hattie and the Children, Loring
and the Children on the Three-wheeler, Enola Tied to the Porch
(Raymond Evans Collection)

Hattie Reading beside Her Piano
(Craig Robinson Collection)

Loring and Hattie with a Buck
(Raymond Evans Collection)

Plow Pushing through Avalanche
(Raymond Evans and Arnold Wilder Collections)

Gordon atop the Derailed Wedge Plow
(Credit: *Life By the Tracks*, pg. 55)

Avalanche of 1921
(Raymond Evans Collections)

Above: Hattie with the Lynx (Credit: *Life by the Tracks*, pg. 9)
Below: Hattie and the Children on a Picnic
(Credit: *Life by the Tracks*, pg. 20)

Afterword

This story, based in truth, presented me with so many facts and photographs that it practically wrote itself. Any inventing I did was to put a bit of meat on the bones of the well-loved tales of the Evans family, the Mount Willard House, and Crawford Notch. Hattie and Loring Evans arrived there in 1903. Loring died on Thanksgiving Day, 1913. Hattie and John Green had worked side by side for nearly forty years. Did they decide together when to retire? I don't know, but I do know they retired at the same time in 1941. According to the family, Hattie's ten-year-old canary died the day she left the house. I named the bird.

The New England storm and resulting flooding in 1927 went down in the record books as the worst natural disaster in Vermont history. Its impact on some areas of New Hampshire was extreme as well. According to her children, this is the only event they remember Hattie being frightened by. And for good reason. Eighty-four Vermonters died, including S. Hollister Jackson, the Lieutenant Governor at the time, and hundreds more were injured. The cost of the damage was estimated at that time to be thirty to thirty-five million dollars. The arrival of a late-season tropical depression had gone inland up through Long Island, Connecticut, and the far eastern edge of New York. The warm, wet air of that storm was met by two high-pressure cold fronts on either side, forcing it to move up over the Green and White mountains of New England. There, the air cooled quickly and dumped between six to as much as fifteen inches of water from late evening on November 2 through late morning on November 4, depending on where it was measured.

It is not known exactly what day Hattie sent her telegram to Gordon (and likely Mildred) to tell him not to come home, but that telegram never made it to Gordon. Assuming they had received her message, she was confident the older two children would be safe where they were. Gordon knew the situation wasn't good when the Friday evening train he always took was canceled because of washouts. And he assumed his mother would be wondering where he was. In Gordon's own words: "I took (scheduled train) Number 154 on Saturday. It could get only as far as North Conway where I got a ride to Glen Station and then walked the rest of the way. I'd walk on the railroad where I could, and partly on the road around the gullies. Cabins had been washed out and people had to be rescued from houses in water up to their shoulders. There were homeless people sleeping in the woods and railroad stations. Trees were down everywhere, but the railroad bridges were mostly untouched, being up so high with plenty of clearance underneath. Fortunately, the railroad managed to escape a lot of damage, but there were no trains running on our section for about five days." It is not known exactly how Mildred made it home, only that she did. (*Life by the Tracks*, Virginia C. Downs, pg.57)

All four children went on to live their own fine lives and all four continued to go home whenever they could, as much to be with each other as to be with Hattie. Gordon graduated from Gray Business School. He was a veteran of the U.S. Army serving in World War II. He and his wife, Helen, had a daughter. Gordon died in 1999. Mildred graduated from Keene Normal School and became a teacher. She married Stillman Robinson, and they had three children. Mildred died in 1996. Raymond was also a WWII veteran. He was employed by the New Hampshire Fish & Game Department and the White Mountain Fish Hatchery. He married Connie, and they had three children. He died in 2001. Enola married Vonley Ruggles and they had three children. She died in 1969. Hattie really did play solitaire waiting for the doctor and gave birth to her last child alone. Hattie enjoyed seeing her children's spouses as well as some of her grandchildren up in that mountain home.

John Green worked as section foreman after Loring was killed and became a surrogate father to the Evans children. I was able to learn that John died in 1941, the same year he retired. His death record indicates that he died in Hanover, New Hampshire. Most importantly to me, and perhaps others, is that he will go down in history as the man who stepped up to the plate.

Hattie moved in with Enola's family in Littleton, New Hampshire, for a short time after retiring, and then with Mildred's family in Portland, Maine. While living in Maine, she kept herself as active as ever, working for the B&M Bean Company, picking over beans in the assembly line. Sometimes she watched the children of parents who both worked. When she worked at the fish pier, she used her own file and knife to cut up fish.

Hattie "lived a remarkable life," as Phil Franklin, president of the Bartlett Historical Society, said in the summer 2021 edition of The Historical Herald, the society's quarterly newsletter.

On June 14, 1954, Hattie died in Portland, Maine. She was 82.

In September 1968, the four Evans children made one last visit to the Mount Willard House. According to *Life by the Tracks*, "Maine Central officials were forced to raze the section house that had been abandoned after the cessation of passenger service in 1958. Vandals had begun to invade the building, posing the threat of track damage and fire in the scenic forest site. Waiting for the first heavy snowfall, railroad employees burned the house to the ground on December 13, 1972. Despite the heavy rumblings of passing trains over the decades, not one crack had marred (the house's) plastered walls."

Similarly, the Crawford House had a notable history. It provided many services, from the employment of all four Evans children to entertaining well-known sports and Hollywood celebrities, entrepreneurial giants, and several U.S. presidents.

The children actually did meet President Harding and other famous people while working at Crawford House. Although I have no way of knowing if Wilbur Wright stayed at the hotel, I do know that Frank Lloyd Wright did. The Crawford House locked its doors for the last time on October 13, 1975. On November 20, 1977, it was destroyed by fire.

The working rails of yesteryear gave way to the Conway Scenic Railroad excursion rides in 1974. As the train slowly climbs past the site of the Mount Willard section house, passengers can see what is left of the homestead—the house's foundation with a small garden growing on the north side, "Hattie's Garden," tended for years by her family. There is also a granite memorial engraved with a picture of Hattie and her children alongside the house with a view of the Notch in the background. Sadly, at the time of this writing, the images of Hattie and her family have been scratched out by vandals. Today, Hattie's legacy lives on in her grandchildren as well as her great and great-great grandchildren's lives.

As for my interest in this story, Loring Evans was my great-great uncle, younger brother of my great grandfather. The stories of Cora and Weston, Nell and Earl, and Millie are based in fact. In a taped interview, my grandfather, Weston, remembered his visit with his uncle as a wonderful time for a young boy. He went on to study civil engineering and eventually became professor and head of the civil engineering department at the University of Maine in Orono. Nell was Loring's sister and Millie was my maternal grandmother, who may or may not have visited Hattie in the Notch. She did, however, live close enough to the Evans family to have heard about Loring's tragic death.

My father made sure we children knew the amazing story of the Mount Willard section house in which his great uncle Loring and wife Hattie had lived. I remember seeing the house from Route 302 far below. I was unimpressed as a child, but over the years, the story grew on me until I knew I needed to write about it. Much of my story is factual, thanks to the testimonies of Hattie and Loring's grandchildren and townsfolk in the Crawford Notch area. Immensely helpful were the interviews of Hattie's children by the late Virginia C. Downs, who wrote *Life by the Tracks*, a wonderful account of many entertaining as well as astounding events.

There are many notable truths in this novel. The major weather and train disasters, including Loring's death, are well documented, as is the upgrade to the Willey Brook bridge in 1905. I could find no accident report about Loring's death that definitively stated why he would not have understood the signals that day.

English Jack really was the Hermit of Crawford Notch. His stories that I included may or may not have been yarns he himself spun. They are, nonetheless, tales that remain untouched to this day. No one who knew him denied that he was a splendid character in their midst. "The Story of Jack: The Hermit of the White Mountains" by James E. Mitchell, 1891, referred to in this novel, is easily found on the Internet.

Other real people and events include Laddie, Sneakers, Joe and Florence Monahan and their children, Bobby Morse, Denny and Ed Meany, Oscar Clemons, Private L. Dudley Leavitt, Charles and Mrs. Morey, and the Maine Central Employees Magazine, first published in 1924. John himself submitted one of his pictures. It was not the winner but did receive mention. Dr. George Shedd, who came by train to assist in the children's births, was a person of some notoriety in the Notch. The children, who were spaced forty feet apart to be picked up, rode the train to school much as children today ride school buses. They went to high school in Whitefield and had to board during the week because the trip home and back by train was too long. They really did name their near miss in Bridgton "Stutz Curve," and tasted ice cream for the first time away from home. Gordon remembers his father reading books to them before bedtime, something I found very charming.

Hattie's father died in an engine explosion when she was one and her mother died when she was twelve. She *was* the first documented woman to have killed a lynx in New Hampshire for a twenty-dollar bounty. However, she killed the lynx in 1929, rather than in 1927 as I have written it.

Hattie and Loring's various civic involvements were revealed in old town documents. Pictures of the inside of the Mount Willard House show that Hattie had both a piano and organ in the house, although I have no idea where they came from or whose they were originally. The pet squirrel and hen in the house, as well as Hattie feeding wild birds by hand, were fond memories her children told in *Life by the Tracks*. She did decide to stay on with the railroad after being given an option to do so. She never remarried after Loring died.

Most of what I invented were the details of Hattie and Loring's lives prior to 1903. After the story was written, I learned that they were actually married in 1892, rather than 1897, and Christmas Day, rather than Loring's birthday. However, I wasn't convinced that these facts made enough difference to rewrite the novel. In deciding on a location for the Evans newlyweds, one document said that the Maine Central Railroad transported their household belongings from Rumford Junction, which isn't far from Lewiston. That city's rich history of the textile industries captured my attention, and I imagined Hattie taking a job at one of the factories. The Reverend and his wife were products of my imagination along with the cat, Boomerang. And lastly, I changed some of the names of real people throughout the novel.

I was once asked if a person reading this book might fall in love with Hattie. I don't know about that, but I know the more I wrote, the more I respected her. My hope is that the reader will feel similarly. Oddly, I did not expect the awe I felt for Hattie's life to diminish in some ways. Let me explain. All these years, when I've thought about what her life was like, I couldn't imagine living it myself. But the more I stepped into her shoes, the more I began "hearing" her say, "I am not to be revered for a life lived one day at a time just as everyone else has lived theirs." So, Hattie, to you, I say, "Well done, good and faithful servant." We'll leave it at that.

Acknowledgments

I am deeply indebted to Virginia C. Downs, though she is no longer with us. Her work, *Life by the Tracks: When Passenger Trains Steamed Through the Notch,* was the foundation for my own. Craig Robinson, grandson of Mildred Evans Robinson, Vernon Evans, grandson of Raymond Evans, and Gary Kezerian, granddaughter of Enola Evans Ruggles, provided me with interviews. Their memories of being with their grandmother were invaluable first-hand information. I am grateful that they entrusted me with family photographs and other items that, themselves, often told the story better than I could.

Richard Alberini, curator, Littleton Historical Museum; Ben English, retired history teacher, train enthusiast, and author; Natalie Fritz, Archivist and Outreach Director, Clark County Historical Society, Springfield, Ohio; Nancy Hayes, Hart's Location Treasurer; Katie Landry, Hart's Location Town Clerk; and Marion L. Varney, author of *Hart's Location in Crawford Notch: New Hampshire's Smallest Town* helped me, along with Internet searches, to fill in details to the well-known stories.

Thanks to Phil Franklin, president of the Bartlett Historical Society, for your time, effort, and keen insight to help me get the facts right.

Special thanks to Jennifer, Pat, Marybeth, and Susie for your support and belief in me and this project. To Francesca and Weston Evans, for introducing me to Loring and Hattie and their children, and for taking me to the Notch many times.

I want to wholeheartedly thank the other members of my family for your consistent encouragement of both my vocational and avocational endeavors. You know who you are, and what you have given me. Mwah!

Thank you, Aimee Adams, for being my editor and supporter extraordinaire. I'm always amazed at how you can see the whole picture enough to move things around in a way that draws the reader into the exact place I intended for them to arrive. What you do is a skill I don't have. So, I'll write, you edit, and we'll keep birthing some new books.

Thank you, pre-readers, Craig Robinson and Charles Smith, for providing me with objective eyes.

Last but by no means least, my profound gratitude goes to my husband, Stan. His railroad knowledge exceeded what I needed, giving me a vast pool of information simply by walking into the next room. When I got all tangled up in computer issues, he patiently untangled them time after time. When I thought I couldn't do this, he wouldn't let me give up, reframing things in a way that bolstered my courage. Thank you for knowing me so well.

About the Author

Mary Anne Evans has been a trained spiritual director since 2009. She leads retreats and workshops on listening skills, telling our stories, dreams, and spirituality. She loves to read and write in her spare time. She lives with her husband, Stan, and together they try not to dote on their grandchildren too much.

Find out more at www.spiritofriverwind.com.

www.ingramcontent.com/pod-product-compliance
Lightning Source LLC
Chambersburg PA
CBHW030916300726
48970CB00001B/186